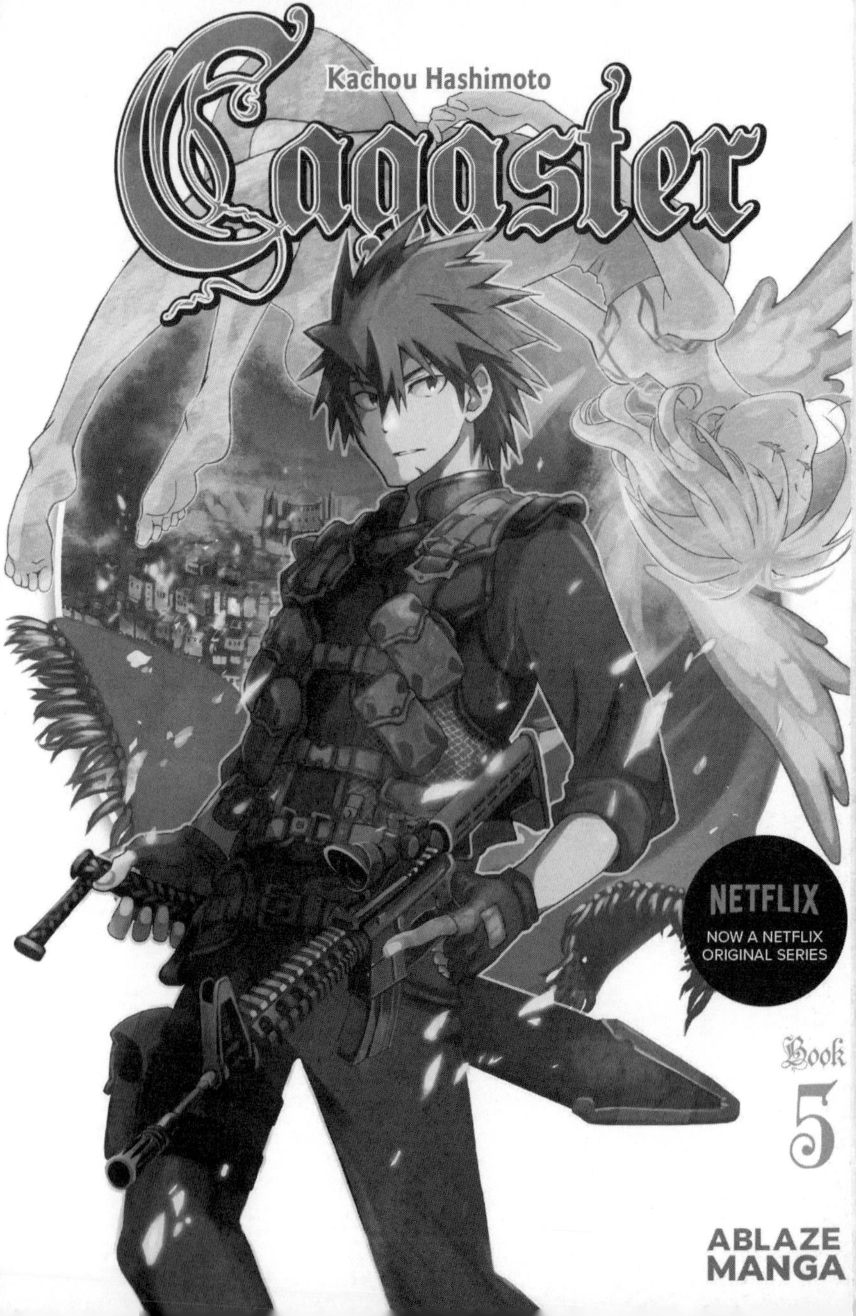
Kachou Hashimoto
Cagaster
NETFLIX
NOW A NETFLIX
ORIGINAL SERIES
Book
5
ABLAZE
MANGA

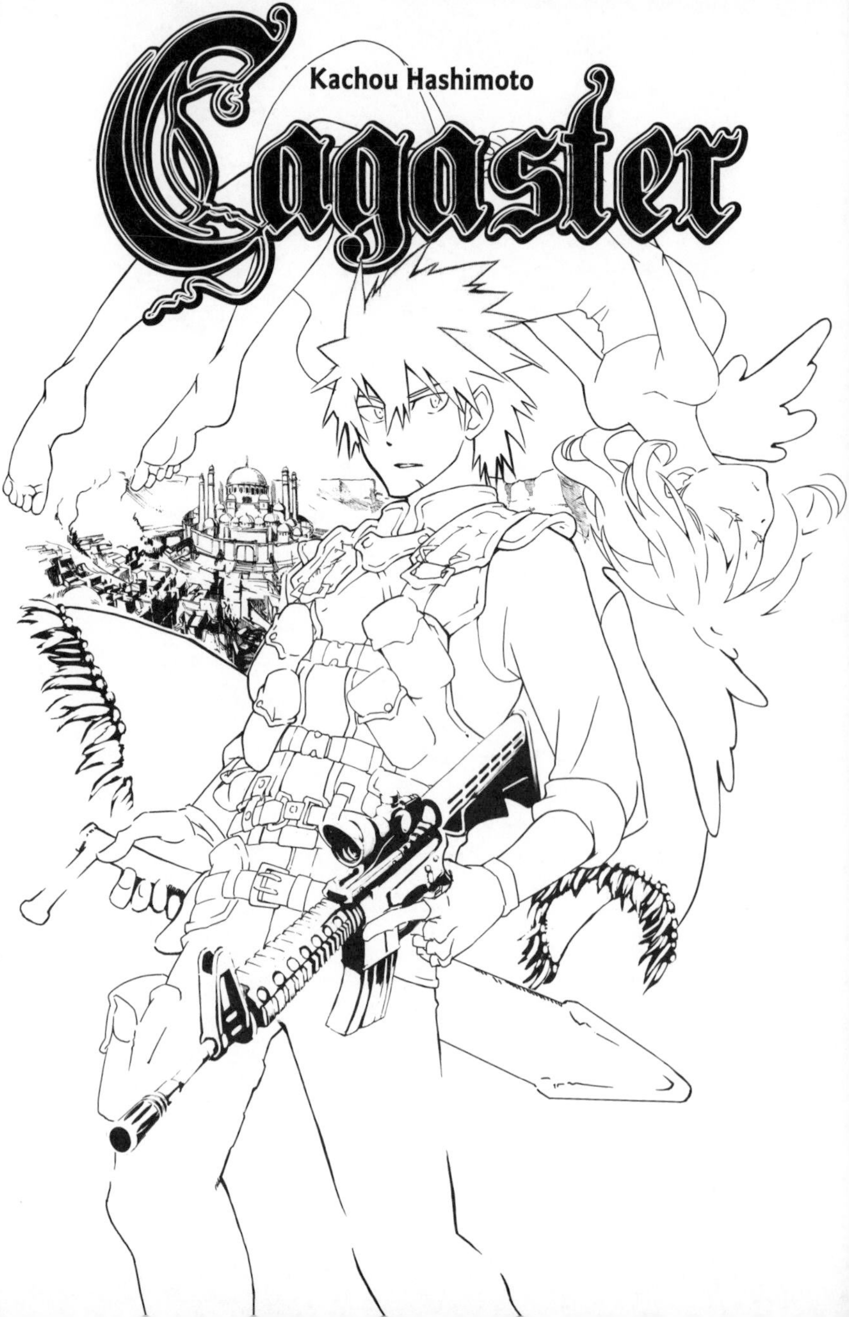
Cagaster
Kachou Hashimoto

FINAL CHAPTER: FOR SOU, IN THE END / PART I

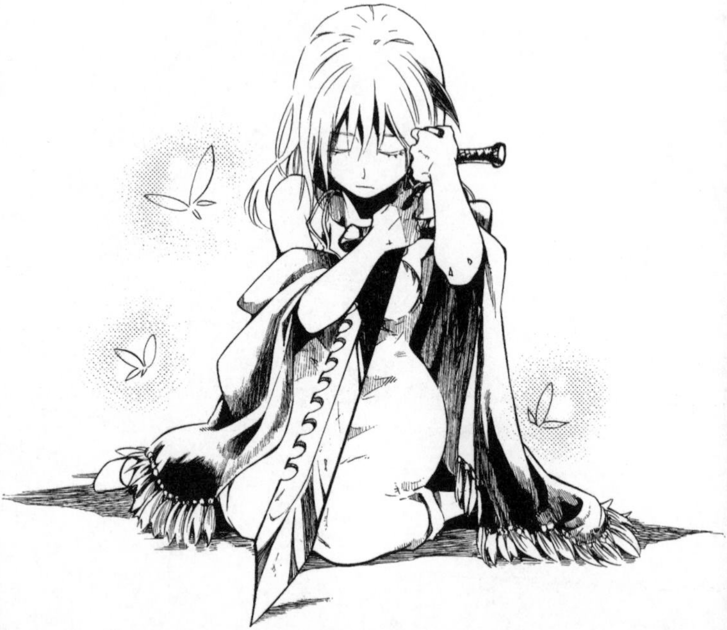

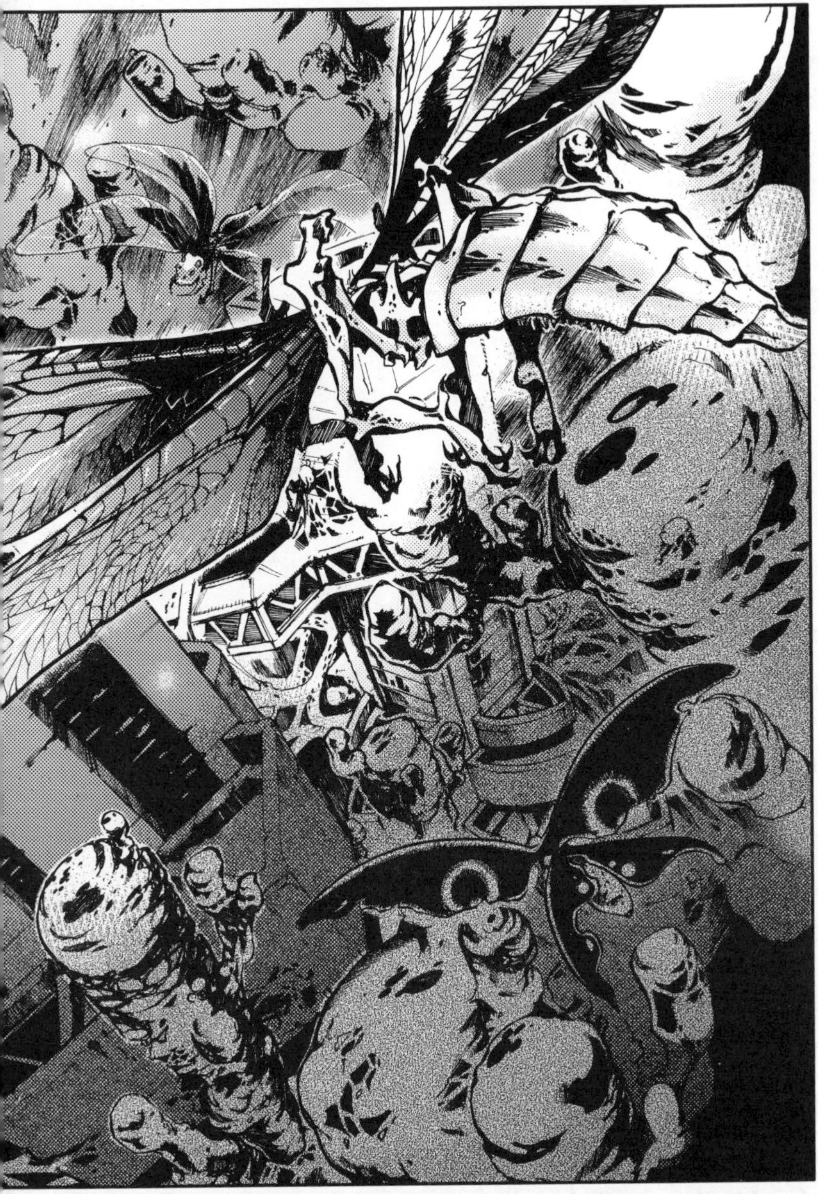

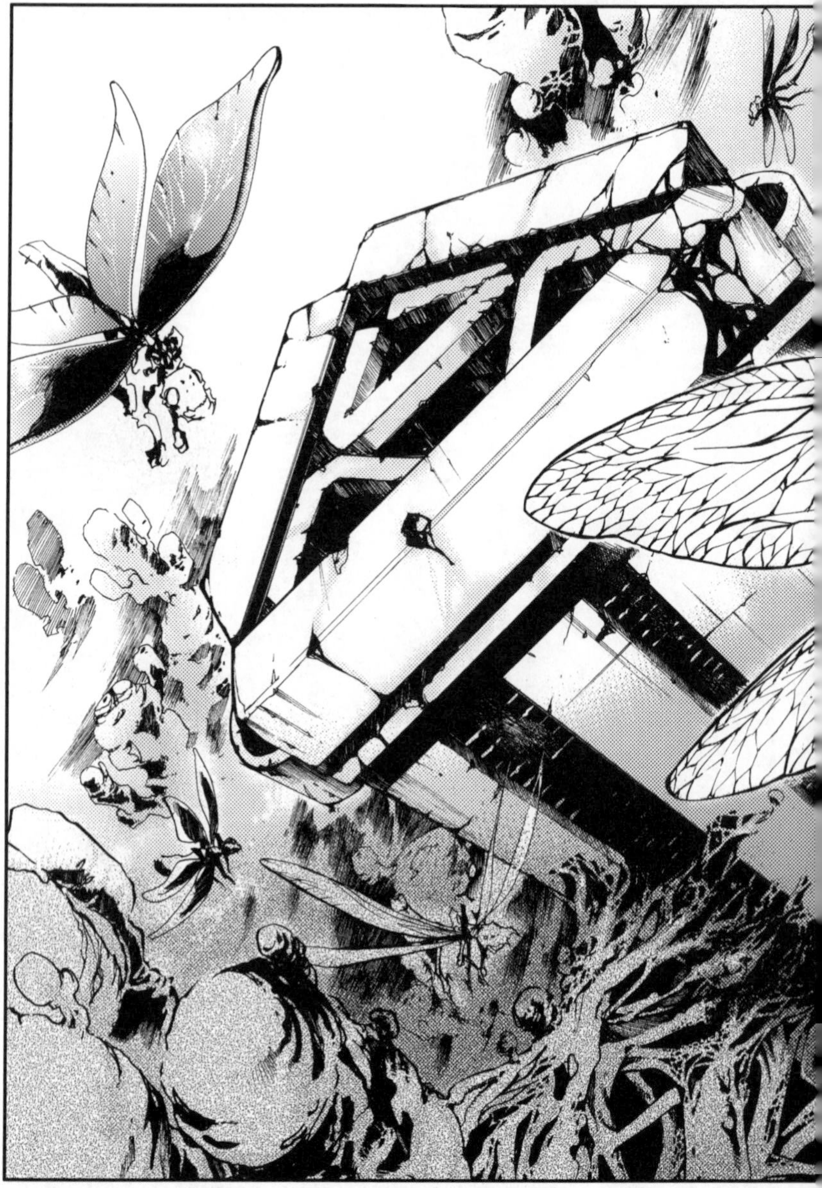

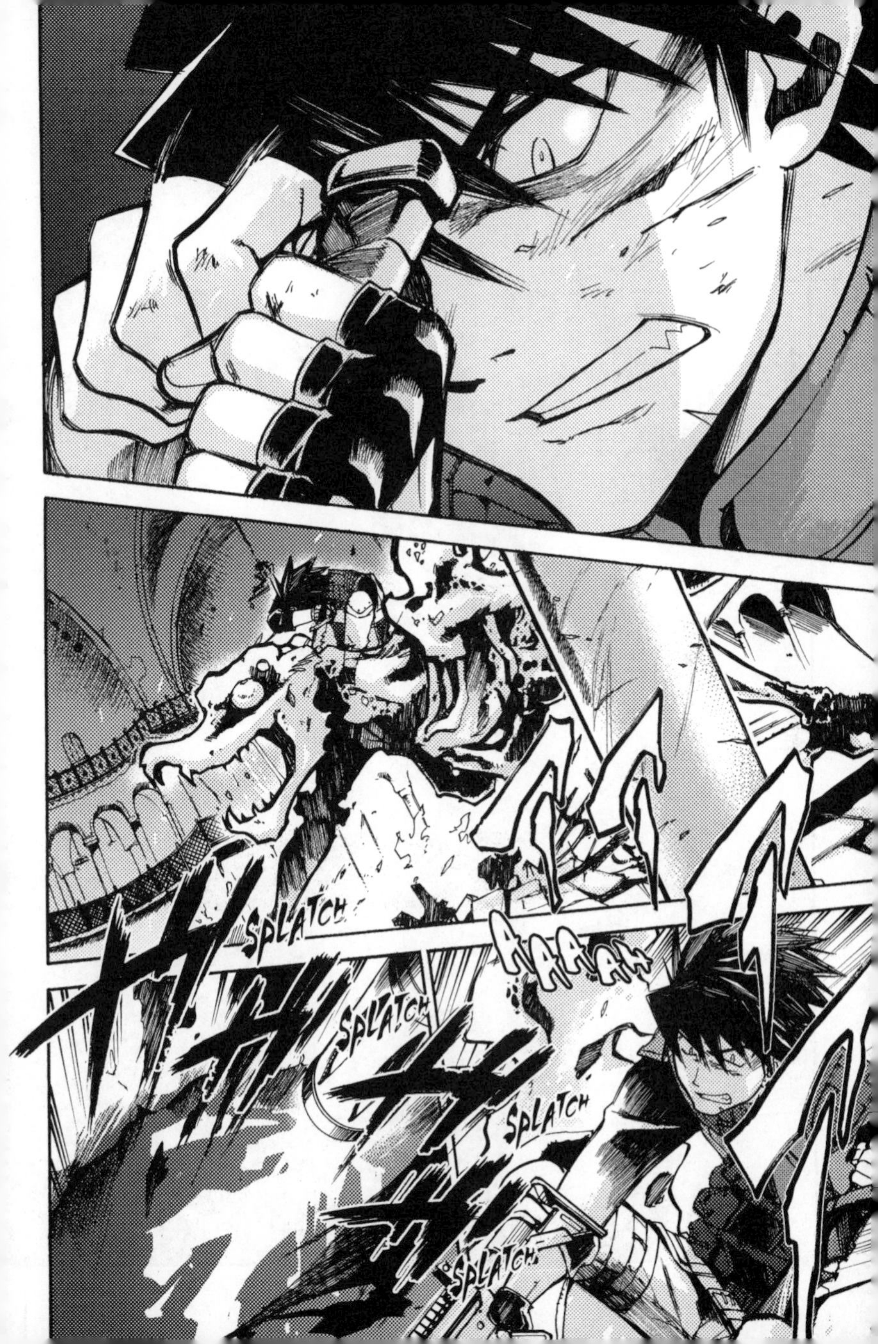
SPLATCH
AAAAH
SPLATCH
SPLATCH
SPLATCH

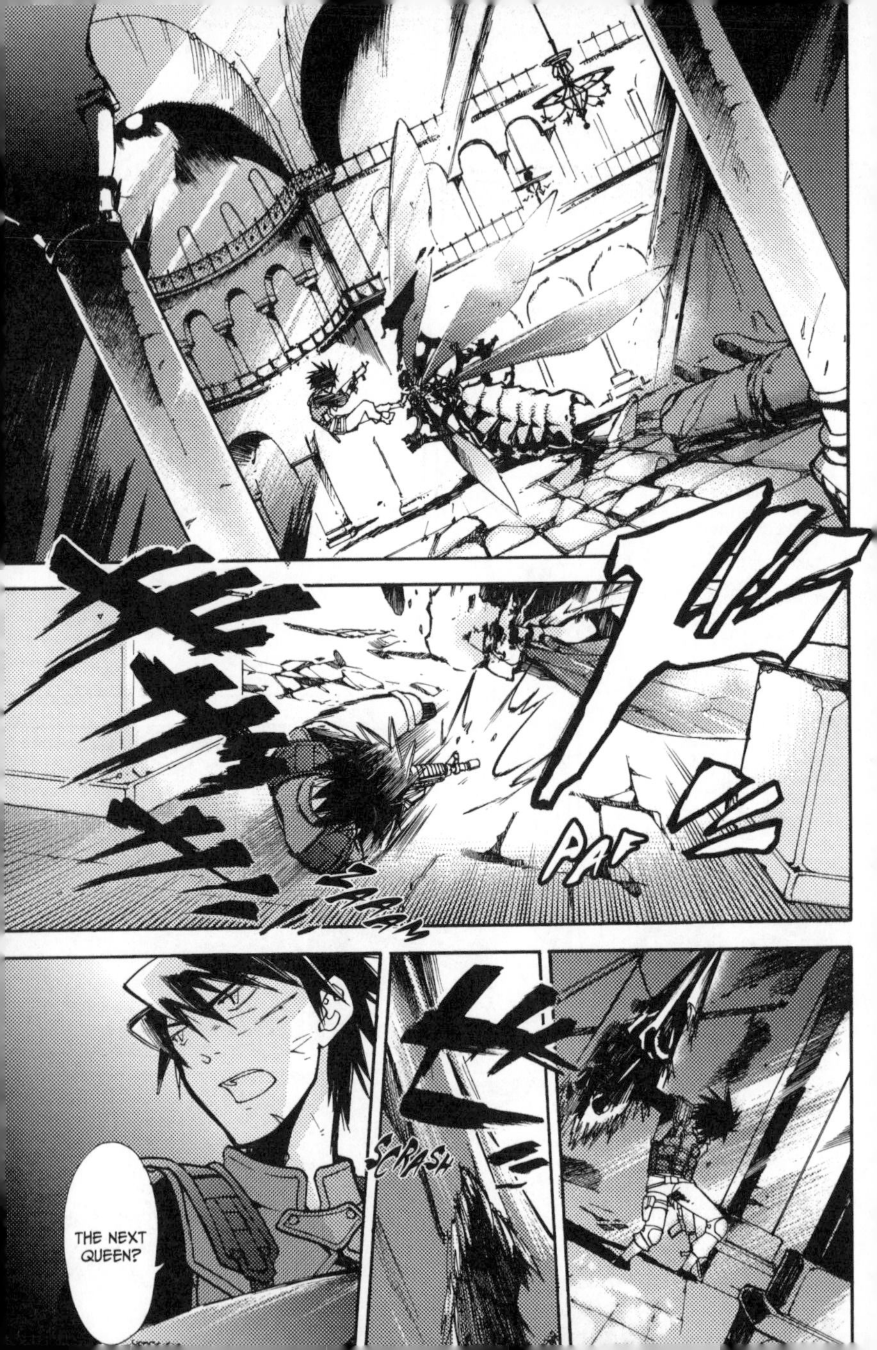
PAF
ZAAAM
SCRASH
THE NEXT QUEEN?

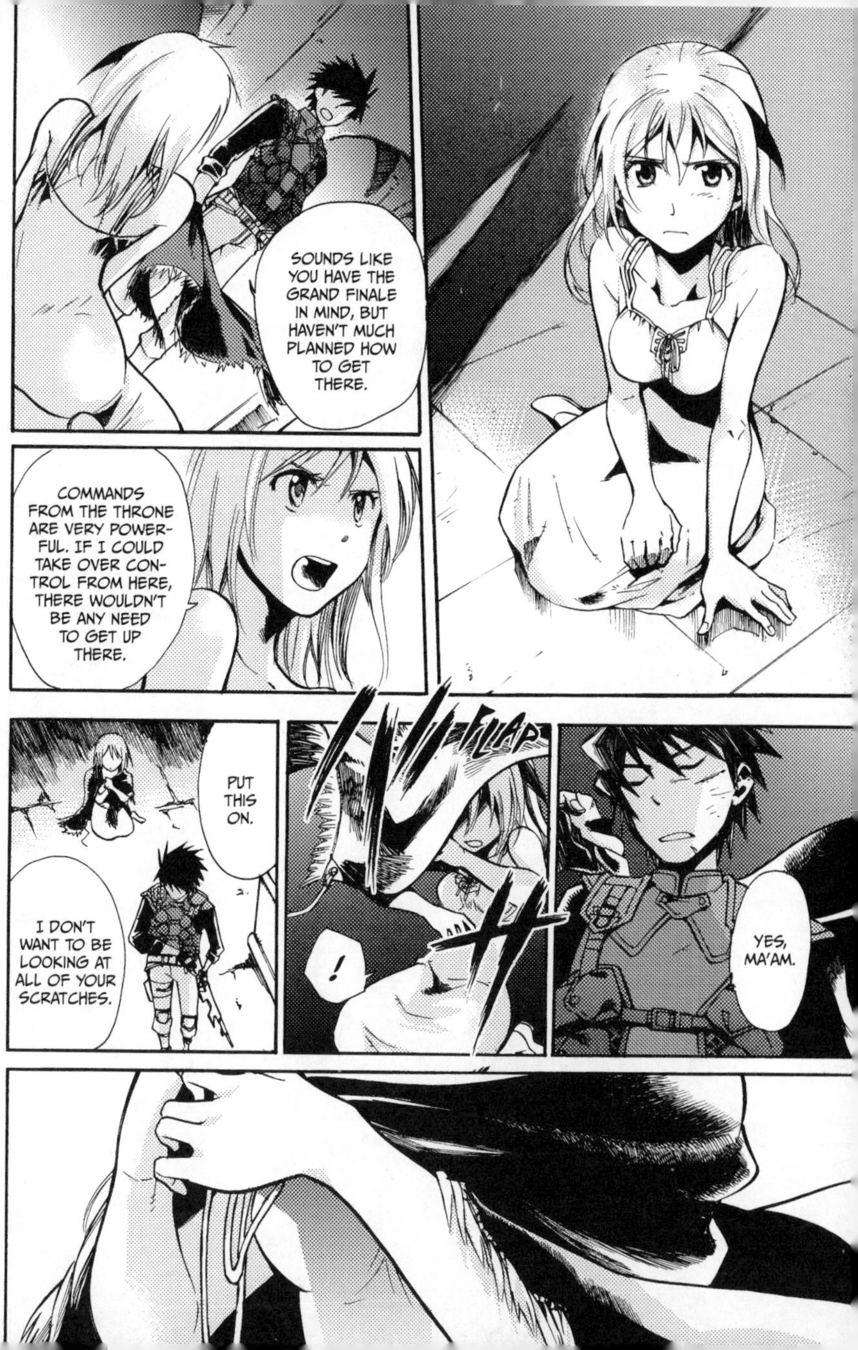
SOUNDS LIKE YOU HAVE THE GRAND FINALE IN MIND, BUT HAVEN'T MUCH PLANNED HOW TO GET THERE.
COMMANDS FROM THE THRONE ARE VERY POWER-FUL. IF I COULD TAKE OVER CON-TROL FROM HERE, THERE WOULDN'T BE ANY NEED TO GET UP THERE.
YES, MA'AM.
FLLLAP
!
PUT THIS ON.
I DON'T WANT TO BE LOOKING AT ALL OF YOUR SCRATCHES.

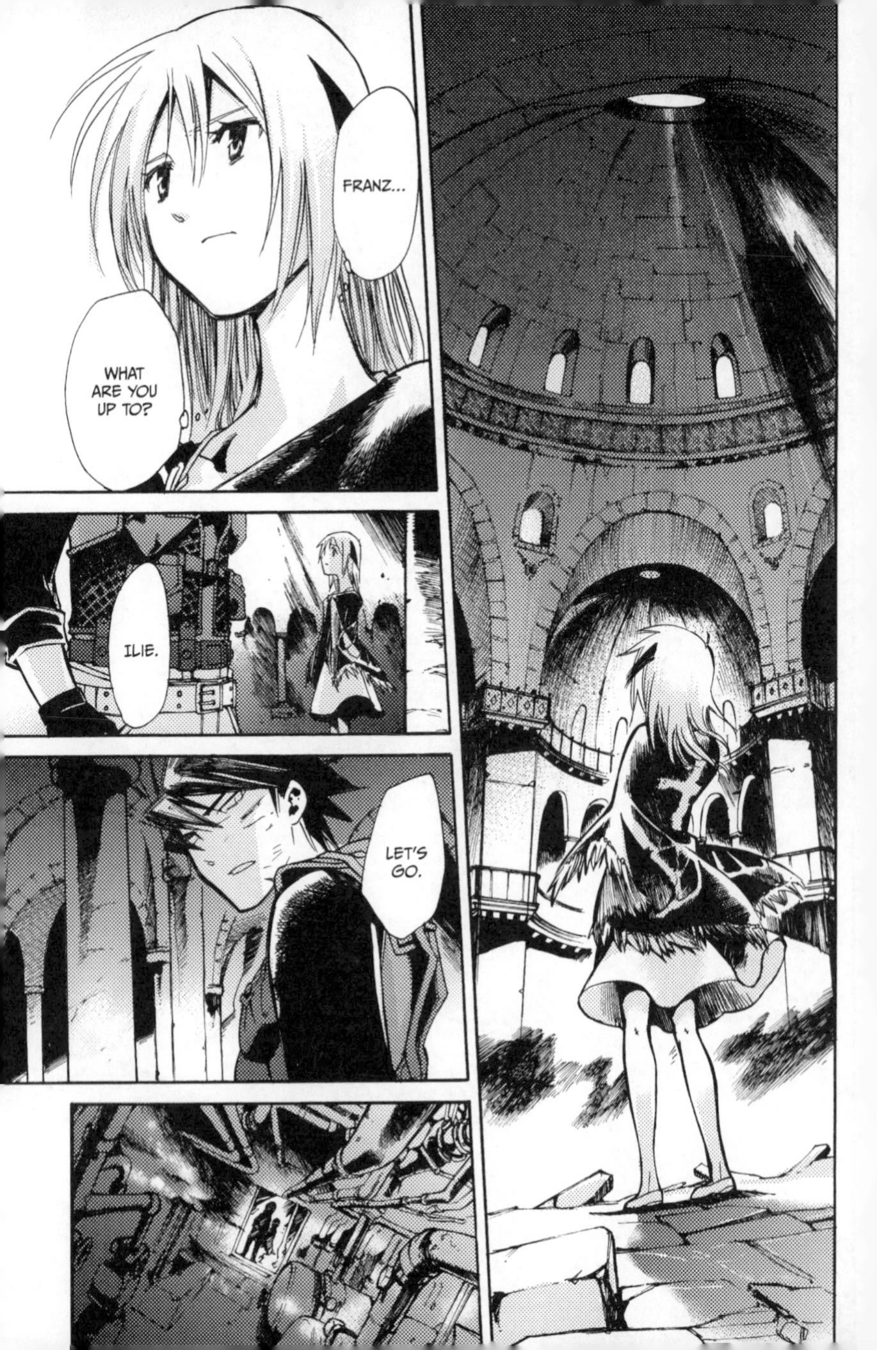
FRANZ...
WHAT ARE YOU UP TO?
ILIE.
LET'S GO.

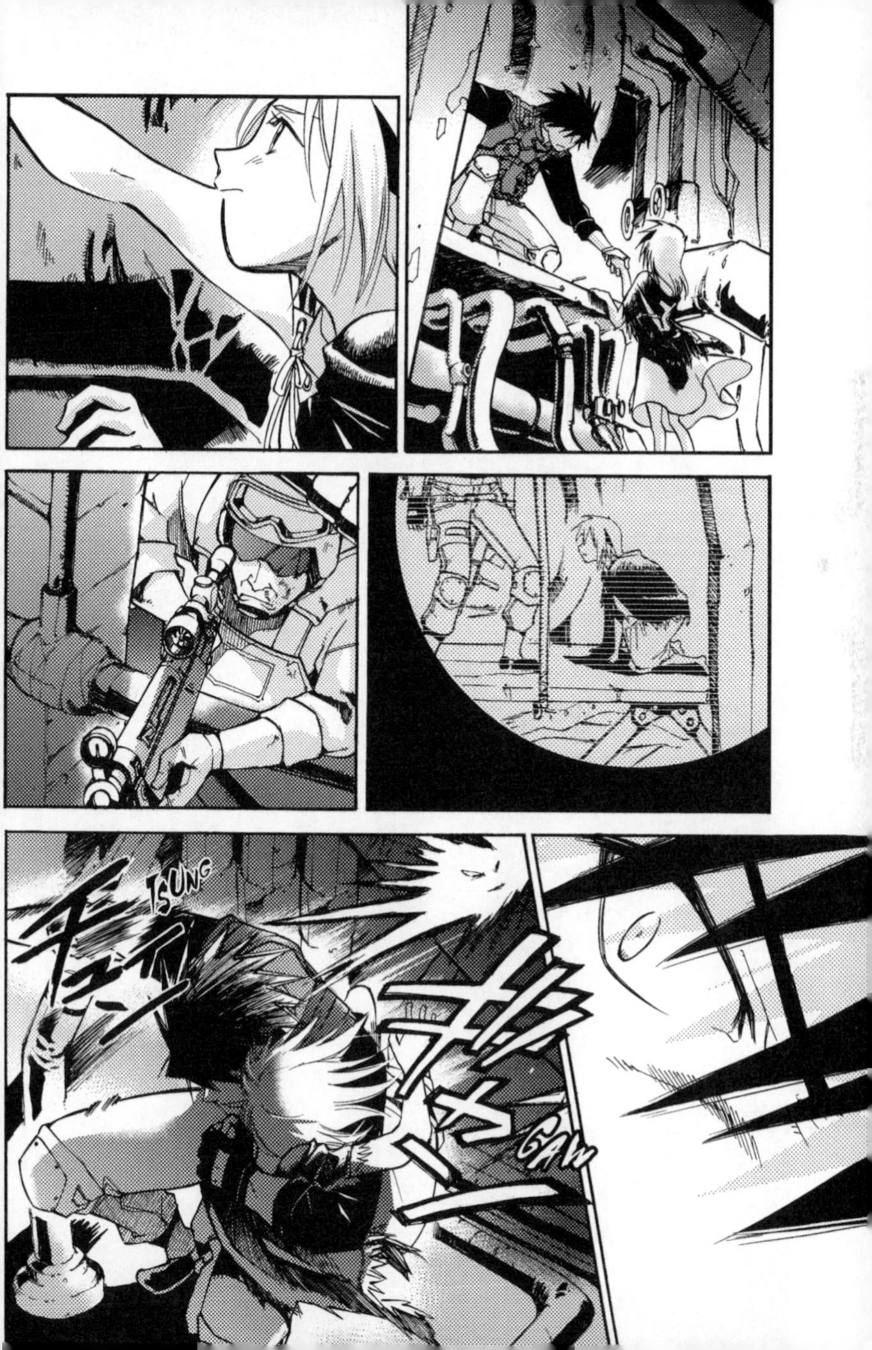
TSUNG
GAW

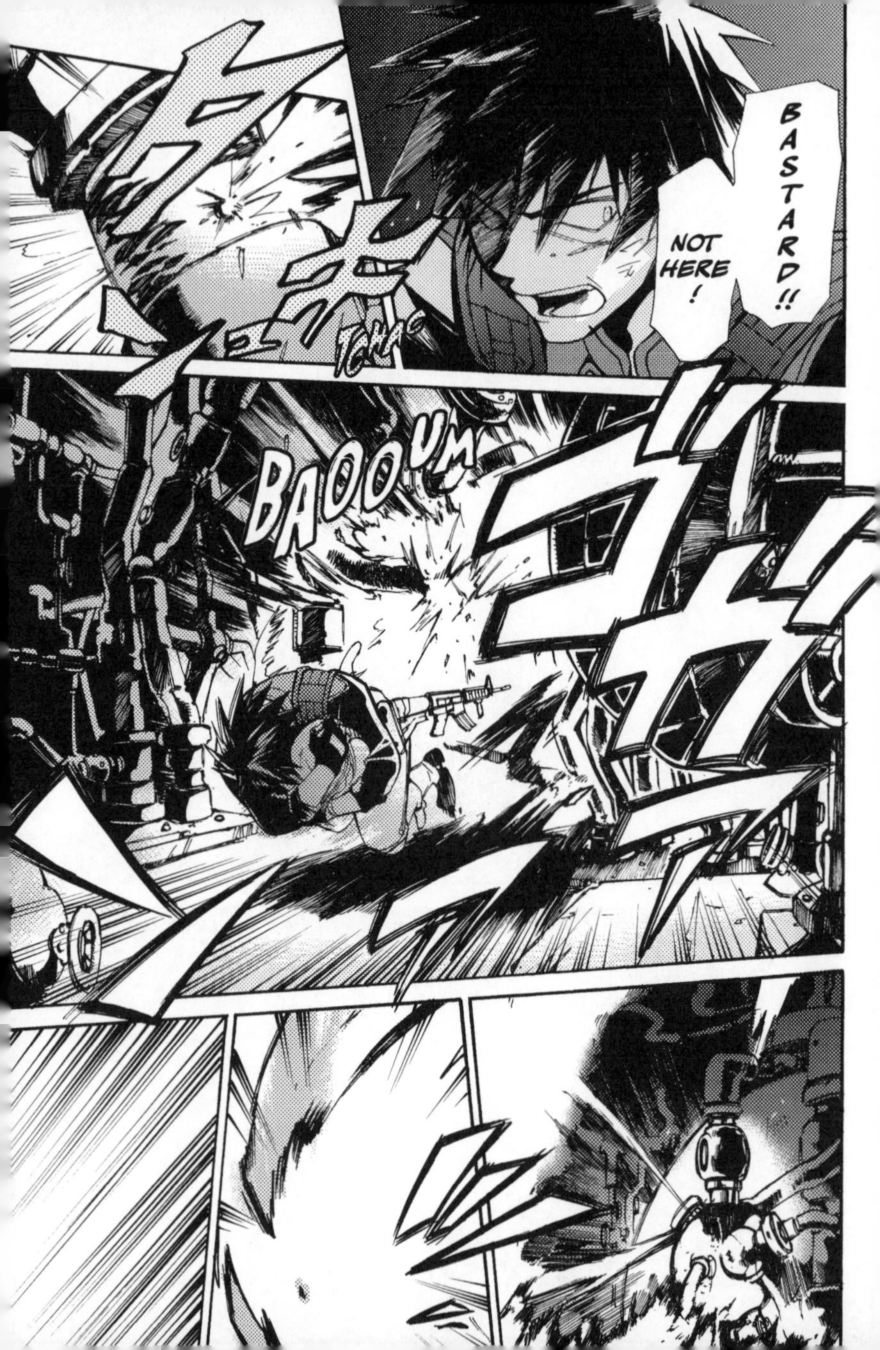
BASTARD!!
NOT HERE!
TCHAC
BAOOUM

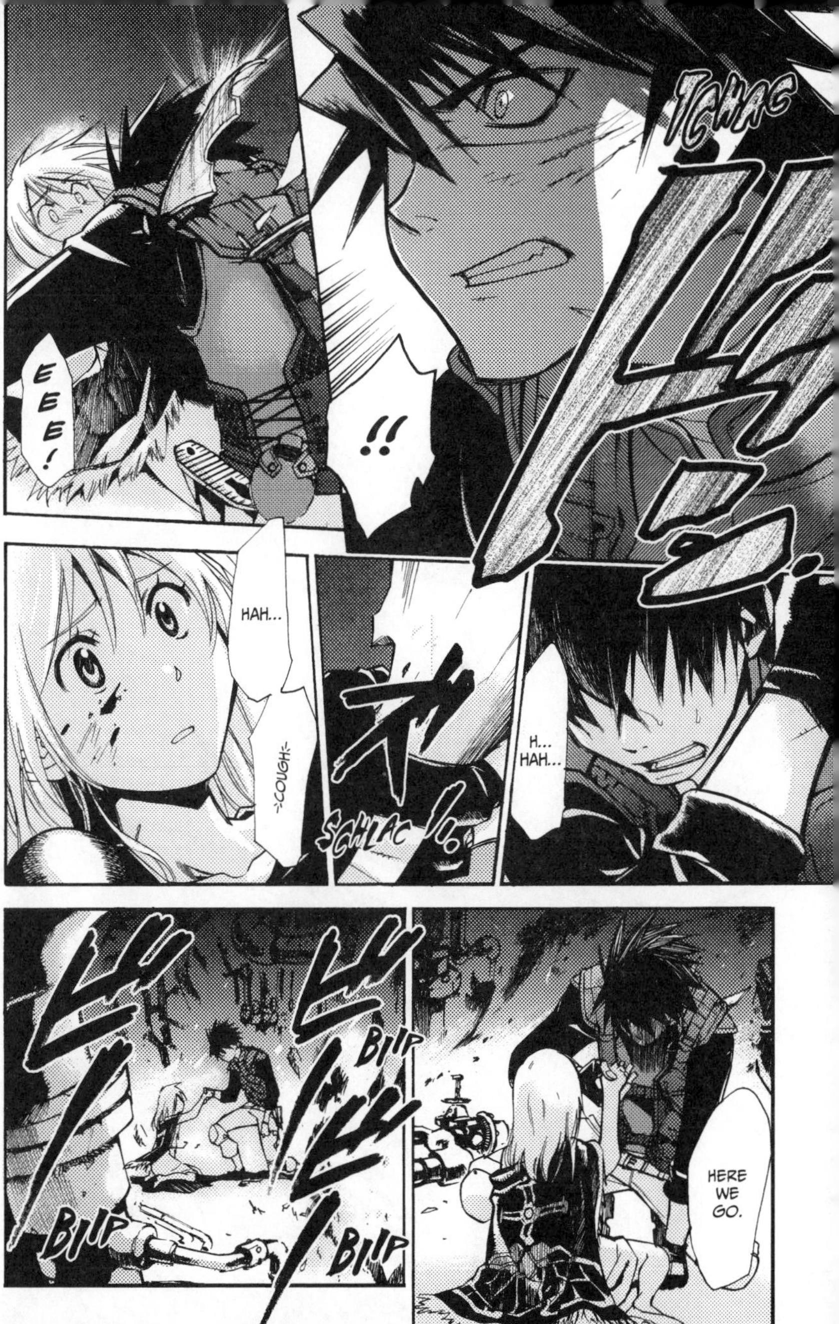
TCHAC
!!
EEE!
H... HAH...
SCHLAC
HAH...
-COUGH-
HERE WE GO.
BIIP
BIIP
BIIP

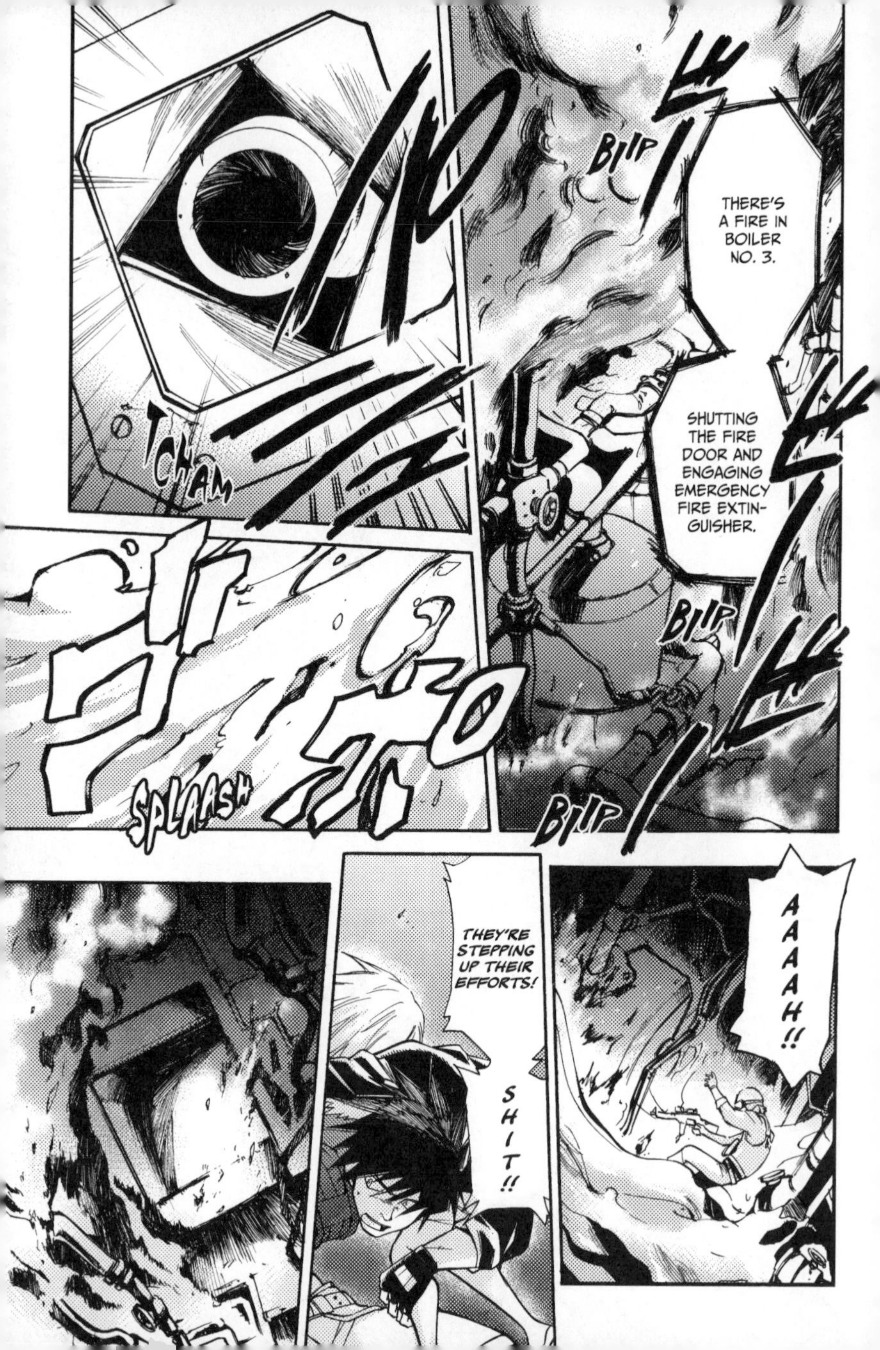
BLIP
THERE'S A FIRE IN BOILER NO. 3.
SHUTTING THE FIRE DOOR AND ENGAGING EMERGENCY FIRE EXTIN-GUISHER.
BLIP
BLIP
TCHAM
SPLAASH
AAAAAH!!
THEY'RE STEPPING UP THEIR EFFORTS!
SHIT!!

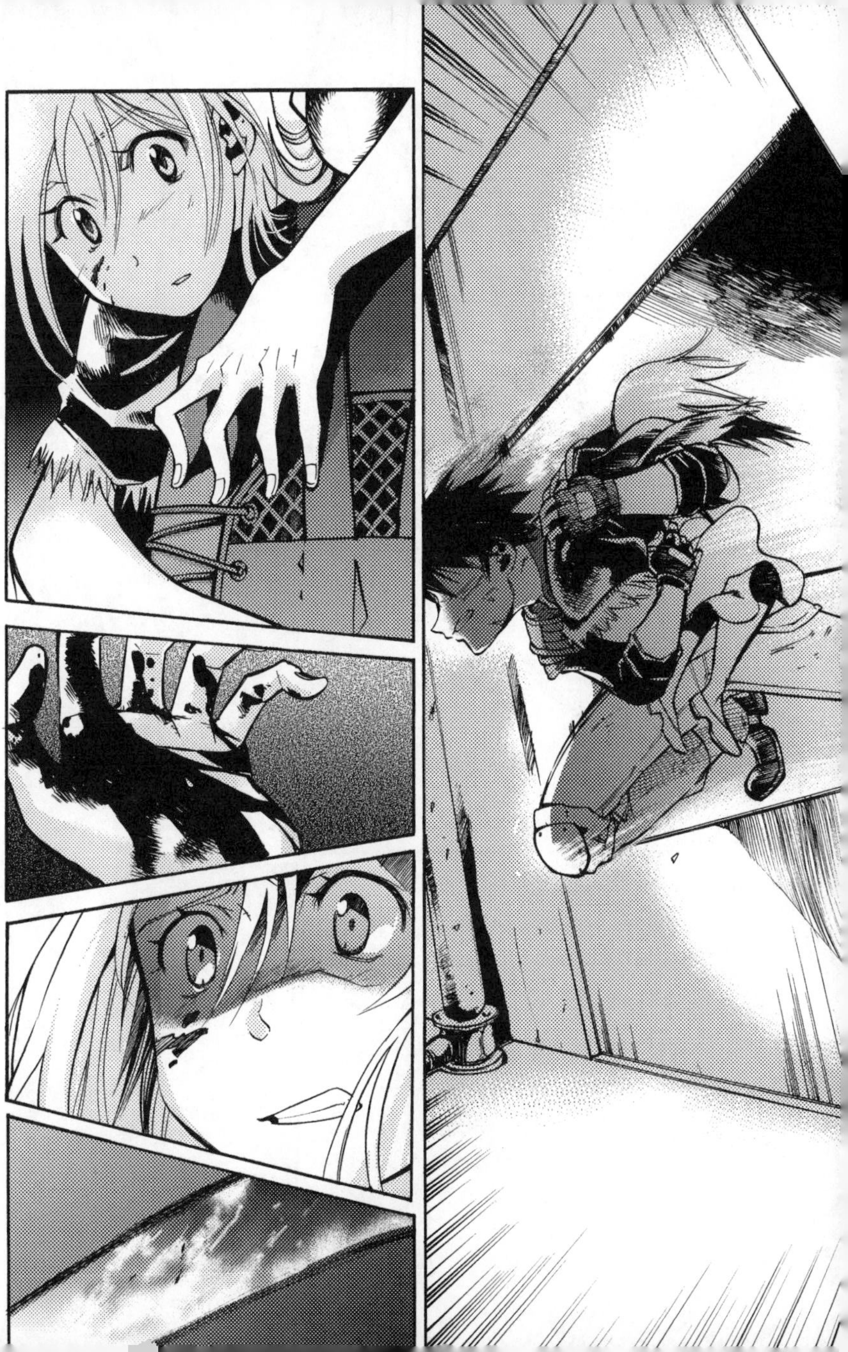

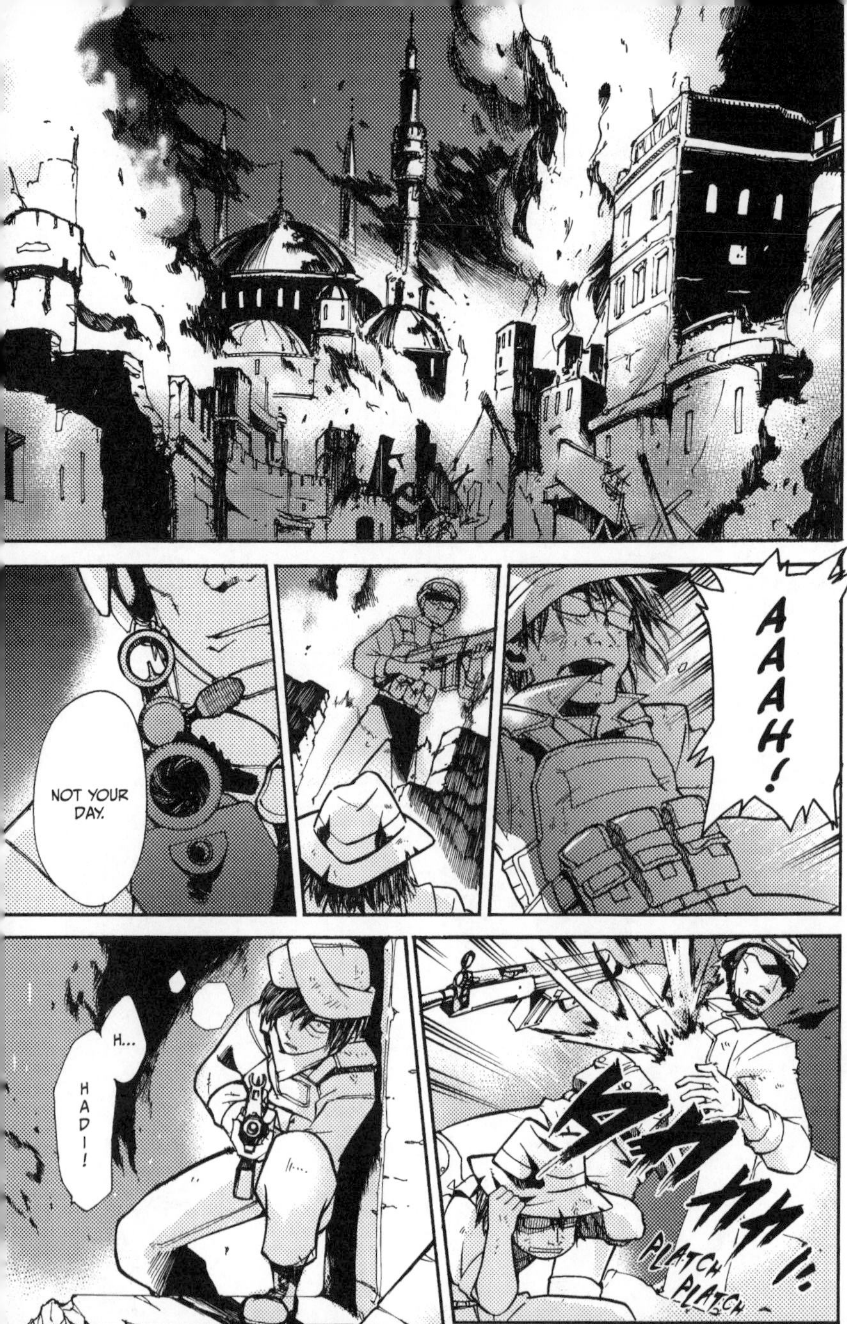
AAAAH!
NOT YOUR DAY.
PLATCH
PLATCH
H...
HADI!

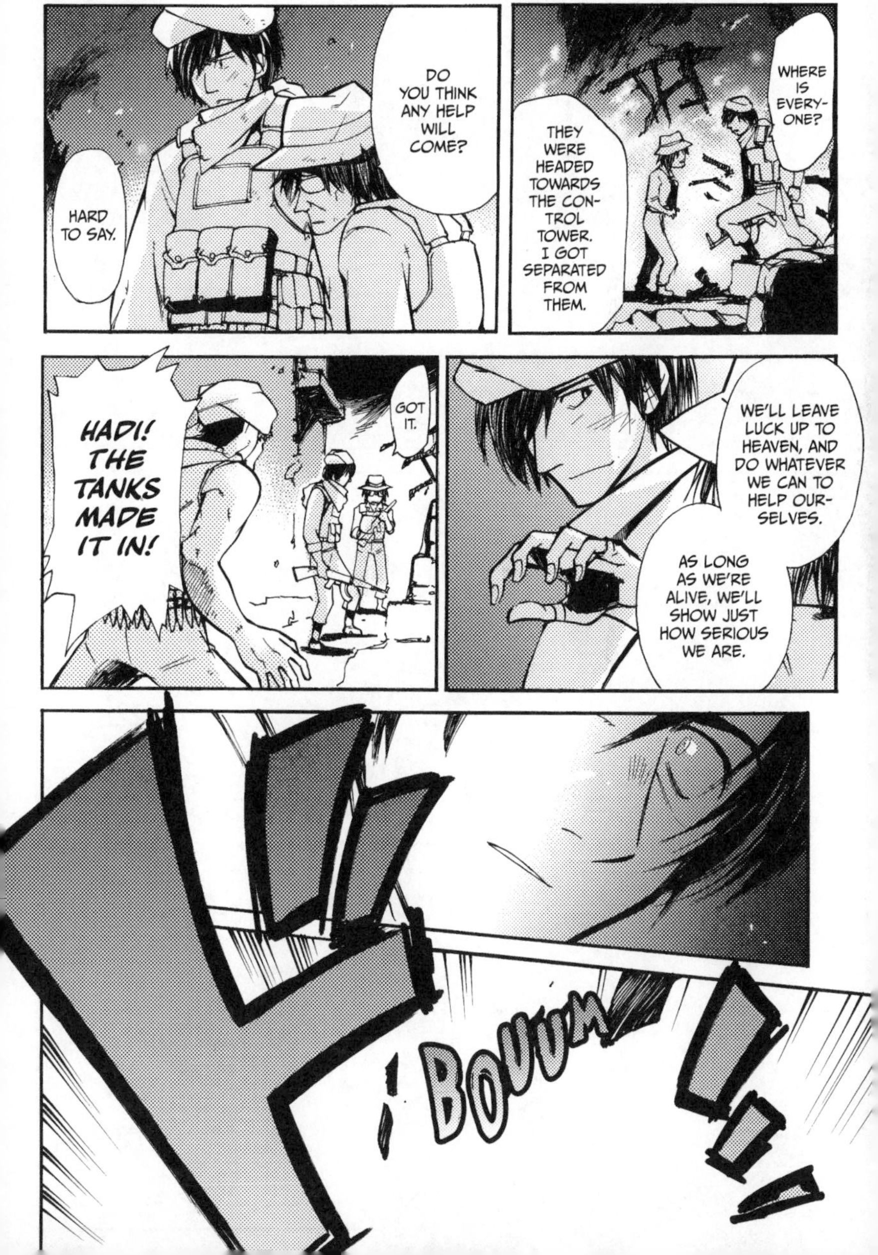
WHERE IS EVERY-ONE?
THEY WERE HEADED TOWARDS THE CON-TROL TOWER. I GOT SEPARATED FROM THEM.
DO YOU THINK ANY HELP WILL COME?
HARD TO SAY.
WE'LL LEAVE LUCK UP TO HEAVEN, AND DO WHATEVER WE CAN TO HELP OUR-SELVES.
AS LONG AS WE'RE ALIVE, WE'LL SHOW JUST HOW SERIOUS WE ARE.
GOT IT.
HADI! THE TANKS MADE IT IN!
¡BOUUM!!

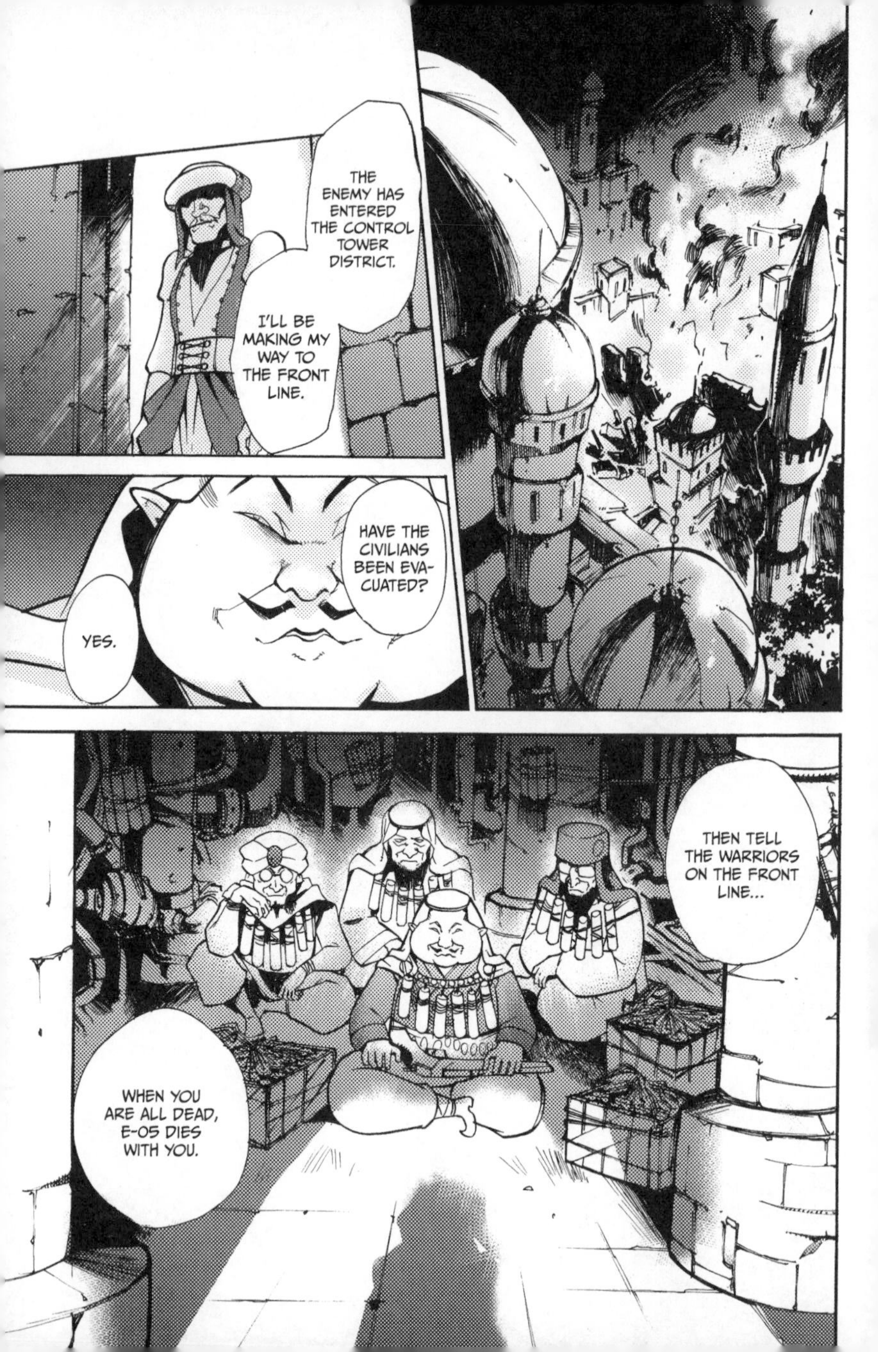
THE ENEMY HAS ENTERED THE CONTROL TOWER DISTRICT.
I'LL BE MAKING MY WAY TO THE FRONT LINE.
HAVE THE CIVILIANS BEEN EVA-CUATED?
YES.
THEN TELL THE WARRIORS ON THE FRONT LINE...
WHEN YOU ARE ALL DEAD, E-05 DIES WITH YOU.

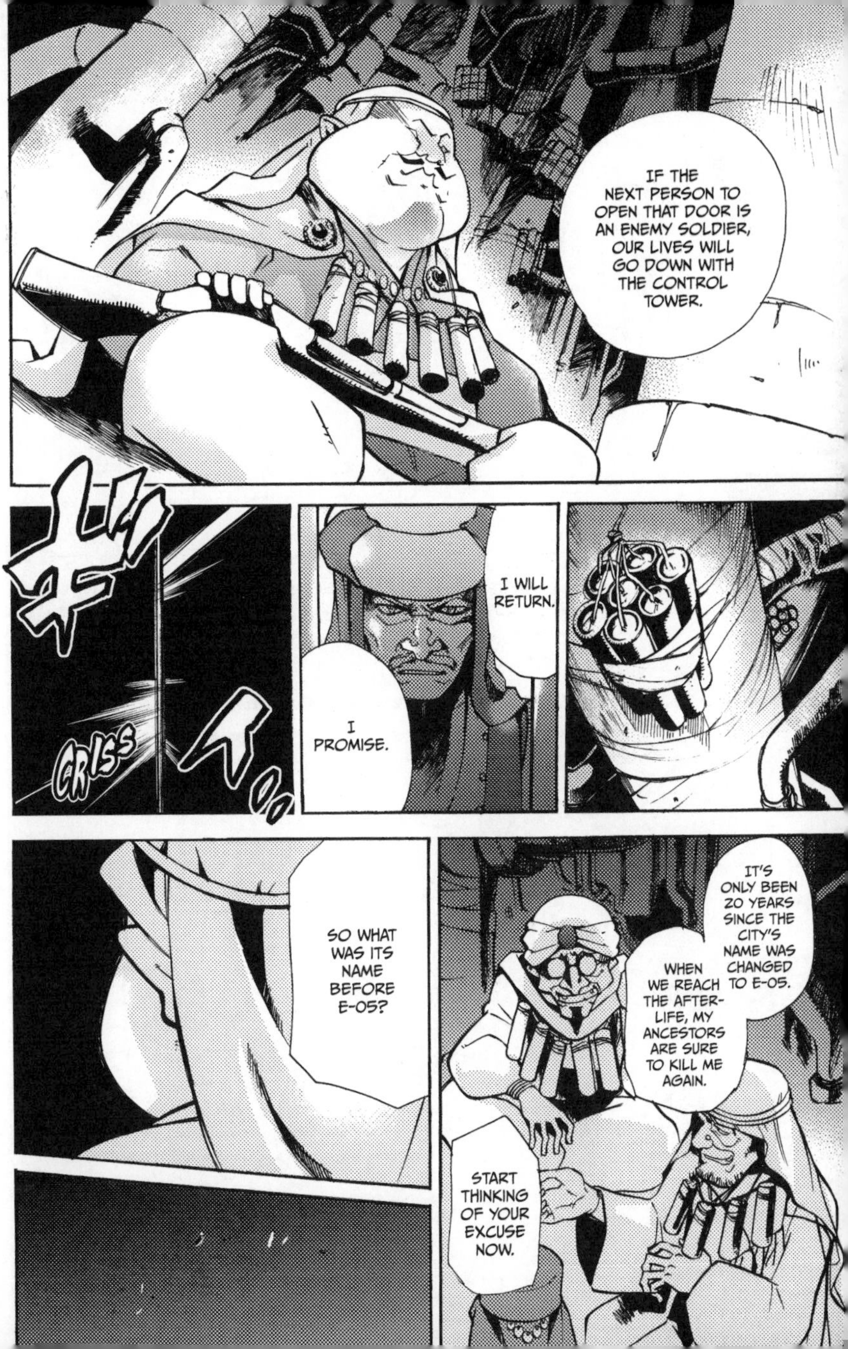
IF THE NEXT PERSON TO OPEN THAT DOOR IS AN ENEMY SOLDIER, OUR LIVES WILL GO DOWN WITH THE CONTROL TOWER.
I WILL RETURN.
I PROMISE.
CRISS
IT'S ONLY BEEN 20 YEARS SINCE THE CITY'S NAME WAS CHANGED TO E-05.
WHEN WE REACH THE AFTER-LIFE, MY ANCESTORS ARE SURE TO KILL ME AGAIN.
START THINKING OF YOUR EXCUSE NOW.
SO WHAT WAS ITS NAME BEFORE E-05?

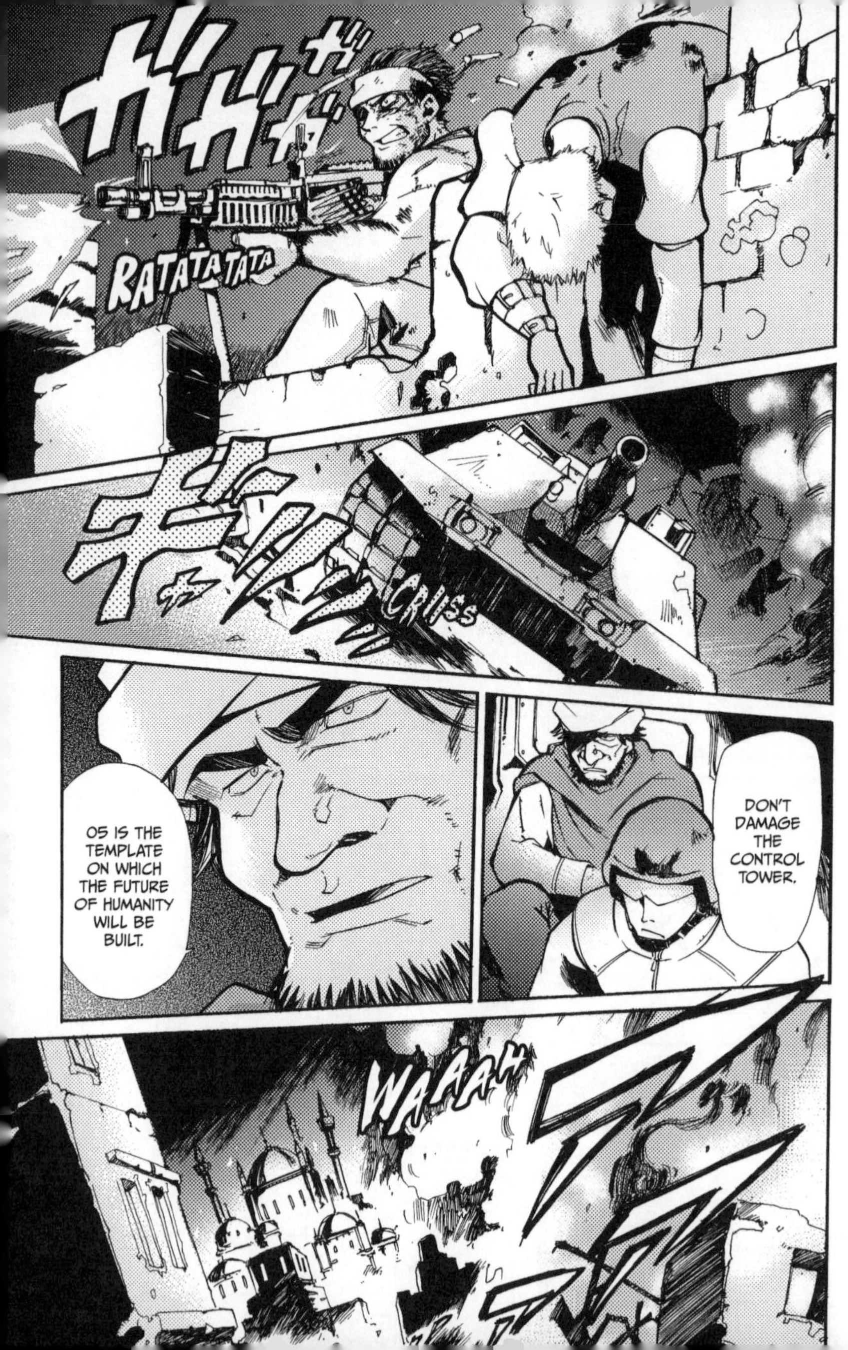
RATATATATA
CRI$$
DON'T DAMAGE THE CONTROL TOWER.
05 IS THE TEMPLATE ON WHICH THE FUTURE OF HUMANITY WILL BE BUILT.
WAAAH

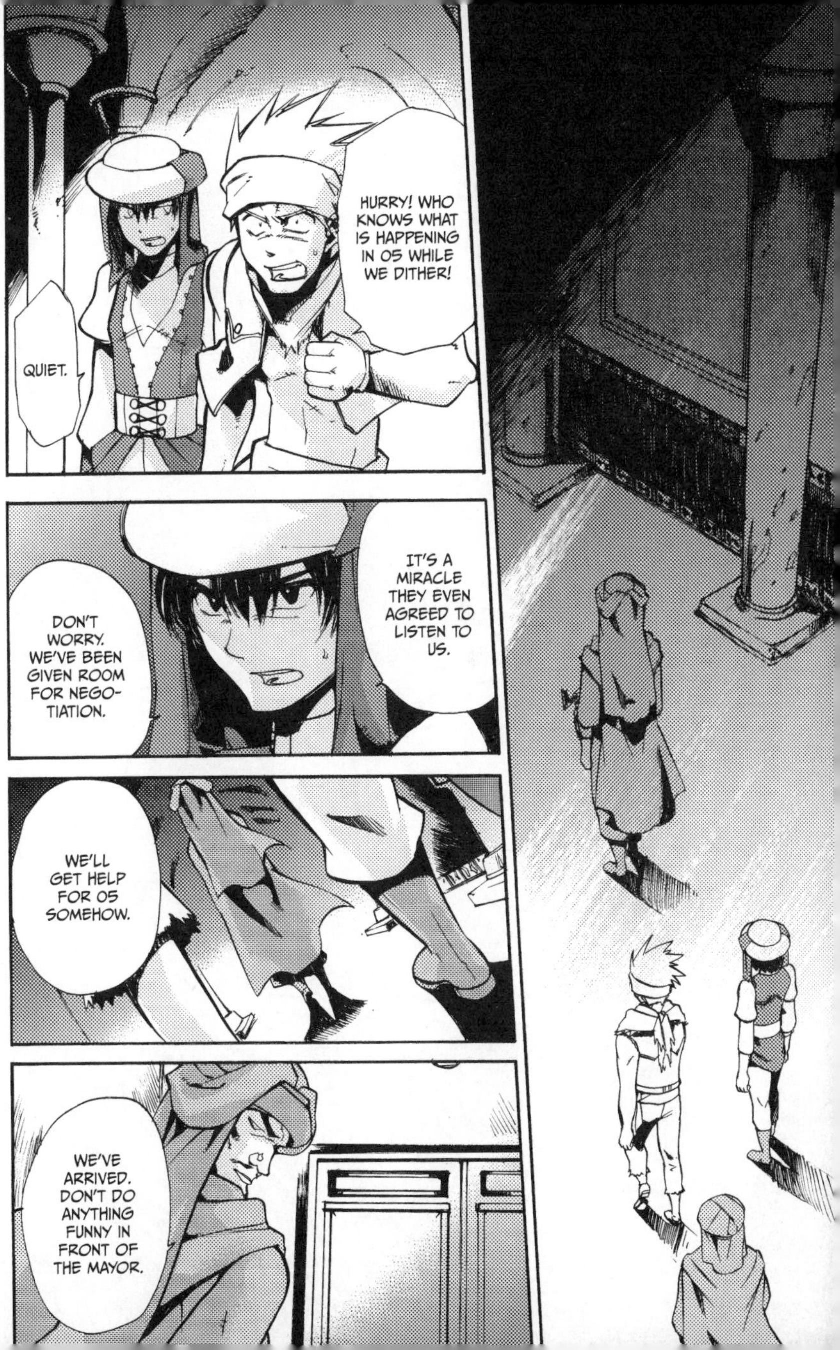
HURRY! WHO KNOWS WHAT IS HAPPENING IN O5 WHILE WE DITHER!
QUIET.
IT'S A MIRACLE THEY EVEN AGREED TO LISTEN TO US.
DON'T WORRY. WE'VE BEEN GIVEN ROOM FOR NEGO-TIATION.
WE'LL GET HELP FOR O5 SOMEHOW.
WE'VE ARRIVED. DON'T DO ANYTHING FUNNY IN FRONT OF THE MAYOR.

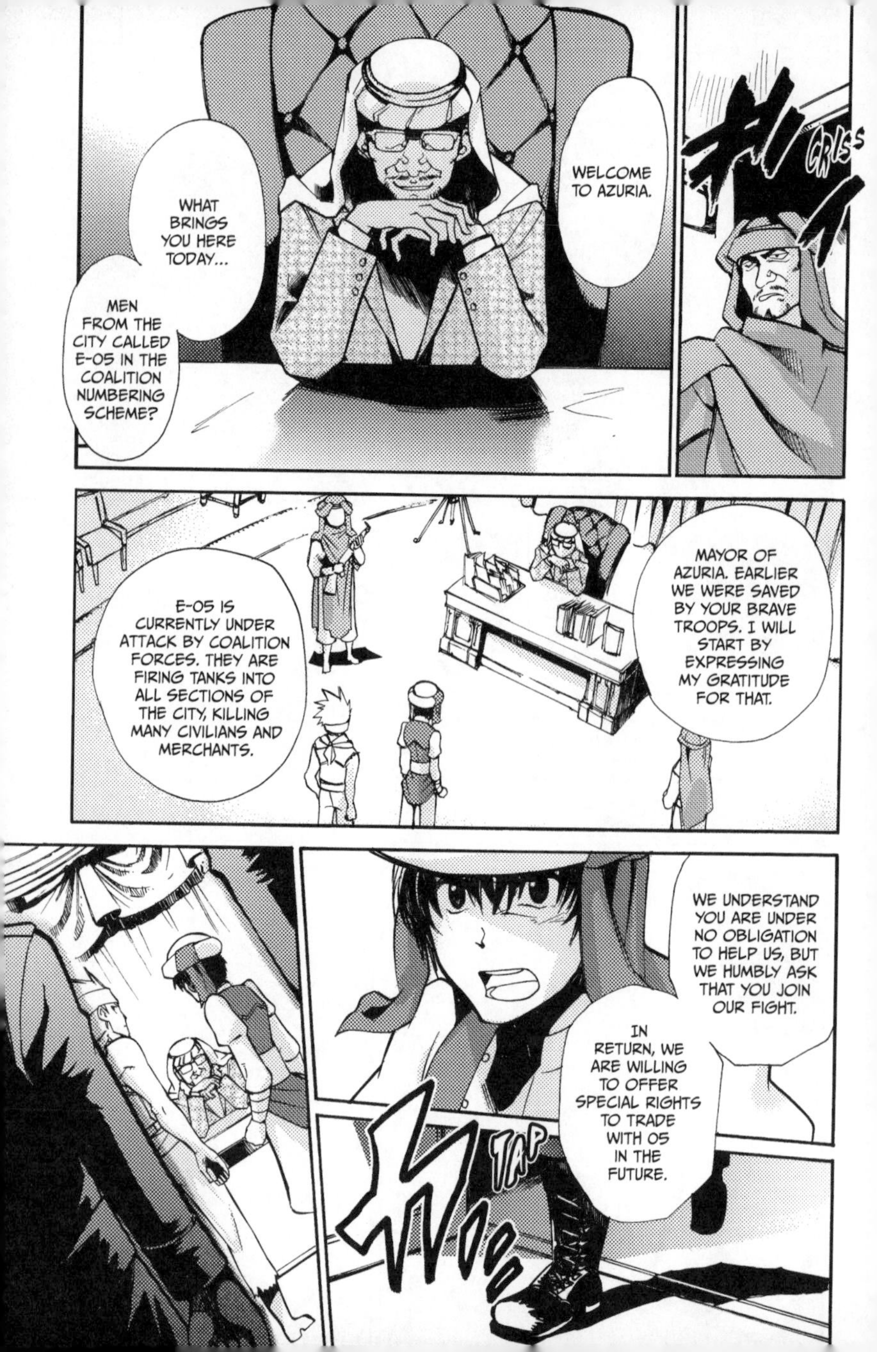
CRISS
WELCOME TO AZURIA.
WHAT BRINGS YOU HERE TODAY...
MEN FROM THE CITY CALLED E-05 IN THE COALITION NUMBERING SCHEME?
MAYOR OF AZURIA. EARLIER WE WERE SAVED BY YOUR BRAVE TROOPS. I WILL START BY EXPRESSING MY GRATITUDE FOR THAT.
E-05 IS CURRENTLY UNDER ATTACK BY COALITION FORCES. THEY ARE FIRING TANKS INTO ALL SECTIONS OF THE CITY, KILLING MANY CIVILIANS AND MERCHANTS.
WE UNDERSTAND YOU ARE UNDER NO OBLIGATION TO HELP US, BUT WE HUMBLY ASK THAT YOU JOIN OUR FIGHT.
IN RETURN, WE ARE WILLING TO OFFER SPECIAL RIGHTS TO TRADE WITH 05 IN THE FUTURE.
TAP

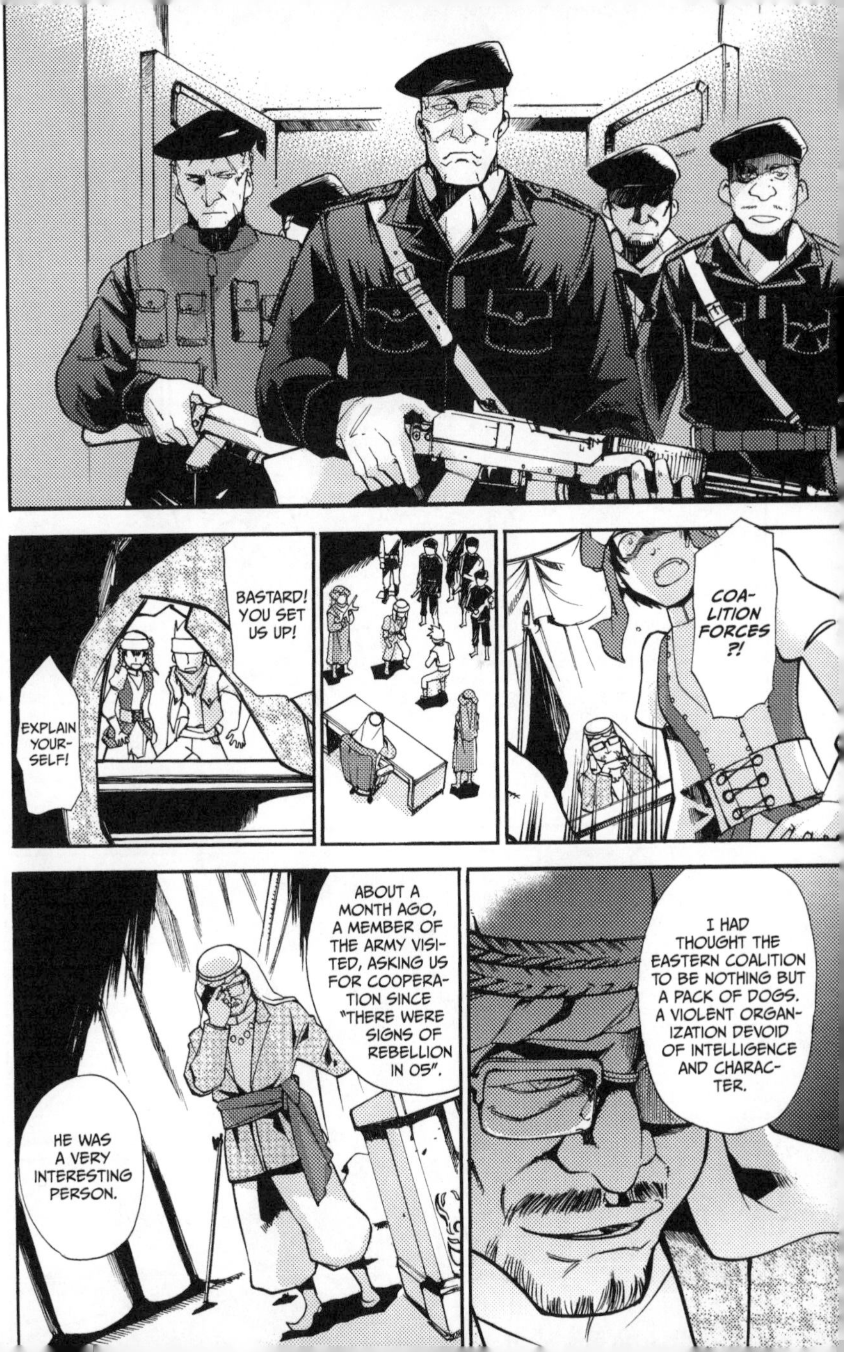
COALITION FORCES?!
BASTARD! YOU SET US UP!
EXPLAIN YOURSELF!
I HAD THOUGHT THE EASTERN COALITION TO BE NOTHING BUT A PACK OF DOGS. A VIOLENT ORGANIZATION DEVOID OF INTELLIGENCE AND CHARACTER.
ABOUT A MONTH AGO, A MEMBER OF THE ARMY VISITED, ASKING US FOR COOPERATION SINCE "THERE WERE SIGNS OF REBELLION IN 05".
HE WAS A VERY INTERESTING PERSON.

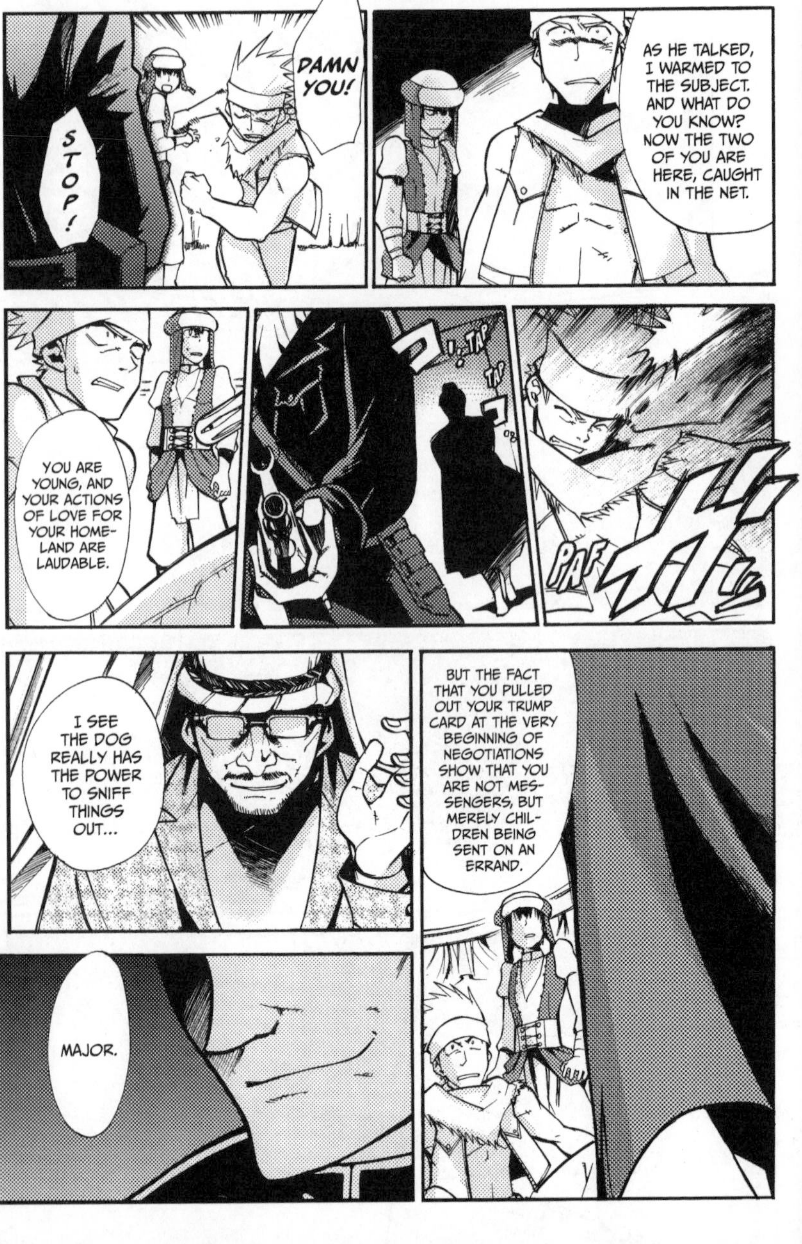
AS HE TALKED, I WARMED TO THE SUBJECT. AND WHAT DO YOU KNOW? NOW THE TWO OF YOU ARE HERE, CAUGHT IN THE NET.
DAMN YOU!
STOP!
PAF
TAP
TAP
YOU ARE YOUNG, AND YOUR ACTIONS OF LOVE FOR YOUR HOME-LAND ARE LAUDABLE.
BUT THE FACT THAT YOU PULLED OUT YOUR TRUMP CARD AT THE VERY BEGINNING OF NEGOTIATIONS SHOW THAT YOU ARE NOT MES-SENGERS, BUT MERELY CHIL-DREN BEING SENT ON AN ERRAND.
I SEE THE DOG REALLY HAS THE POWER TO SNIFF THINGS OUT...
MAJOR.

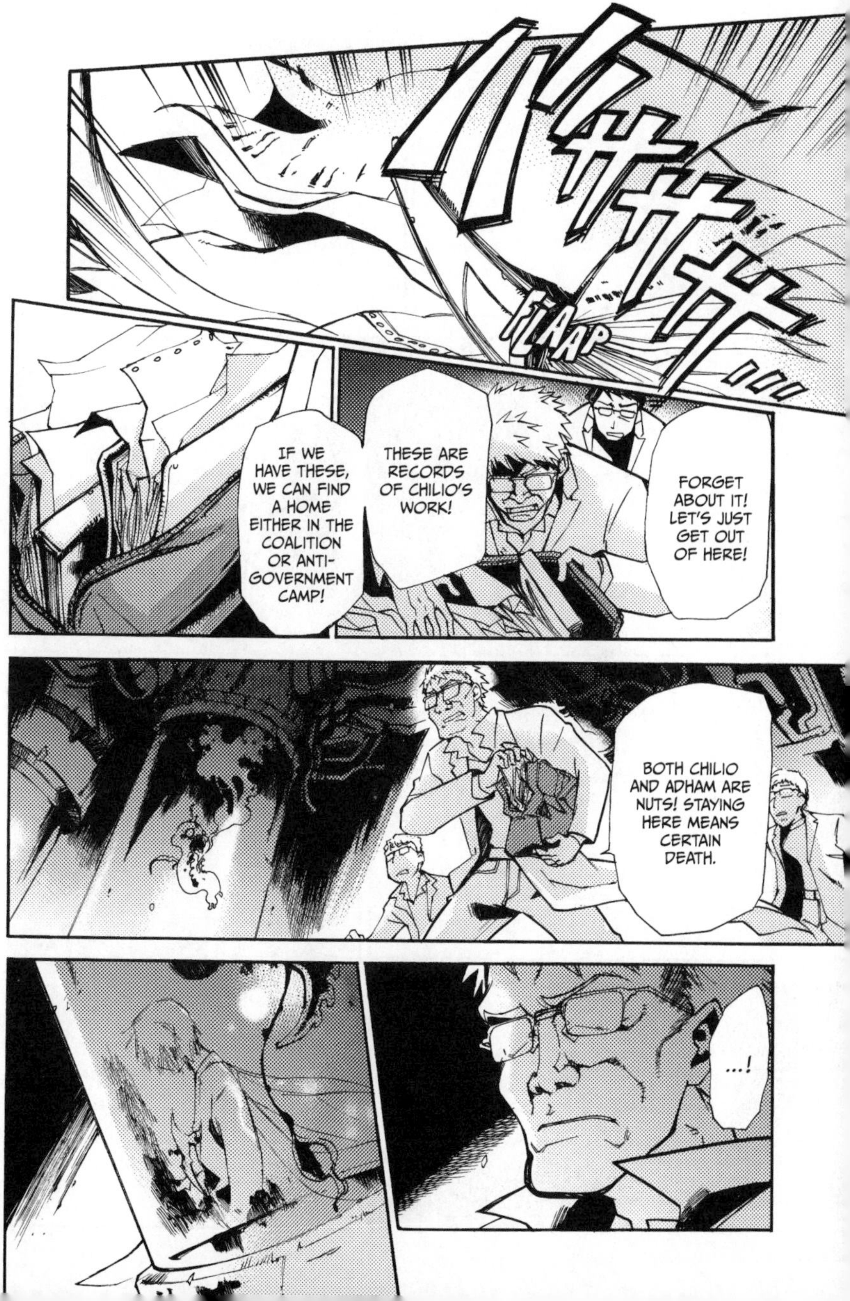
FLAAP
FORGET ABOUT IT! LET'S JUST GET OUT OF HERE!
THESE ARE RECORDS OF CHILIO'S WORK!
IF WE HAVE THESE, WE CAN FIND A HOME EITHER IN THE COALITION OR ANTI-GOVERNMENT CAMP!
BOTH CHILIO AND ADHAM ARE NUTS! STAYING HERE MEANS CERTAIN DEATH.
...!

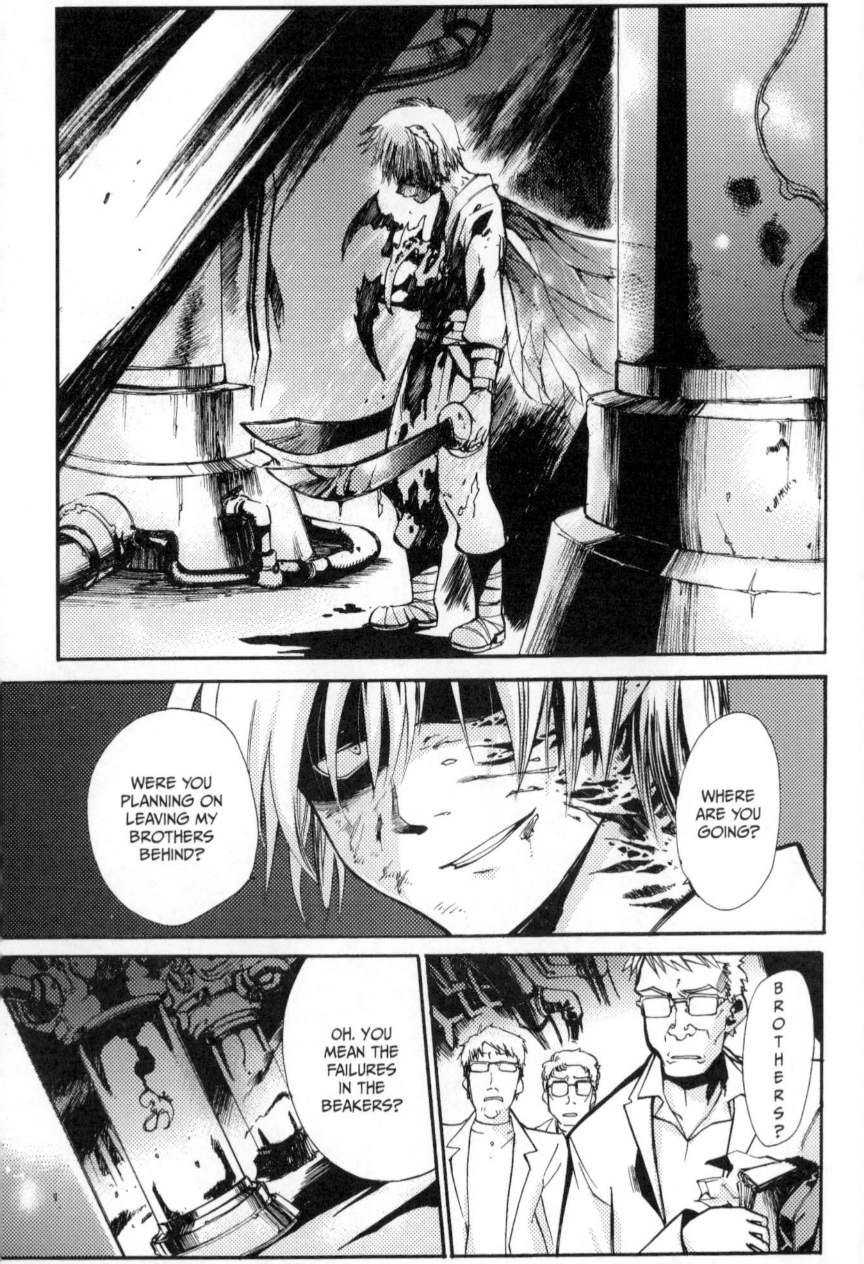
WHERE ARE YOU GOING?
WERE YOU PLANNING ON LEAVING MY BROTHERS BEHIND?
BROTHERS?
OH. YOU MEAN THE FAILURES IN THE BEAKERS?

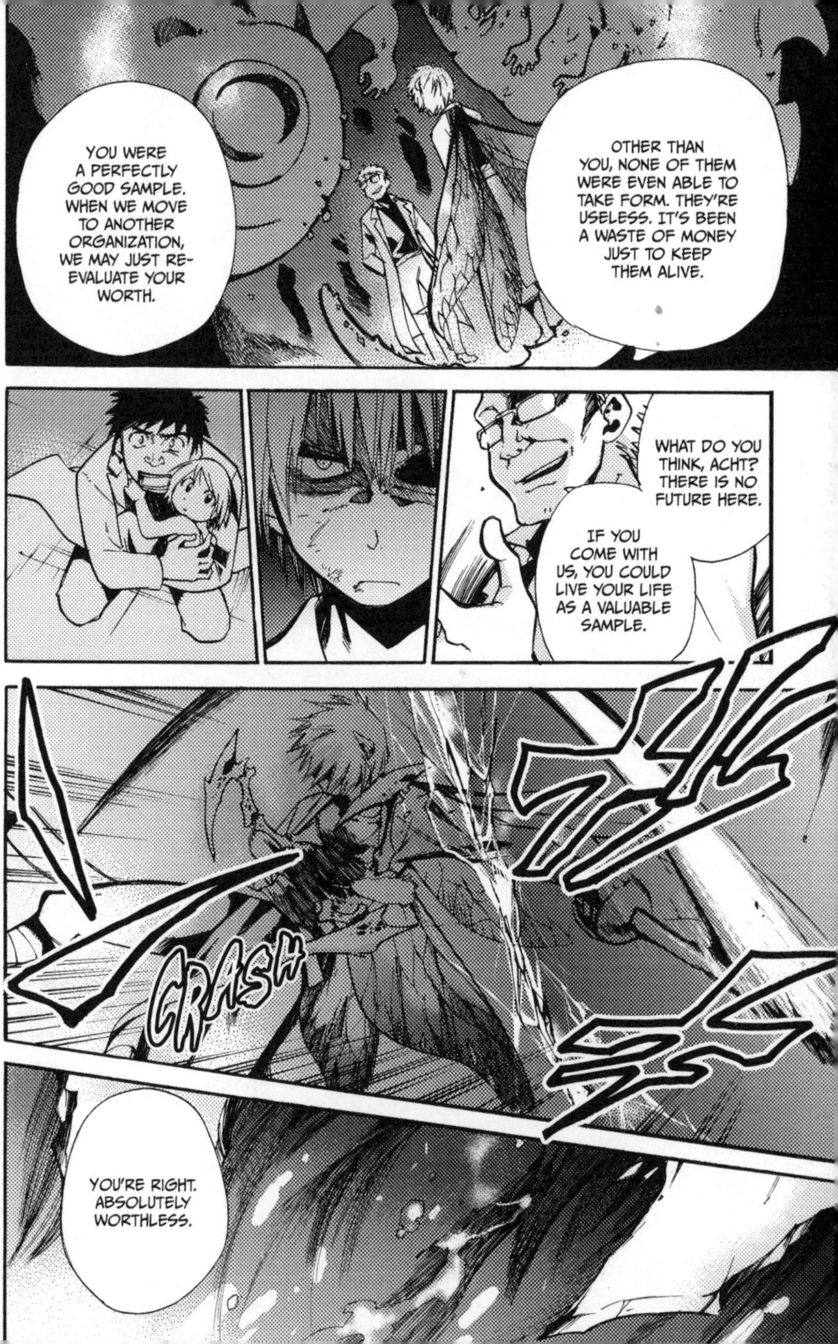
OTHER THAN YOU, NONE OF THEM WERE EVEN ABLE TO TAKE FORM. THEY'RE USELESS. IT'S BEEN A WASTE OF MONEY JUST TO KEEP THEM ALIVE.
YOU WERE A PERFECTLY GOOD SAMPLE. WHEN WE MOVE TO ANOTHER ORGANIZATION, WE MAY JUST RE-EVALUATE YOUR WORTH.
WHAT DO YOU THINK, ACHT? THERE IS NO FUTURE HERE.
IF YOU COME WITH US, YOU COULD LIVE YOUR LIFE AS A VALUABLE SAMPLE.
CRASH
YOU'RE RIGHT. ABSOLUTELY WORTHLESS.

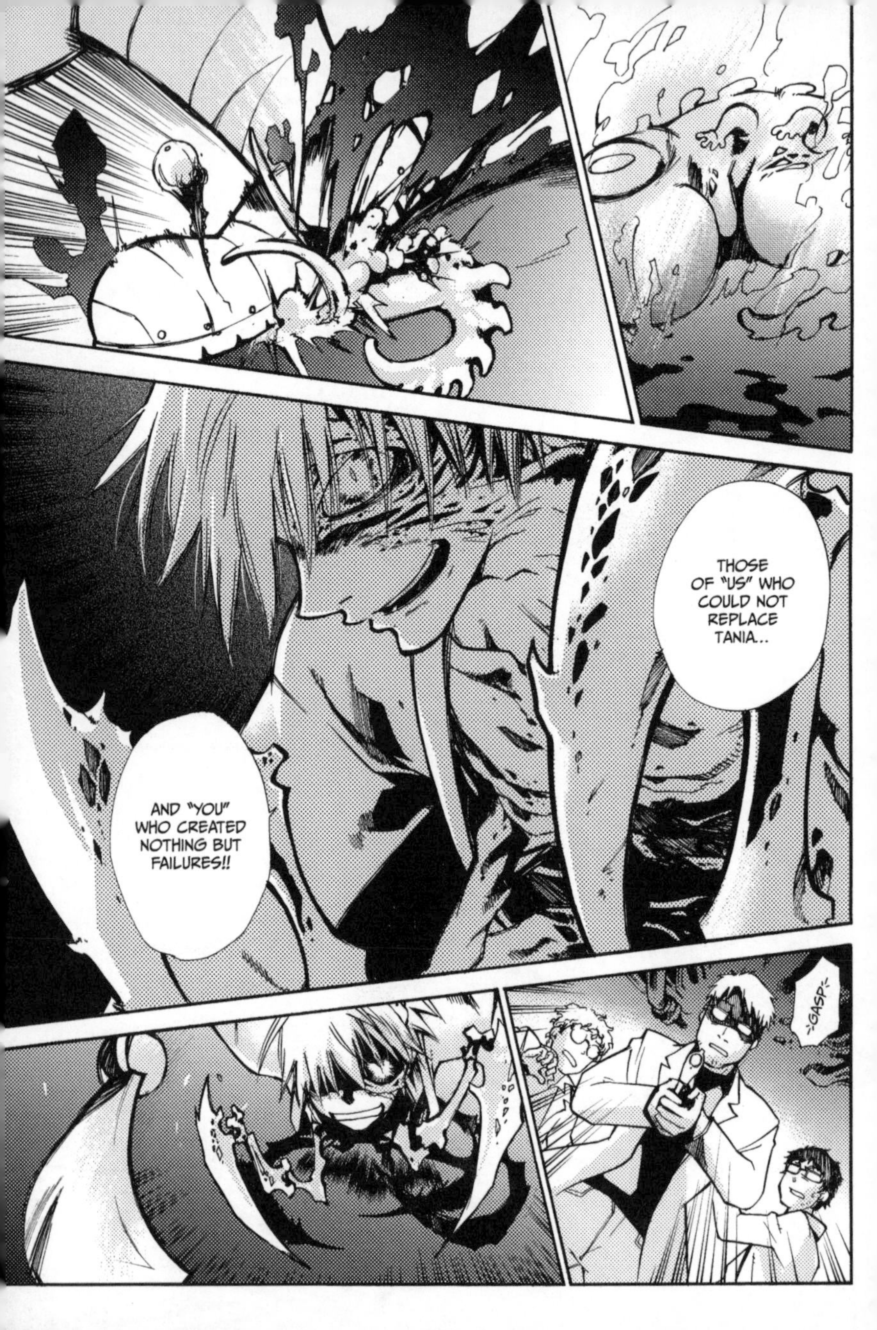
THOSE OF "US" WHO COULD NOT REPLACE TANIA..
AND "YOU" WHO CREATED NOTHING BUT FAILURES!!
GASP

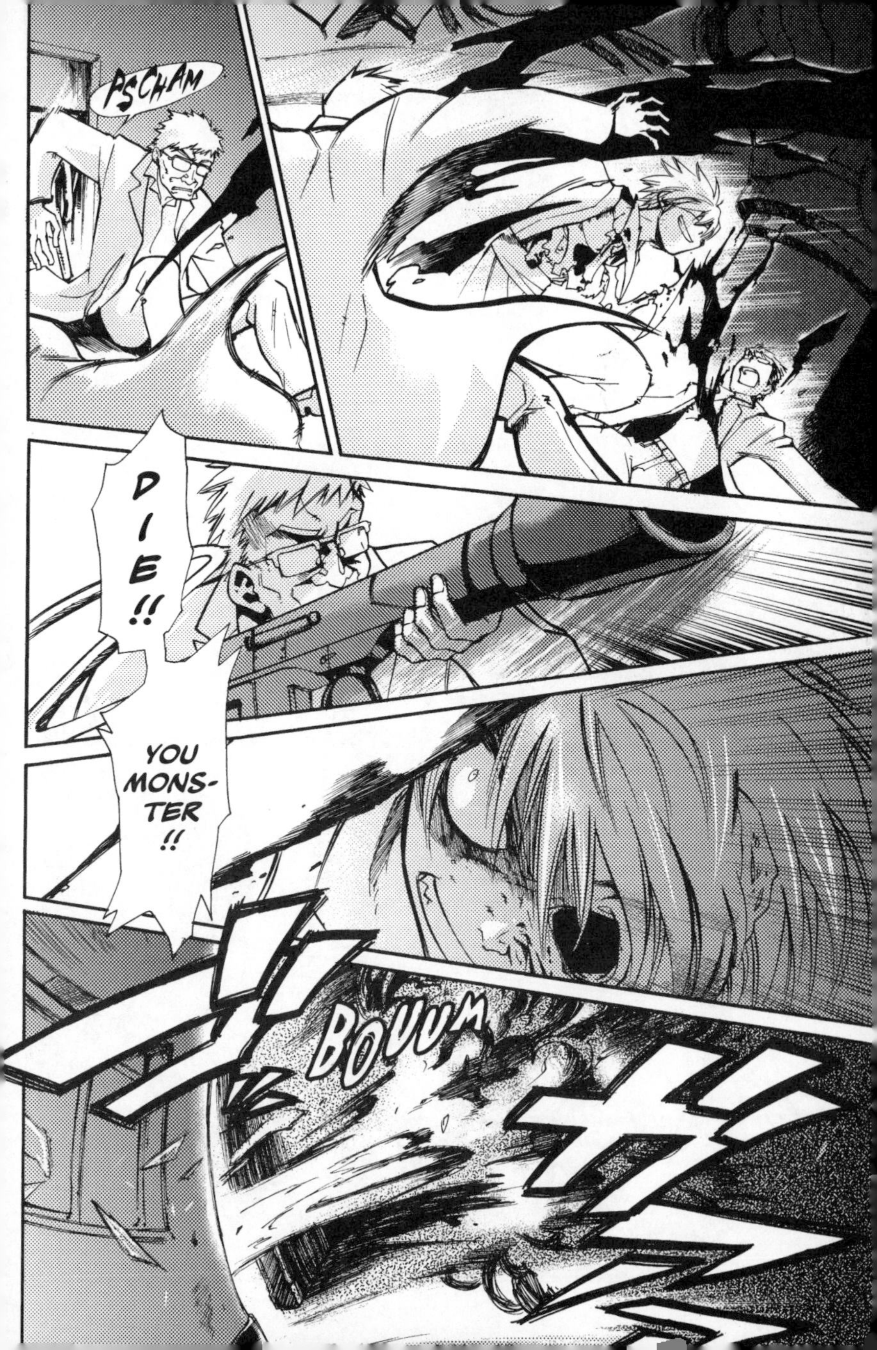
PSCHAM
DIE!!
YOU MONSTER!!
BOUUM

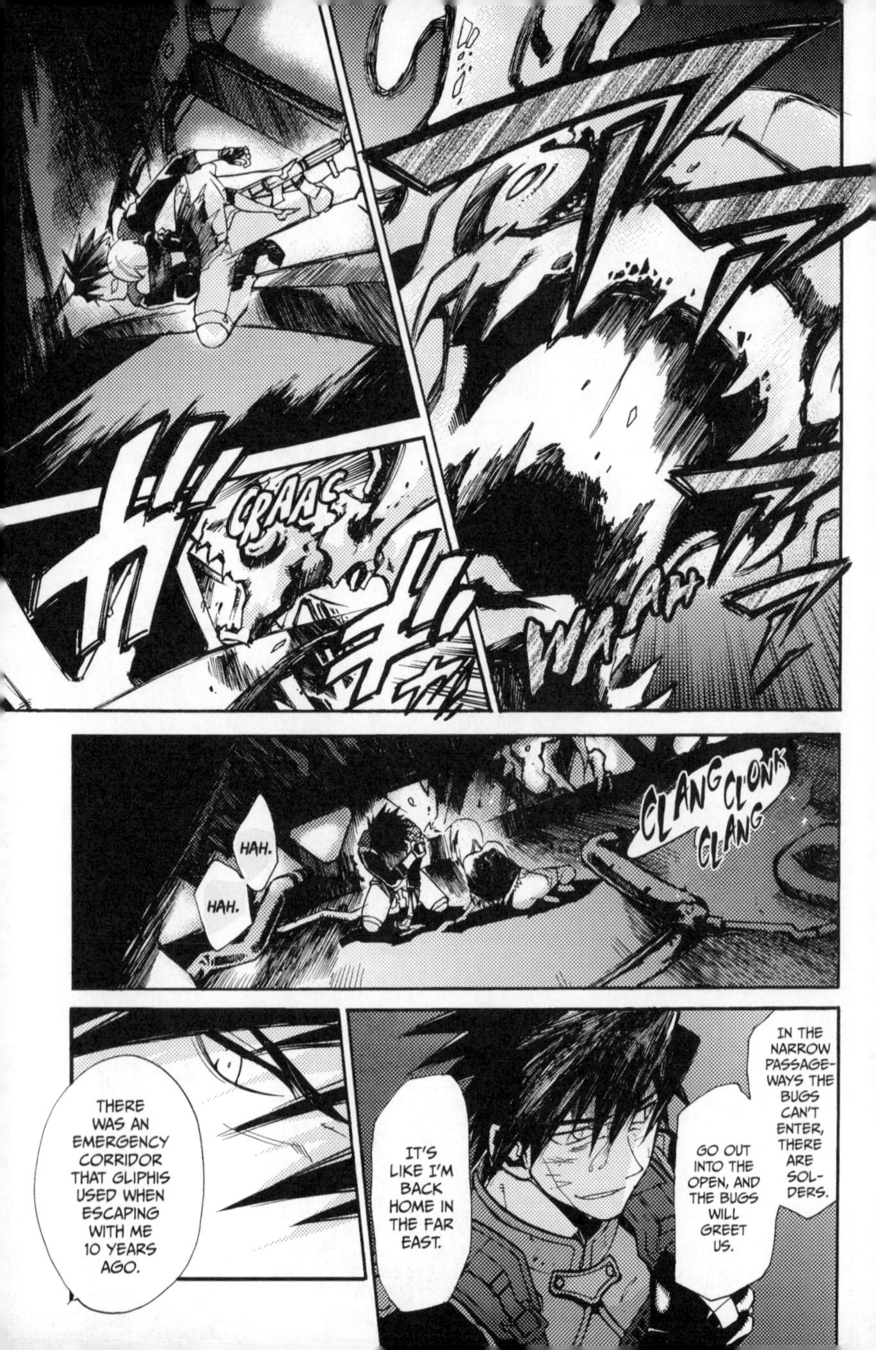
WAAAH
CRAAC
HAH.
HAH.
CLANG CLONK CLANG
IN THE NARROW PASSAGEWAYS THE BUGS CAN'T ENTER, THERE ARE SOLDERS.
GO OUT INTO THE OPEN, AND THE BUGS WILL GREET US.
IT'S LIKE I'M BACK HOME IN THE FAR EAST.
THERE WAS AN EMERGENCY CORRIDOR THAT GLIPHIS USED WHEN ESCAPING WITH ME 10 YEARS AGO.

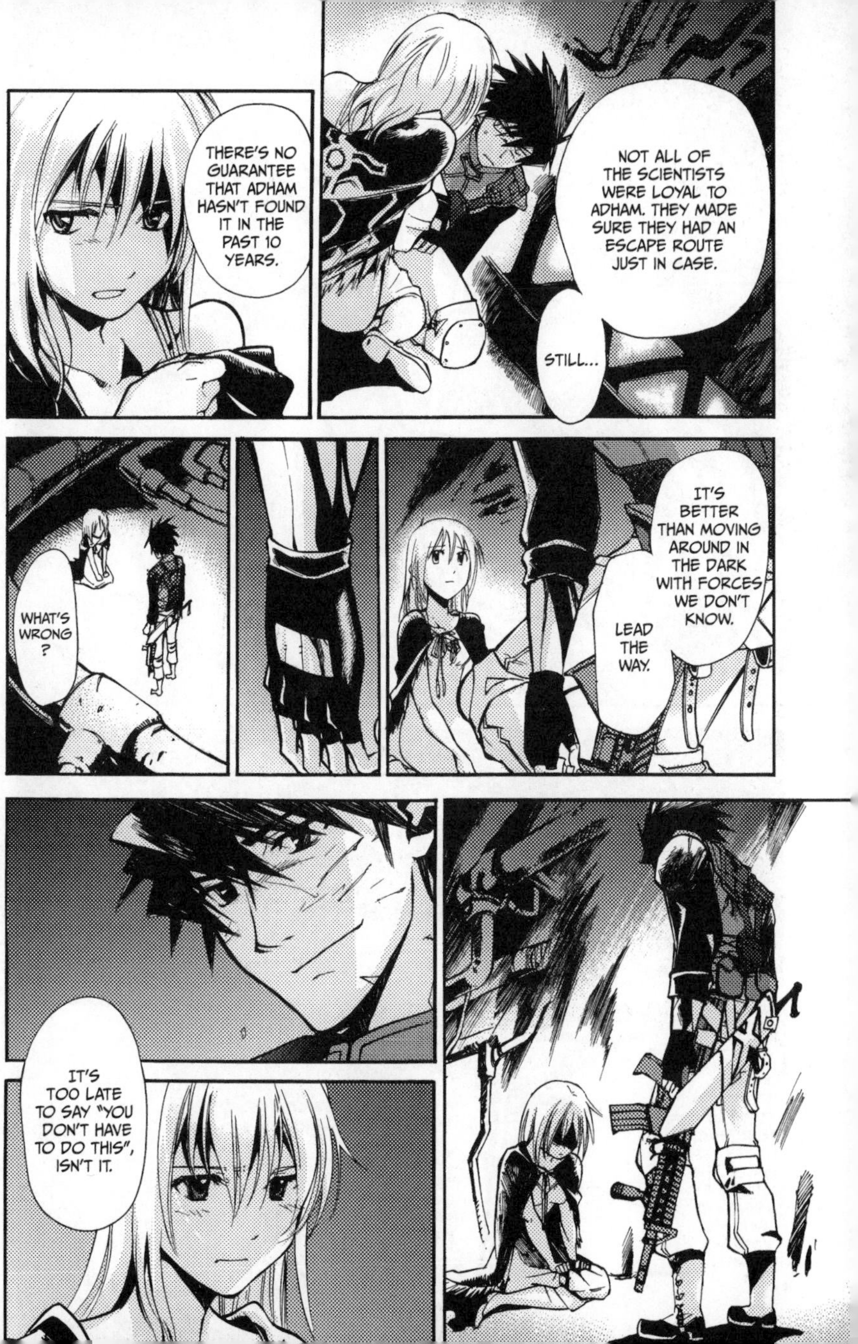
NOT ALL OF THE SCIENTISTS WERE LOYAL TO ADHAM. THEY MADE SURE THEY HAD AN ESCAPE ROUTE JUST IN CASE.
STILL...
THERE'S NO GUARANTEE THAT ADHAM HASN'T FOUND IT IN THE PAST 10 YEARS.
IT'S BETTER THAN MOVING AROUND IN THE DARK WITH FORCES WE DON'T KNOW.
LEAD THE WAY.
WHAT'S WRONG ?
IT'S TOO LATE TO SAY "YOU DON'T HAVE TO DO THIS", ISN'T IT.

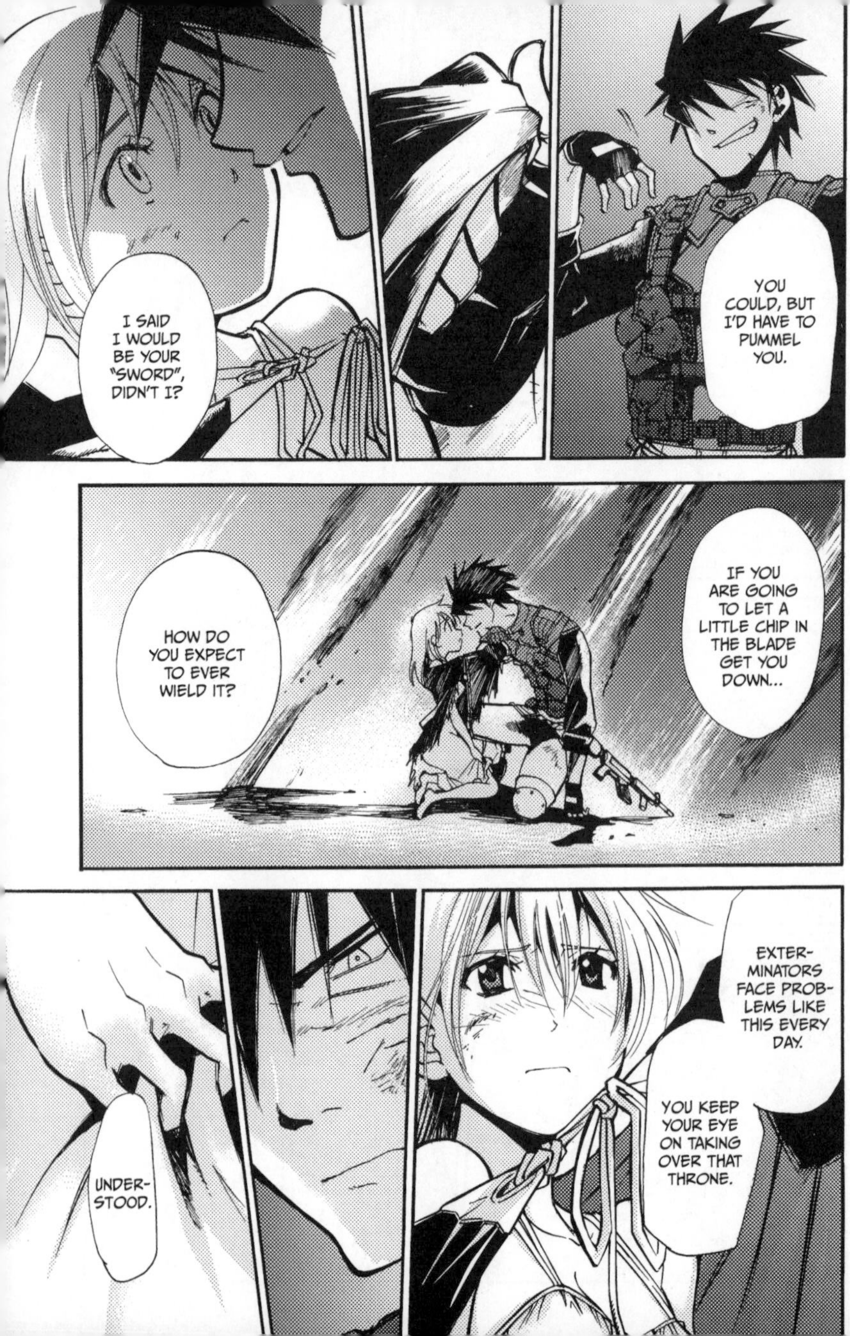
YOU COULD, BUT I'D HAVE TO PUMMEL YOU.
I SAID I WOULD BE YOUR "SWORD", DIDN'T I?
IF YOU ARE GOING TO LET A LITTLE CHIP IN THE BLADE GET YOU DOWN...
HOW DO YOU EXPECT TO EVER WIELD IT?
EXTER-MINATORS FACE PROB-LEMS LIKE THIS EVERY DAY.
YOU KEEP YOUR EYE ON TAKING OVER THAT THRONE.
UNDER-STOOD.

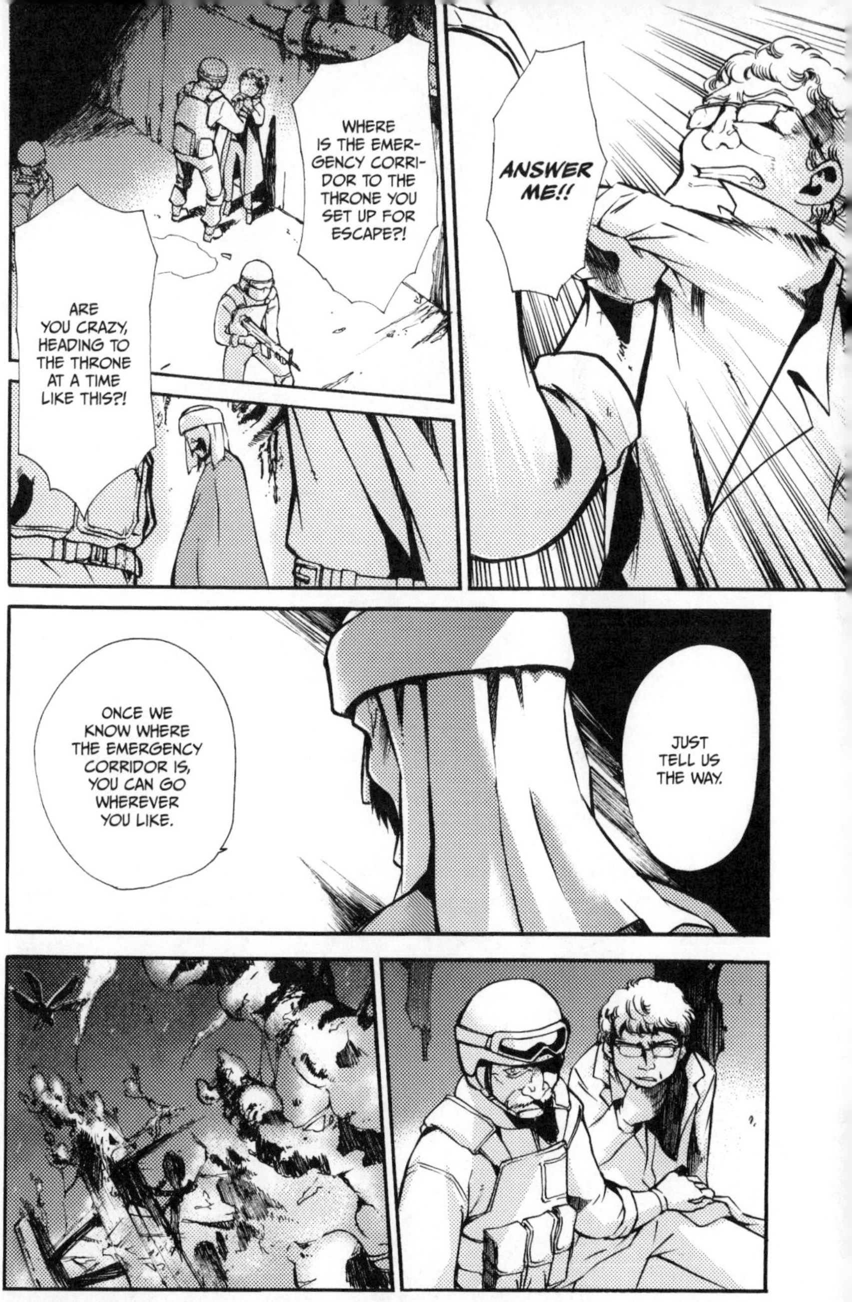
ANSWER ME!!
WHERE IS THE EMERGENCY CORRIDOR TO THE THRONE YOU SET UP FOR ESCAPE?!
ARE YOU CRAZY, HEADING TO THE THRONE AT A TIME LIKE THIS?!
JUST TELL US THE WAY.
ONCE WE KNOW WHERE THE EMERGENCY CORRIDOR IS, YOU CAN GO WHEREVER YOU LIKE.

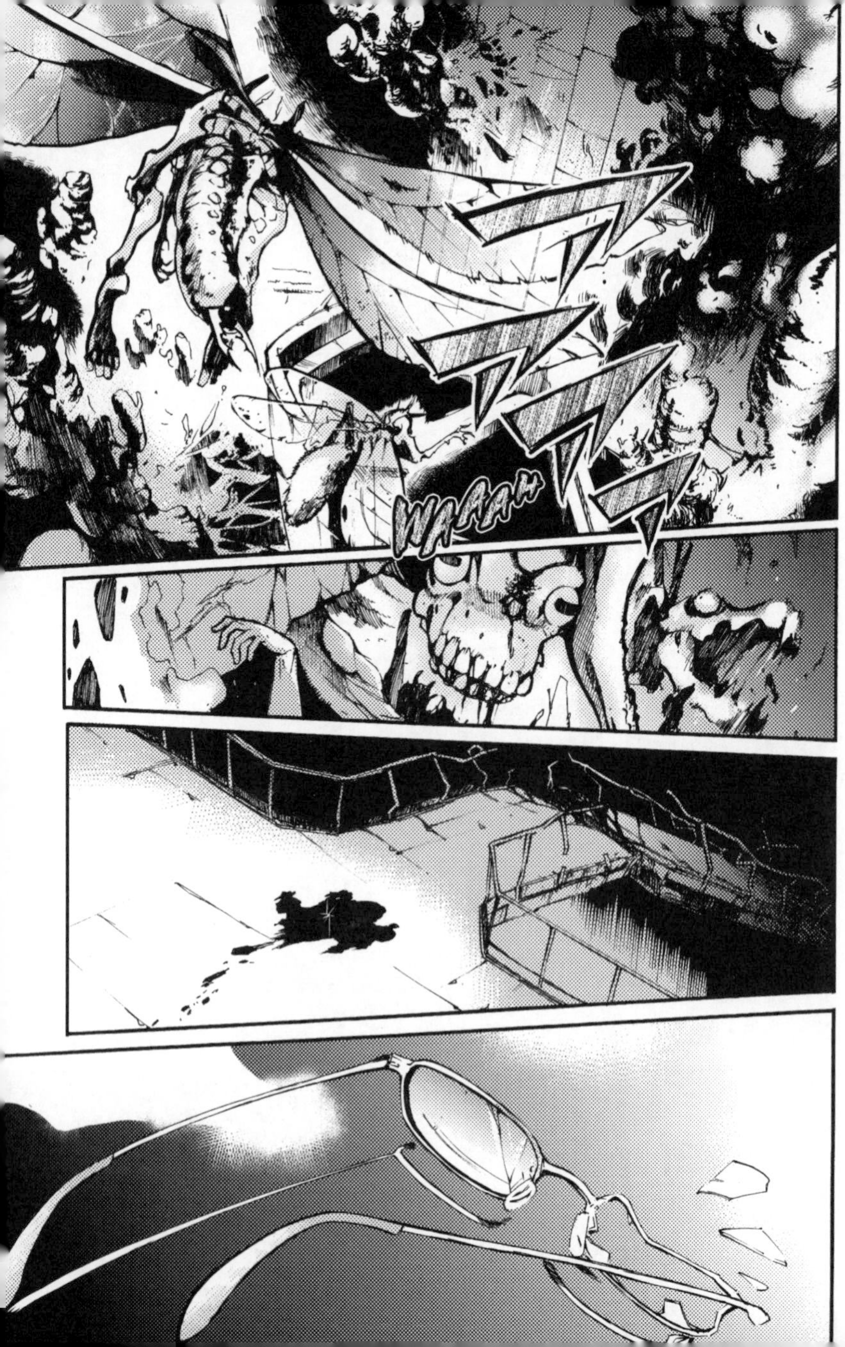
WAAAAH

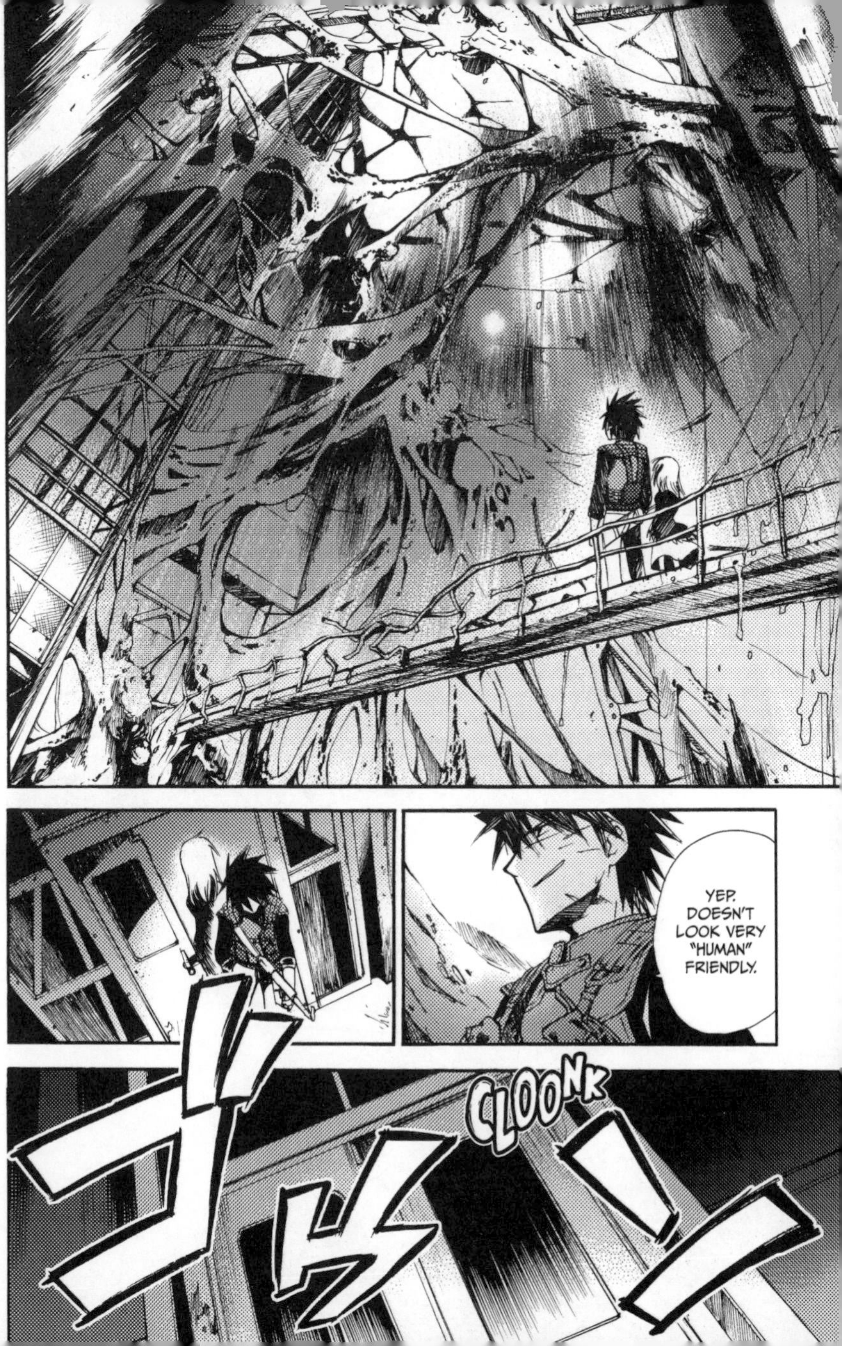
YEP. DOESN'T LOOK VERY "HUMAN" FRIENDLY.
CLOONK

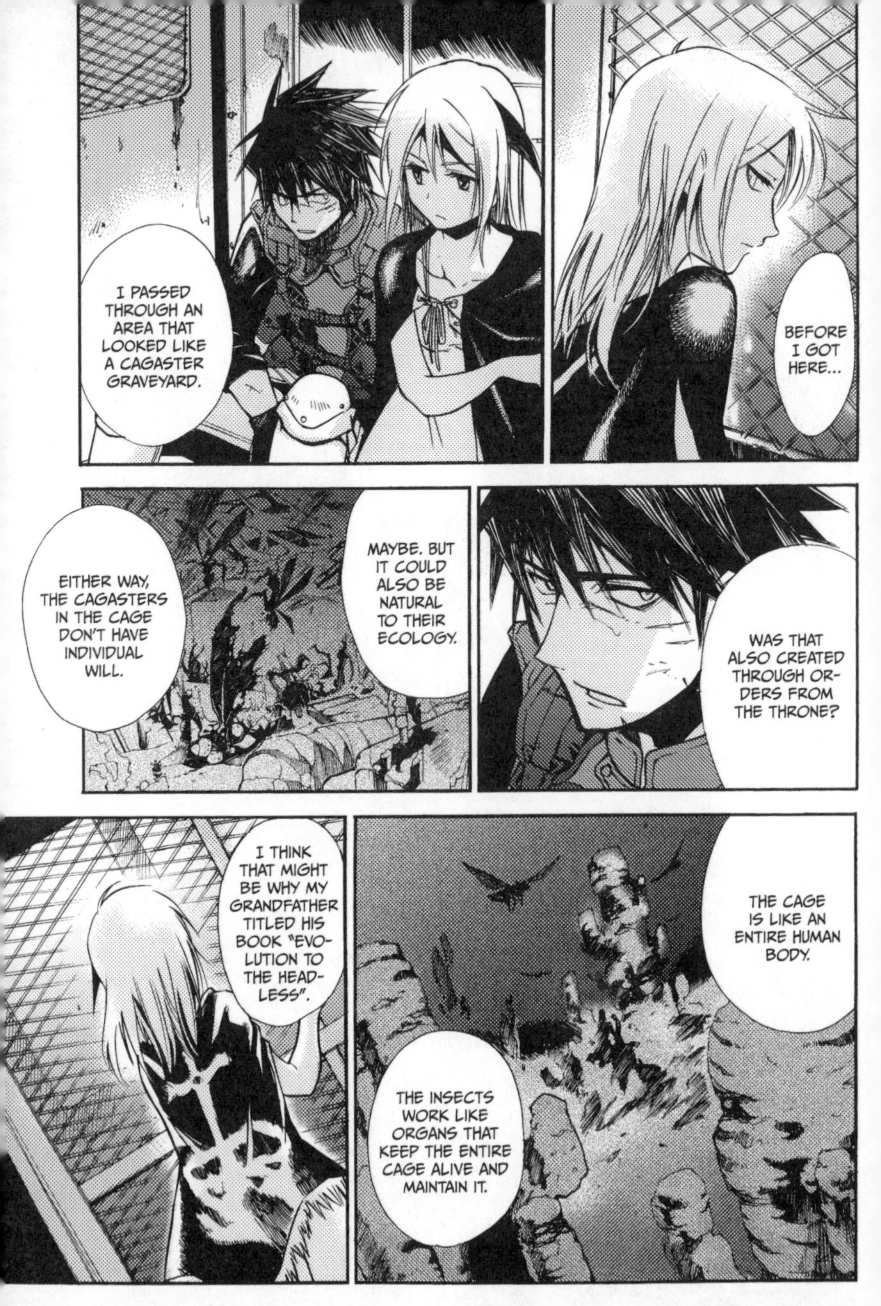

BEFORE I GOT HERE...
I PASSED THROUGH AN AREA THAT LOOKED LIKE A CAGASTER GRAVEYARD.
WAS THAT ALSO CREATED THROUGH OR-DERS FROM THE THRONE?
MAYBE. BUT IT COULD ALSO BE NATURAL TO THEIR ECOLOGY.
EITHER WAY, THE CAGASTERS IN THE CAGE DON'T HAVE INDIVIDUAL WILL.
THE CAGE IS LIKE AN ENTIRE HUMAN BODY.
THE INSECTS WORK LIKE ORGANS THAT KEEP THE ENTIRE CAGE ALIVE AND MAINTAIN IT.
I THINK THAT MIGHT BE WHY MY GRANDFATHER TITLED HIS BOOK "EVO-LUTION TO THE HEAD-LESS".

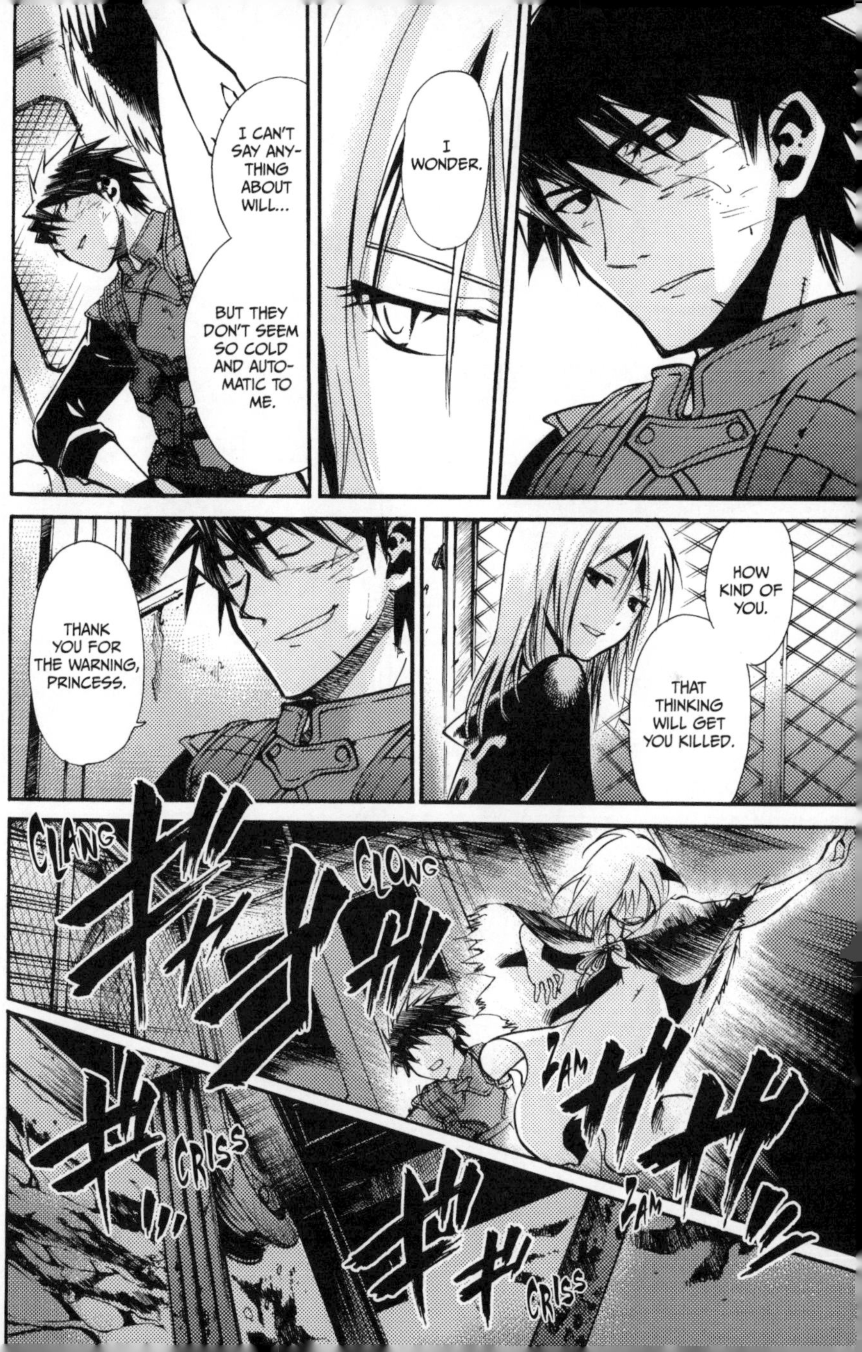
I WONDER.
I CAN'T SAY ANYTHING ABOUT WILL...
BUT THEY DON'T SEEM SO COLD AND AUTOMATIC TO ME.
HOW KIND OF YOU.
THAT THINKING WILL GET YOU KILLED.
THANK YOU FOR THE WARNING, PRINCESS.
CLONG
CLANG
ZAM
ZAM
CRISS
CRISS

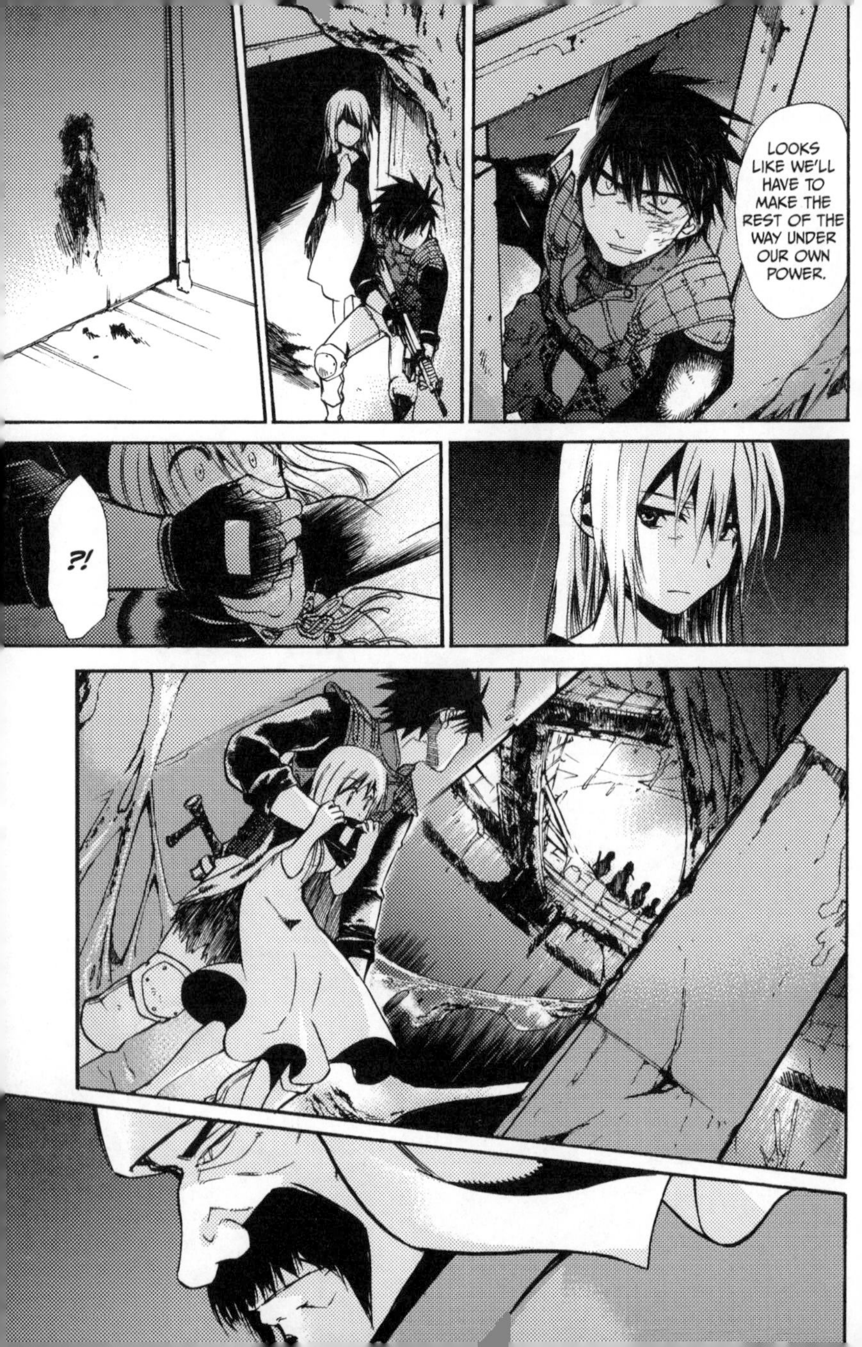
LOOKS LIKE WE'LL HAVE TO MAKE THE REST OF THE WAY UNDER OUR OWN POWER.
?!

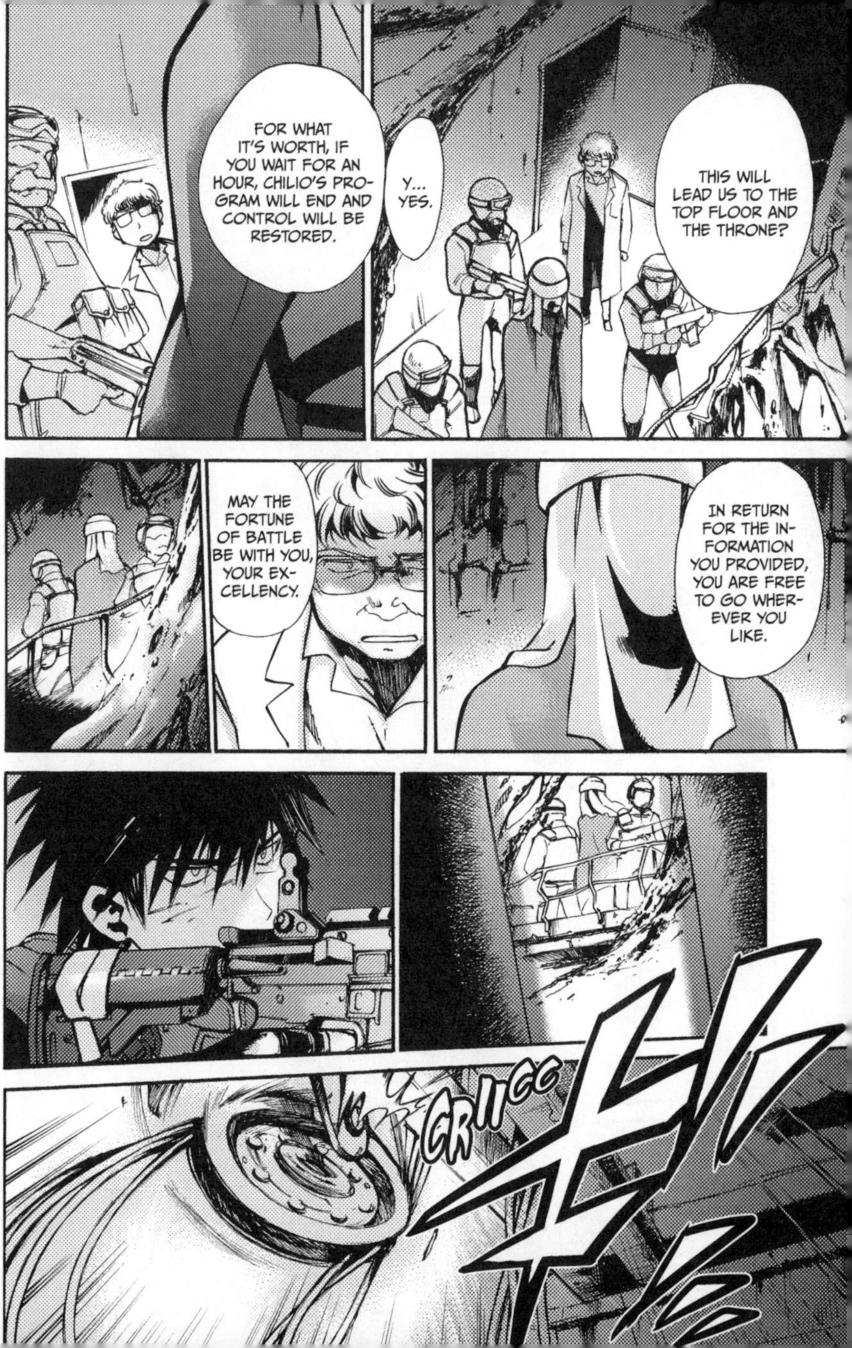
THIS WILL LEAD US TO THE TOP FLOOR AND THE THRONE?
Y... YES.
FOR WHAT IT'S WORTH, IF YOU WAIT FOR AN HOUR, CHILIO'S PROGRAM WILL END AND CONTROL WILL BE RESTORED.
IN RETURN FOR THE INFORMATION YOU PROVIDED, YOU ARE FREE TO GO WHEREVER YOU LIKE.
MAY THE FORTUNE OF BATTLE BE WITH YOU, YOUR EXCELLENCY.
GRIIGG

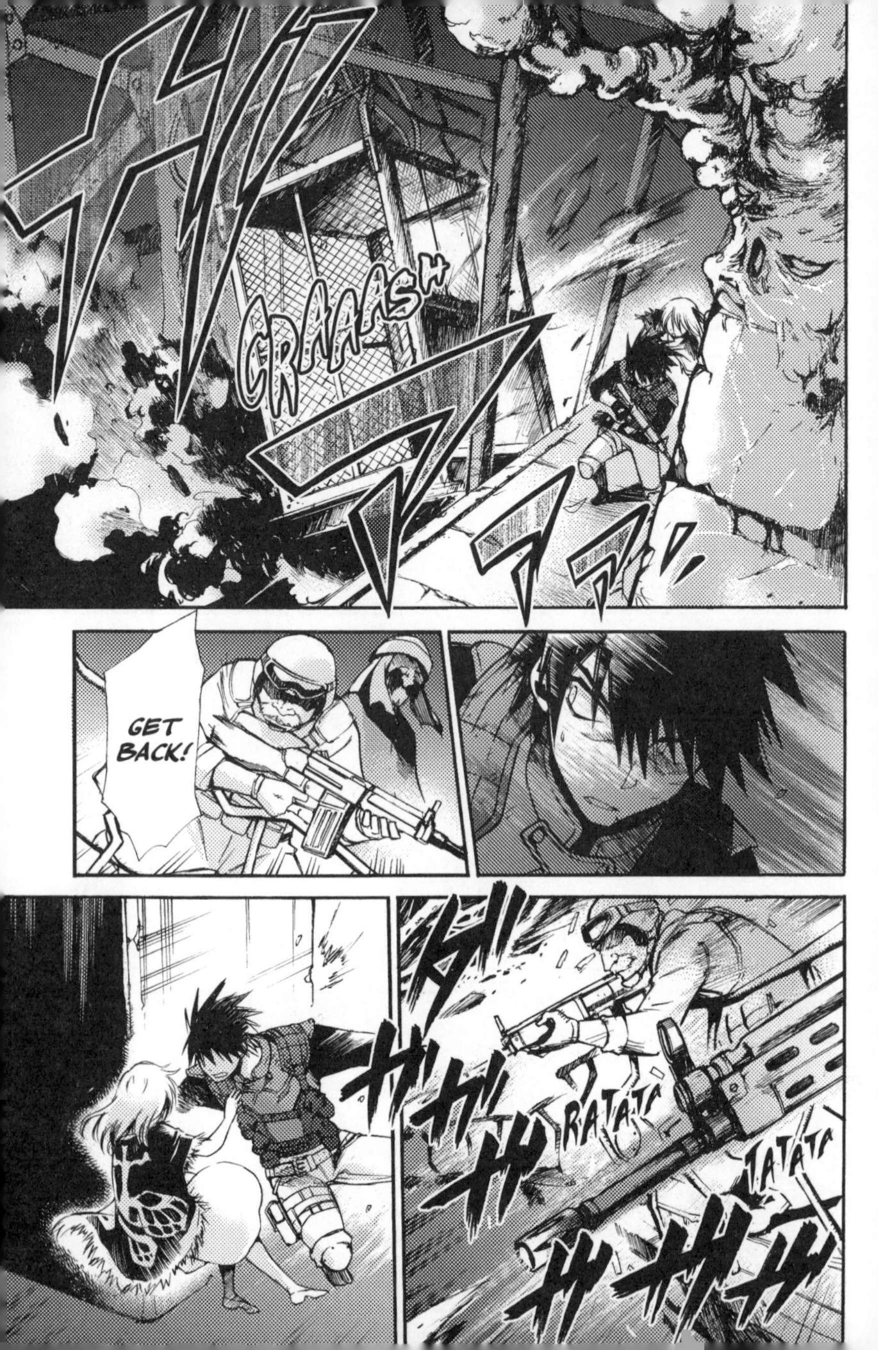
CRAAASH
GET BACK!
RATATA
TATATA

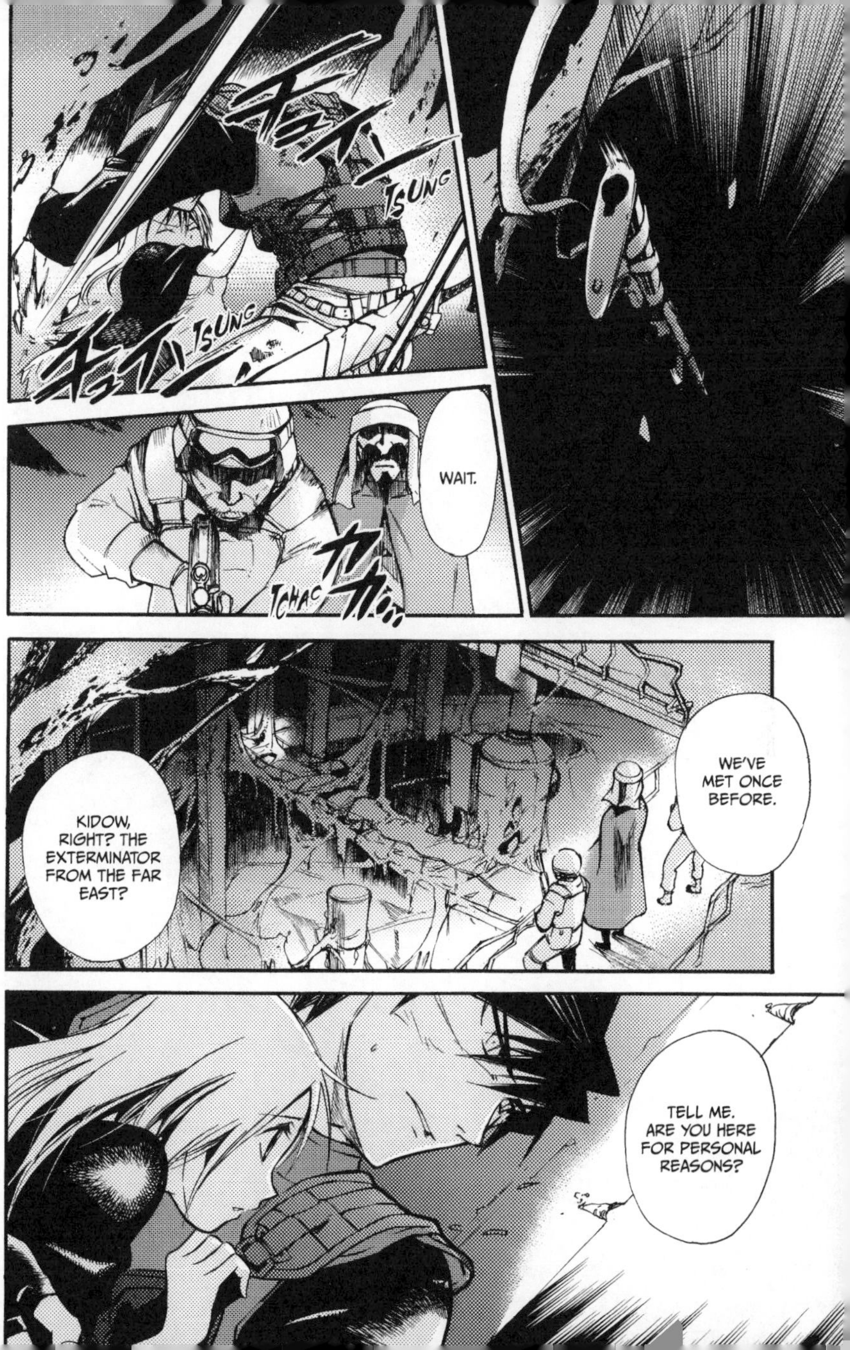
TSUNG
TSUNG
WAIT.
TCHAC
WE'VE MET ONCE BEFORE.
KIDOW, RIGHT? THE EXTERMINATOR FROM THE FAR EAST?
TELL ME. ARE YOU HERE FOR PERSONAL REASONS?

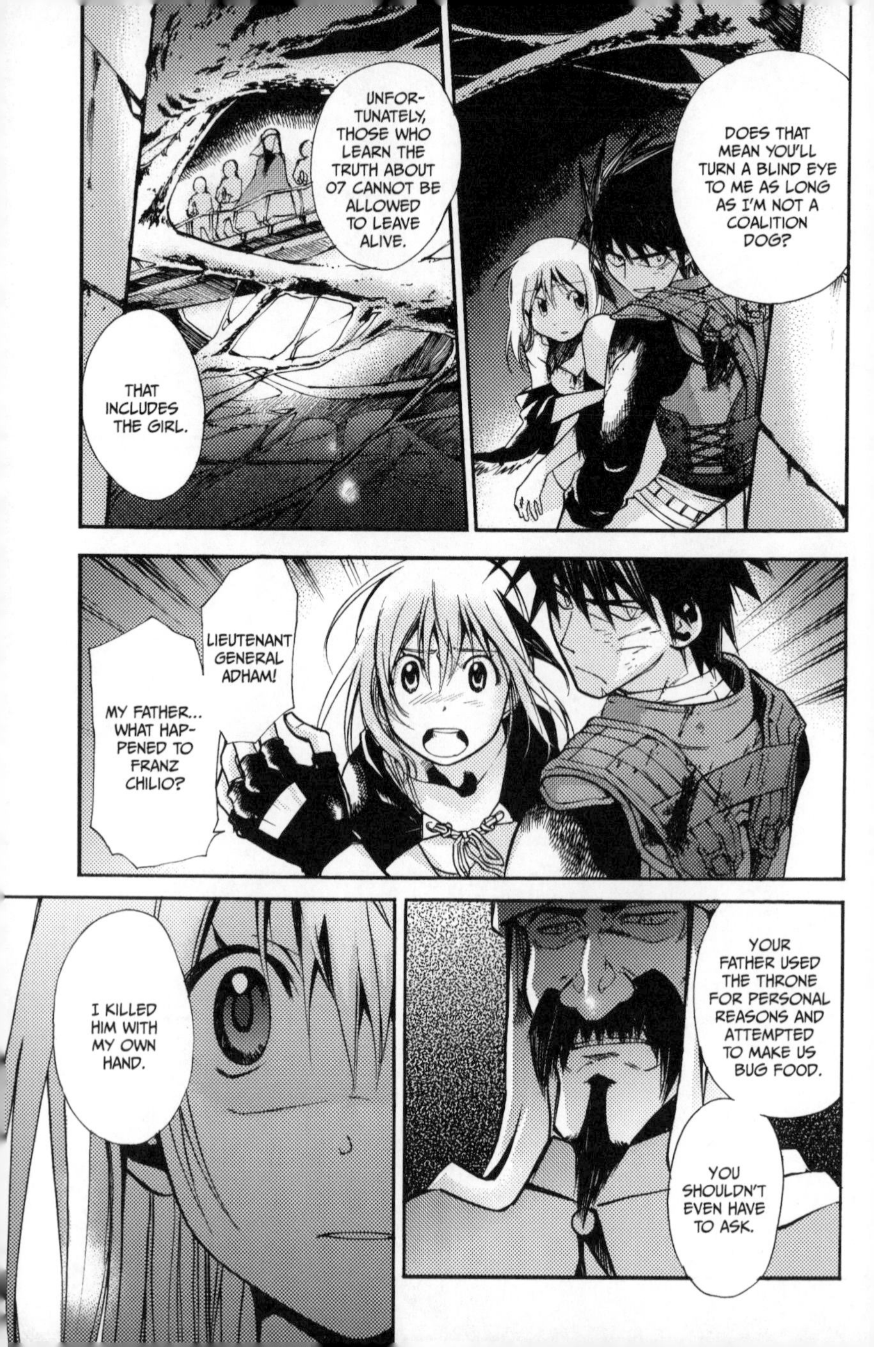
DOES THAT MEAN YOU'LL TURN A BLIND EYE TO ME AS LONG AS I'M NOT A COALITION DOG?
UNFORTUNATELY, THOSE WHO LEARN THE TRUTH ABOUT 07 CANNOT BE ALLOWED TO LEAVE ALIVE.
THAT INCLUDES THE GIRL.
LIEUTENANT GENERAL ADHAM!
MY FATHER... WHAT HAPPENED TO FRANZ CHILIO?
YOUR FATHER USED THE THRONE FOR PERSONAL REASONS AND ATTEMPTED TO MAKE US BUG FOOD.
YOU SHOULDN'T EVEN HAVE TO ASK.
I KILLED HIM WITH MY OWN HAND.

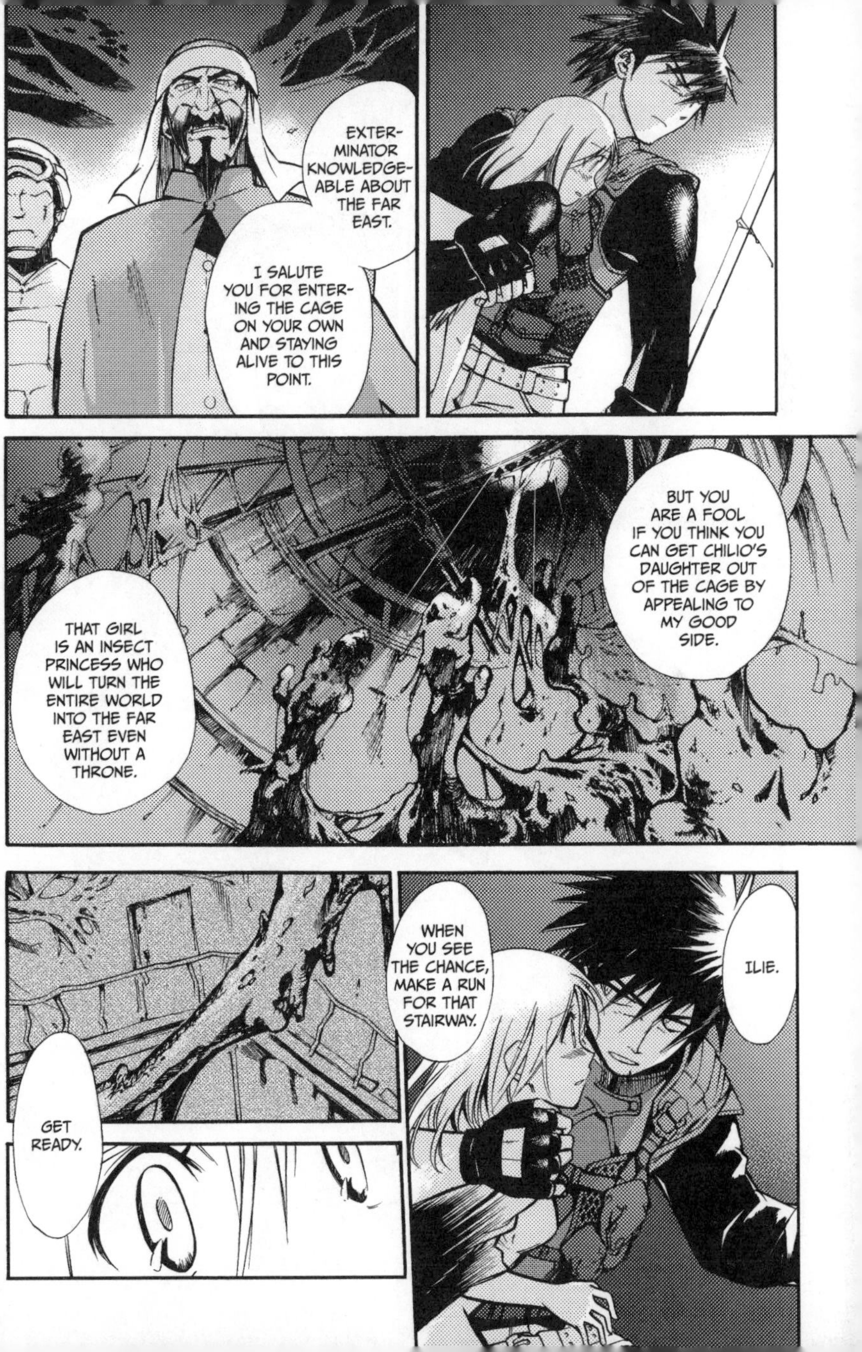
EXTER-MINATOR KNOWLEDGE-ABLE ABOUT THE FAR EAST.
I SALUTE YOU FOR ENTER-ING THE CAGE ON YOUR OWN AND STAYING ALIVE TO THIS POINT.
BUT YOU ARE A FOOL IF YOU THINK YOU CAN GET CHILIO'S DAUGHTER OUT OF THE CAGE BY APPEALING TO MY GOOD SIDE.
THAT GIRL IS AN INSECT PRINCESS WHO WILL TURN THE ENTIRE WORLD INTO THE FAR EAST EVEN WITHOUT A THRONE.
ILIE.
WHEN YOU SEE THE CHANCE, MAKE A RUN FOR THAT STAIRWAY.
GET READY.

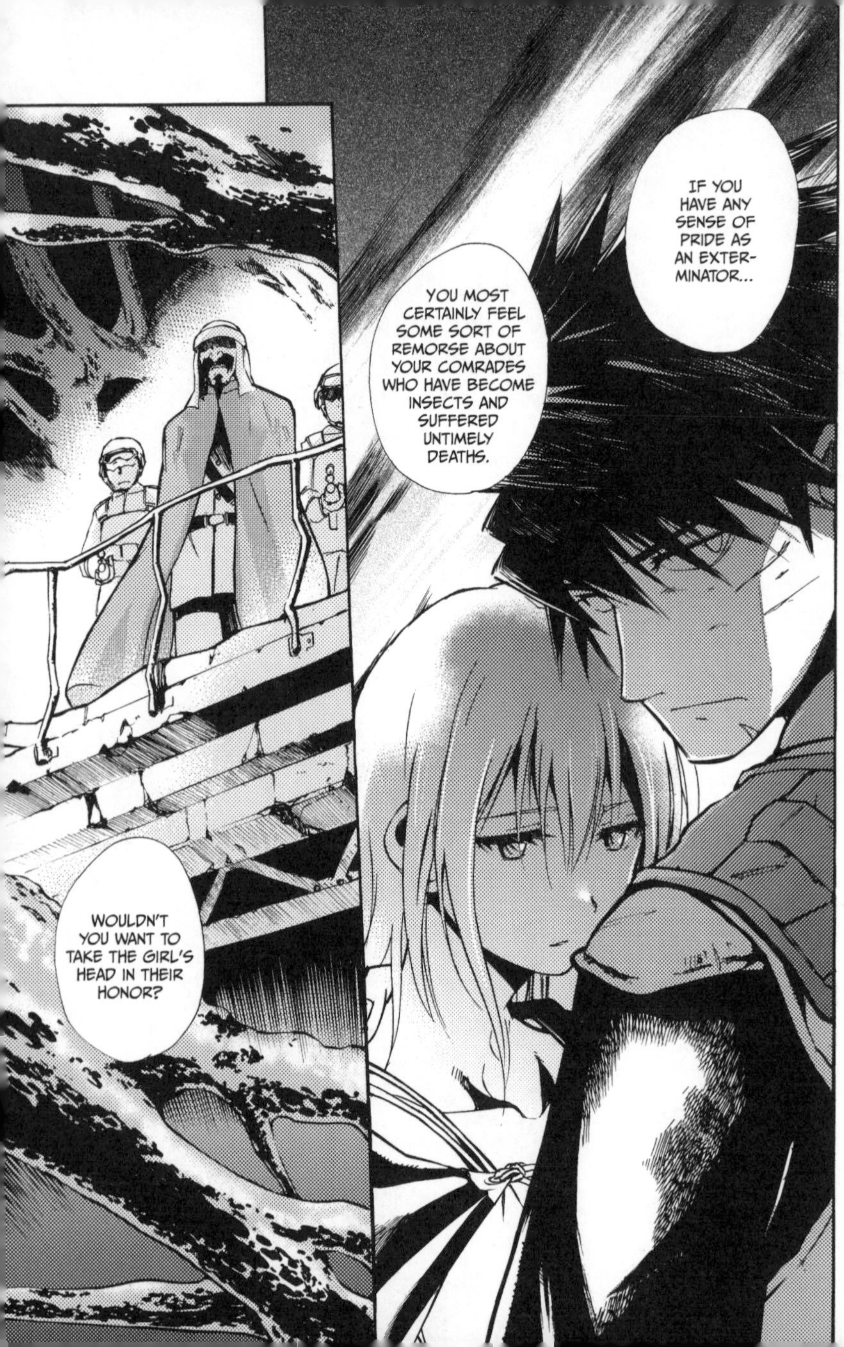
IF YOU HAVE ANY SENSE OF PRIDE AS AN EXTER-MINATOR...
YOU MOST CERTAINLY FEEL SOME SORT OF REMORSE ABOUT YOUR COMRADES WHO HAVE BECOME INSECTS AND SUFFERED UNTIMELY DEATHS.
WOULDN'T YOU WANT TO TAKE THE GIRL'S HEAD IN THEIR HONOR?

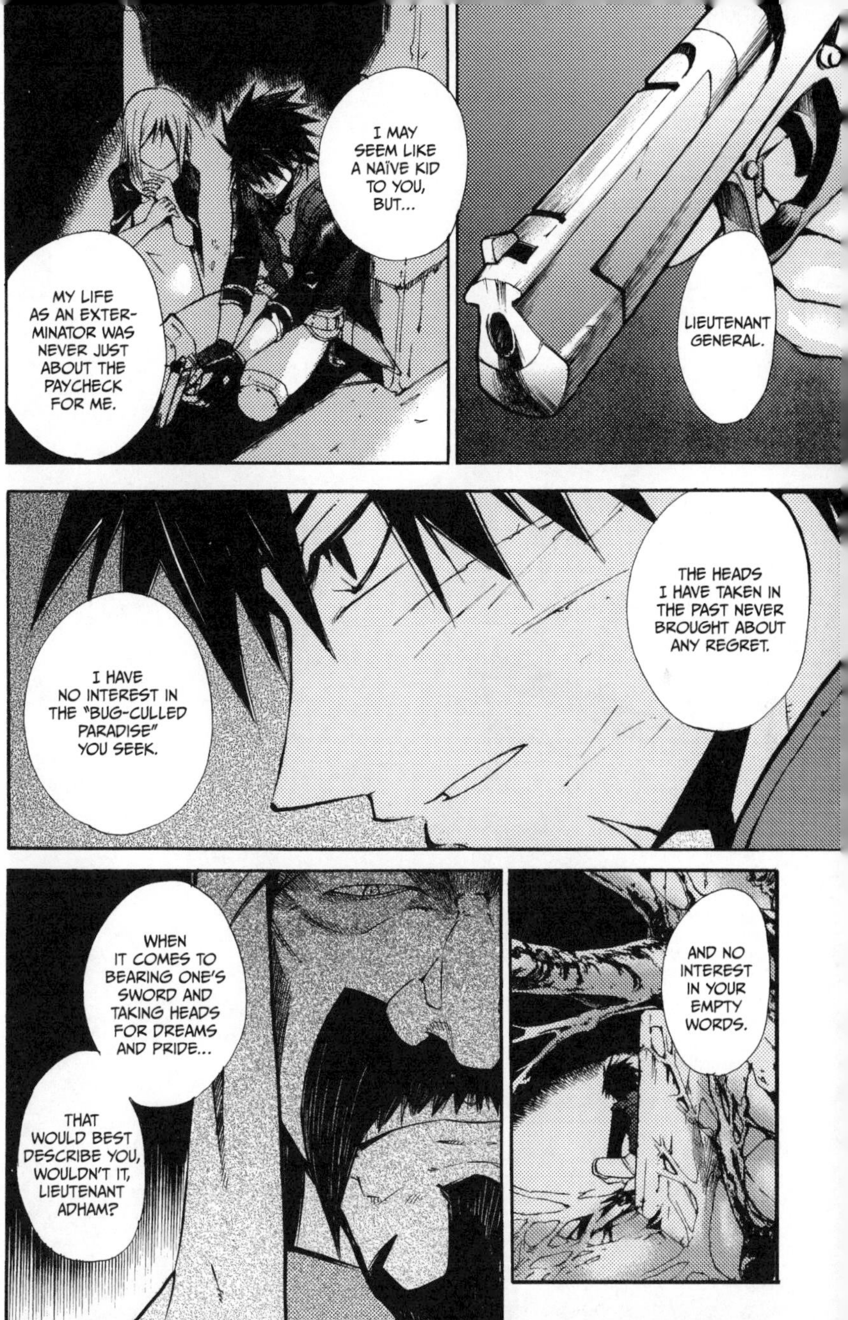
LIEUTENANT GENERAL.
I MAY SEEM LIKE A NAÏVE KID TO YOU, BUT...
MY LIFE AS AN EXTER-MINATOR WAS NEVER JUST ABOUT THE PAYCHECK FOR ME.
THE HEADS I HAVE TAKEN IN THE PAST NEVER BROUGHT ABOUT ANY REGRET.
I HAVE NO INTEREST IN THE "BUG-CULLED PARADISE" YOU SEEK.
AND NO INTEREST IN YOUR EMPTY WORDS.
WHEN IT COMES TO BEARING ONE'S SWORD AND TAKING HEADS FOR DREAMS AND PRIDE...
THAT WOULD BEST DESCRIBE YOU, WOULDN'T IT, LIEUTENANT ADHAM?

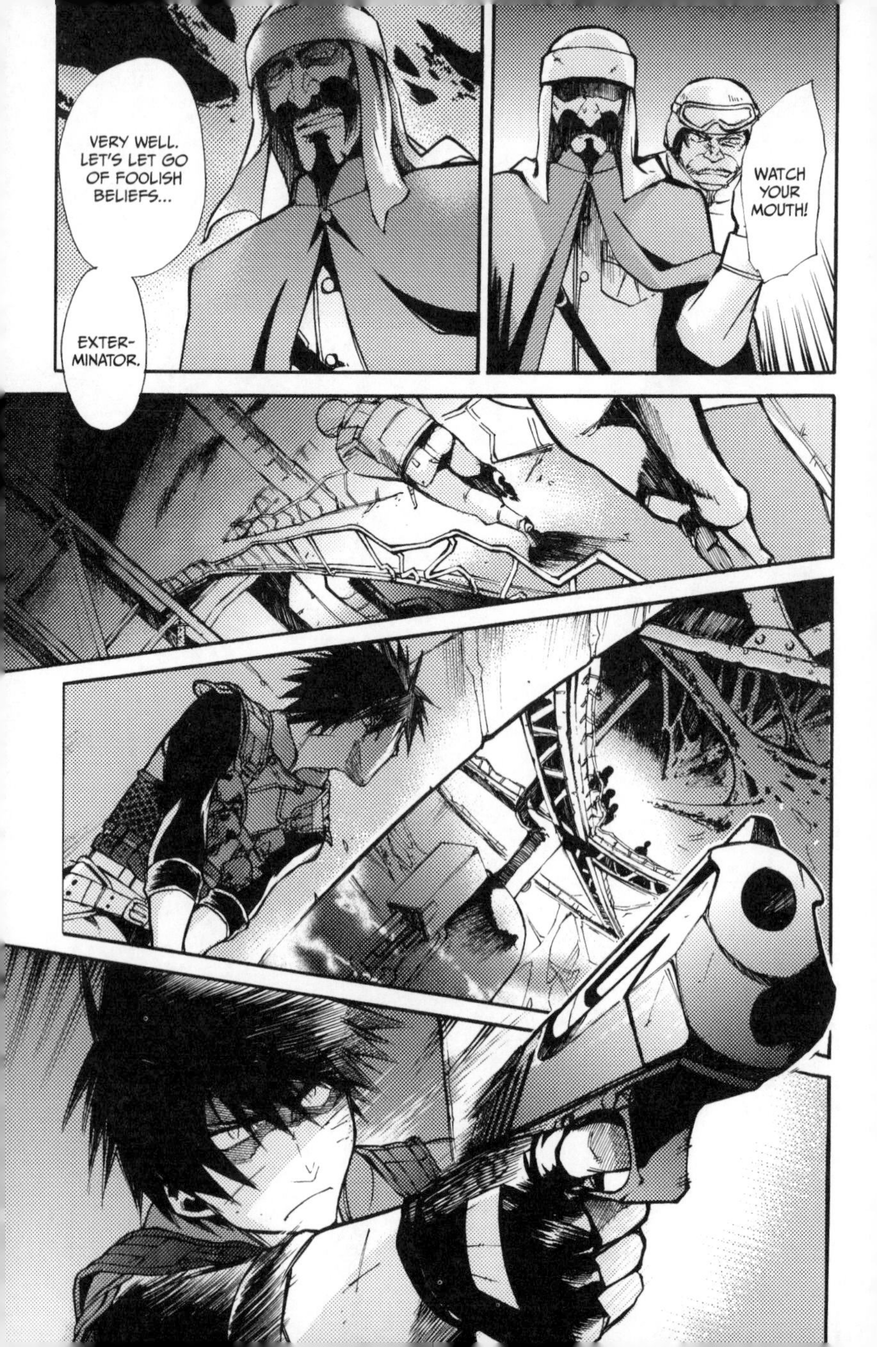
WATCH YOUR MOUTH!
VERY WELL. LET'S LET GO OF FOOLISH BELIEFS...
EXTER-MINATOR.

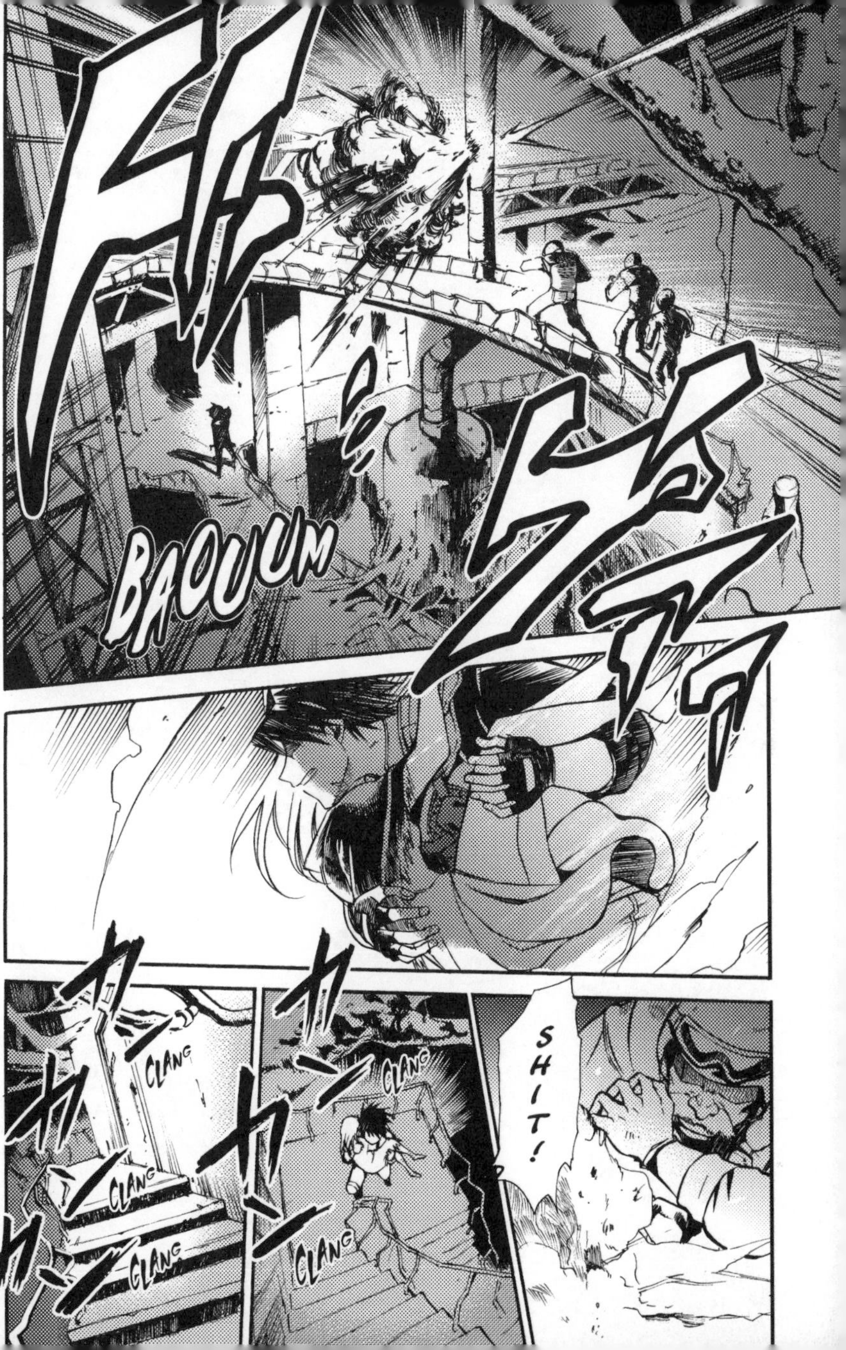
BAOUUM
SHIT!
CLANG
CLANG
CLANG
CLANG
CLANG

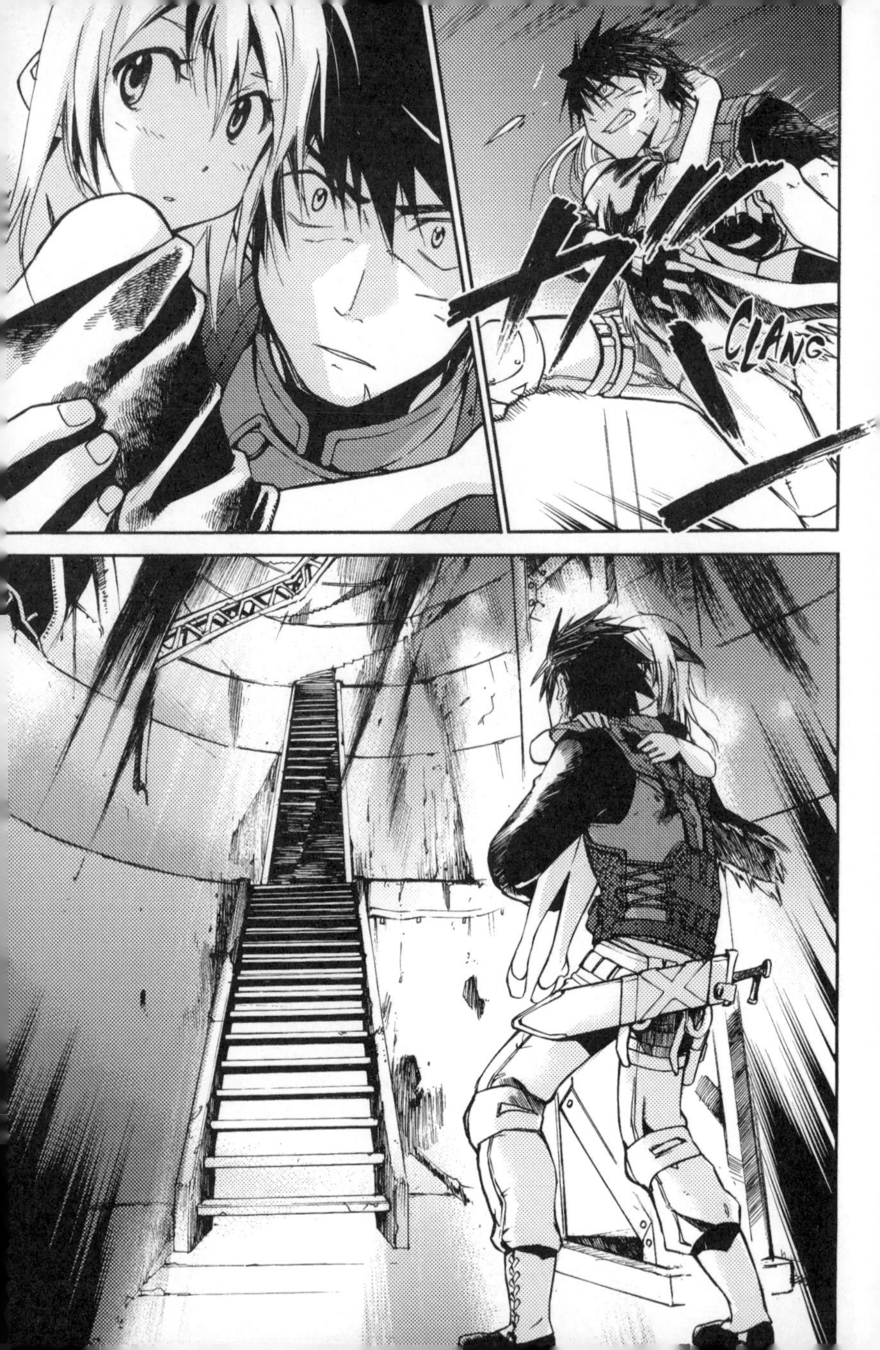
CLANG

YOU GO AHEAD.

I'LL STAY BEHIND TO BUY TIME...

AND CATCH UP TO YOU LATER.

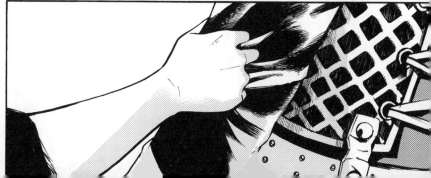

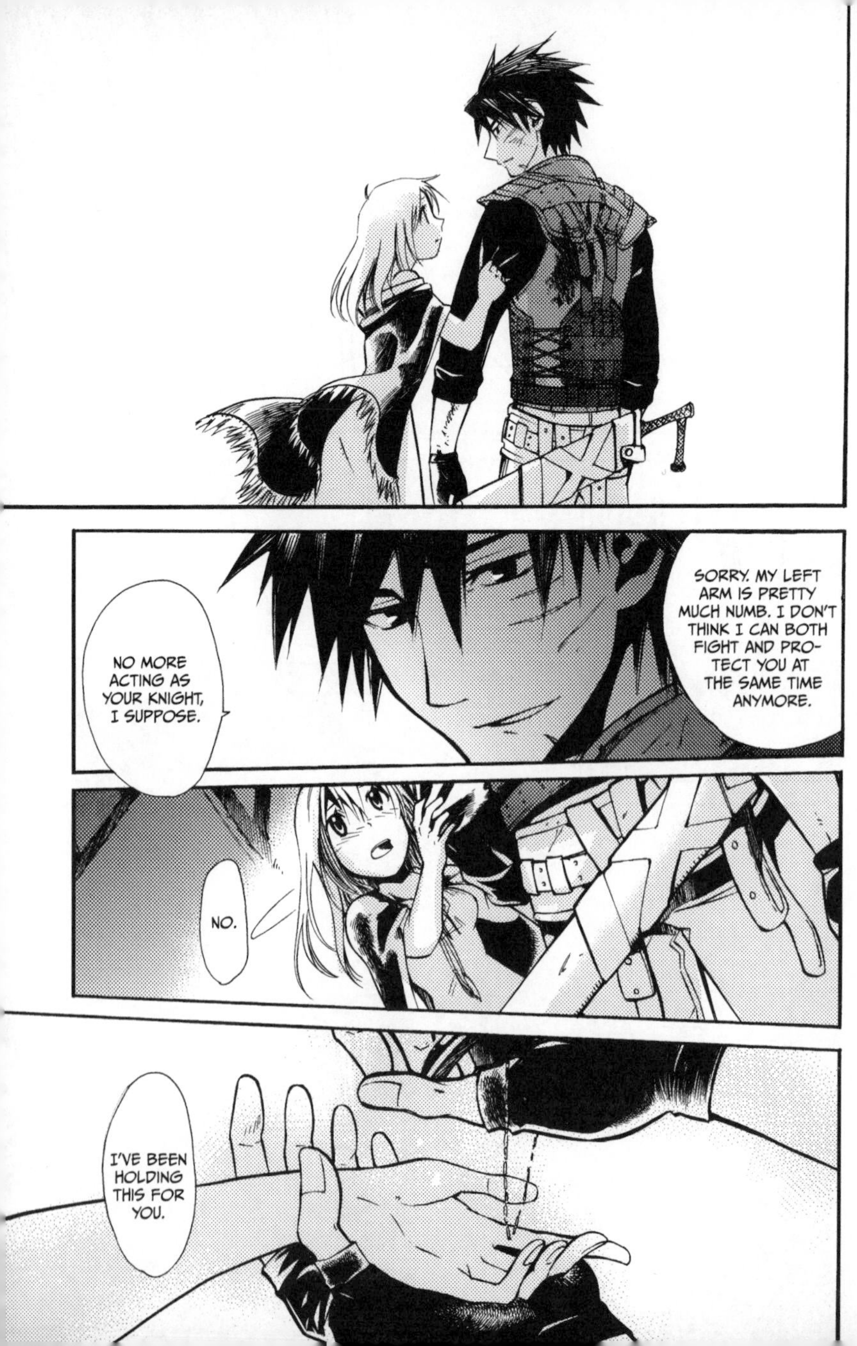
SORRY. MY LEFT ARM IS PRETTY MUCH NUMB. I DON'T THINK I CAN BOTH FIGHT AND PRO-TECT YOU AT THE SAME TIME ANYMORE.
NO MORE ACTING AS YOUR KNIGHT, I SUPPOSE.
NO.
I'VE BEEN HOLDING THIS FOR YOU.

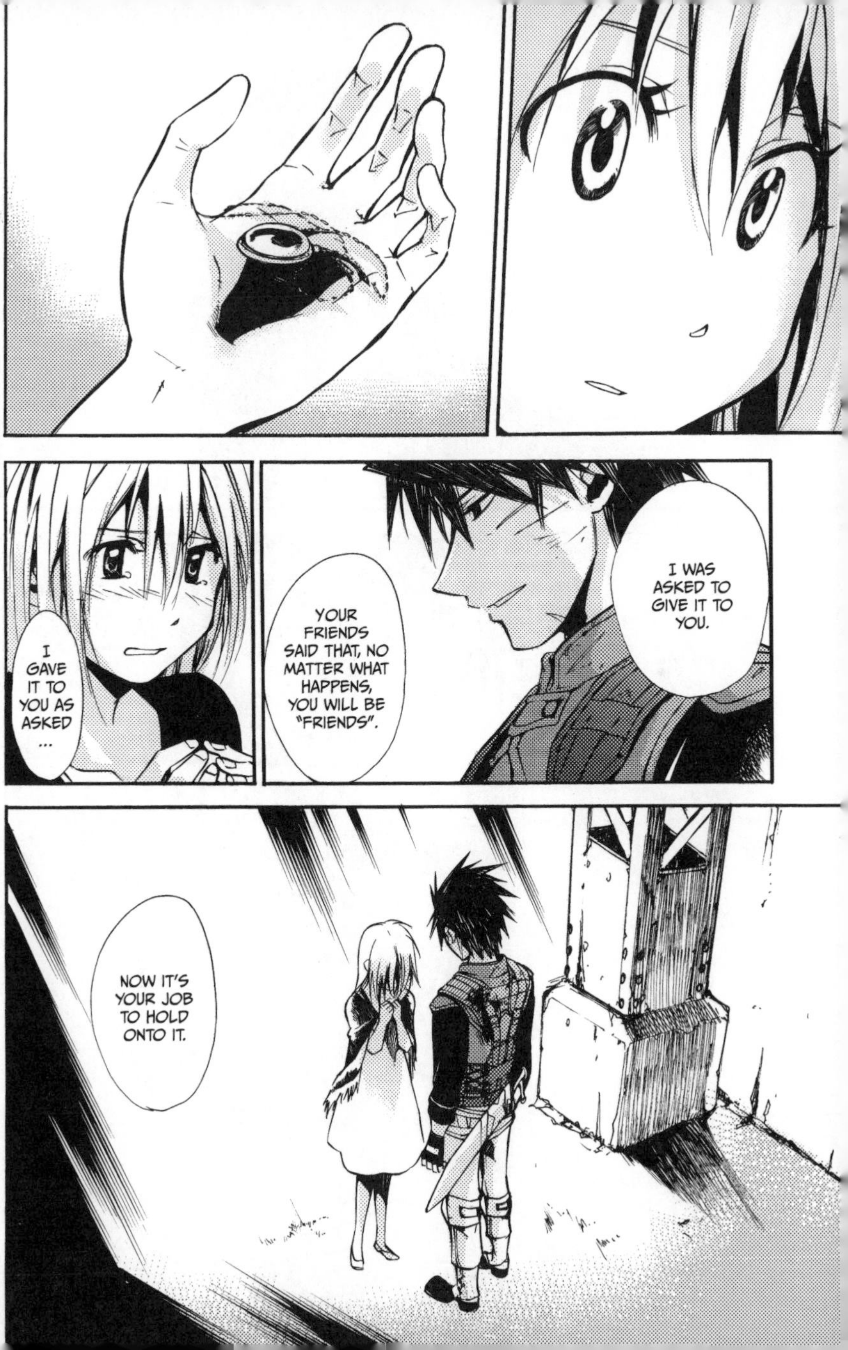
I WAS ASKED TO GIVE IT TO YOU.
YOUR FRIENDS SAID THAT, NO MATTER WHAT HAPPENS, YOU WILL BE "FRIENDS".
I GAVE IT TO YOU AS ASKED ...
NOW IT'S YOUR JOB TO HOLD ONTO IT.

ILIE.

I'M SORRY I HIT YOU THE FIRST TIME WE MET.

IF GIVEN THE OPPORTUNITY TO MEET YOU FOR THE FIRST TIME AGAIN, I WOULD USE THAT HAND TO TAKE YOURS.

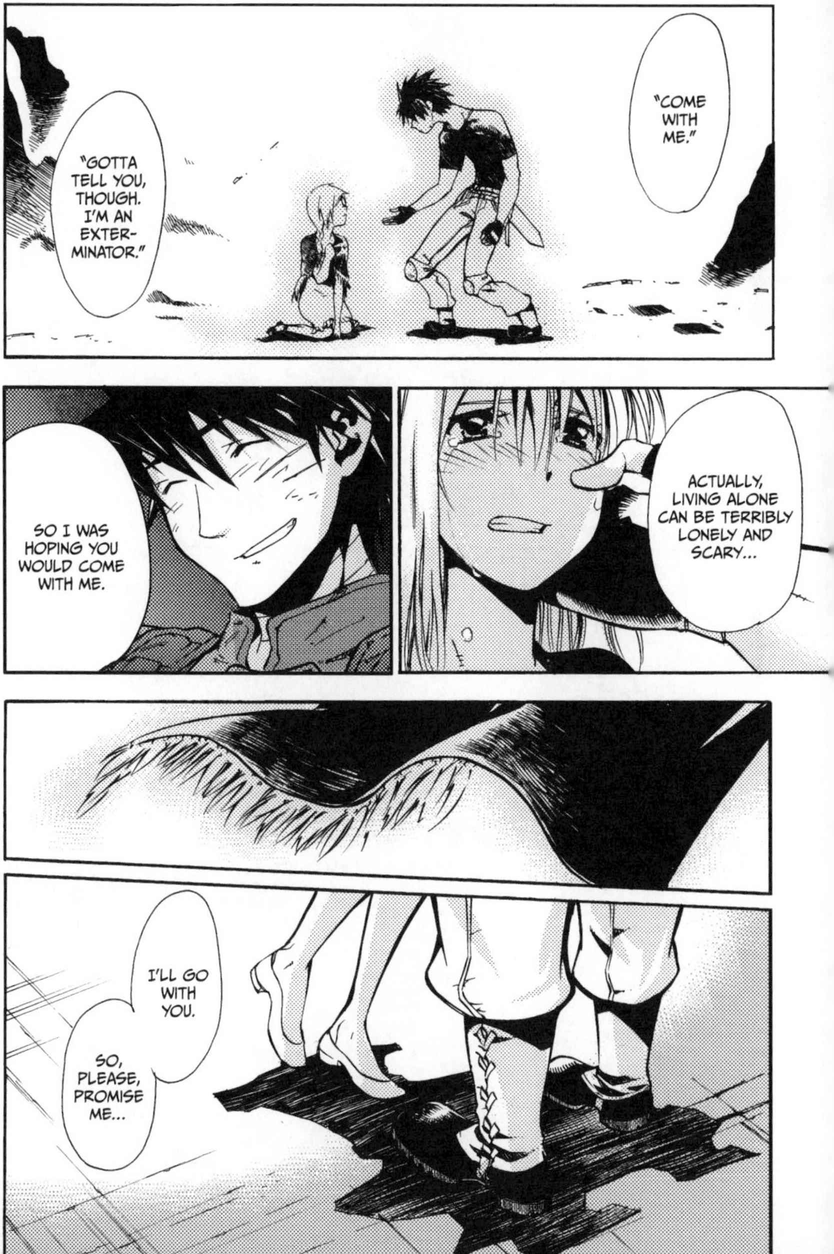
"COME WITH ME."
"GOTTA TELL YOU, THOUGH. I'M AN EXTER-MINATOR."
ACTUALLY, LIVING ALONE CAN BE TERRIBLY LONELY AND SCARY...
SO I WAS HOPING YOU WOULD COME WITH ME.
I'LL GO WITH YOU.
SO, PLEASE, PROMISE ME...

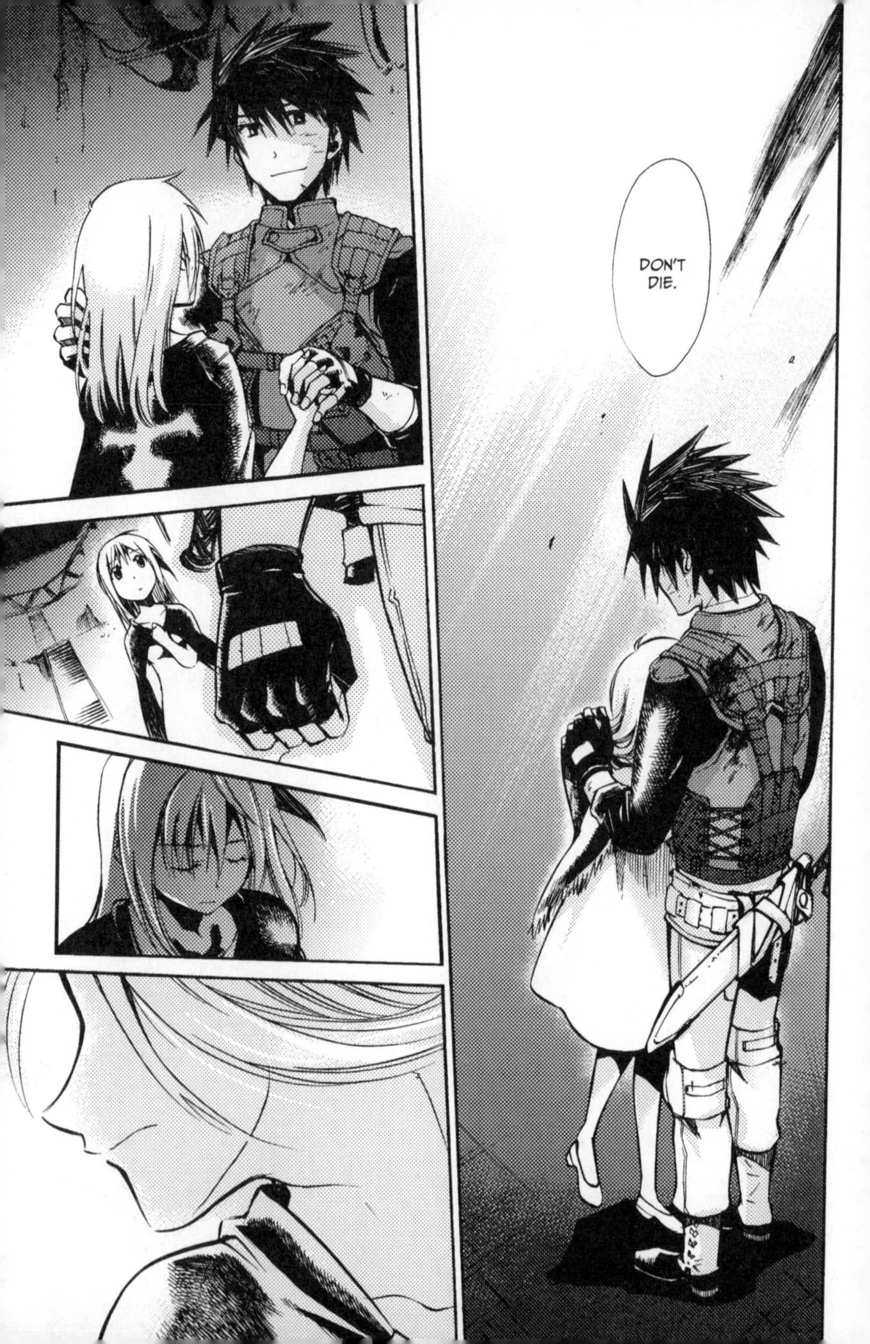
DON'T DIE.

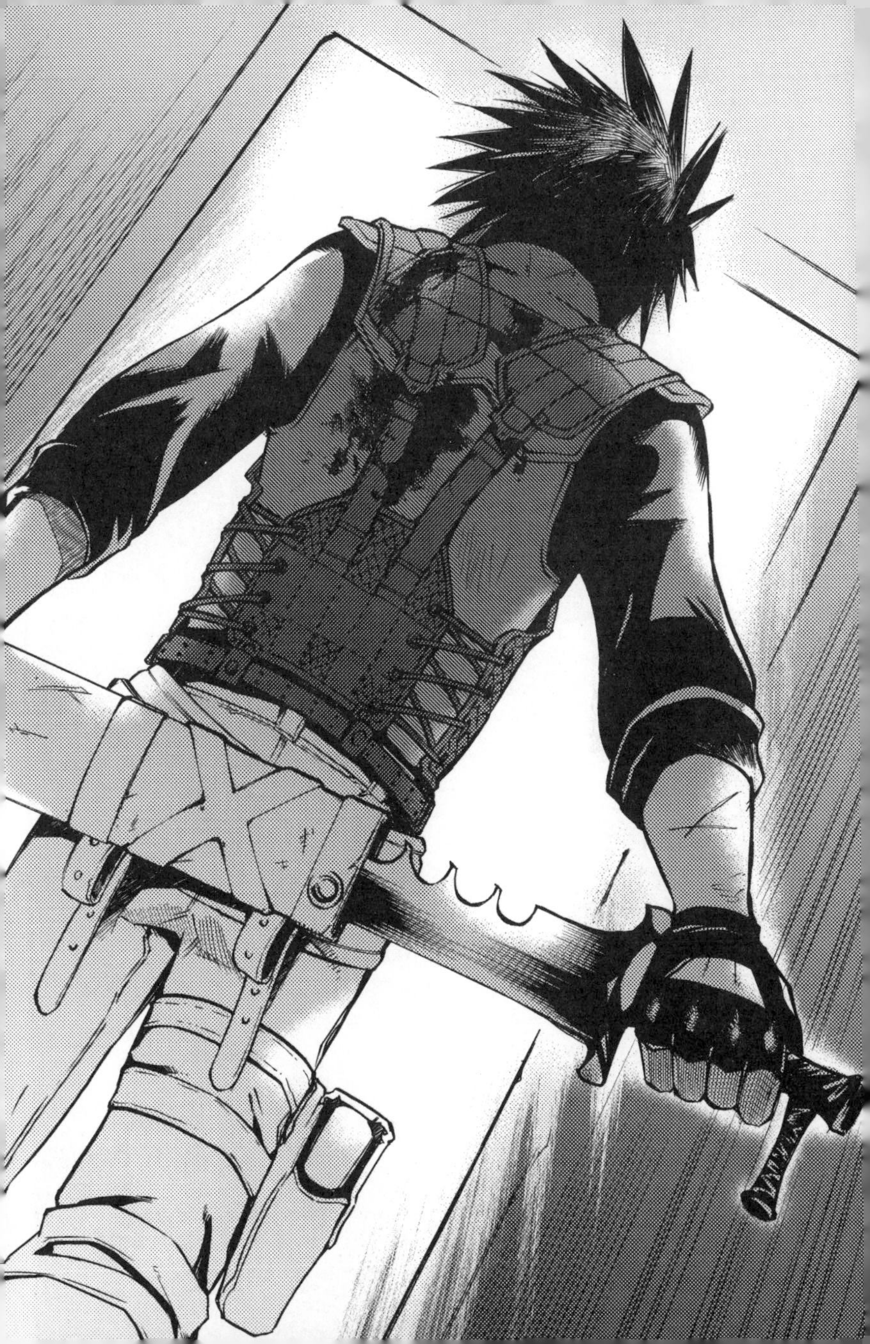

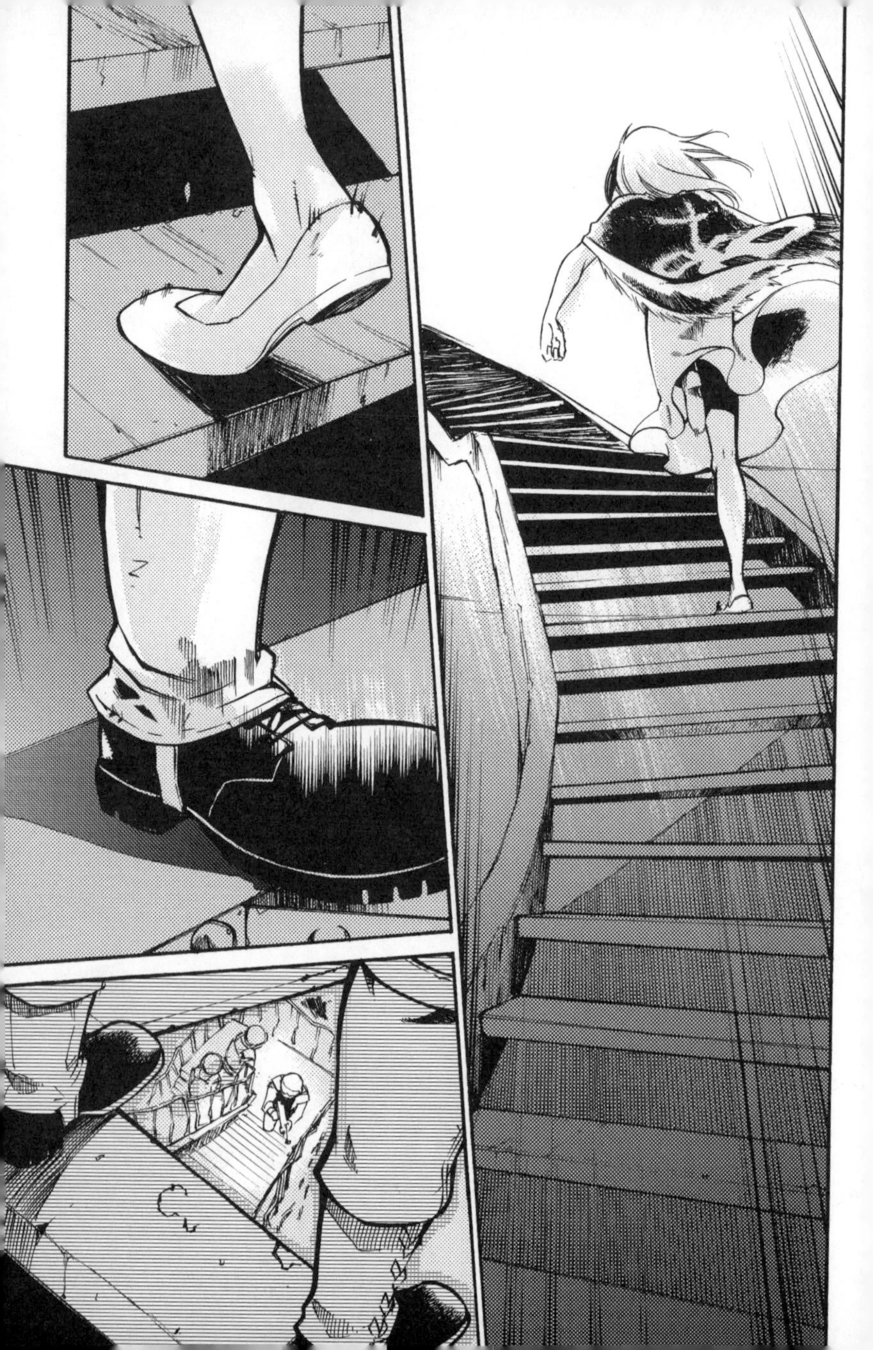

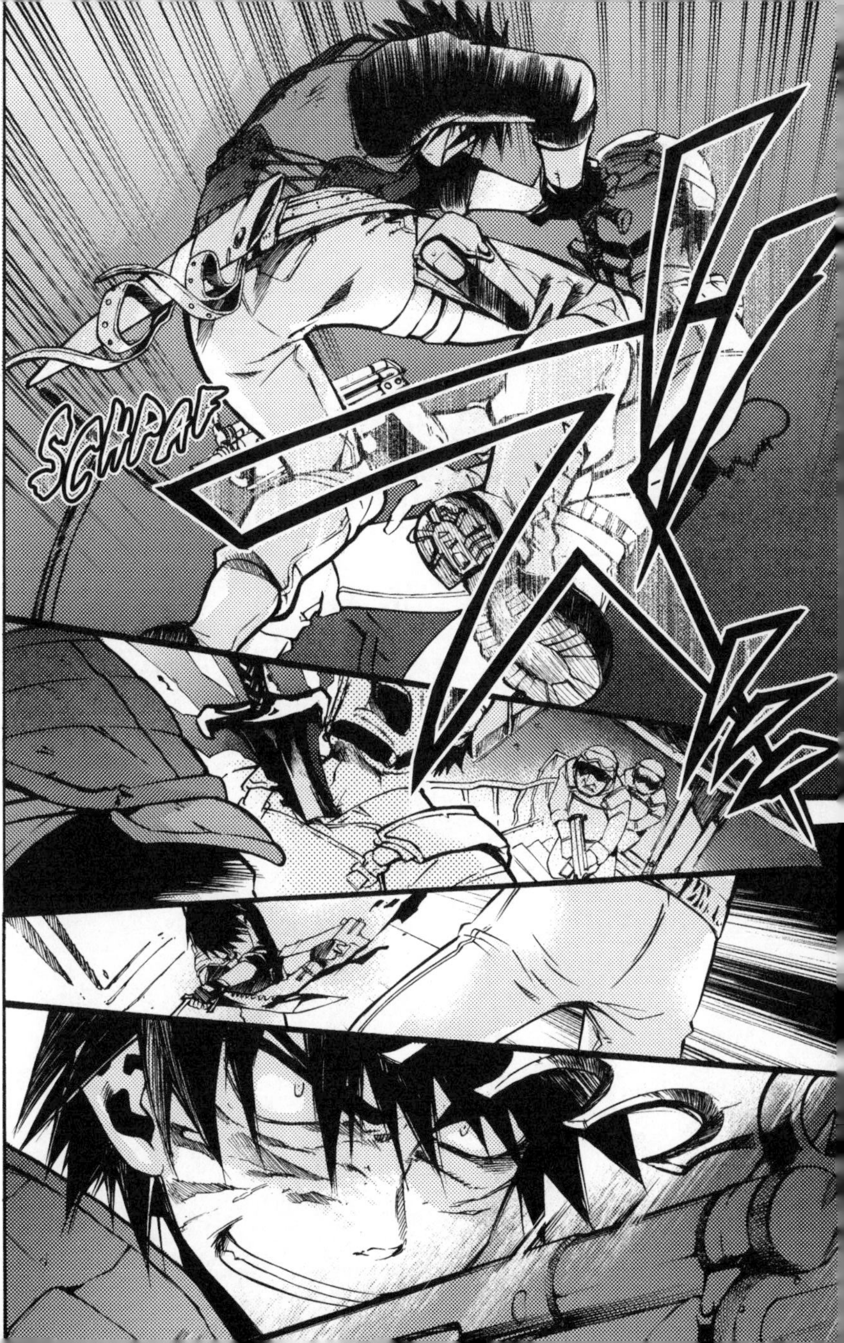
SCHPAF

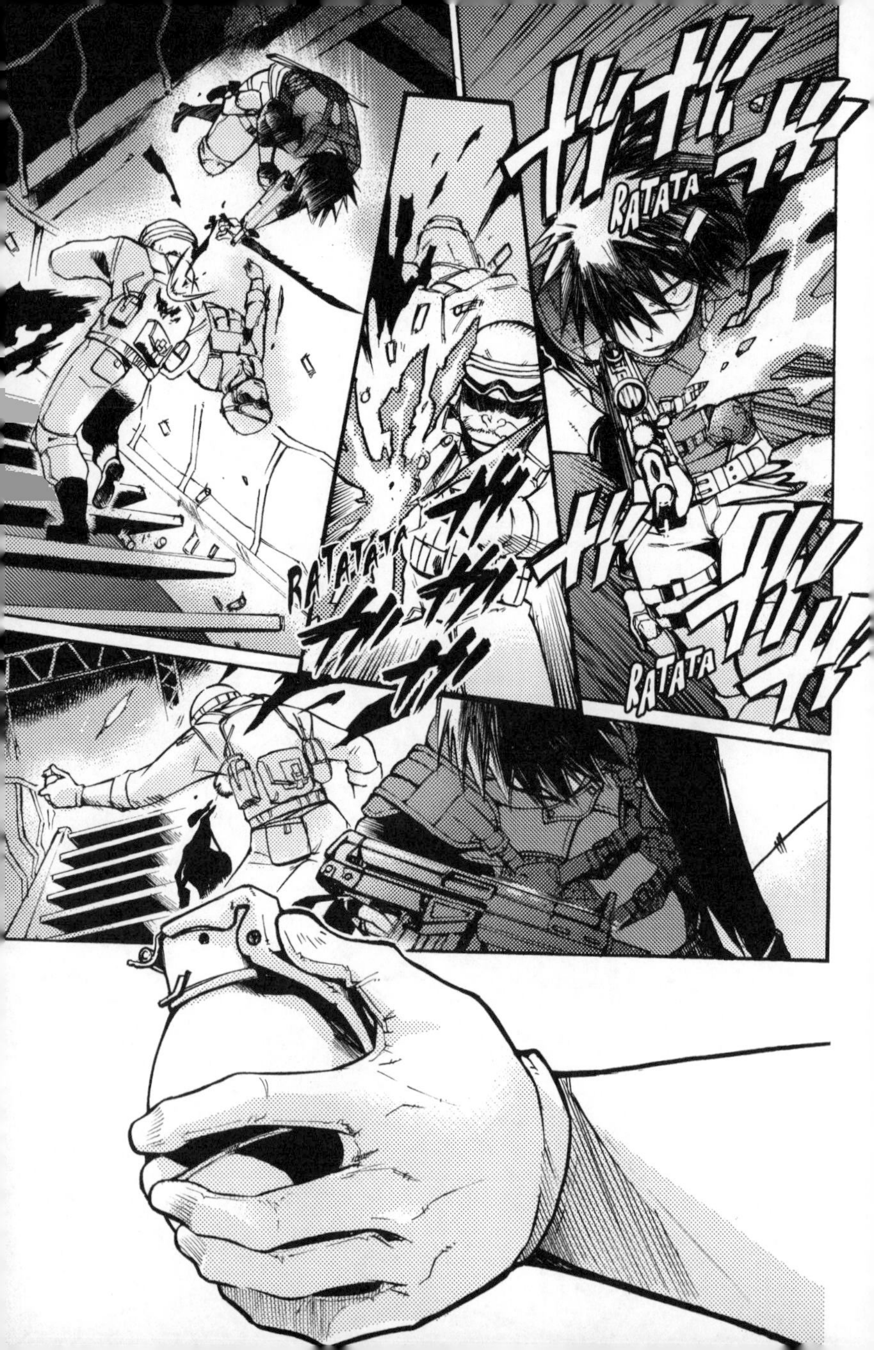
RATATA
RATATA
RATATATA

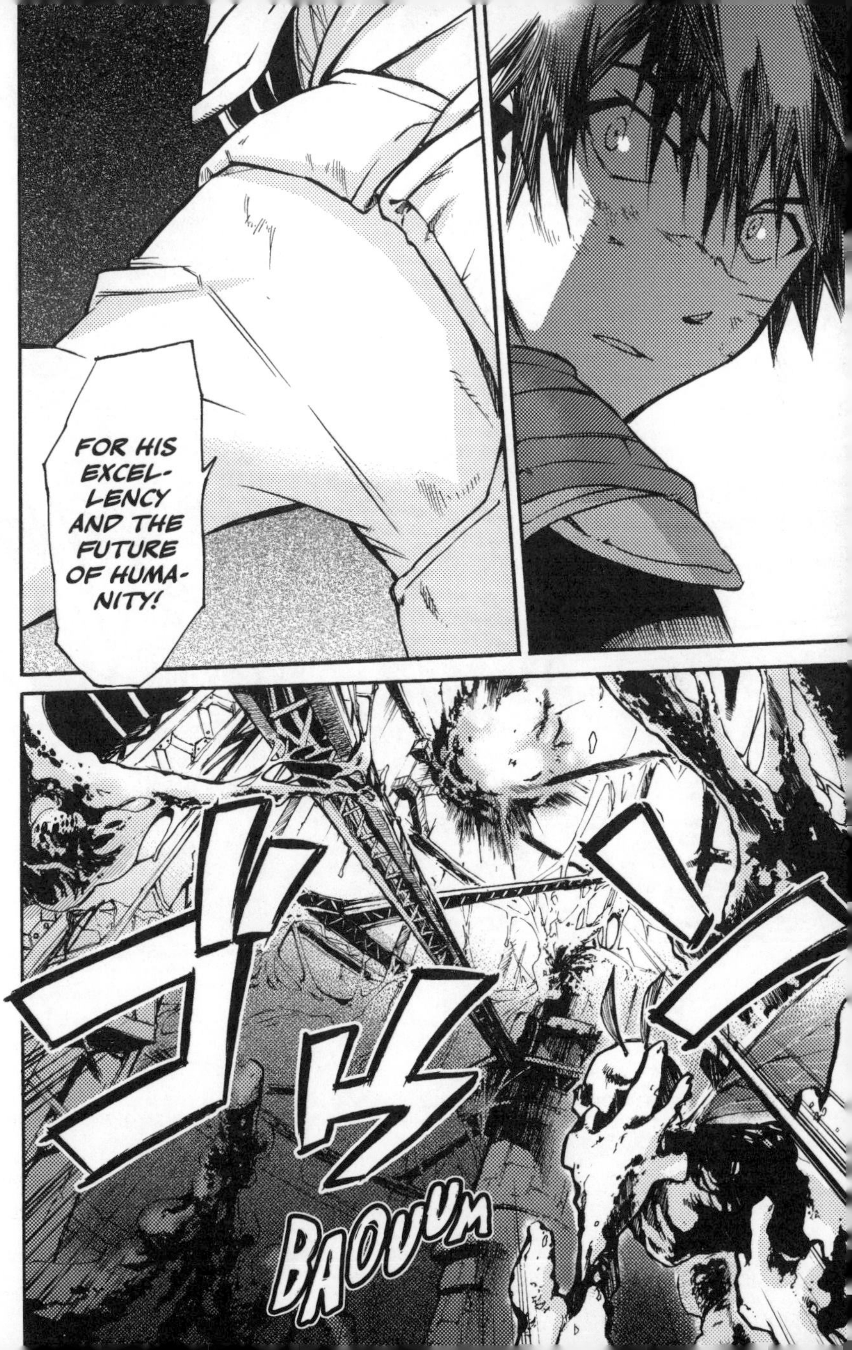
FOR HIS EXCEL-LENCY AND THE FUTURE OF HUMA-NITY!
BAOUUM

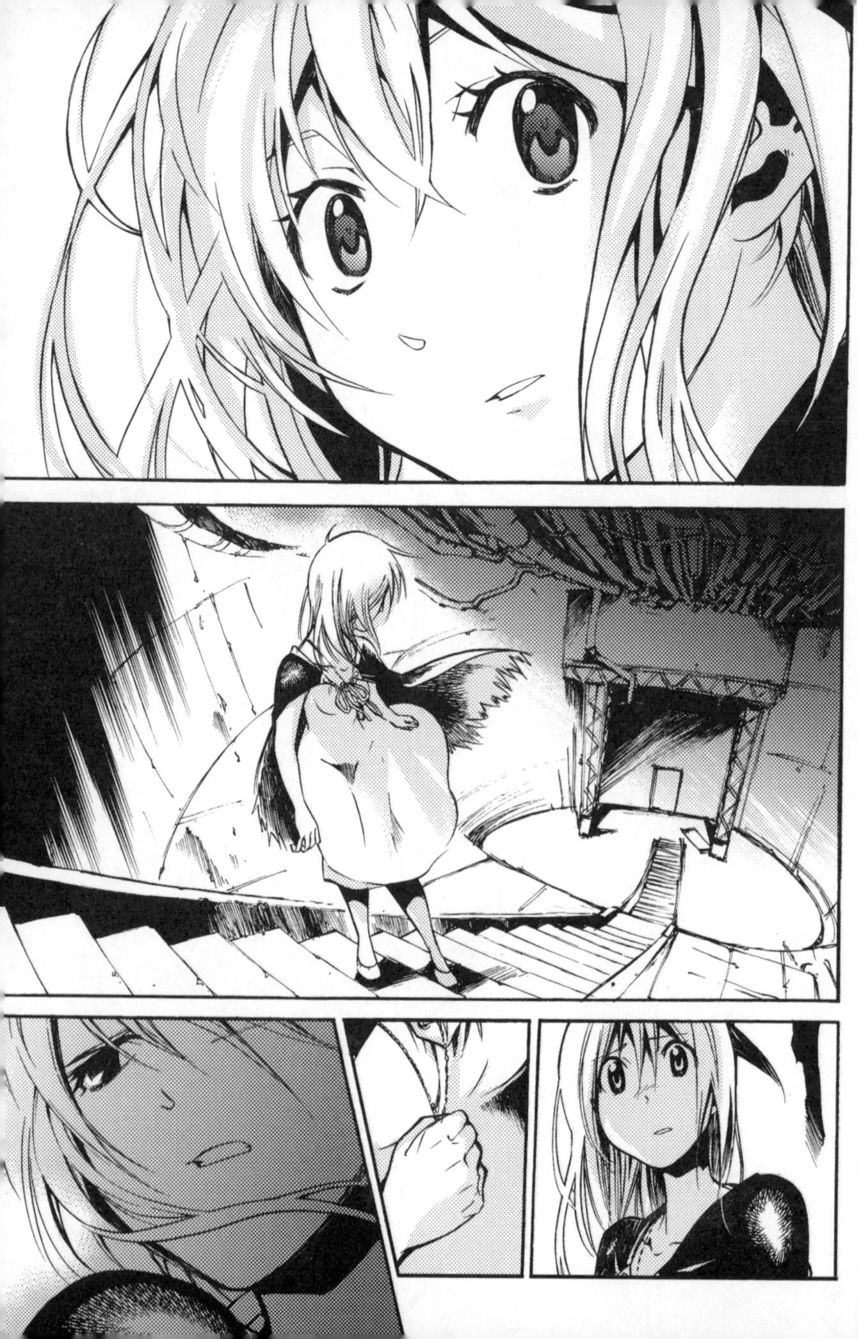

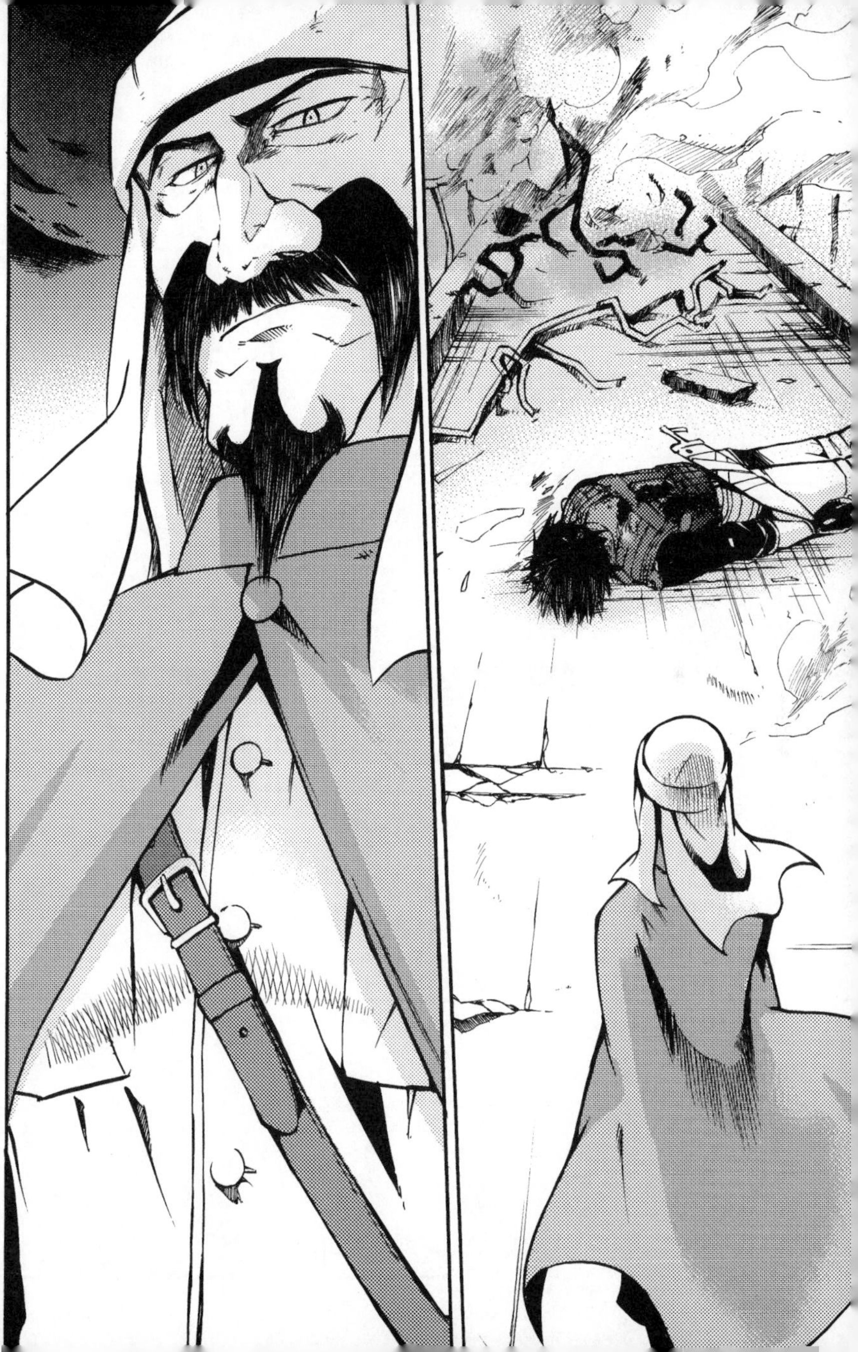

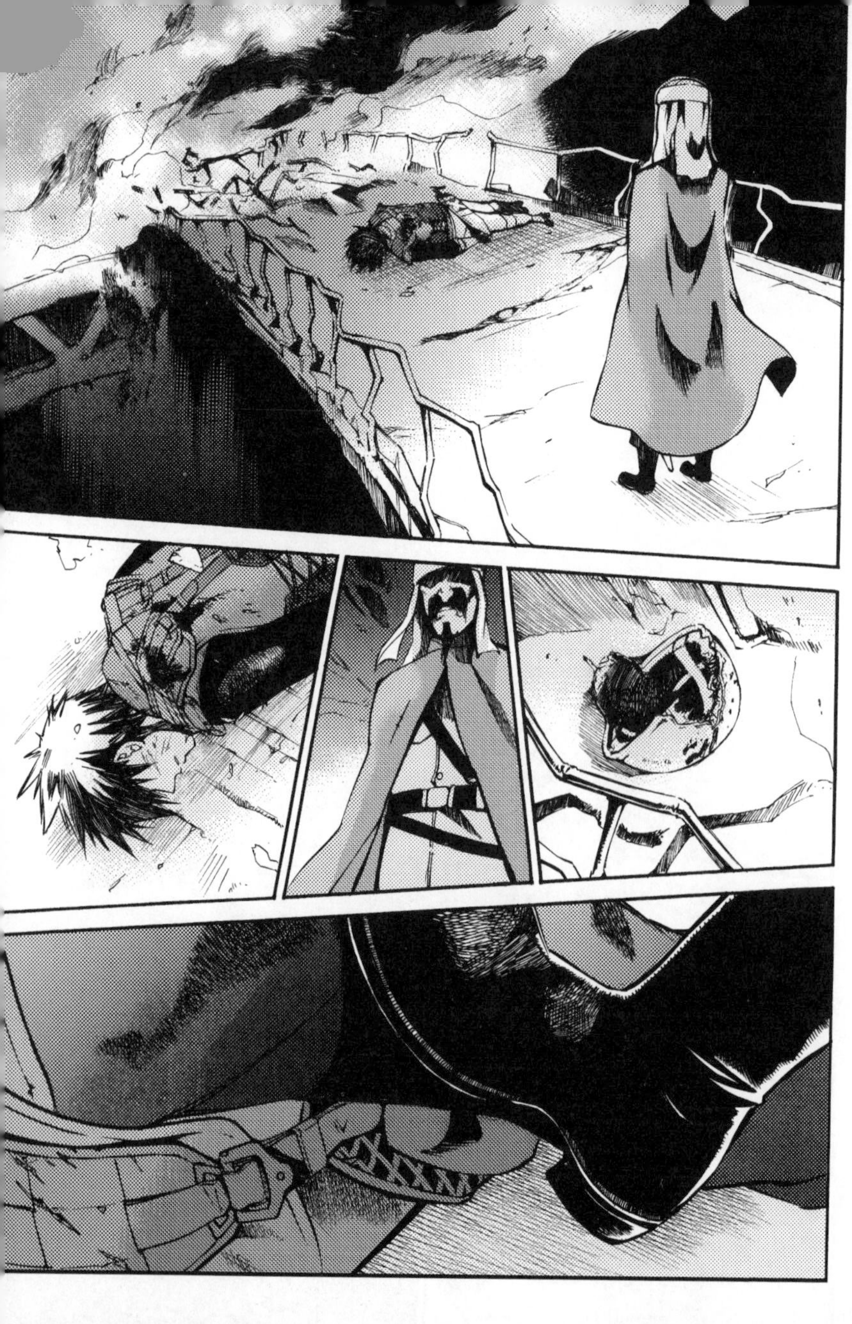

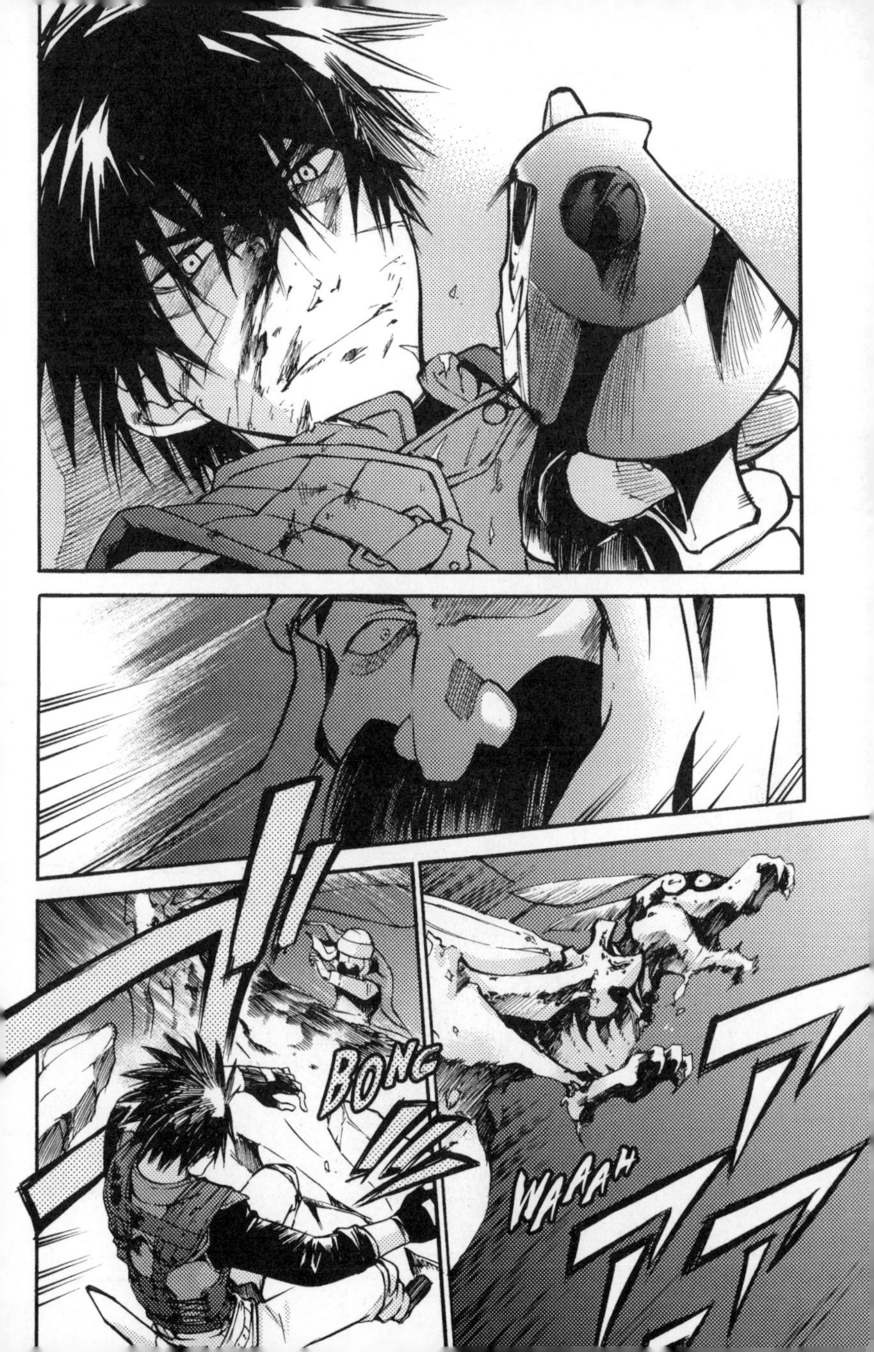
BONG
WAAAH

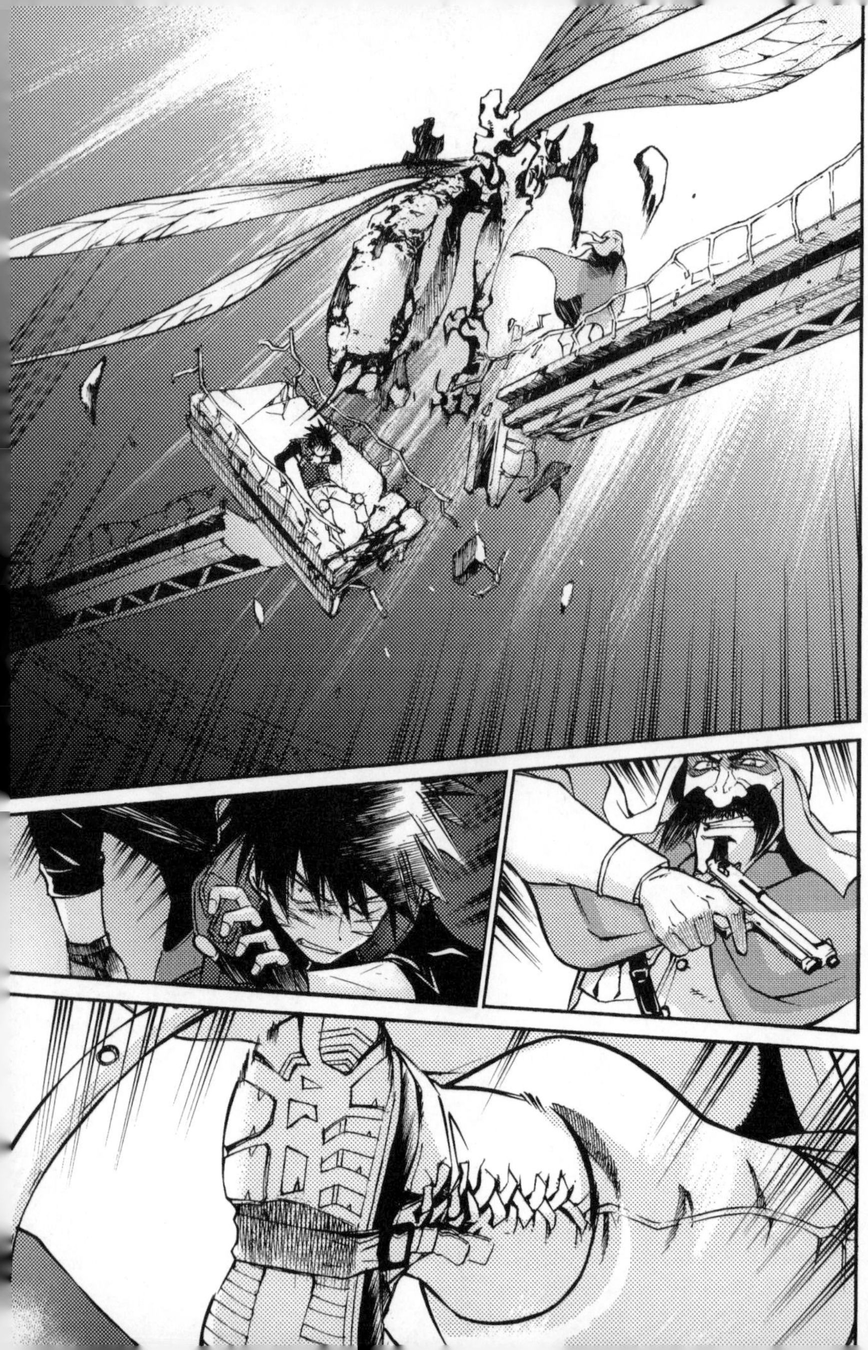

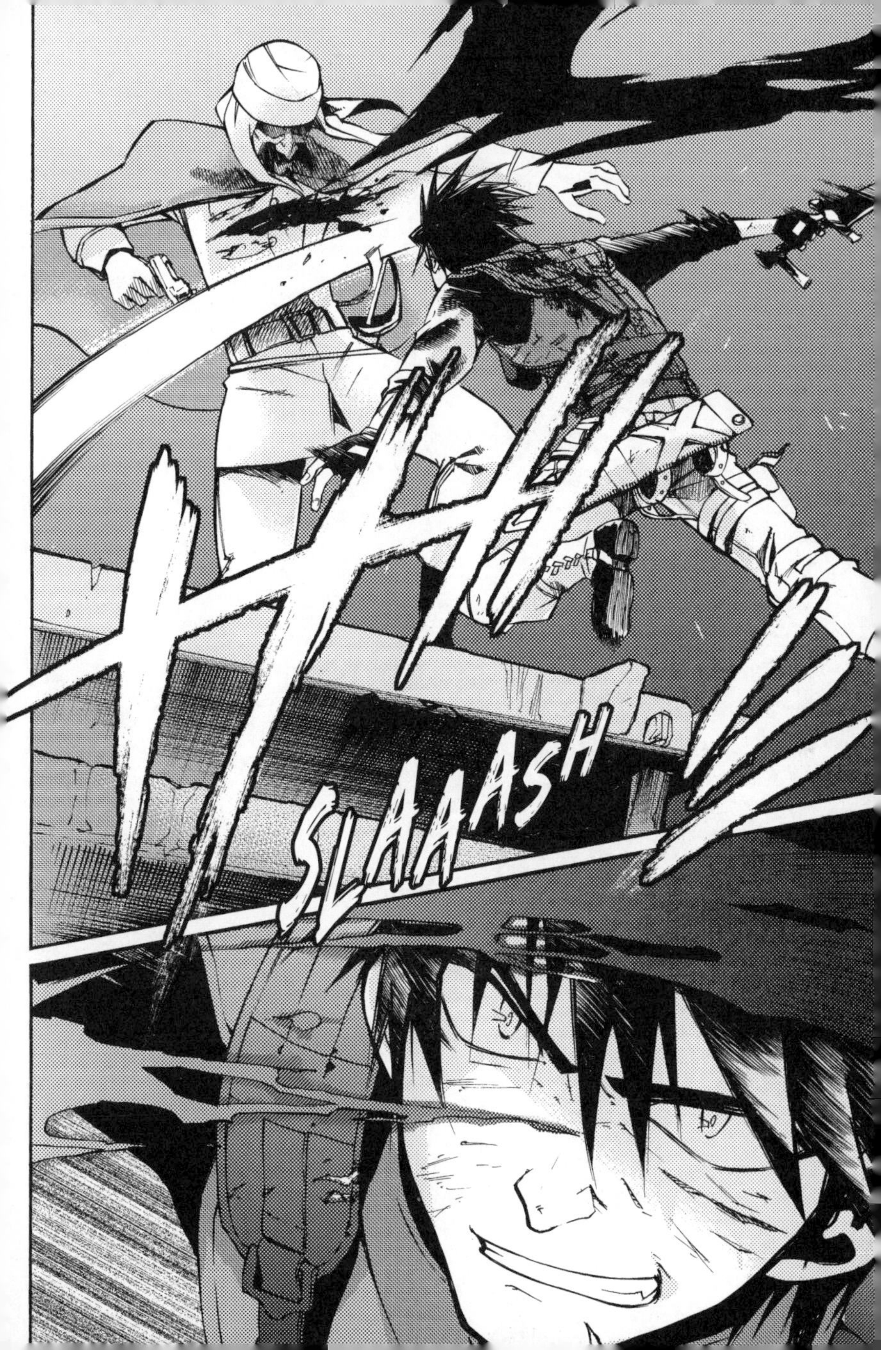
SLAAASH

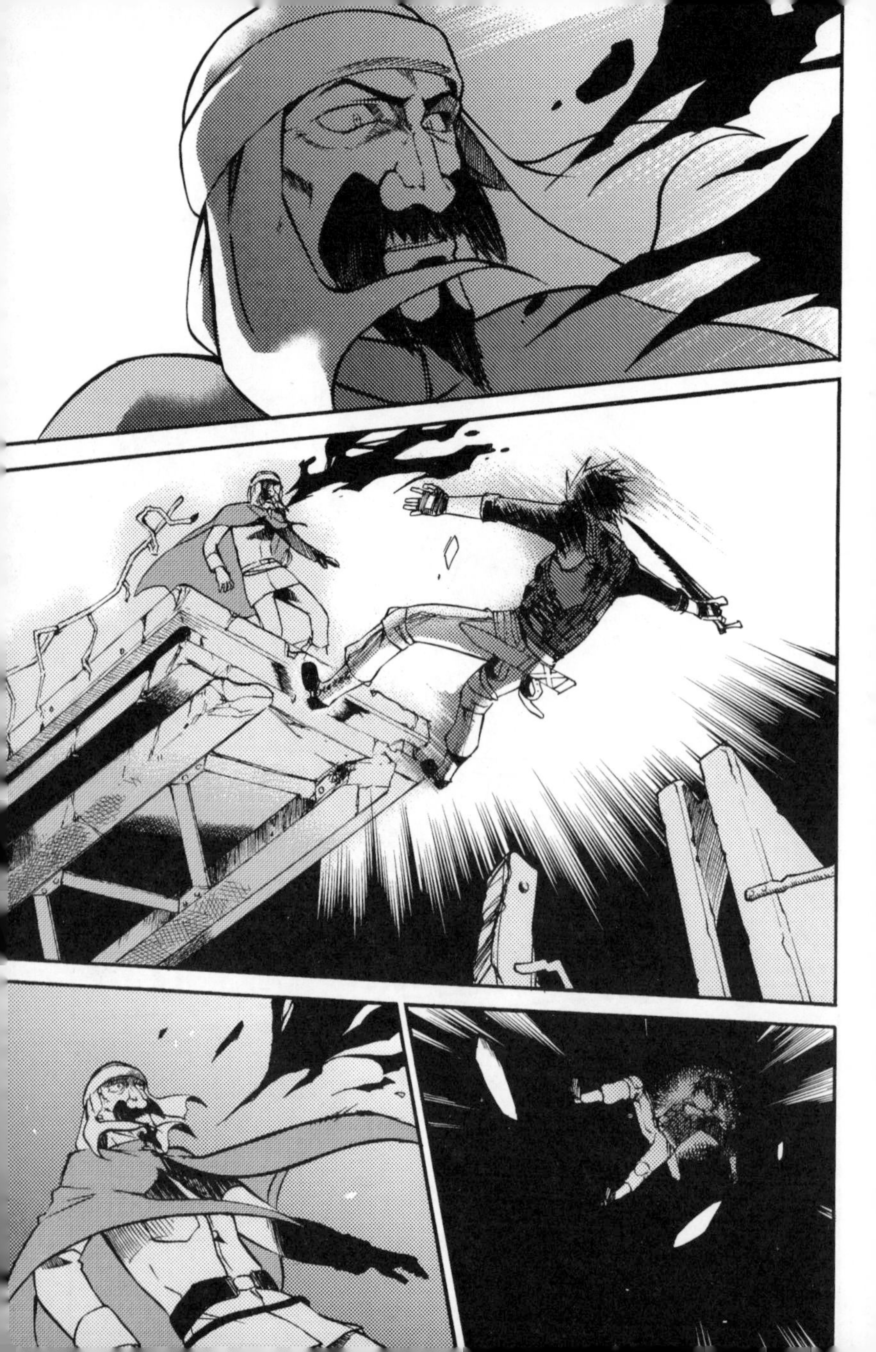

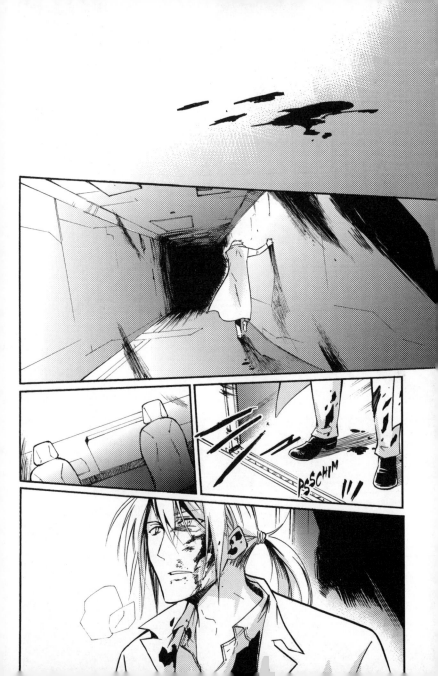

PSSCHIM

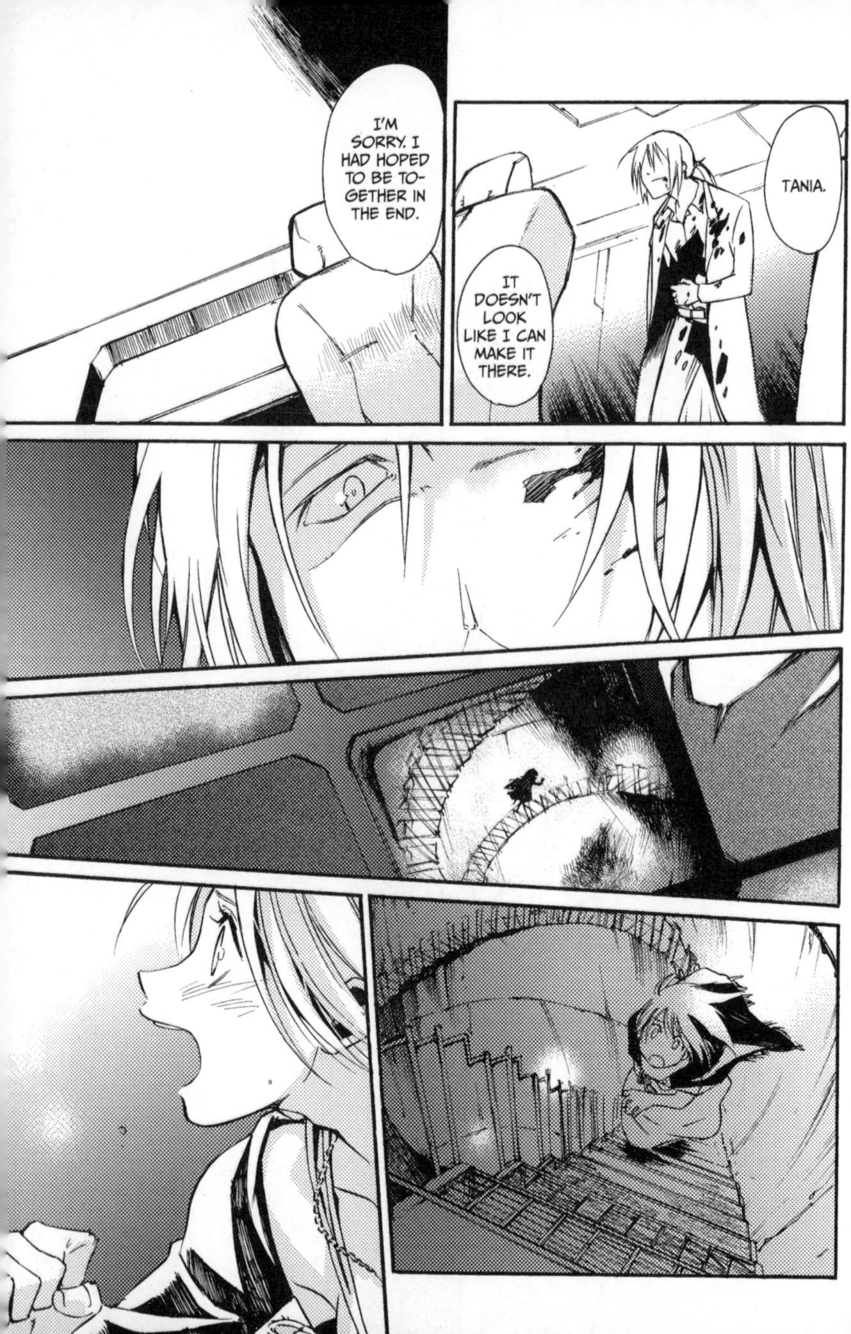
TANIA.
IT DOESN'T LOOK LIKE I CAN MAKE IT THERE.
I'M SORRY. I HAD HOPED TO BE TO-GETHER IN THE END.

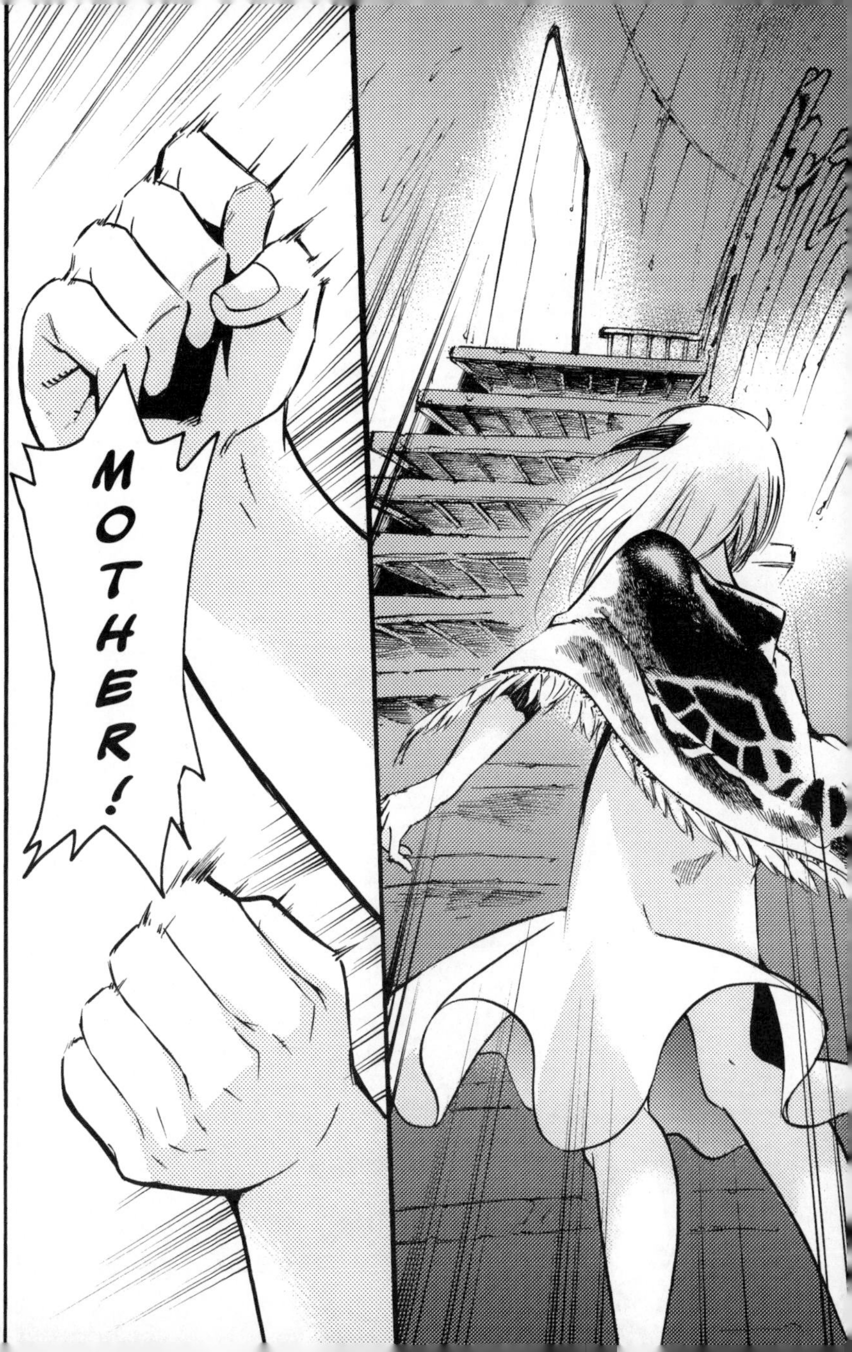
MOTHER!

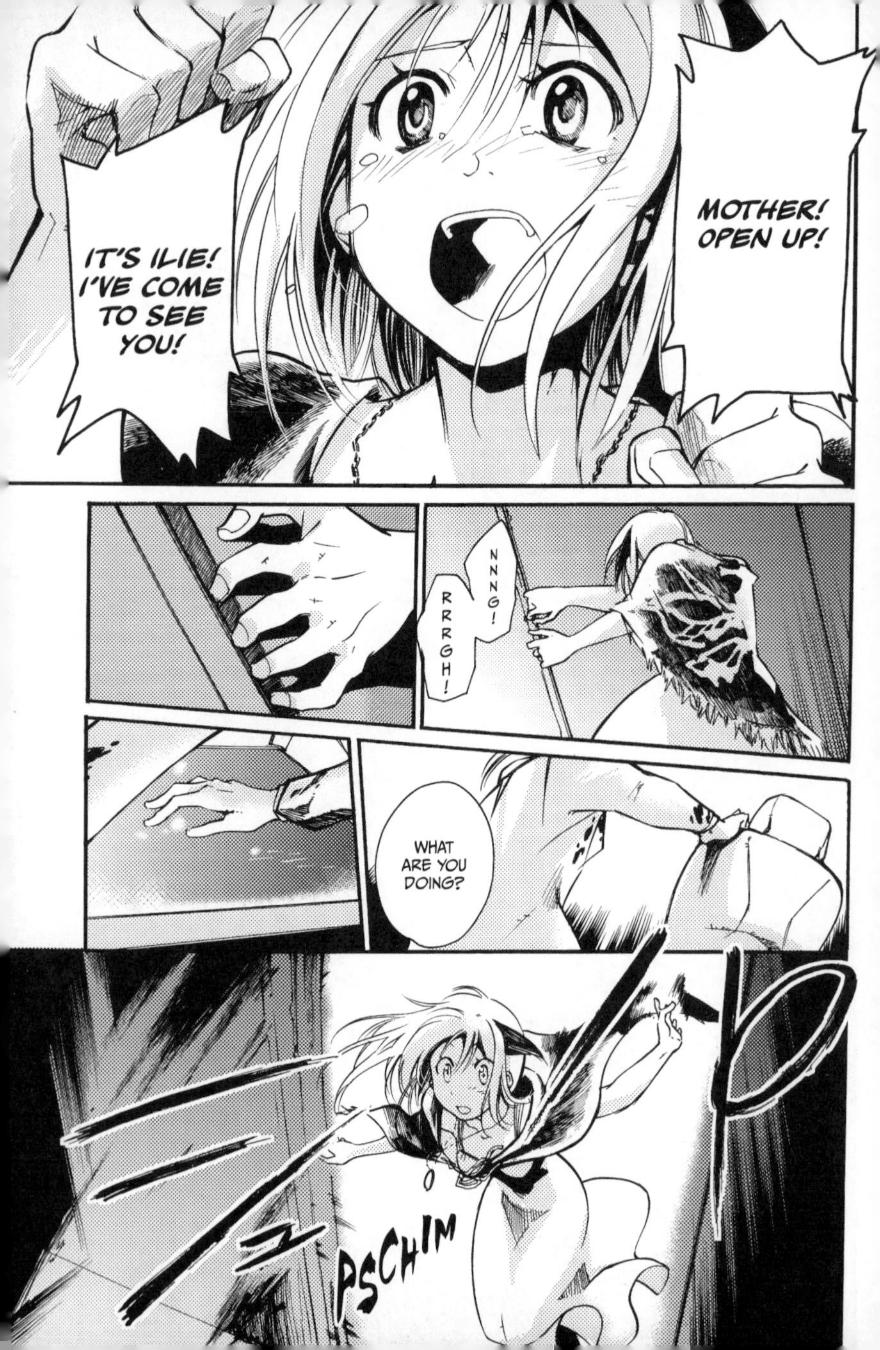
MOTHER! OPEN UP!
IT'S ILIE! I'VE COME TO SEE YOU!
NNNG!
RRRGH!
WHAT ARE YOU DOING?
PSCHIM

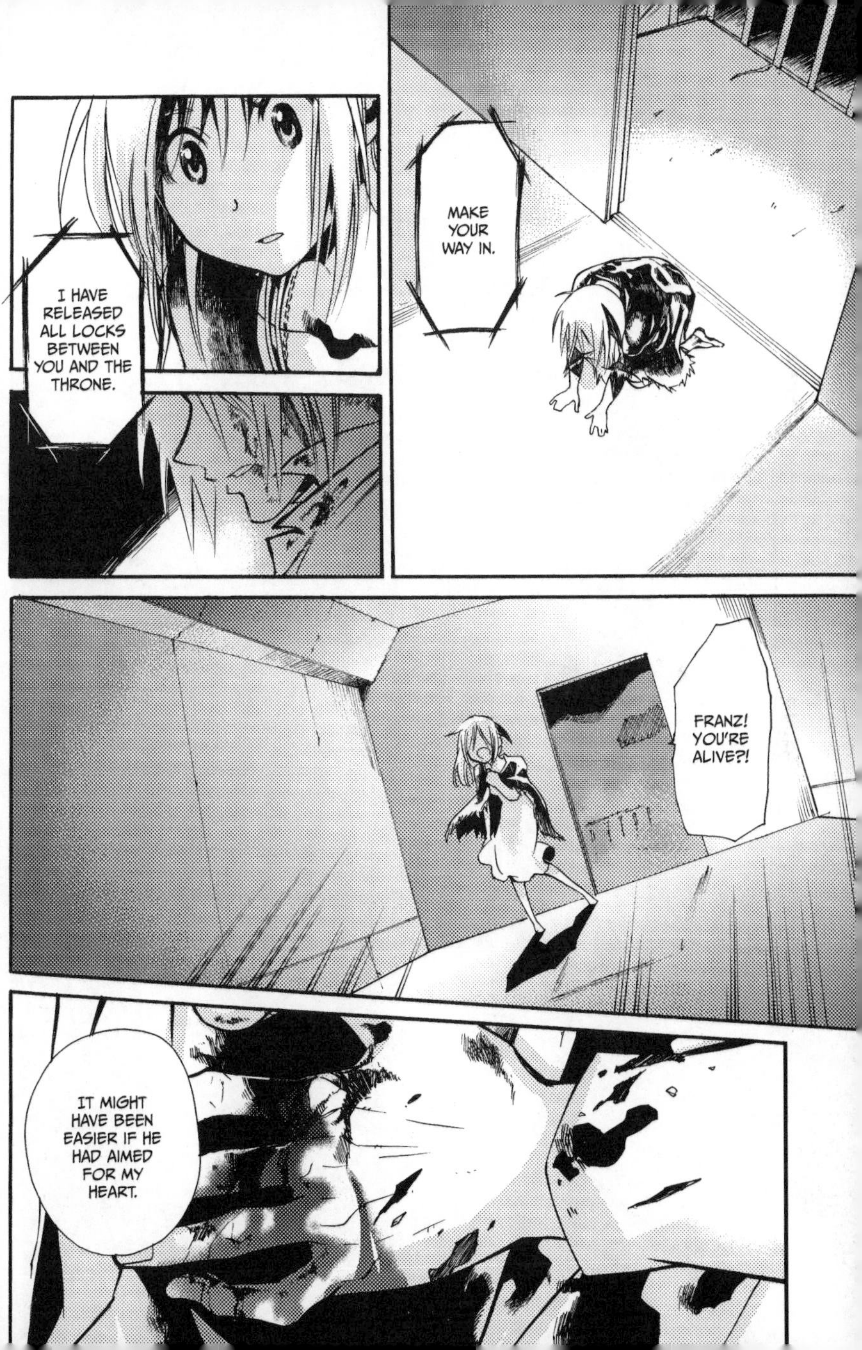
MAKE YOUR WAY IN.
I HAVE RELEASED ALL LOCKS BETWEEN YOU AND THE THRONE.
FRANZ! YOU'RE ALIVE?!
IT MIGHT HAVE BEEN EASIER IF HE HAD AIMED FOR MY HEART.

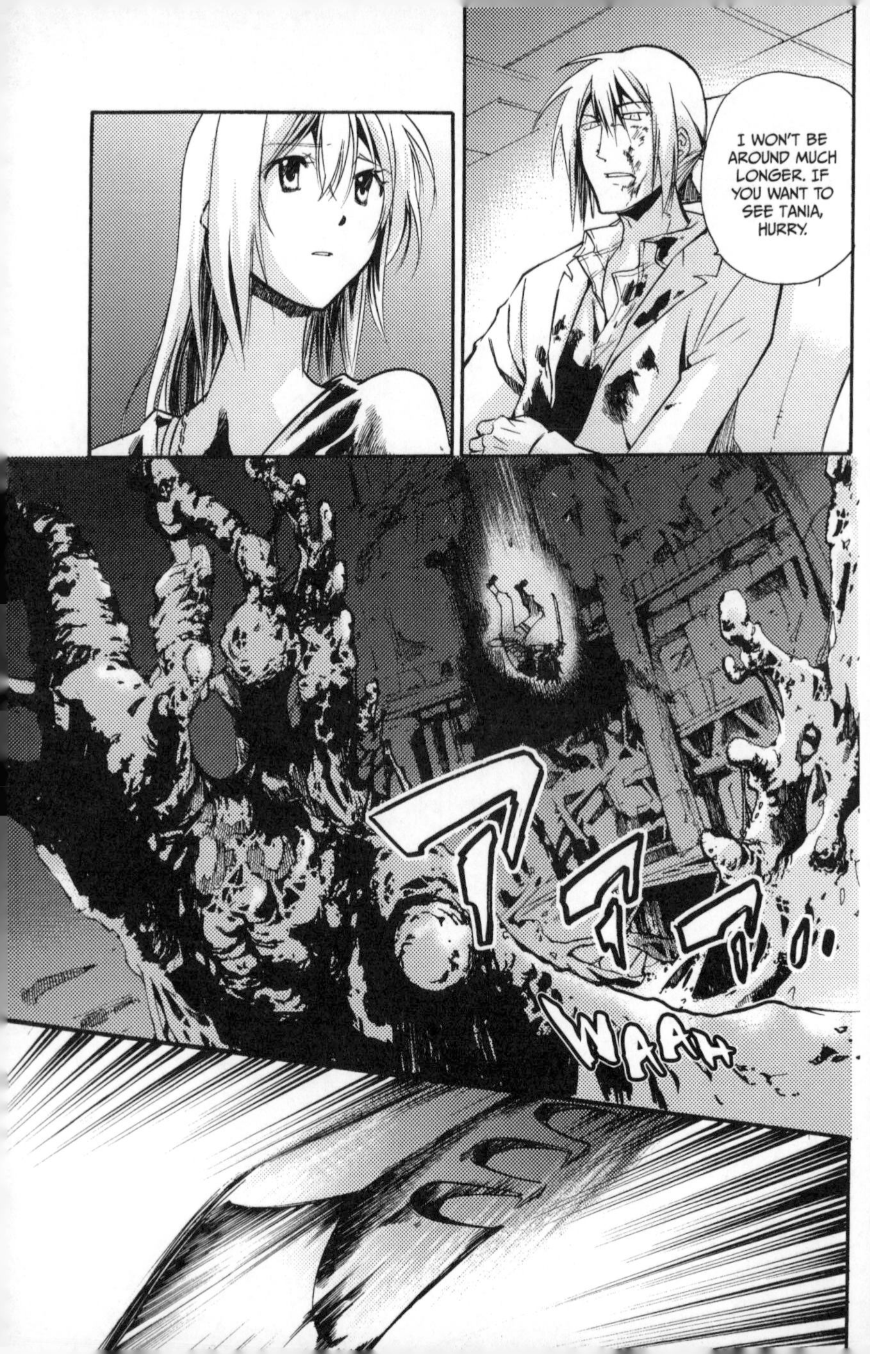
I WON'T BE AROUND MUCH LONGER. IF YOU WANT TO SEE TANIA, HURRY.
WAAH

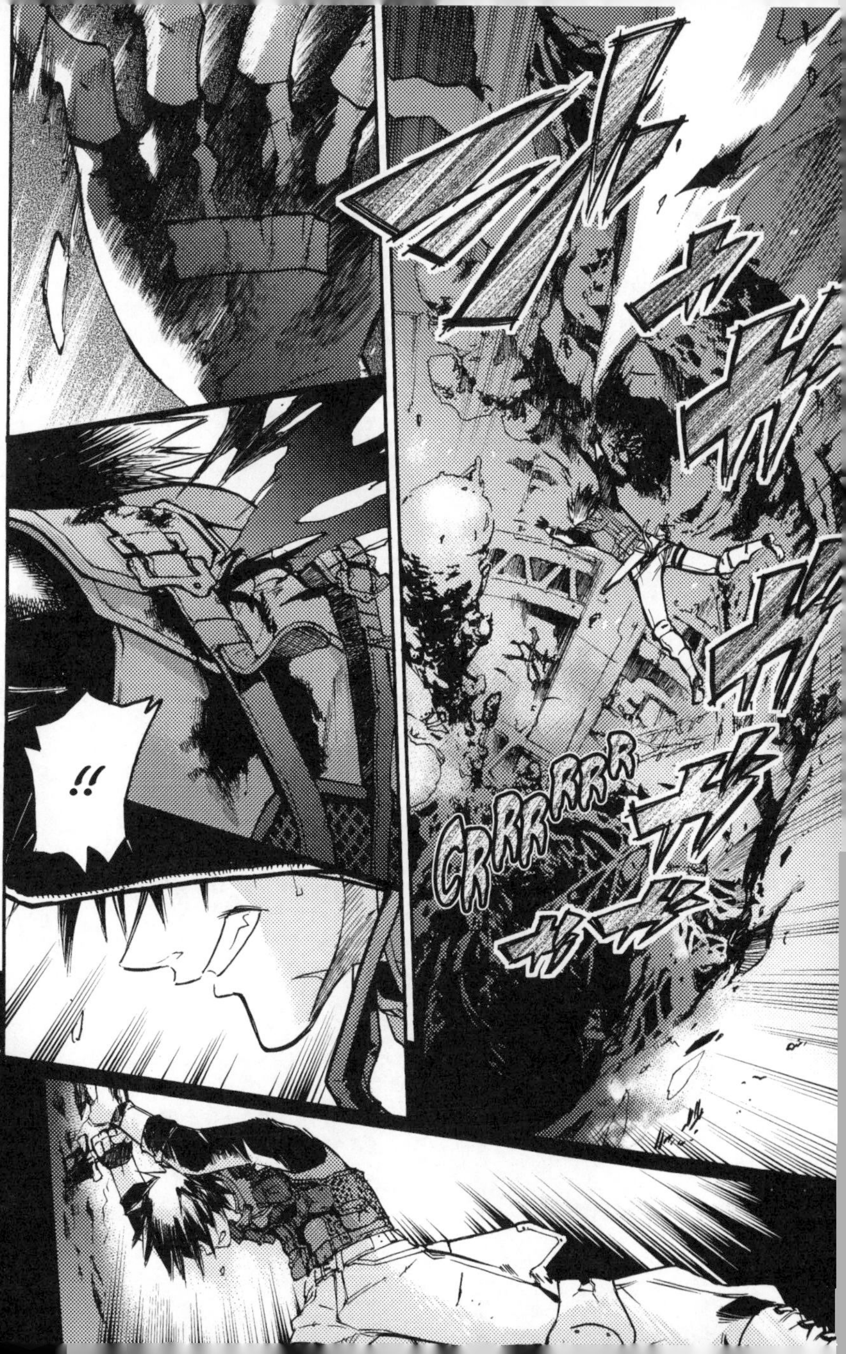
CRRRRRR
!!

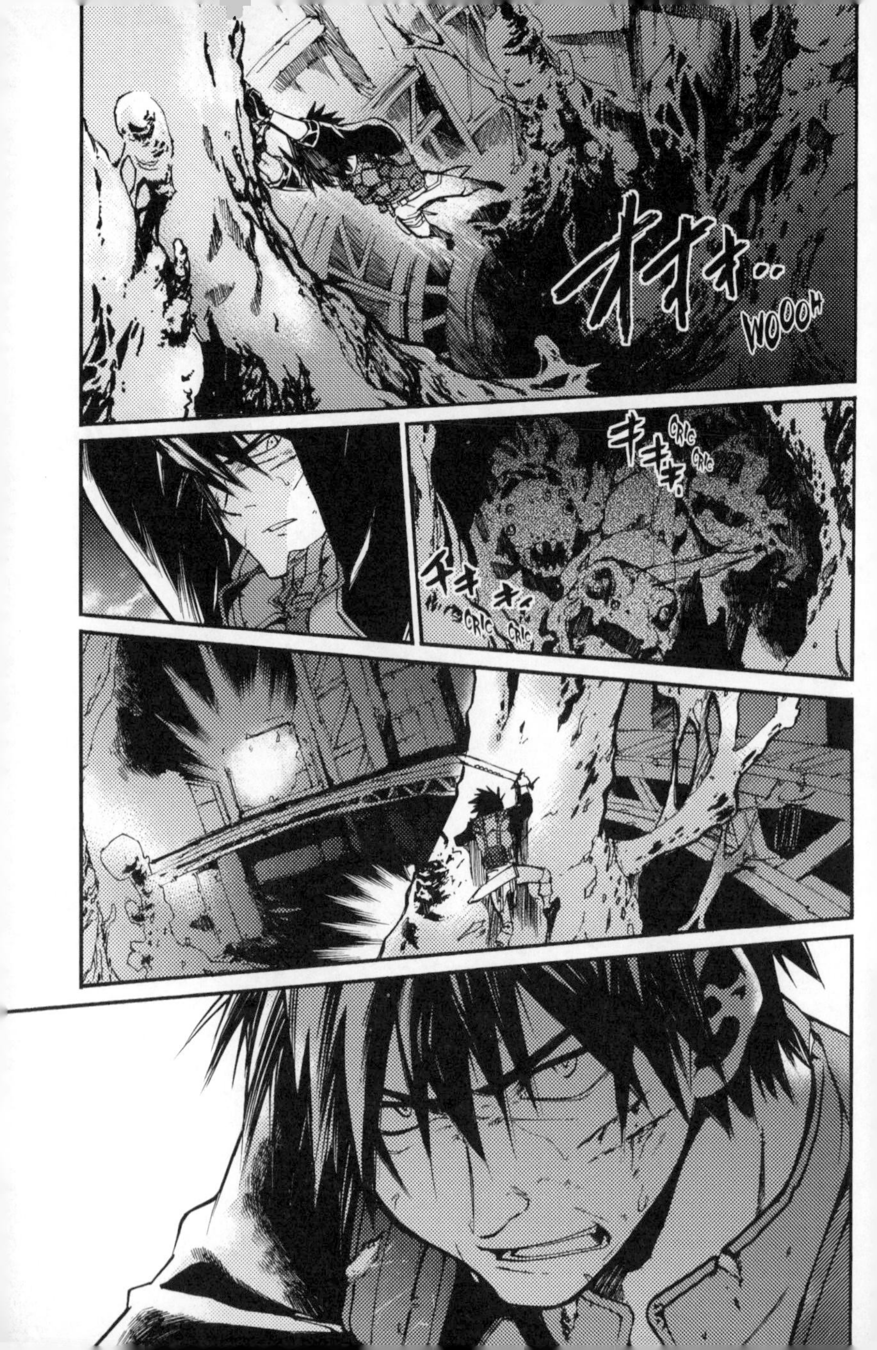
オォォ..
WOOOH
キキキ.
GRIC GRIC
チキキィ
GRIC GRIC

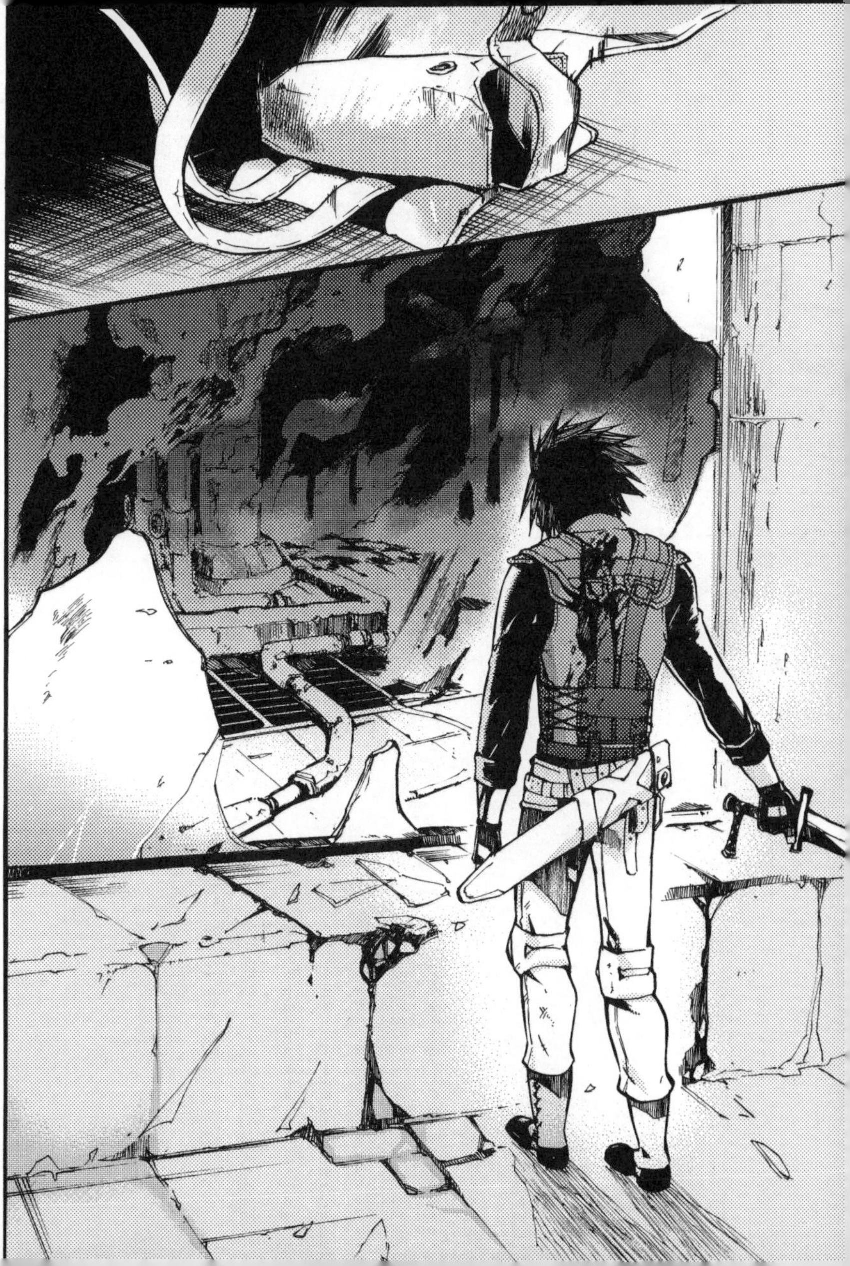

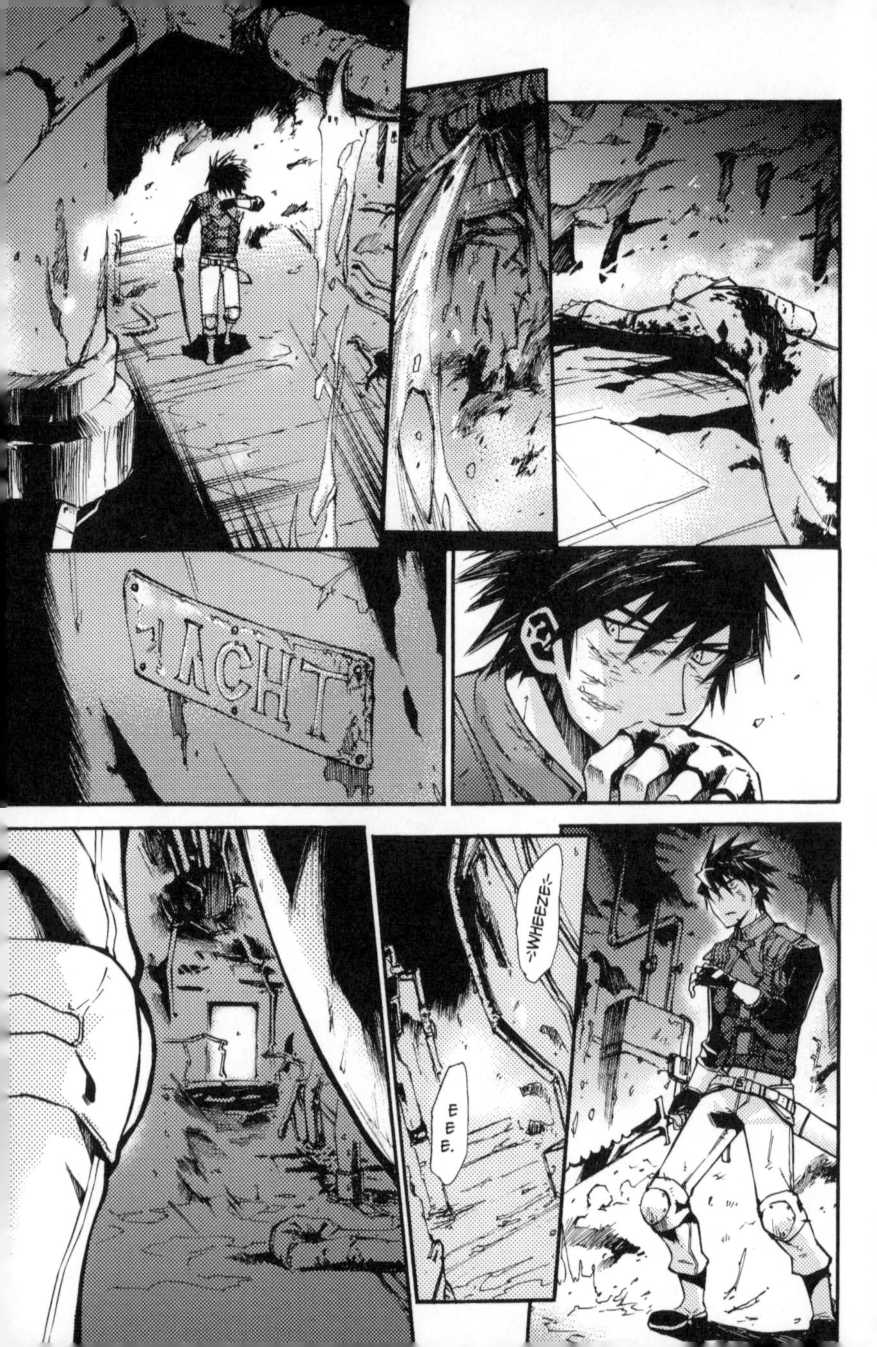
ACHT
WHEEZE
EEE.

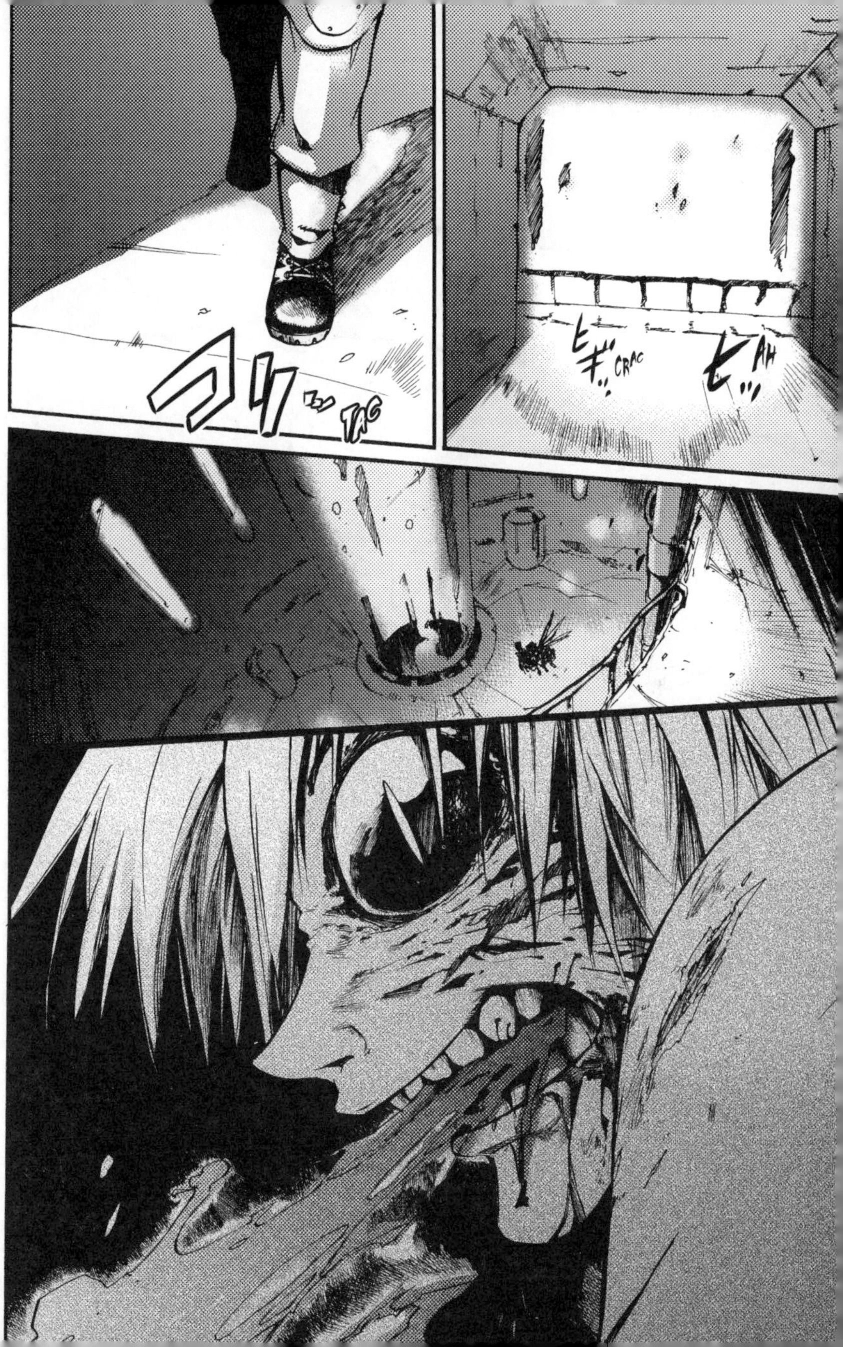
CRAC
AH
コツ
TAC

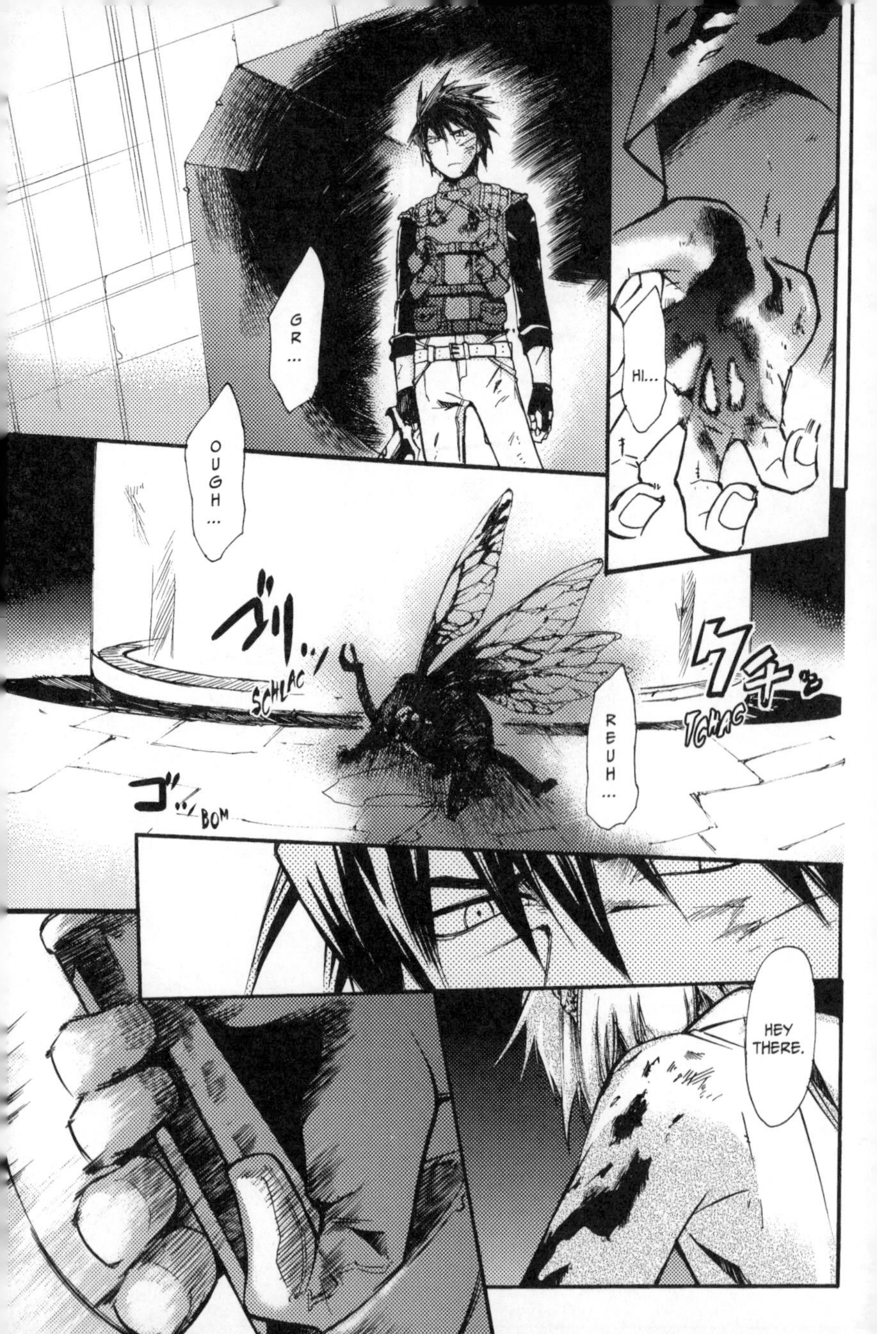
HI...
GR...
OUGH...
クチッ
TCHAC
ゴリッ
SCHLAC
REUH...
ゴッ
BOM
HEY THERE.

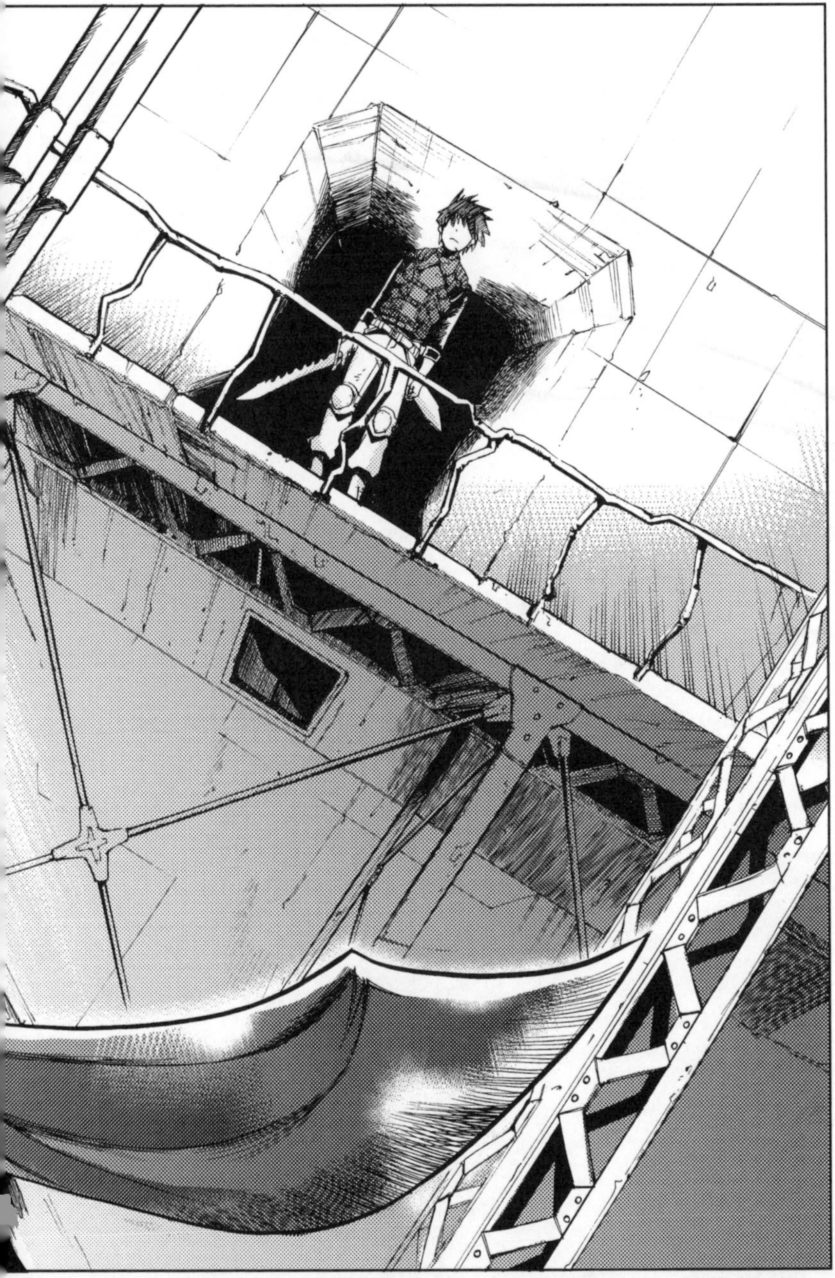

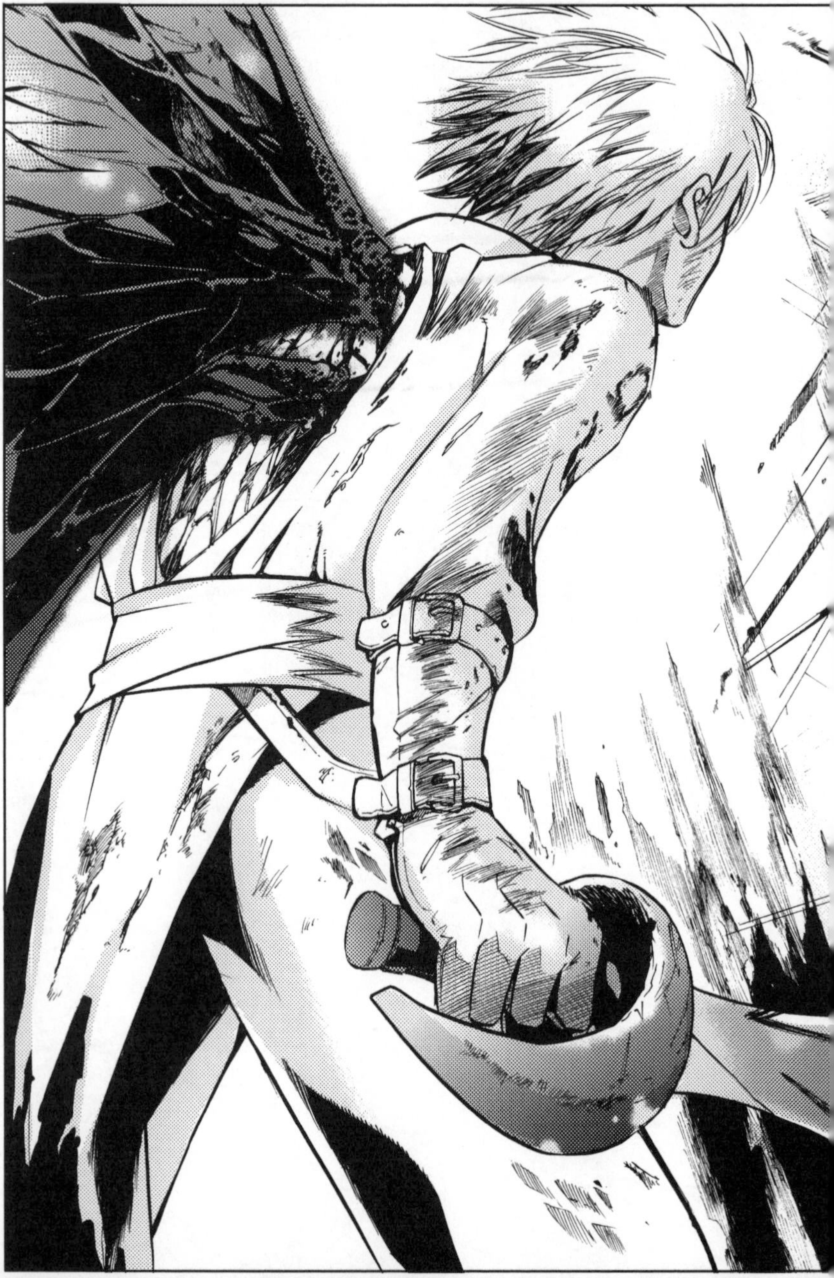

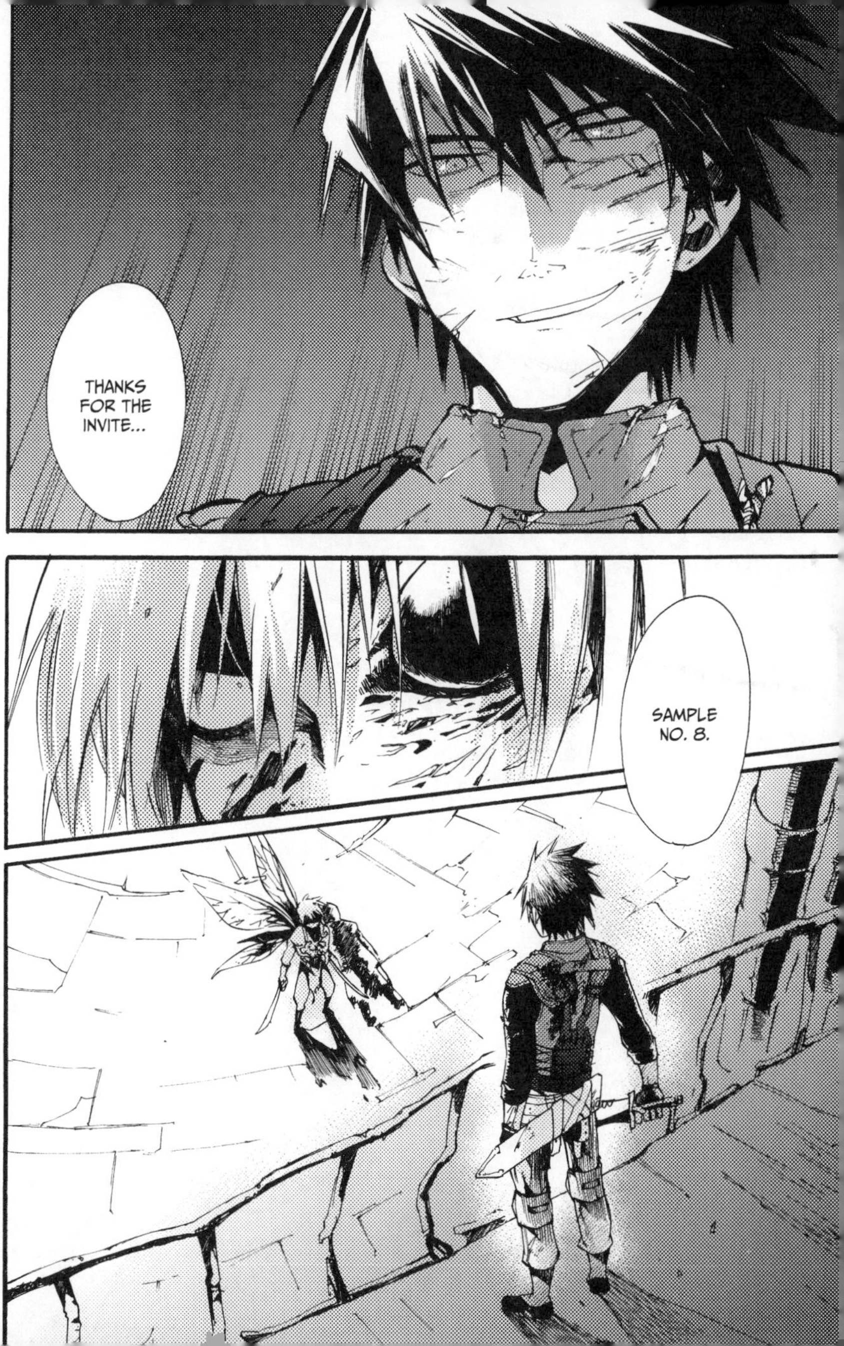
THANKS FOR THE INVITE...
SAMPLE NO. 8.

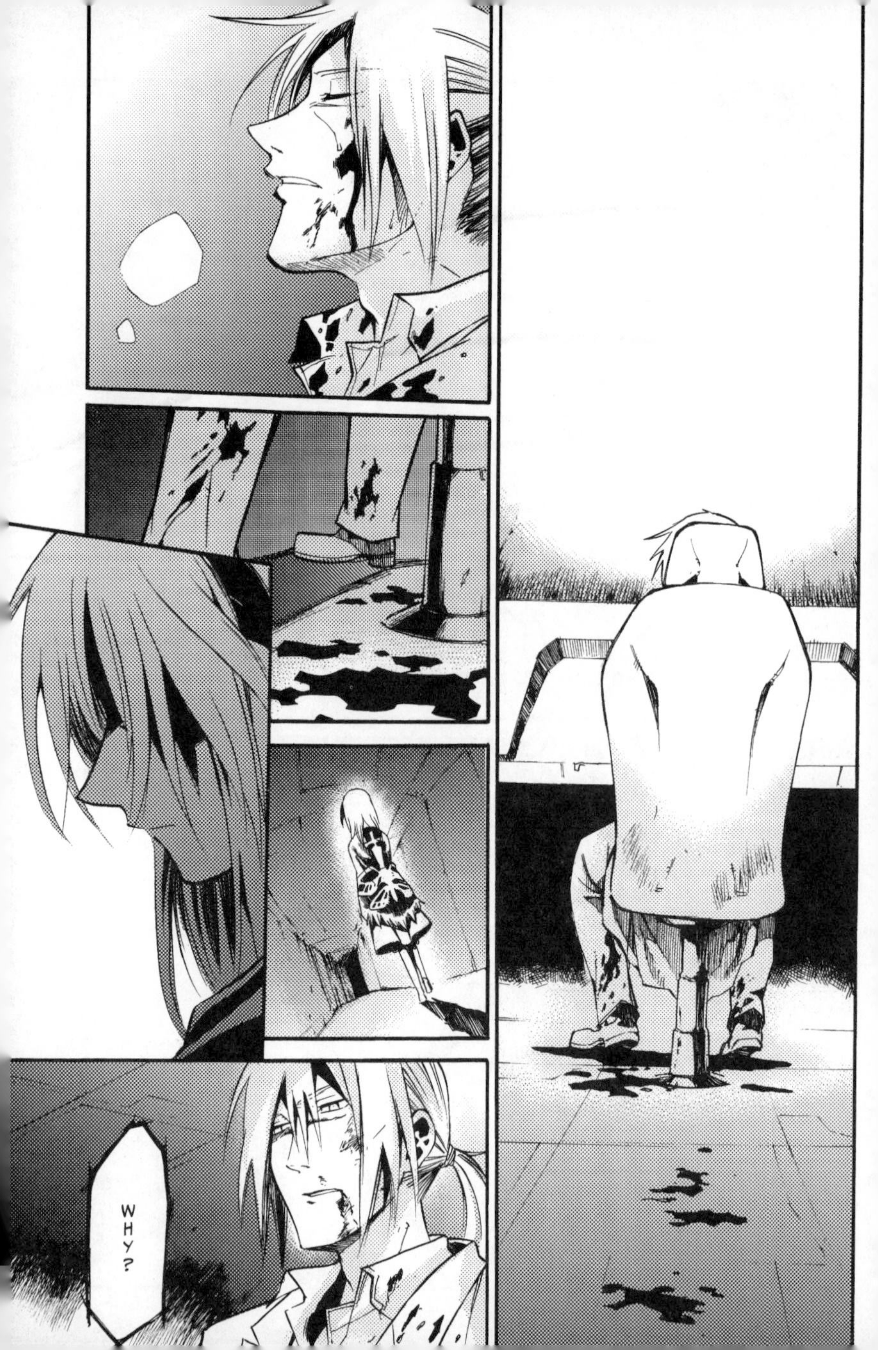
WHY?

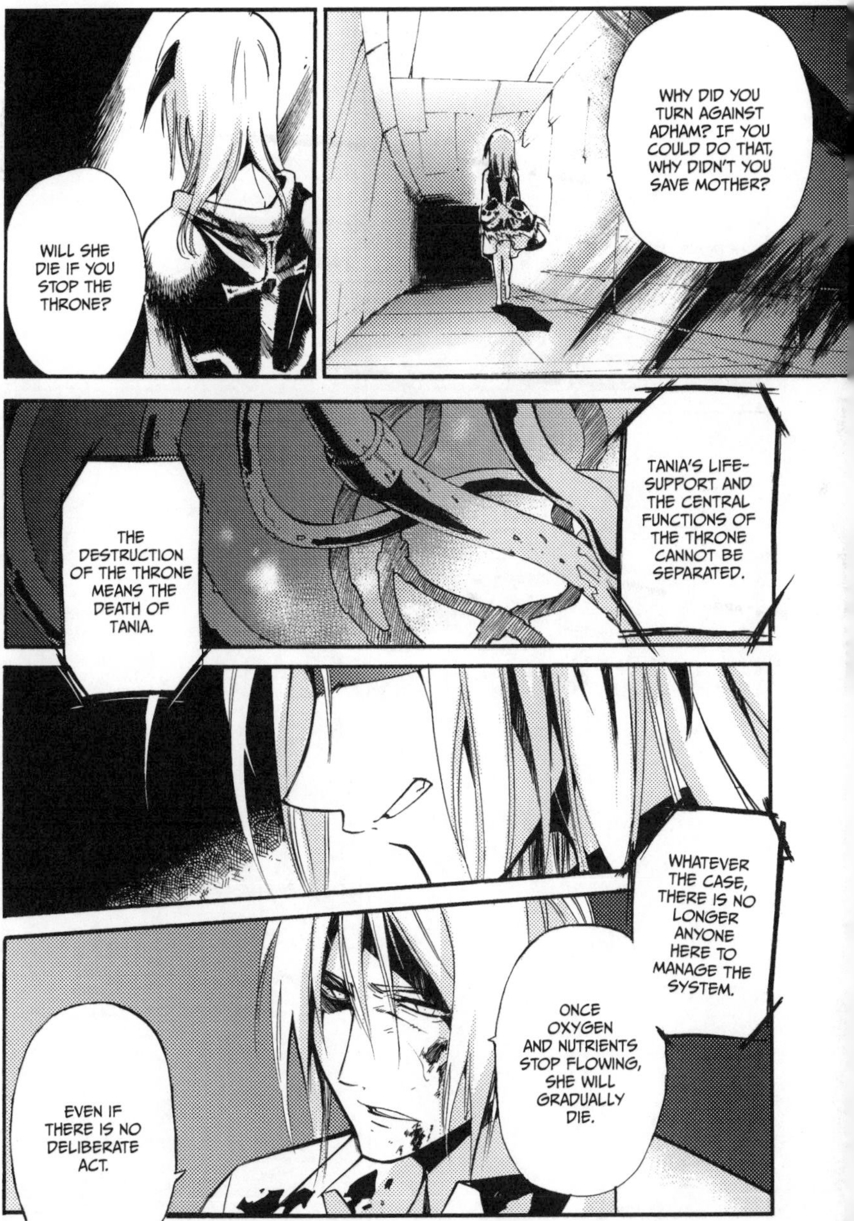
WHY DID YOU TURN AGAINST ADHAM? IF YOU COULD DO THAT, WHY DIDN'T YOU SAVE MOTHER?
WILL SHE DIE IF YOU STOP THE THRONE?
TANIA'S LIFE-SUPPORT AND THE CENTRAL FUNCTIONS OF THE THRONE CANNOT BE SEPARATED.
THE DESTRUCTION OF THE THRONE MEANS THE DEATH OF TANIA.
WHATEVER THE CASE, THERE IS NO LONGER ANYONE HERE TO MANAGE THE SYSTEM.
ONCE OXYGEN AND NUTRIENTS STOP FLOWING, SHE WILL GRADUALLY DIE.
EVEN IF THERE IS NO DELIBERATE ACT.

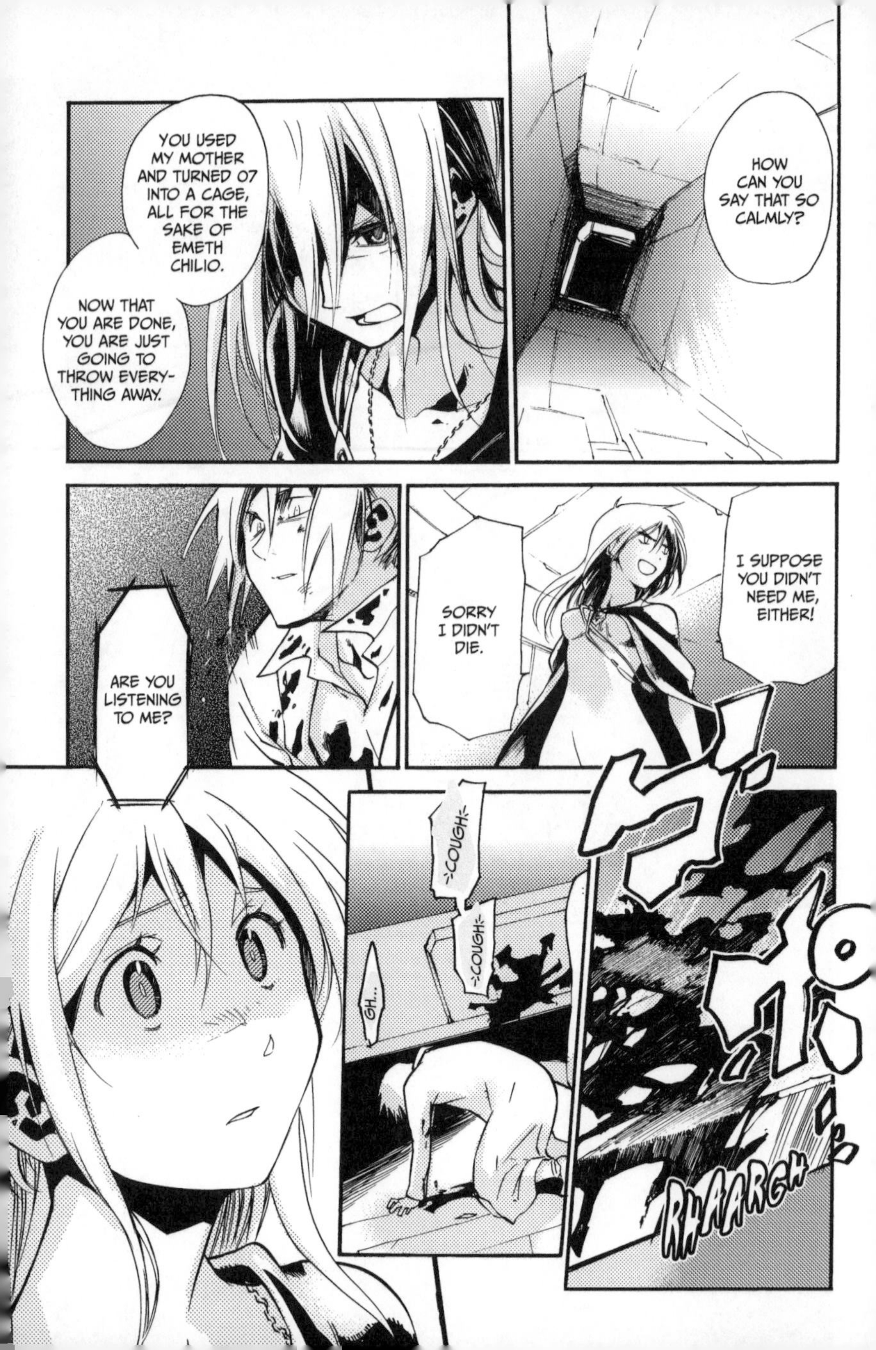
HOW CAN YOU SAY THAT SO CALMLY?
YOU USED MY MOTHER AND TURNED 07 INTO A CAGE, ALL FOR THE SAKE OF EMETH CHILIO.
NOW THAT YOU ARE DONE, YOU ARE JUST GOING TO THROW EVERY-THING AWAY.
I SUPPOSE YOU DIDN'T NEED ME, EITHER!
SORRY I DIDN'T DIE.
ARE YOU LISTENING TO ME?
RHAARGH
COUGH
COUGH
GH...

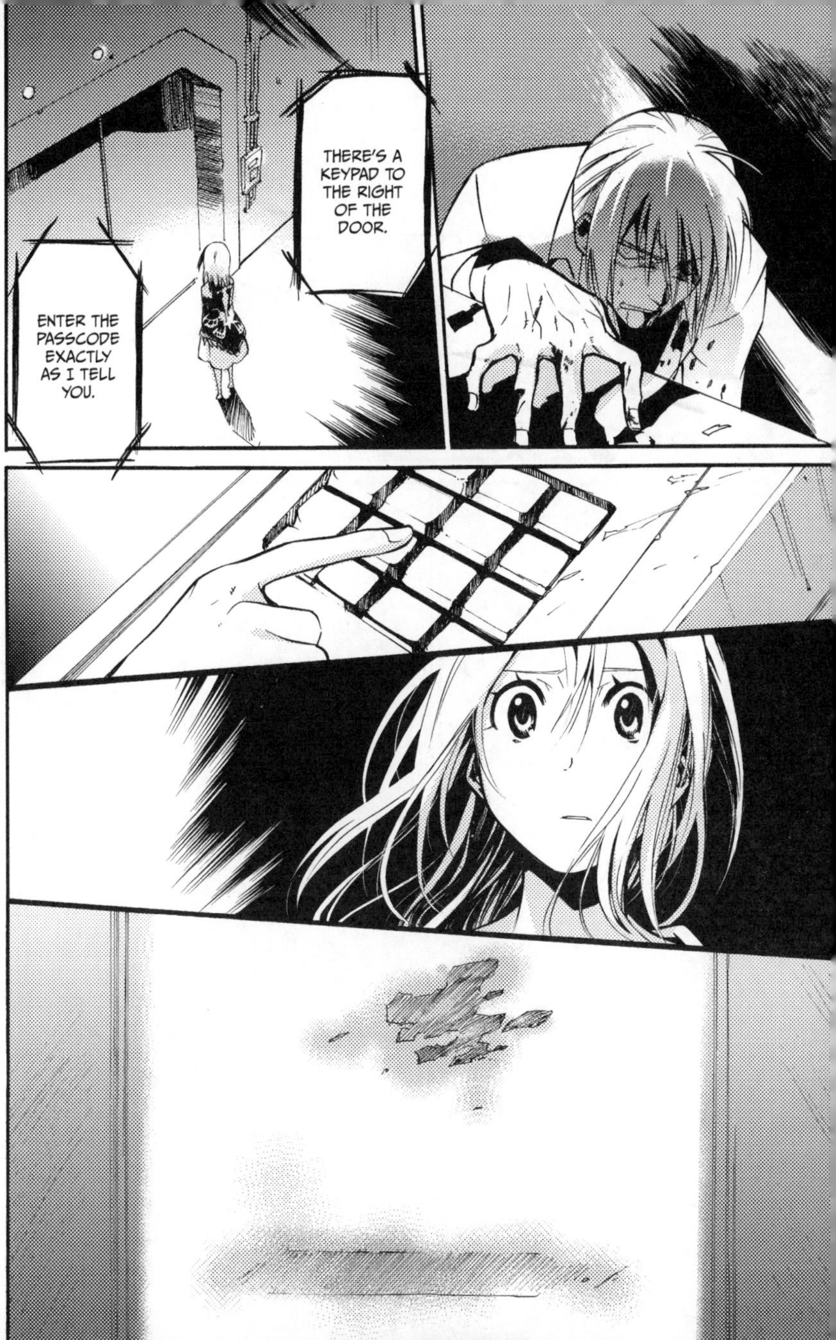
THERE'S A KEYPAD TO THE RIGHT OF THE DOOR.
ENTER THE PASSCODE EXACTLY AS I TELL YOU.

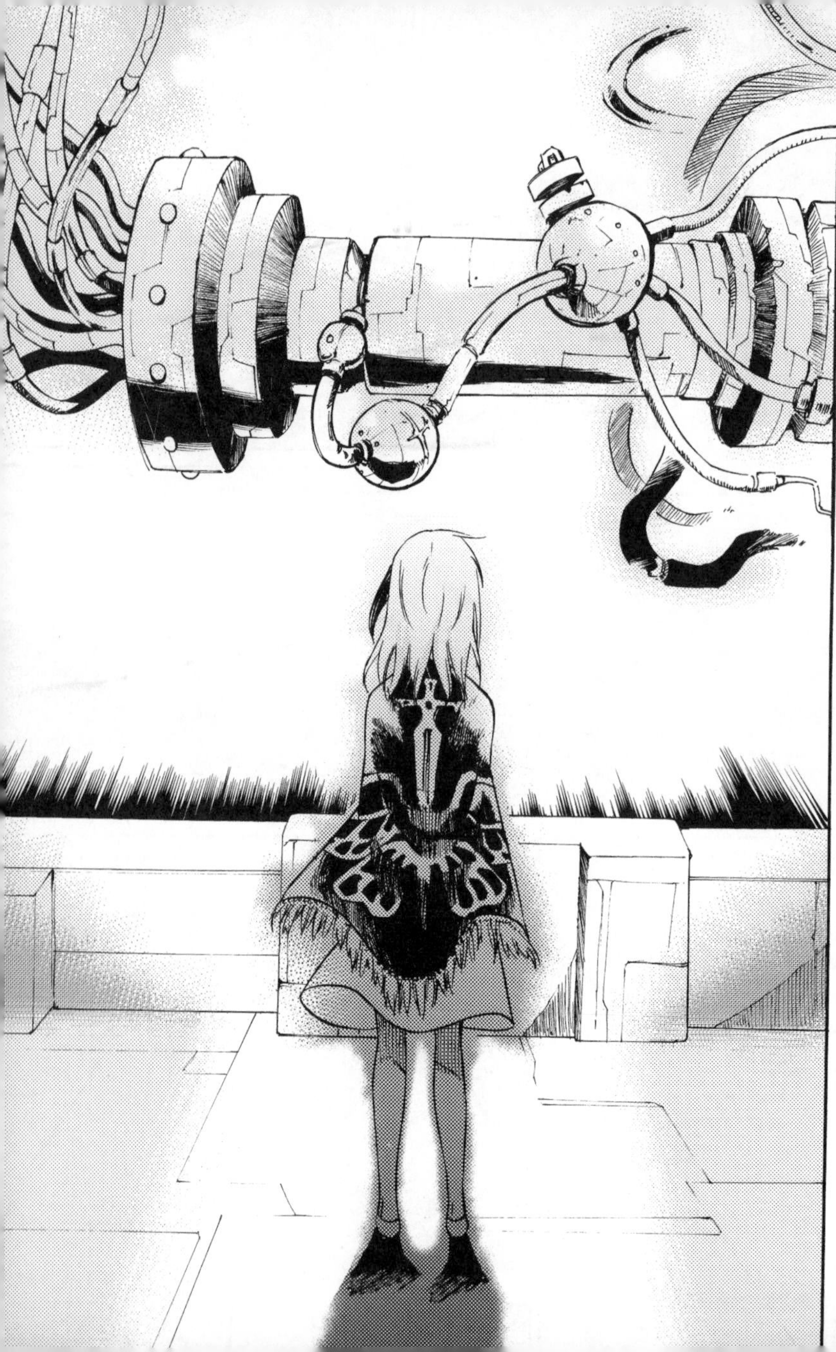

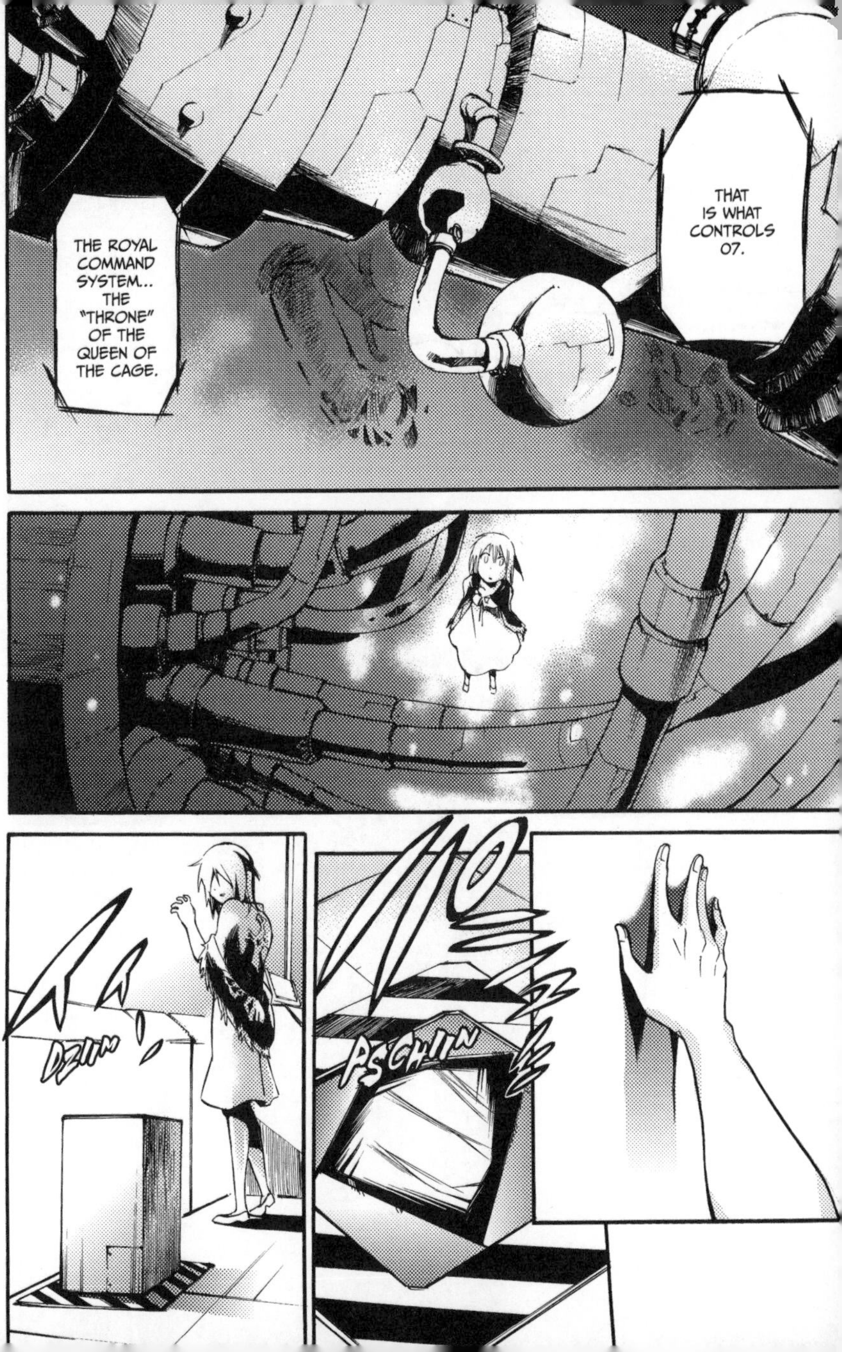
THAT IS WHAT CONTROLS 07.
THE ROYAL COMMAND SYSTEM... THE "THRONE" OF THE QUEEN OF THE CAGE.
PSCHIIN
DZIIN

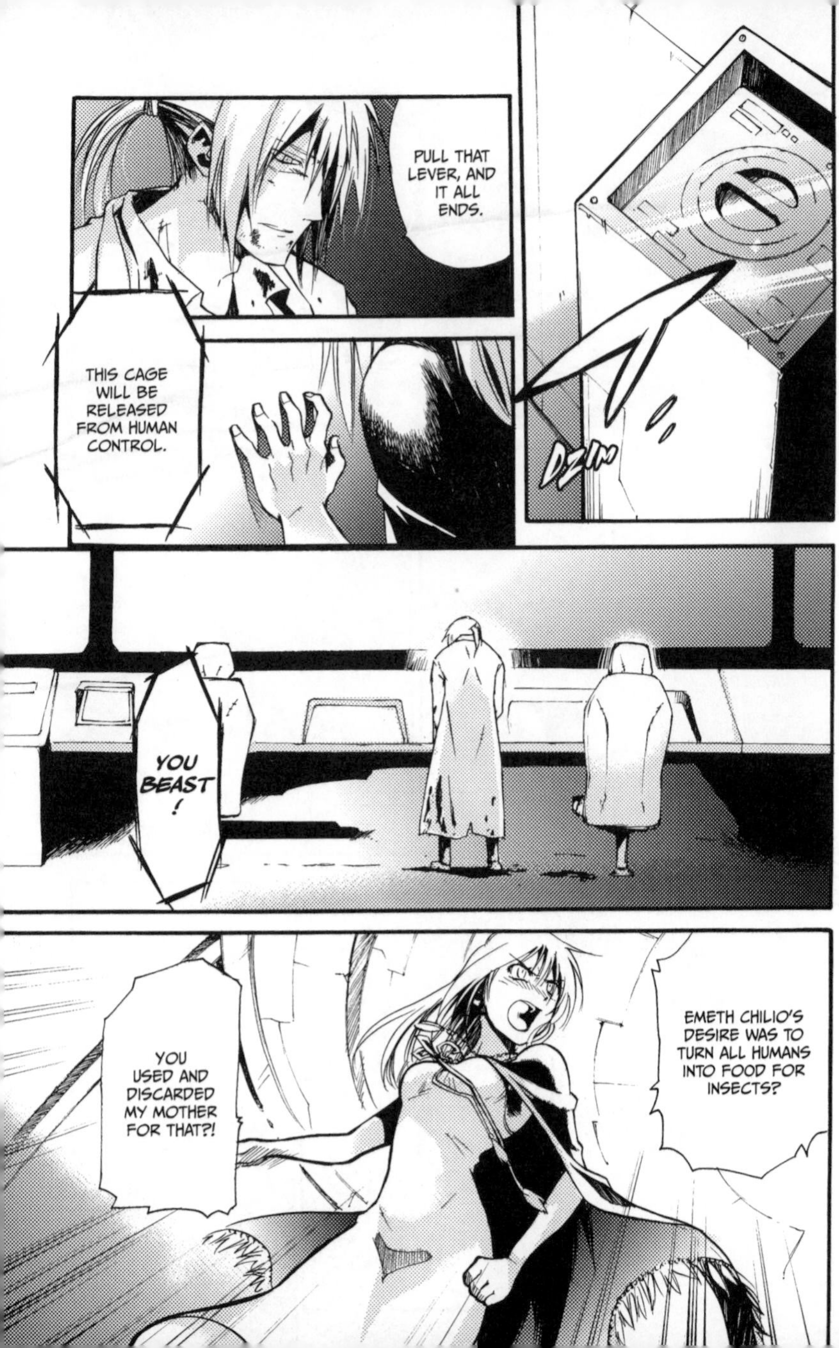
DZIN
PULL THAT LEVER, AND IT ALL ENDS.
THIS CAGE WILL BE RELEASED FROM HUMAN CONTROL.
YOU BEAST!
EMETH CHILIO'S DESIRE WAS TO TURN ALL HUMANS INTO FOOD FOR INSECTS?
YOU USED AND DISCARDED MY MOTHER FOR THAT?!

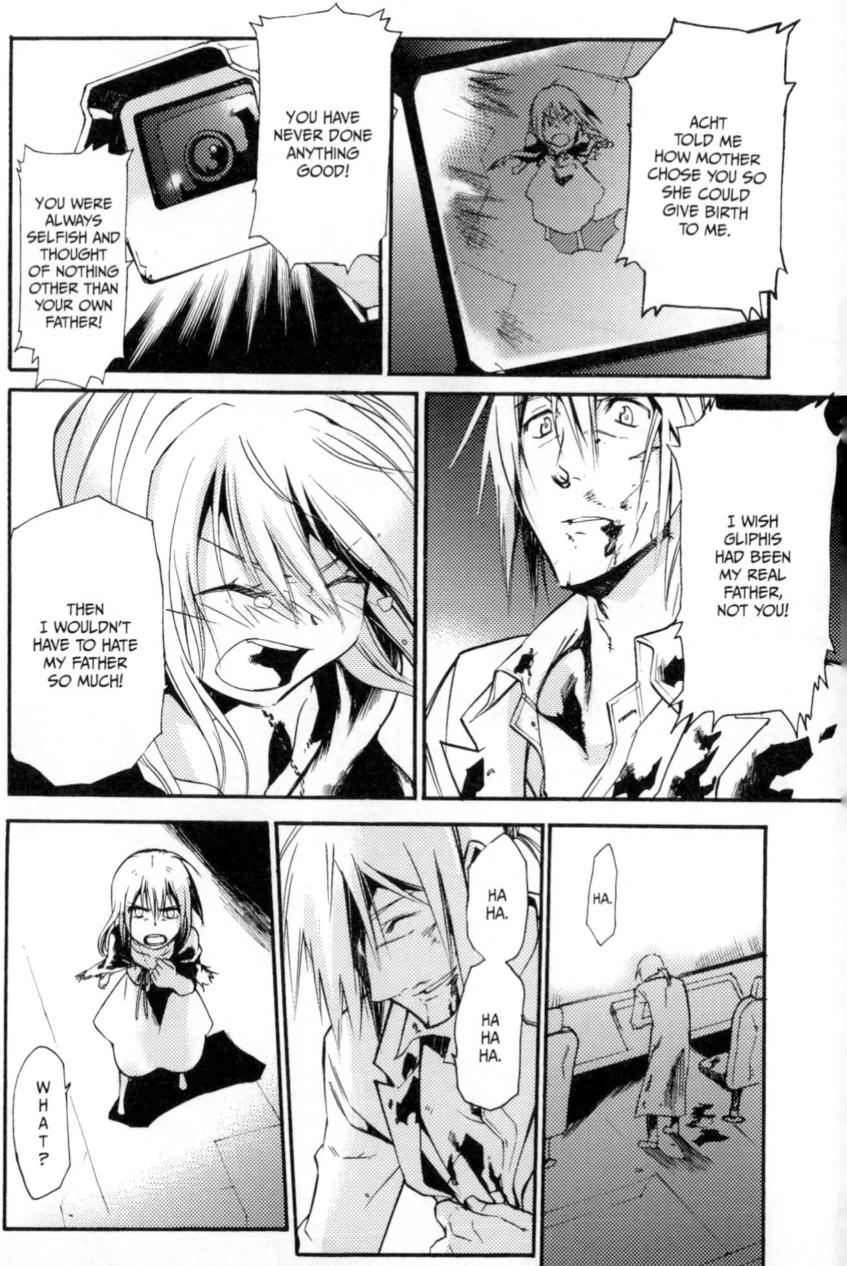
ACHT TOLD ME HOW MOTHER CHOSE YOU SO SHE COULD GIVE BIRTH TO ME.
YOU HAVE NEVER DONE ANYTHING GOOD!
YOU WERE ALWAYS SELFISH AND THOUGHT OF NOTHING OTHER THAN YOUR OWN FATHER!
I WISH GLIPHIS HAD BEEN MY REAL FATHER, NOT YOU!
THEN I WOULDN'T HAVE TO HATE MY FATHER SO MUCH!
HA.
HA HA.
HA HA HA.
WHAT?

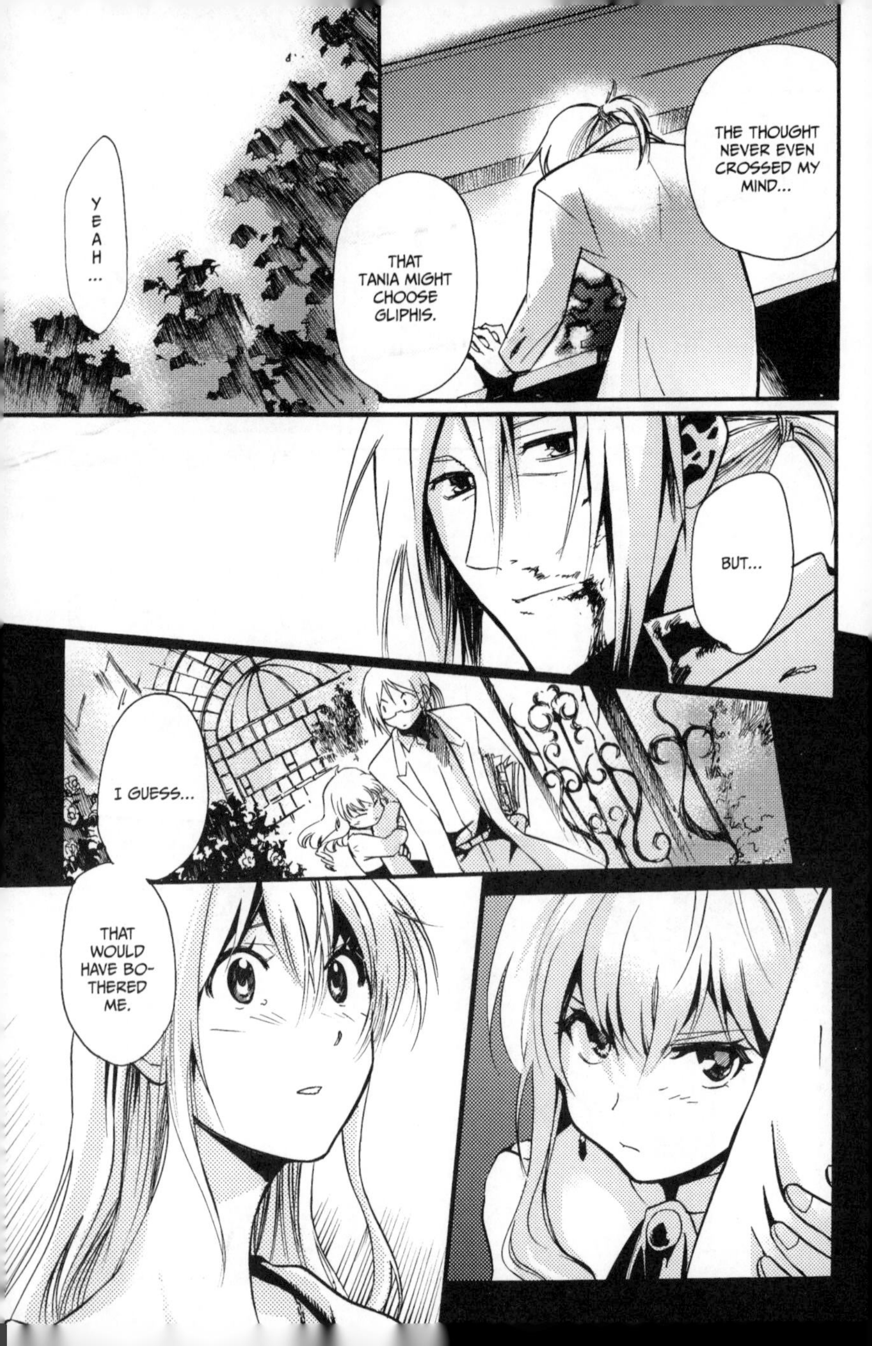
THE THOUGHT NEVER EVEN CROSSED MY MIND...
THAT TANIA MIGHT CHOOSE GLIPHIS.
YEAH...
BUT...
I GUESS...
THAT WOULD HAVE BO-THERED ME.

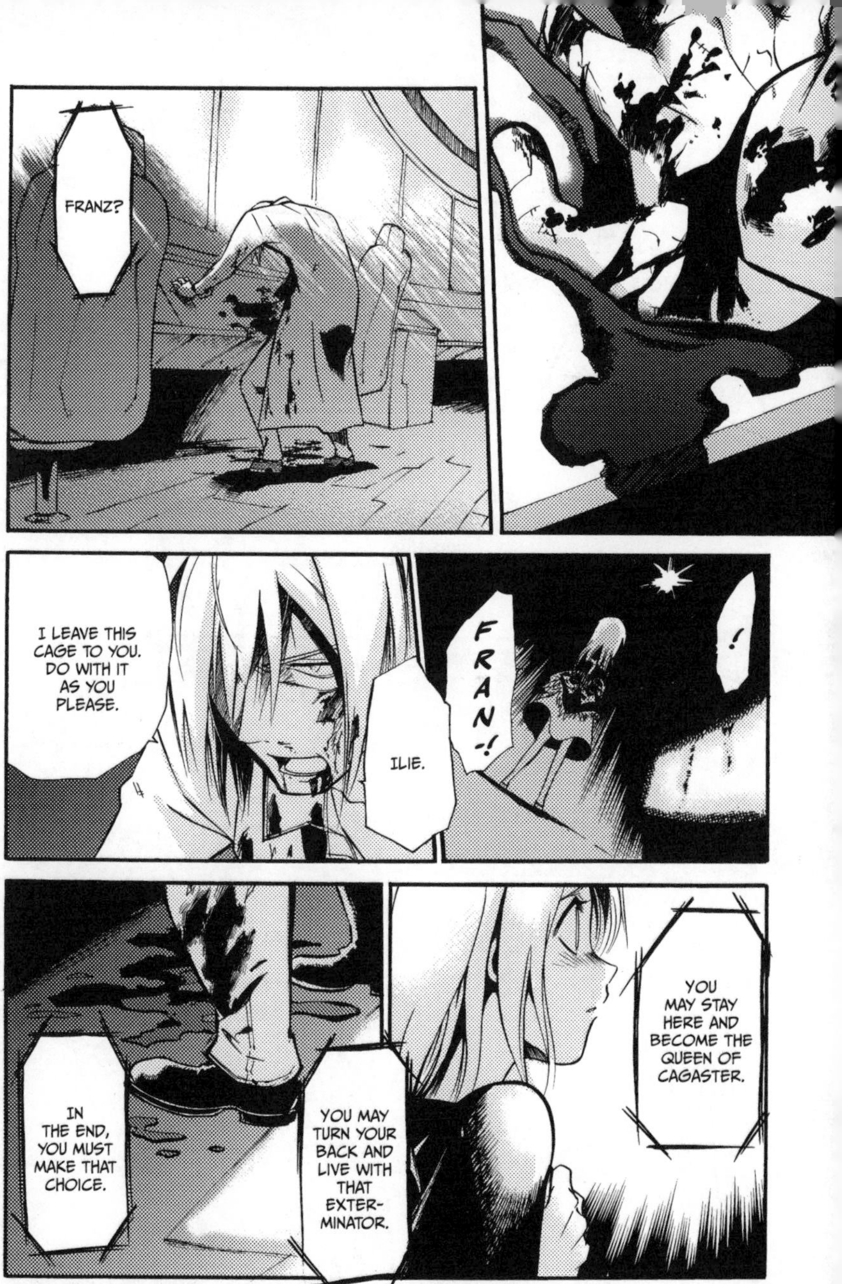
FRANZ?
!
FRAN-!
ILIE.
I LEAVE THIS CAGE TO YOU. DO WITH IT AS YOU PLEASE.
YOU MAY STAY HERE AND BECOME THE QUEEN OF CAGASTER.
YOU MAY TURN YOUR BACK AND LIVE WITH THAT EXTER- MINATOR.
IN THE END, YOU MUST MAKE THAT CHOICE.

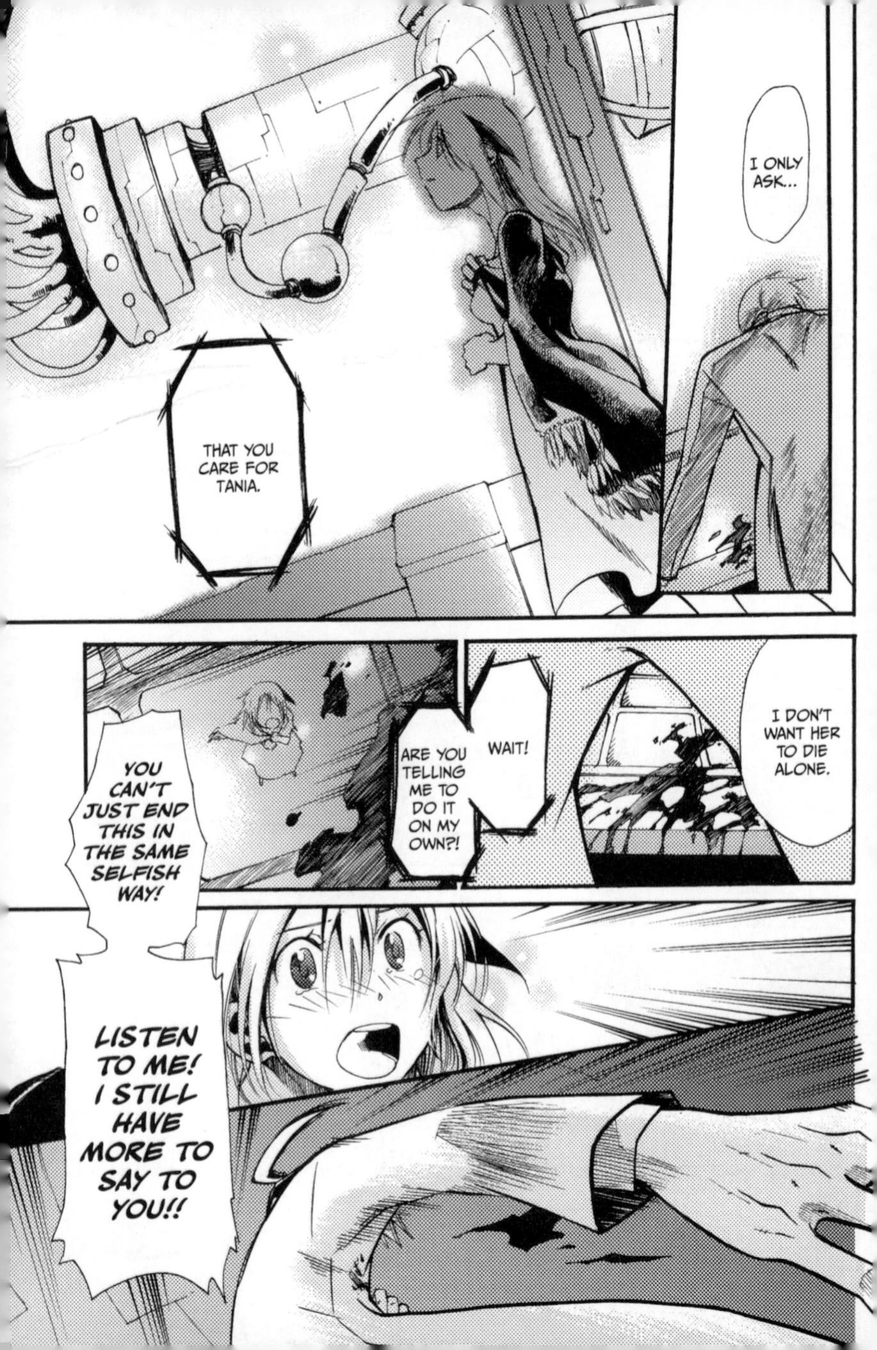
I ONLY ASK...
THAT YOU CARE FOR TANIA.
I DON'T WANT HER TO DIE ALONE.
WAIT!
ARE YOU TELLING ME TO DO IT ON MY OWN?!
YOU CAN'T JUST END THIS IN THE SAME SELFISH WAY!
LISTEN TO ME! I STILL HAVE MORE TO SAY TO YOU!!

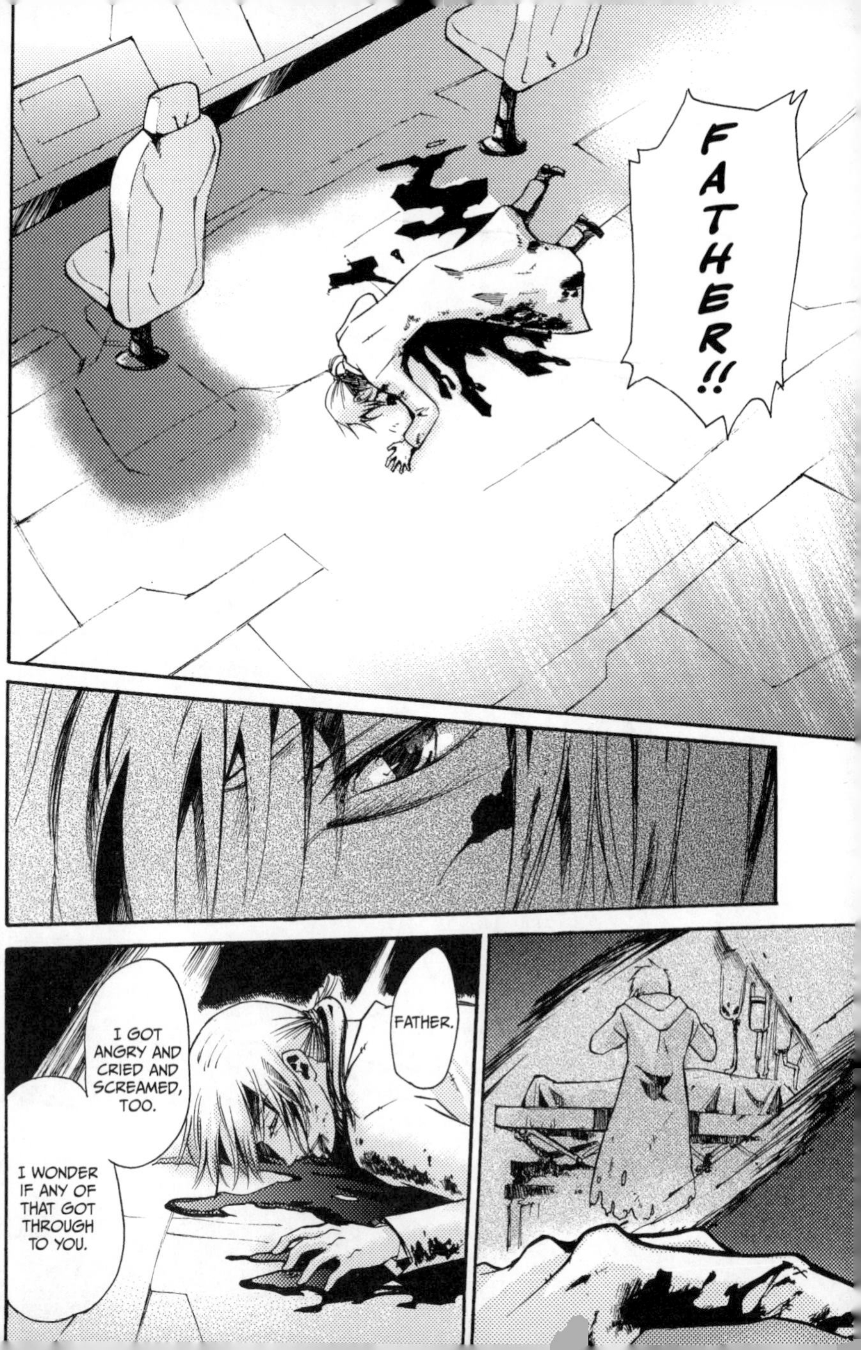
FATHER!!
FATHER.
I GOT ANGRY AND CRIED AND SCREAMED, TOO.
I WONDER IF ANY OF THAT GOT THROUGH TO YOU.

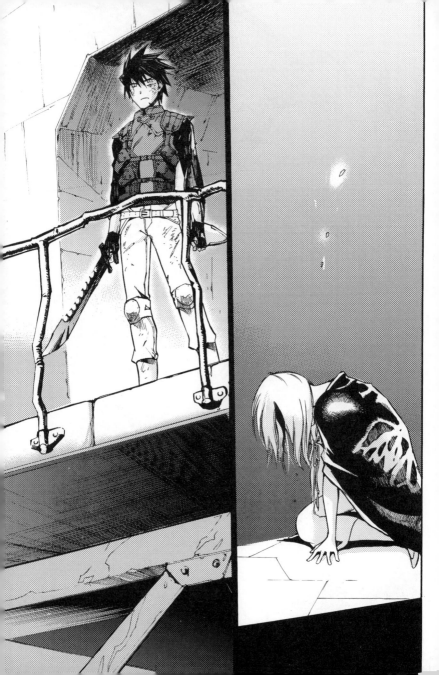

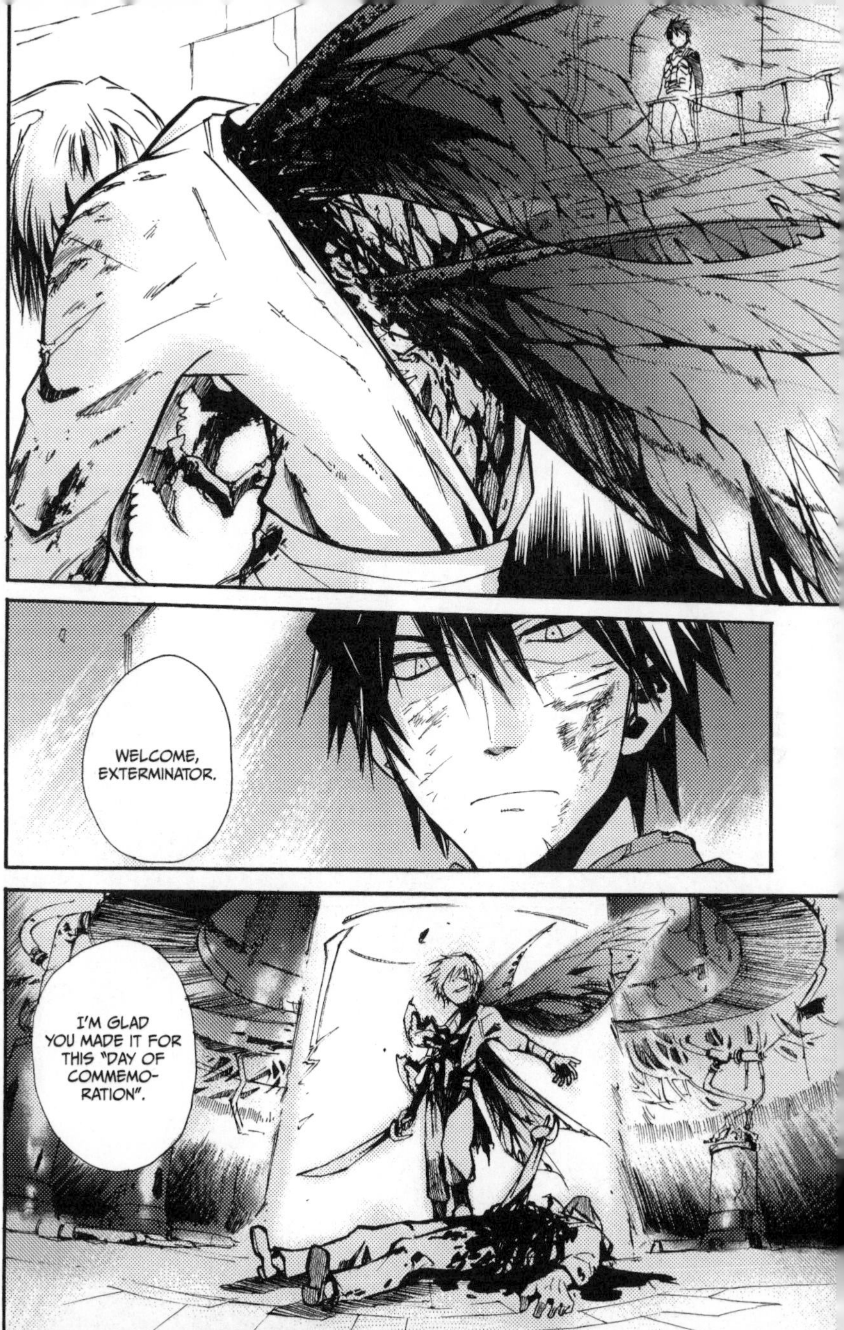
WELCOME, EXTERMINATOR.
I'M GLAD YOU MADE IT FOR THIS "DAY OF COMMEMO-RATION".

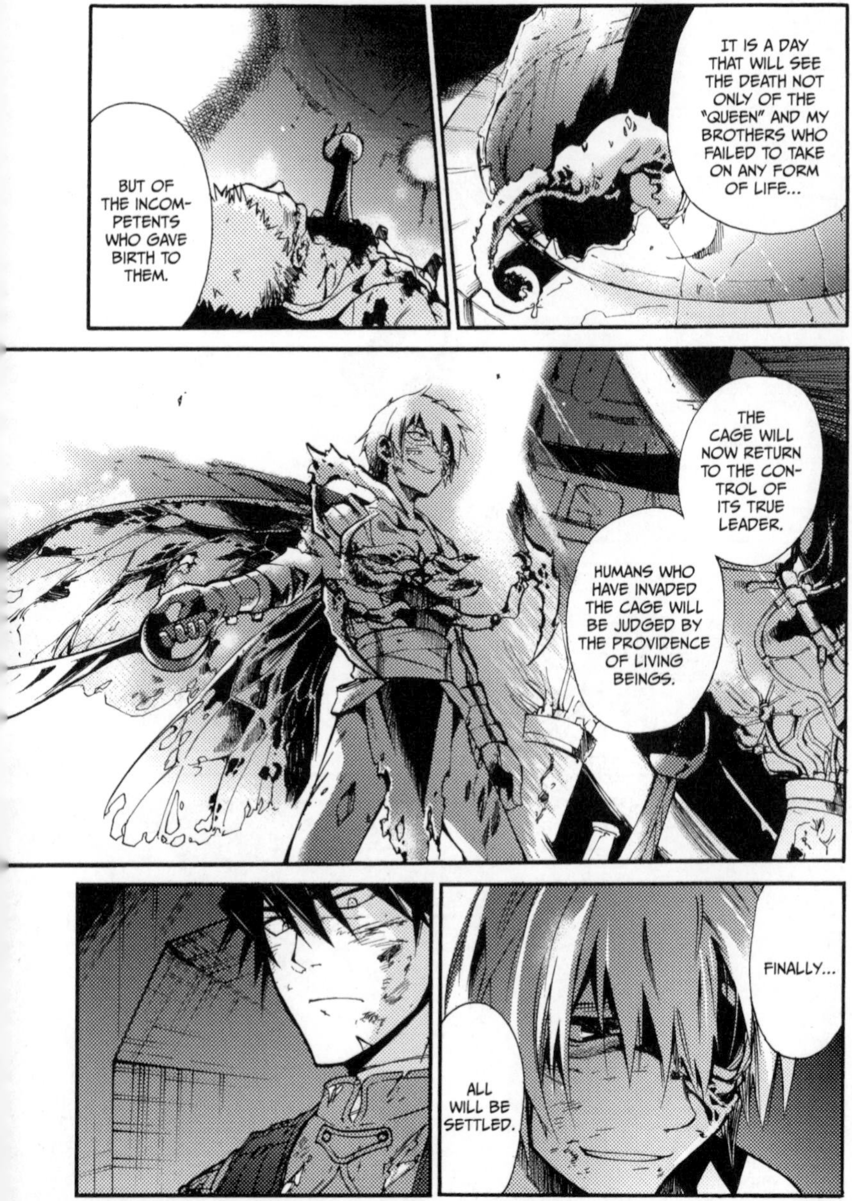
IT IS A DAY THAT WILL SEE THE DEATH NOT ONLY OF THE "QUEEN" AND MY BROTHERS WHO FAILED TO TAKE ON ANY FORM OF LIFE...
BUT OF THE INCOMPETENTS WHO GAVE BIRTH TO THEM.
THE CAGE WILL NOW RETURN TO THE CONTROL OF ITS TRUE LEADER.
HUMANS WHO HAVE INVADED THE CAGE WILL BE JUDGED BY THE PROVIDENCE OF LIVING BEINGS.
FINALLY...
ALL WILL BE SETTLED.

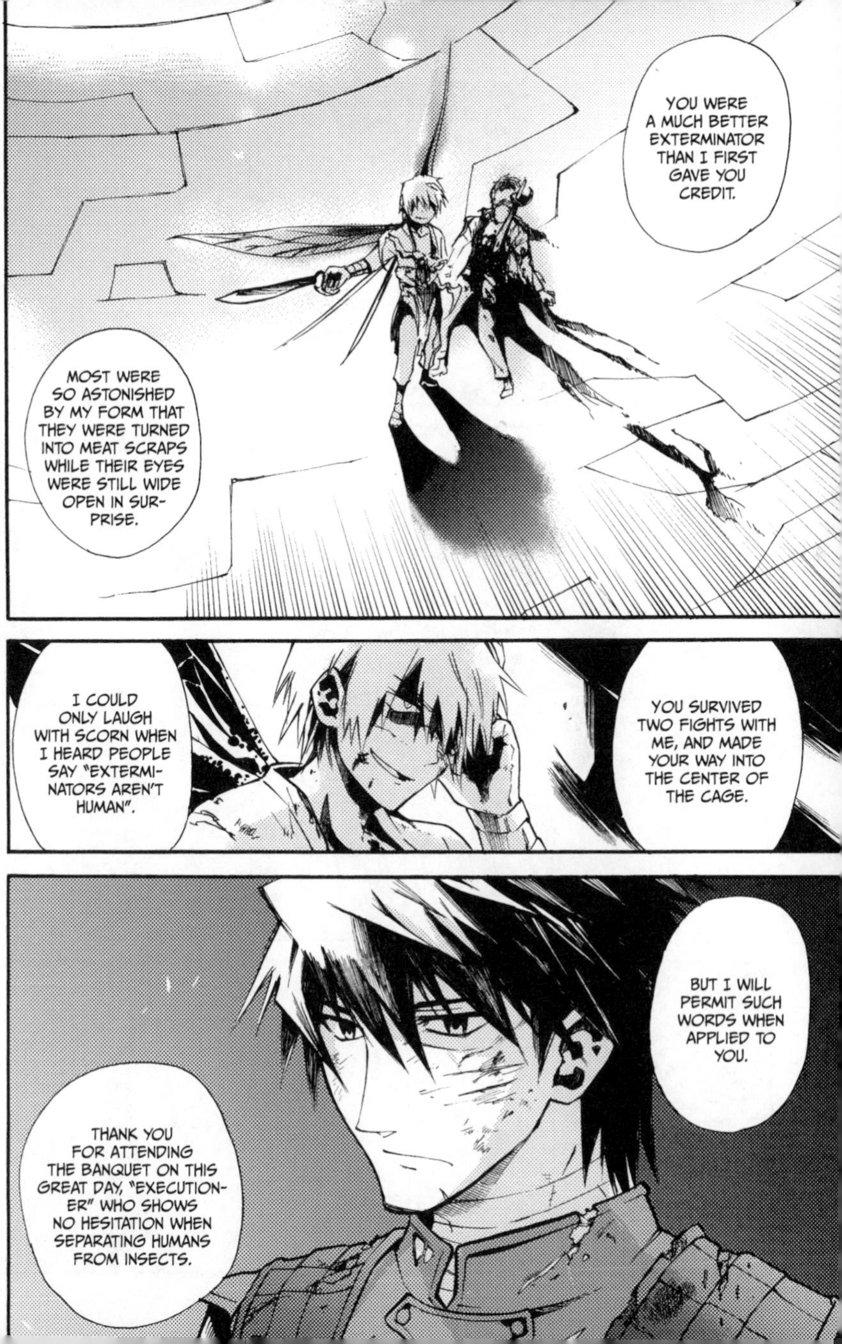
YOU WERE A MUCH BETTER EXTERMINATOR THAN I FIRST GAVE YOU CREDIT.
MOST WERE SO ASTONISHED BY MY FORM THAT THEY WERE TURNED INTO MEAT SCRAPS WHILE THEIR EYES WERE STILL WIDE OPEN IN SUR-PRISE.
YOU SURVIVED TWO FIGHTS WITH ME, AND MADE YOUR WAY INTO THE CENTER OF THE CAGE.
I COULD ONLY LAUGH WITH SCORN WHEN I HEARD PEOPLE SAY "EXTERMI-NATORS AREN'T HUMAN".
BUT I WILL PERMIT SUCH WORDS WHEN APPLIED TO YOU.
THANK YOU FOR ATTENDING THE BANQUET ON THIS GREAT DAY, "EXECUTION-ER" WHO SHOWS NO HESITATION WHEN SEPARATING HUMANS FROM INSECTS.

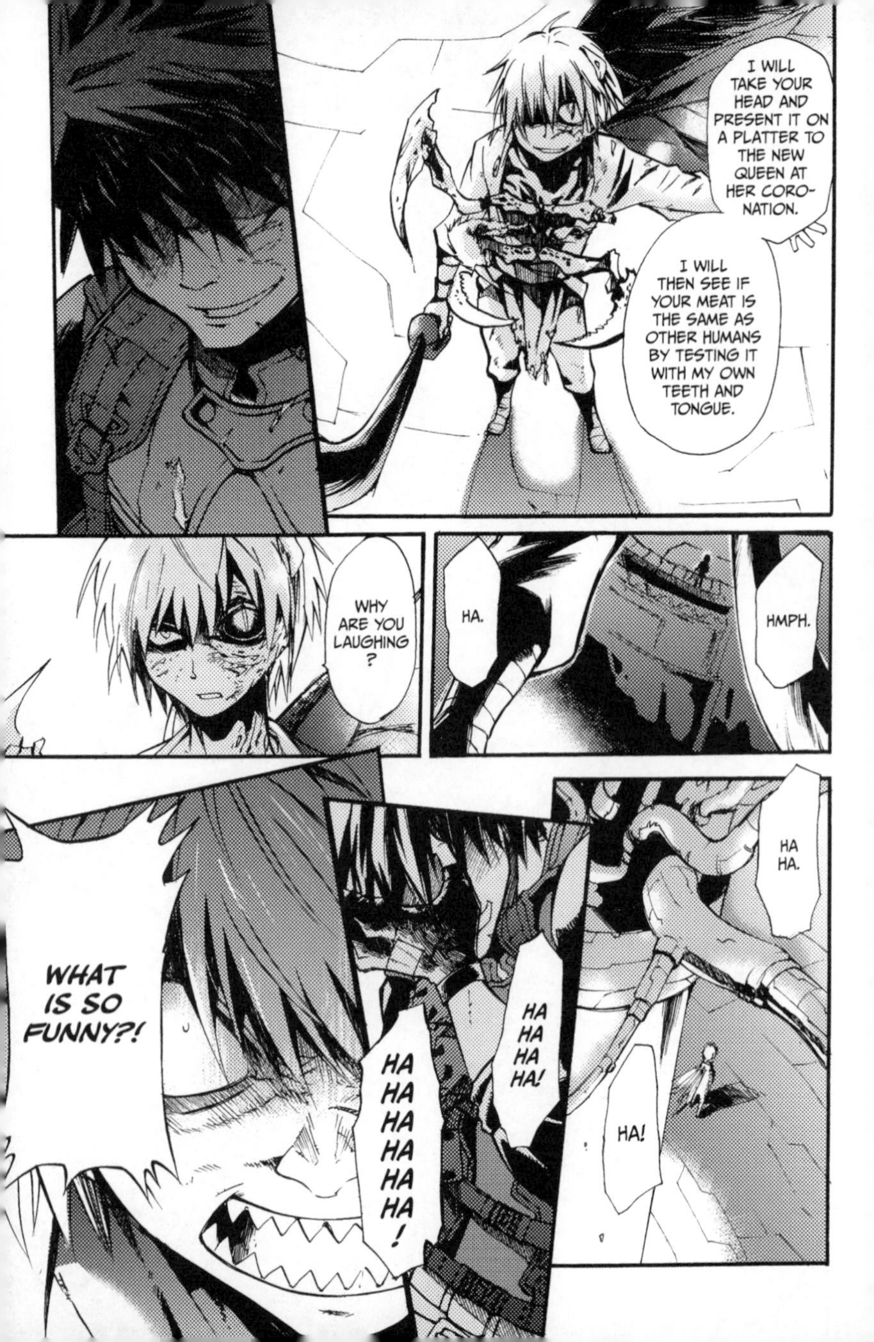
I WILL TAKE YOUR HEAD AND PRESENT IT ON A PLATTER TO THE NEW QUEEN AT HER CORONATION.
I WILL THEN SEE IF YOUR MEAT IS THE SAME AS OTHER HUMANS BY TESTING IT WITH MY OWN TEETH AND TONGUE.
HMPH.
HA.
WHY ARE YOU LAUGHING?
HA HA.
HA!
HA HA HA HA!
HA HA HA HA HA HA!
WHAT IS SO FUNNY?!

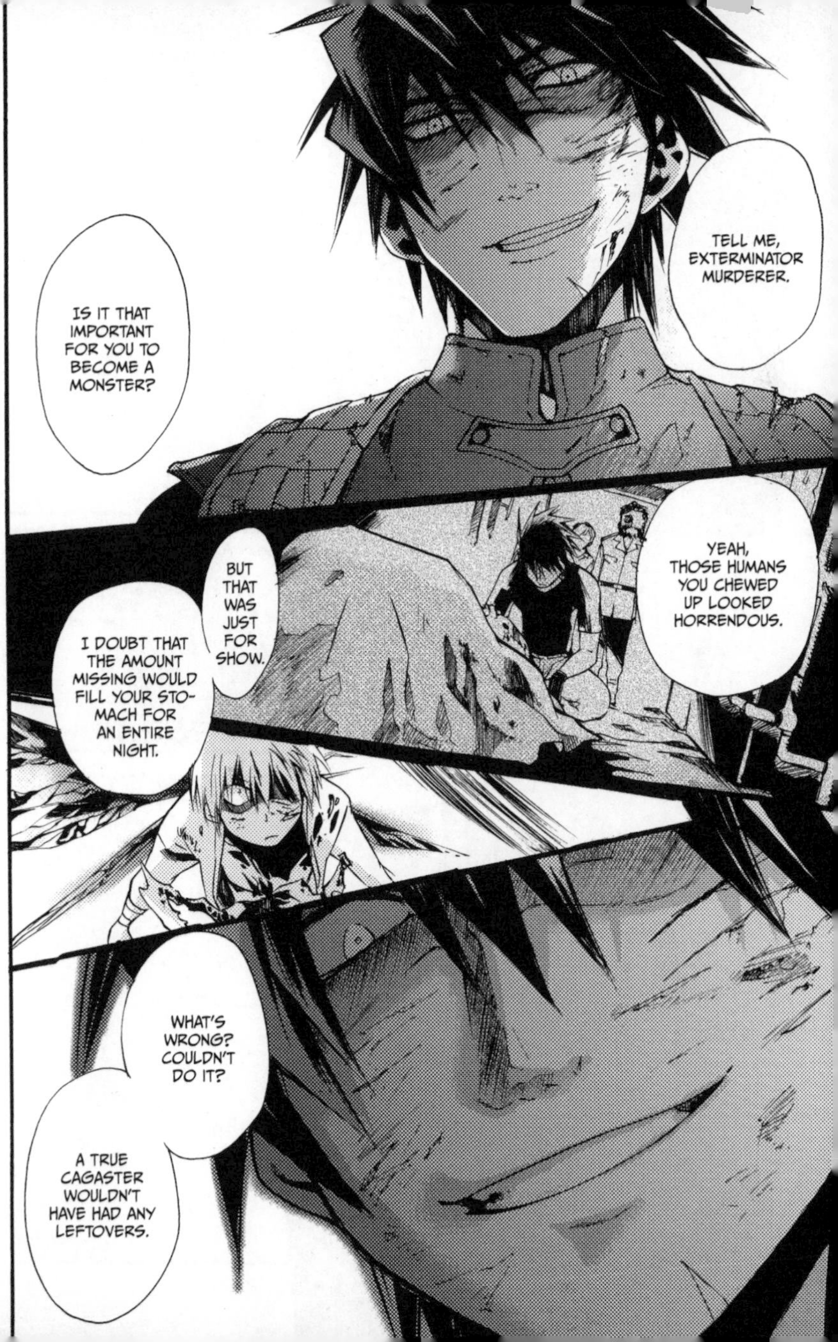
TELL ME, EXTERMINATOR MURDERER.
IS IT THAT IMPORTANT FOR YOU TO BECOME A MONSTER?
YEAH, THOSE HUMANS YOU CHEWED UP LOOKED HORRENDOUS.
BUT THAT WAS JUST FOR SHOW.
I DOUBT THAT THE AMOUNT MISSING WOULD FILL YOUR STO-MACH FOR AN ENTIRE NIGHT.
WHAT'S WRONG? COULDN'T DO IT?
A TRUE CAGASTER WOULDN'T HAVE HAD ANY LEFTOVERS.

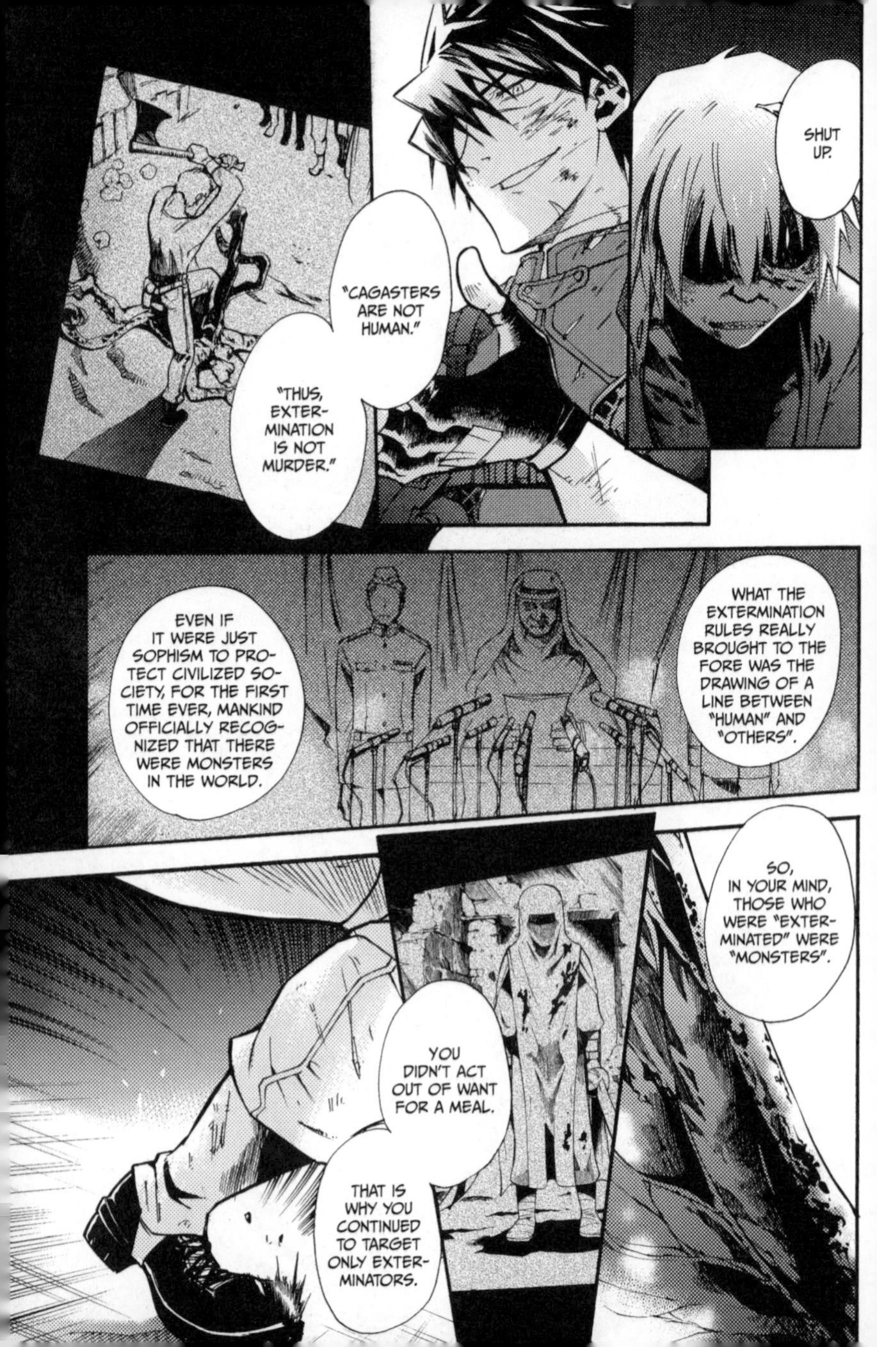
SHUT UP.
"CAGASTERS ARE NOT HUMAN."
"THUS, EXTER-MINATION IS NOT MURDER."
WHAT THE EXTERMINATION RULES REALLY BROUGHT TO THE FORE WAS THE DRAWING OF A LINE BETWEEN "HUMAN" AND "OTHERS".
EVEN IF IT WERE JUST SOPHISM TO PRO-TECT CIVILIZED SO-CIETY, FOR THE FIRST TIME EVER, MANKIND OFFICIALLY RECOG-NIZED THAT THERE WERE MONSTERS IN THE WORLD.
SO, IN YOUR MIND, THOSE WHO WERE "EXTER-MINATED" WERE "MONSTERS".
YOU DIDN'T ACT OUT OF WANT FOR A MEAL.
THAT IS WHY YOU CONTINUED TO TARGET ONLY EXTER-MINATORS.

EVEN AS YOU SLURPED UP DIRTY EXTERMINATOR BLOOD, YOU SAID TO YOURSELF "NEXT TIME I WILL REALLY SHOW THEM WHO IS A MONSTER"!!

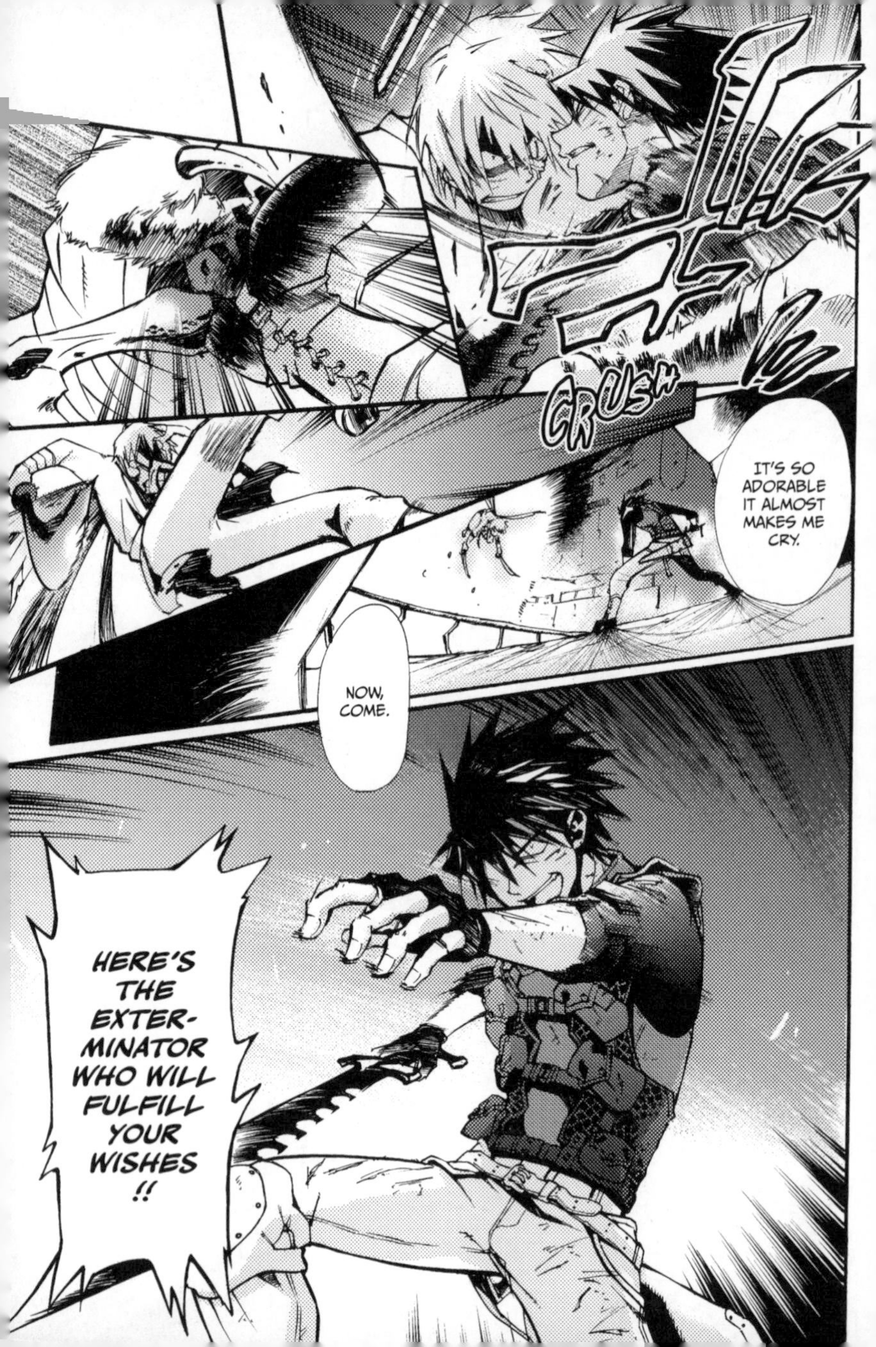
CRUSH
IT'S SO ADORABLE IT ALMOST MAKES ME CRY.
NOW, COME.
HERE'S THE EXTERMINATOR WHO WILL FULFILL YOUR WISHES!!

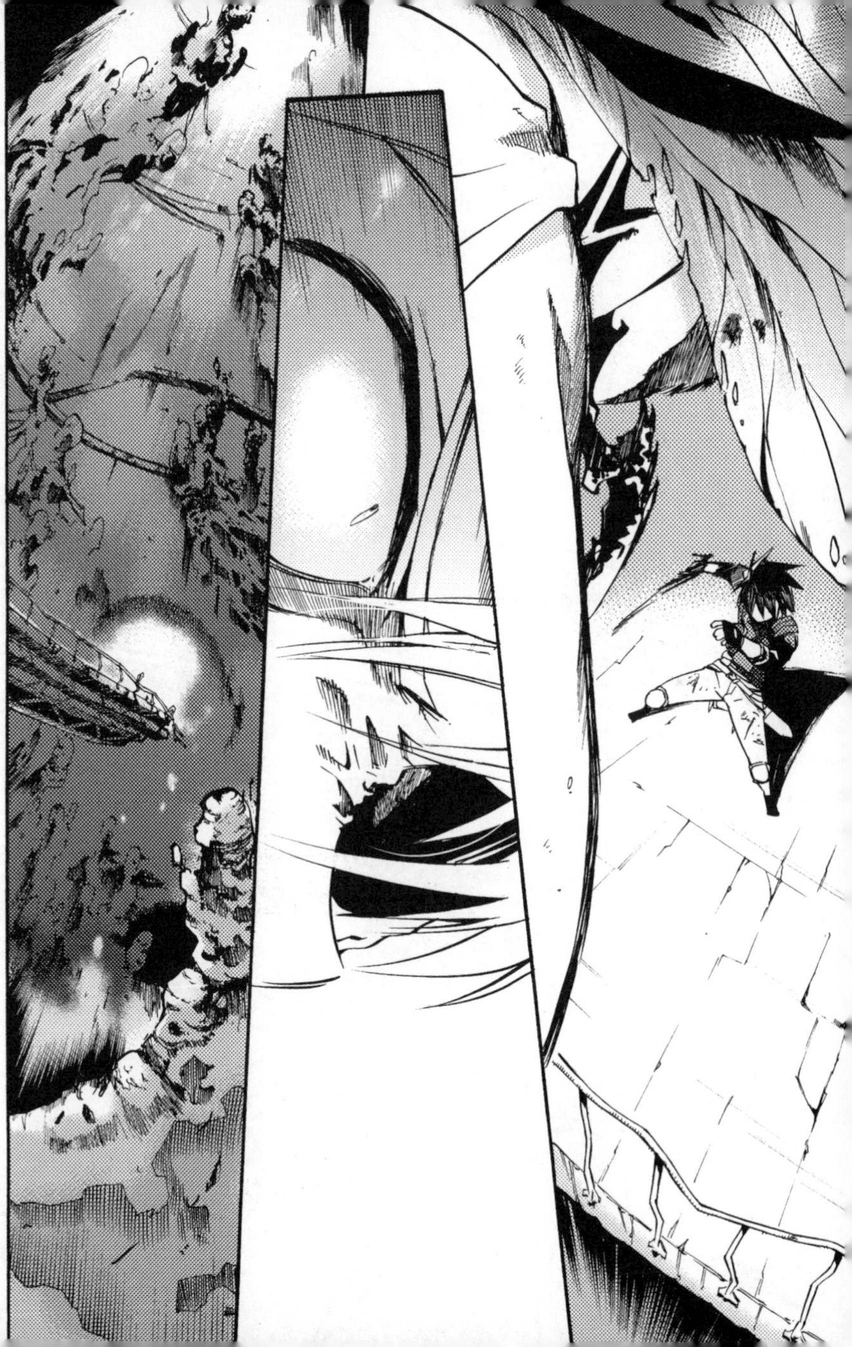

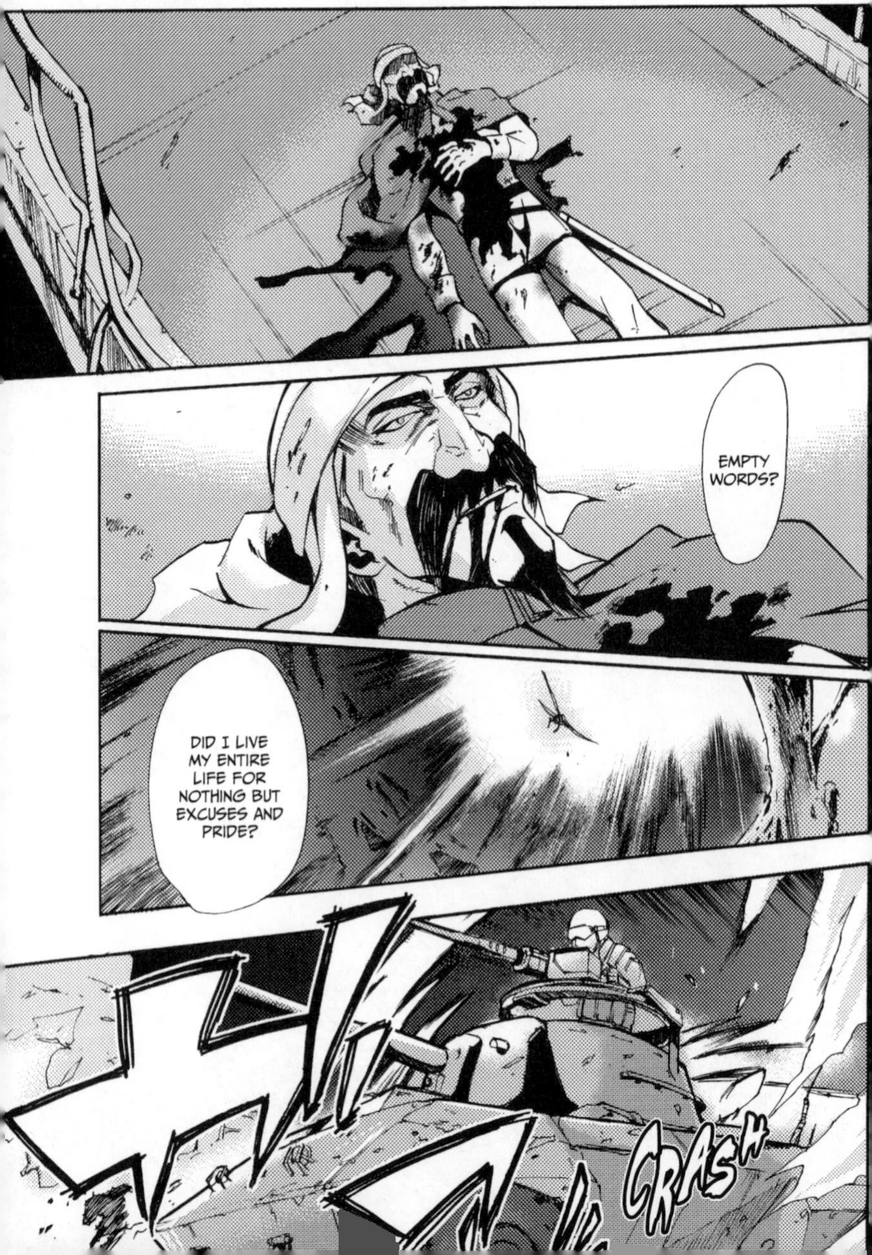
EMPTY WORDS?
DID I LIVE MY ENTIRE LIFE FOR NOTHING BUT EXCUSES AND PRIDE?
CRASH

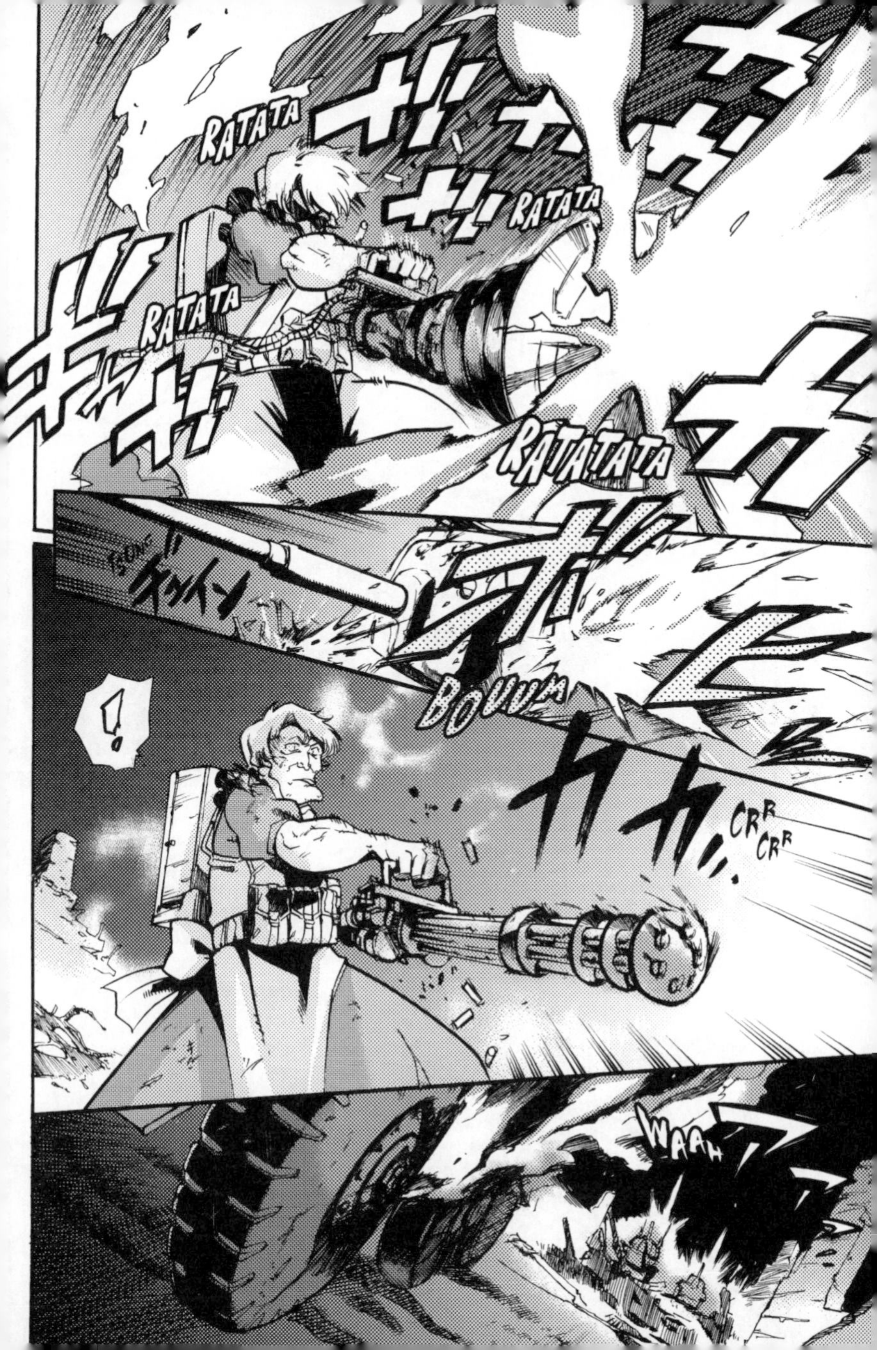
RATATA
RATATA
RATATA
RATATATA
TSONG
BOUUM
!
CRR CRR
WAAH

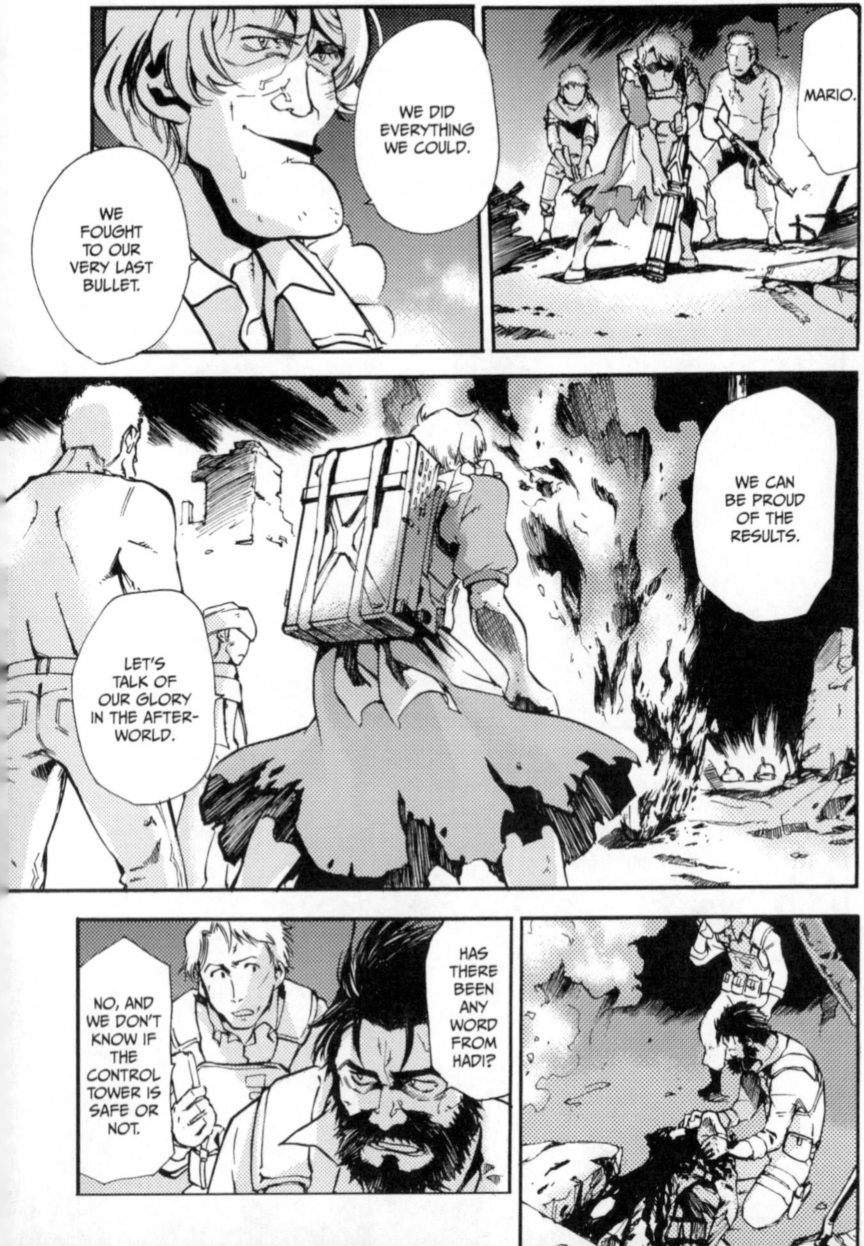
MARIO.
WE DID EVERYTHING WE COULD.
WE FOUGHT TO OUR VERY LAST BULLET.
WE CAN BE PROUD OF THE RESULTS.
LET'S TALK OF OUR GLORY IN THE AFTER-WORLD.
HAS THERE BEEN ANY WORD FROM HADI?
NO, AND WE DON'T KNOW IF THE CONTROL TOWER IS SAFE OR NOT.

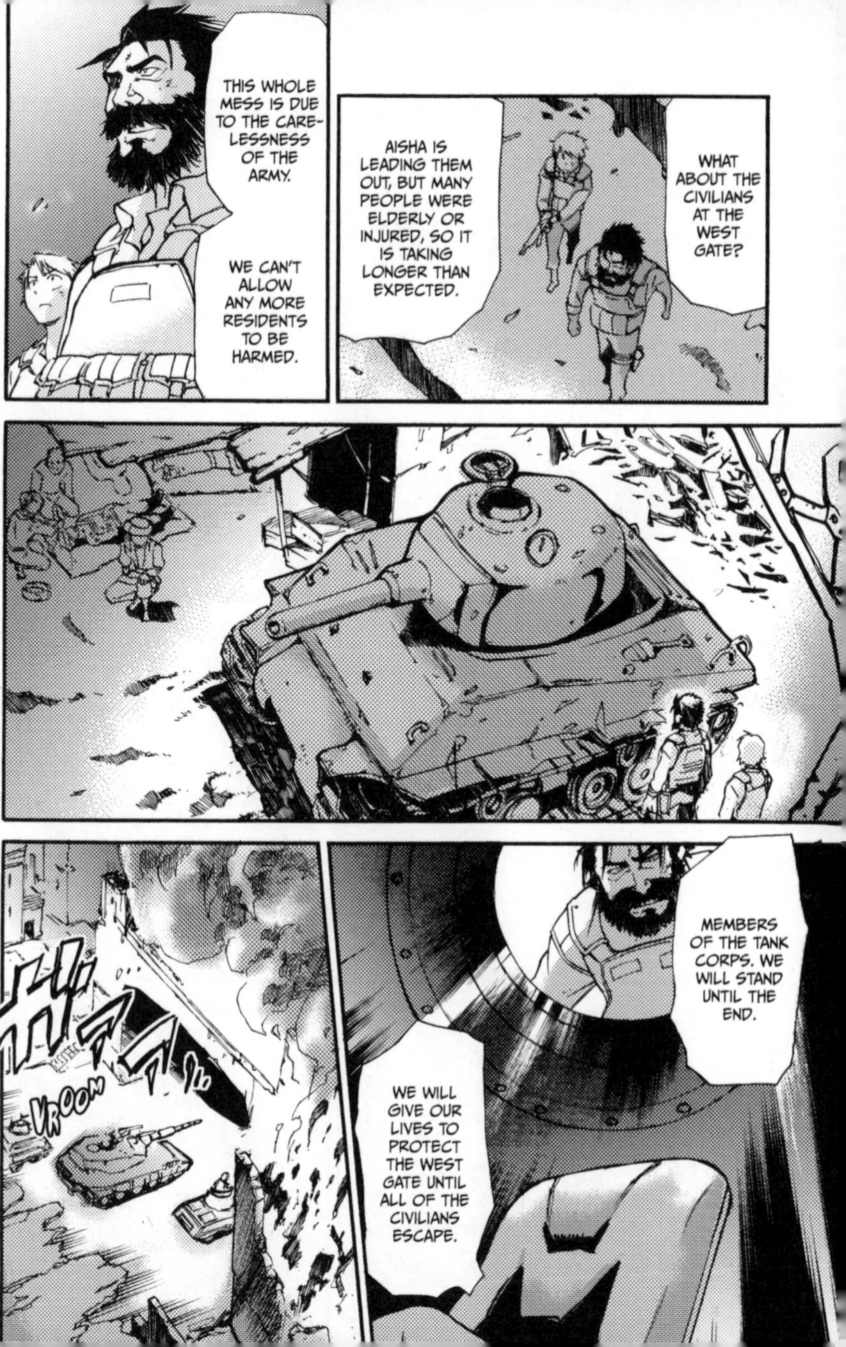
WHAT ABOUT THE CIVILIANS AT THE WEST GATE?
AISHA IS LEADING THEM OUT, BUT MANY PEOPLE WERE ELDERLY OR INJURED, SO IT IS TAKING LONGER THAN EXPECTED.
THIS WHOLE MESS IS DUE TO THE CARE-LESSNESS OF THE ARMY.
WE CAN'T ALLOW ANY MORE RESIDENTS TO BE HARMED.
MEMBERS OF THE TANK CORPS. WE WILL STAND UNTIL THE END.
WE WILL GIVE OUR LIVES TO PROTECT THE WEST GATE UNTIL ALL OF THE CIVILIANS ESCAPE.
VROOM

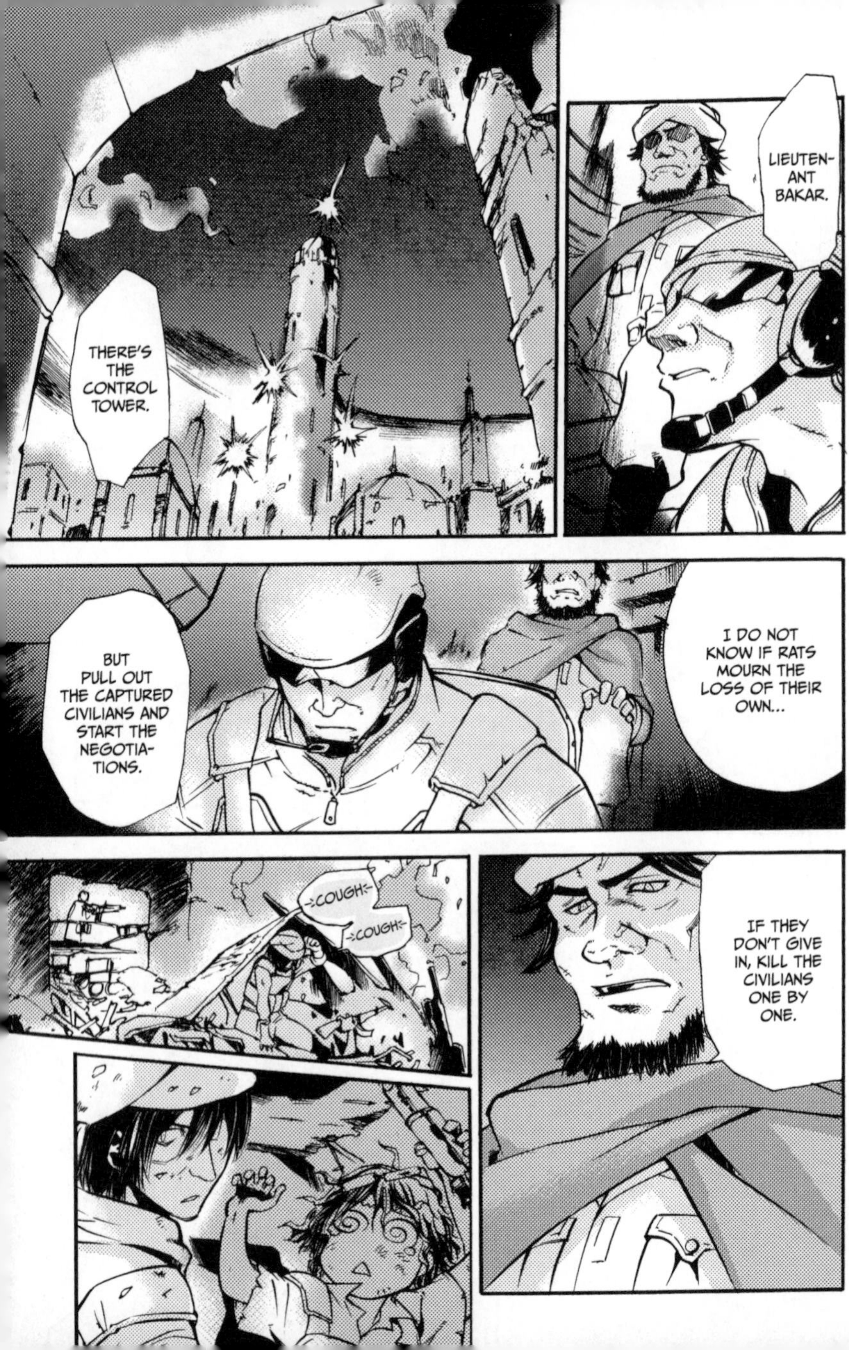
LIEUTEN-
ANT
BAKAR.
THERE'S THE CONTROL TOWER.
I DO NOT KNOW IF RATS MOURN THE LOSS OF THEIR OWN...
BUT PULL OUT THE CAPTURED CIVILIANS AND START THE NEGOTIA-
TIONS.
IF THEY DON'T GIVE IN, KILL THE CIVILIANS ONE BY ONE.
COUGH
COUGH

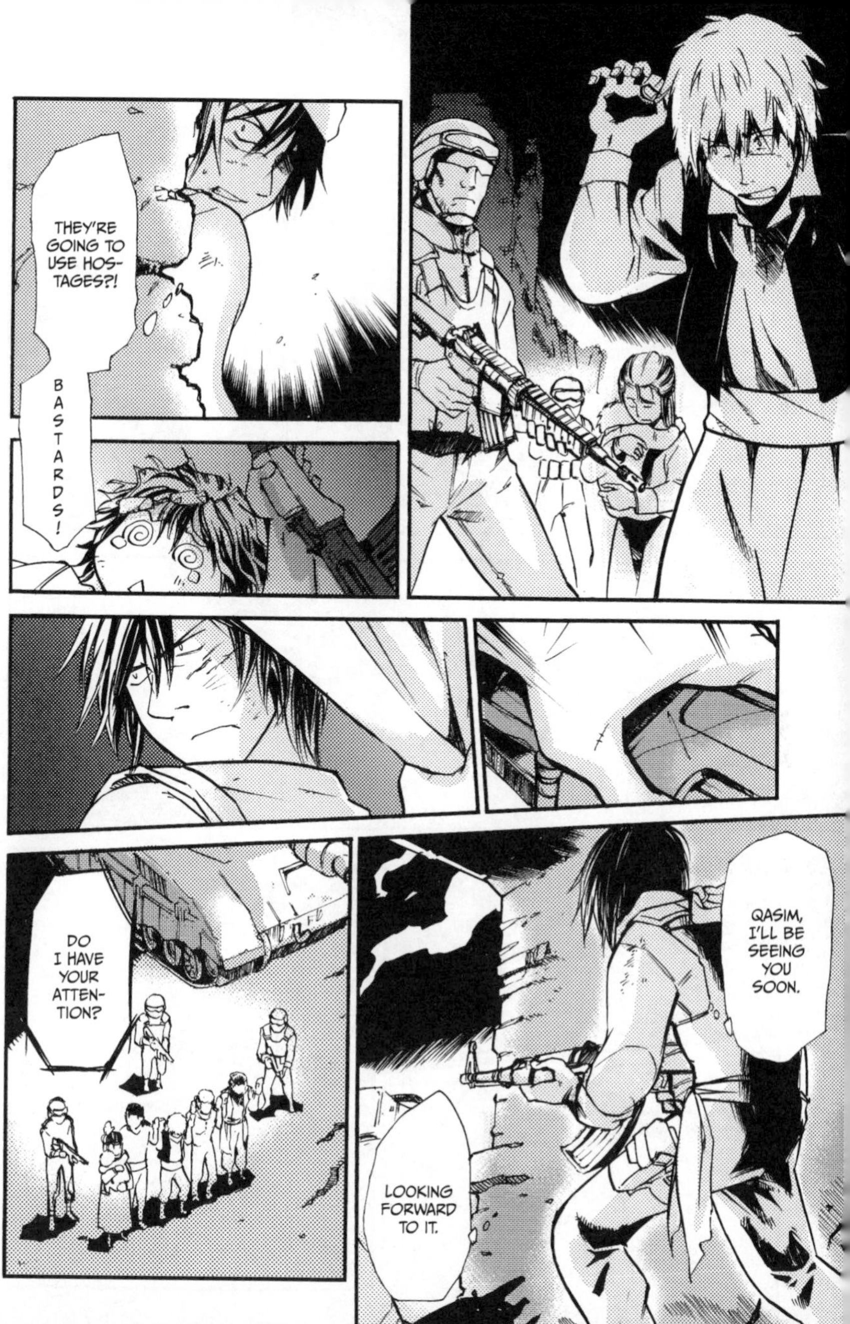
THEY'RE GOING TO USE HOSTAGES?!
BASTARDS!
QASIM, I'LL BE SEEING YOU SOON.
LOOKING FORWARD TO IT.
DO I HAVE YOUR ATTENTION?

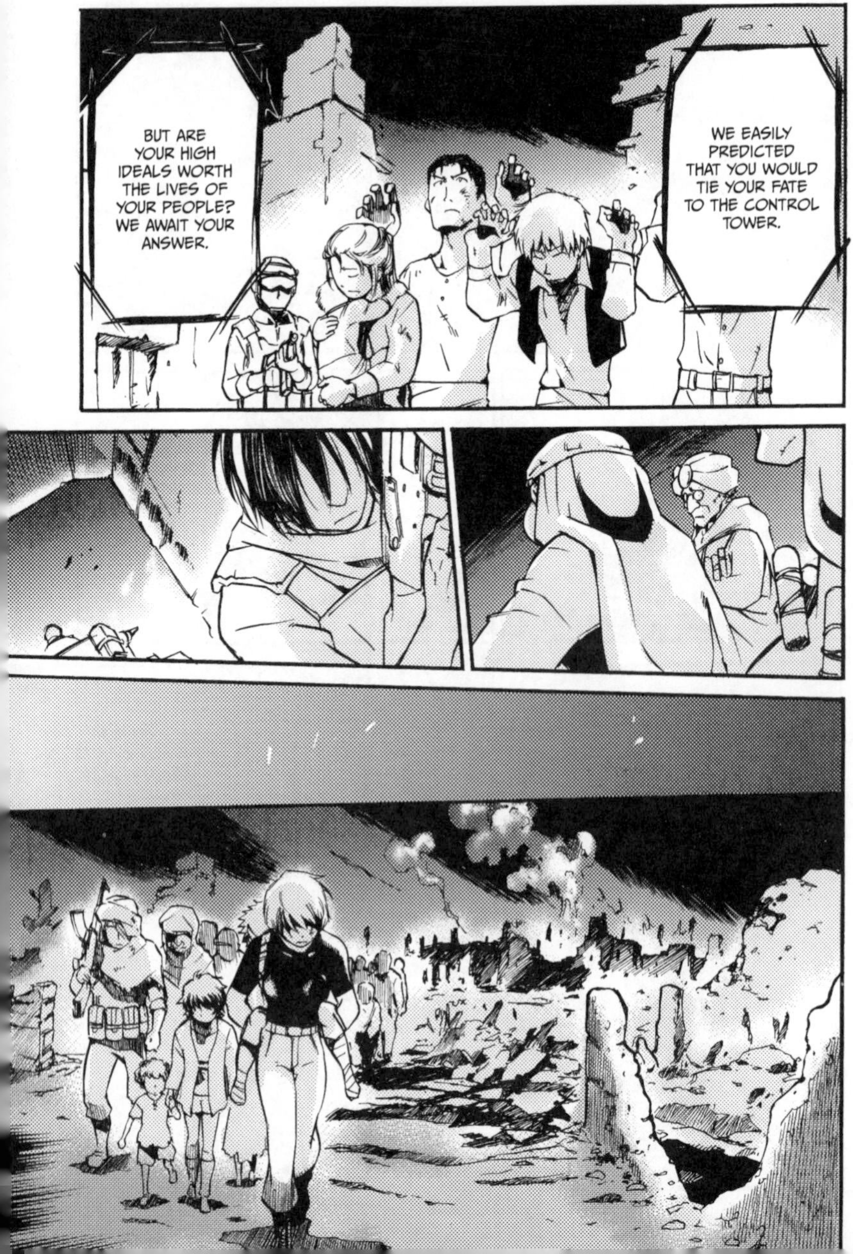
WE EASILY PREDICTED THAT YOU WOULD TIE YOUR FATE TO THE CONTROL TOWER.
BUT ARE YOUR HIGH IDEALS WORTH THE LIVES OF YOUR PEOPLE? WE AWAIT YOUR ANSWER.

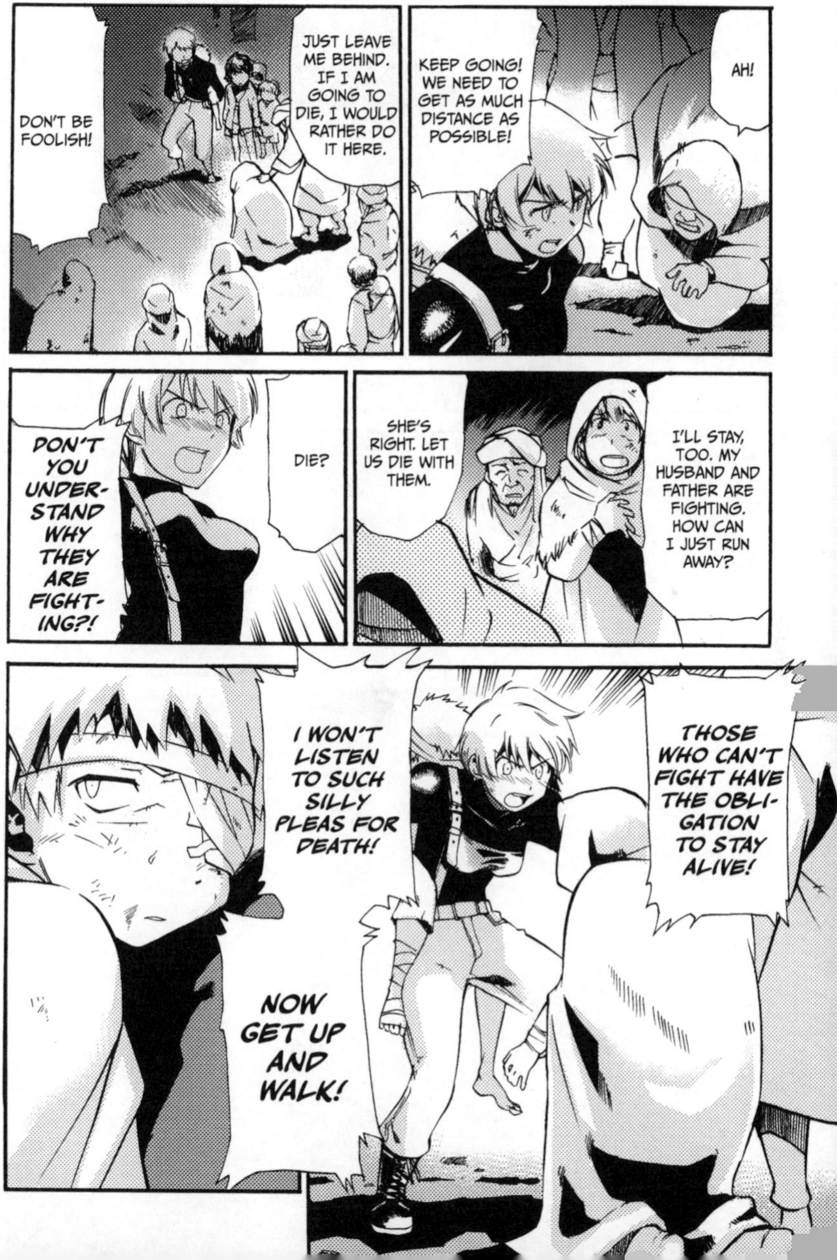
AH!
KEEP GOING! WE NEED TO GET AS MUCH DISTANCE AS POSSIBLE!
JUST LEAVE ME BEHIND. IF I AM GOING TO DIE, I WOULD RATHER DO IT HERE.
DON'T BE FOOLISH!
I'LL STAY, TOO. MY HUSBAND AND FATHER ARE FIGHTING. HOW CAN I JUST RUN AWAY?
SHE'S RIGHT. LET US DIE WITH THEM.
DIE?
DON'T YOU UNDERSTAND WHY THEY ARE FIGHTING?!
THOSE WHO CAN'T FIGHT HAVE THE OBLIGATION TO STAY ALIVE!
I WON'T LISTEN TO SUCH SILLY PLEAS FOR DEATH!
NOW GET UP AND WALK!

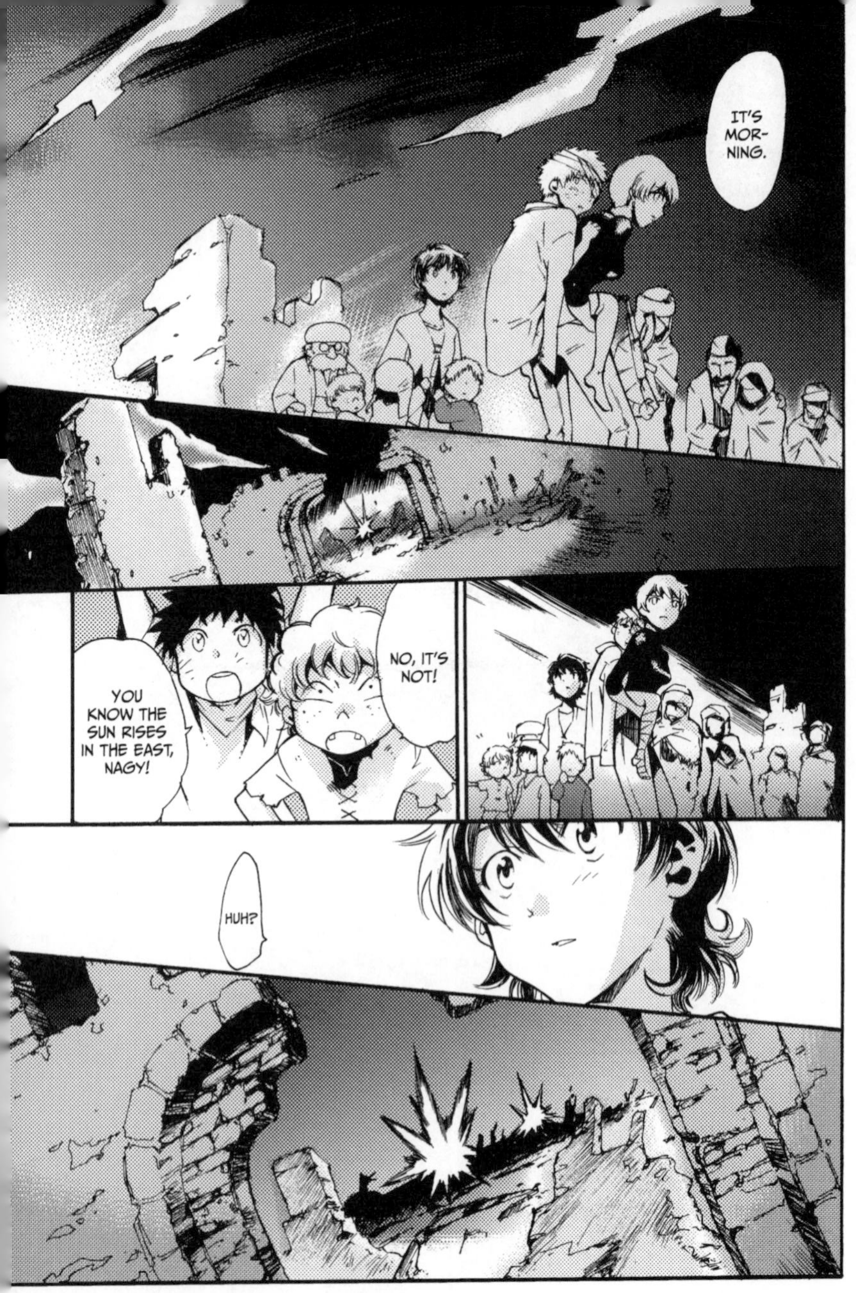
IT'S MOR-NING.
NO, IT'S NOT!
YOU KNOW THE SUN RISES IN THE EAST, NAGY!
HUH?

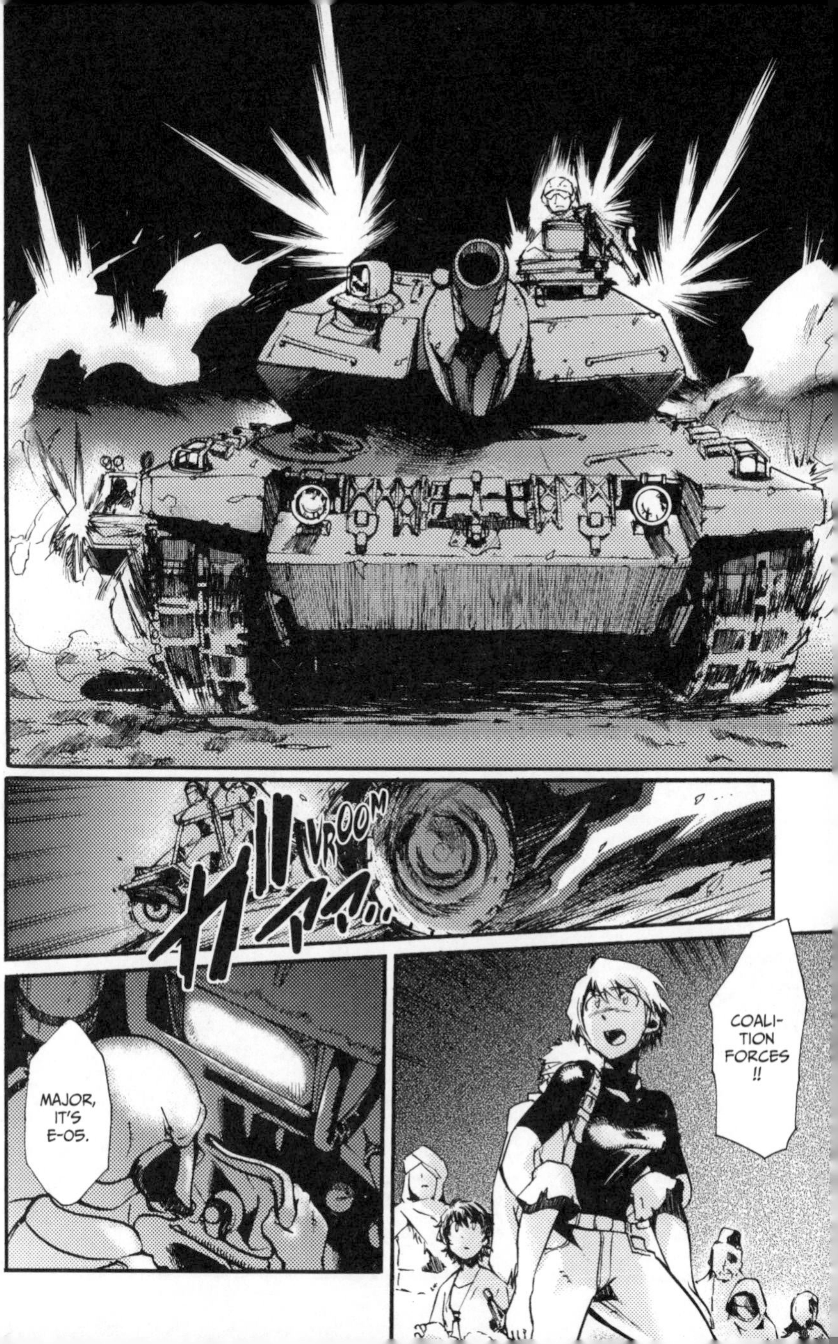
VROOM
COALI-
TION
FORCES
!!
MAJOR,
IT'S
E-05.

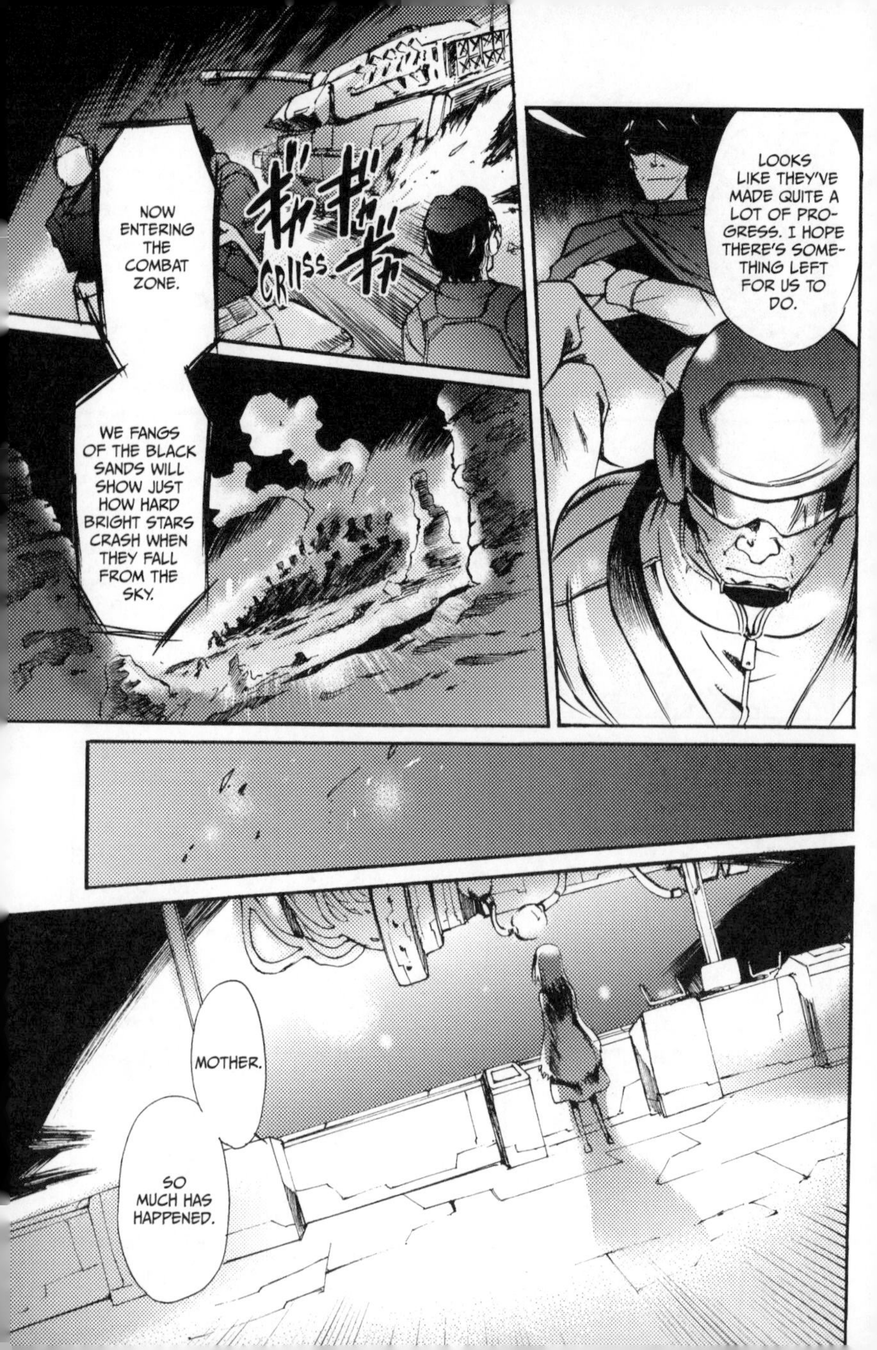
LOOKS LIKE THEY'VE MADE QUITE A LOT OF PROGRESS. I HOPE THERE'S SOMETHING LEFT FOR US TO DO.
NOW ENTERING THE COMBAT ZONE.
CRIISS
WE FANGS OF THE BLACK SANDS WILL SHOW JUST HOW HARD BRIGHT STARS CRASH WHEN THEY FALL FROM THE SKY.
MOTHER.
SO MUCH HAS HAPPENED.

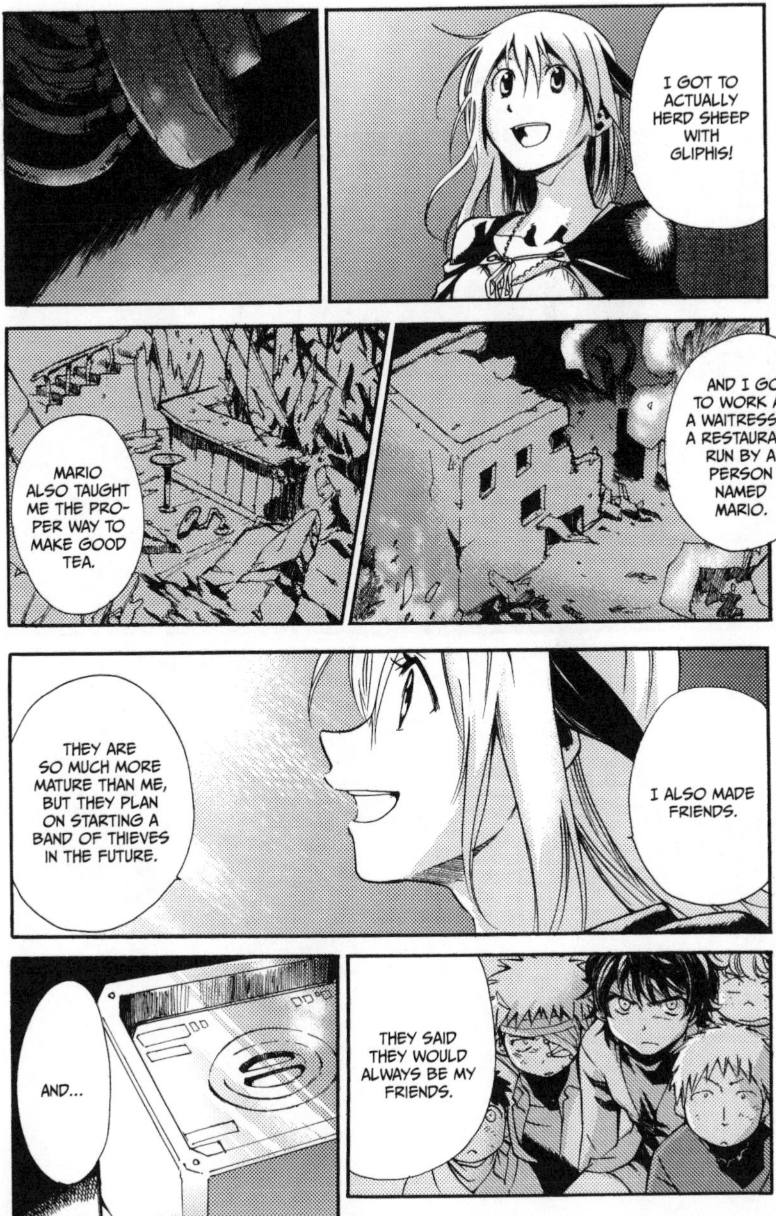
I GOT TO ACTUALLY HERD SHEEP WITH GLIPHIS!
AND I GOT TO WORK AS A WAITRESS AT A RESTAURANT RUN BY A PERSON NAMED MARIO.
MARIO ALSO TAUGHT ME THE PRO-PER WAY TO MAKE GOOD TEA.
I ALSO MADE FRIENDS.
THEY ARE SO MUCH MORE MATURE THAN ME, BUT THEY PLAN ON STARTING A BAND OF THIEVES IN THE FUTURE.
THEY SAID THEY WOULD ALWAYS BE MY FRIENDS.
AND...

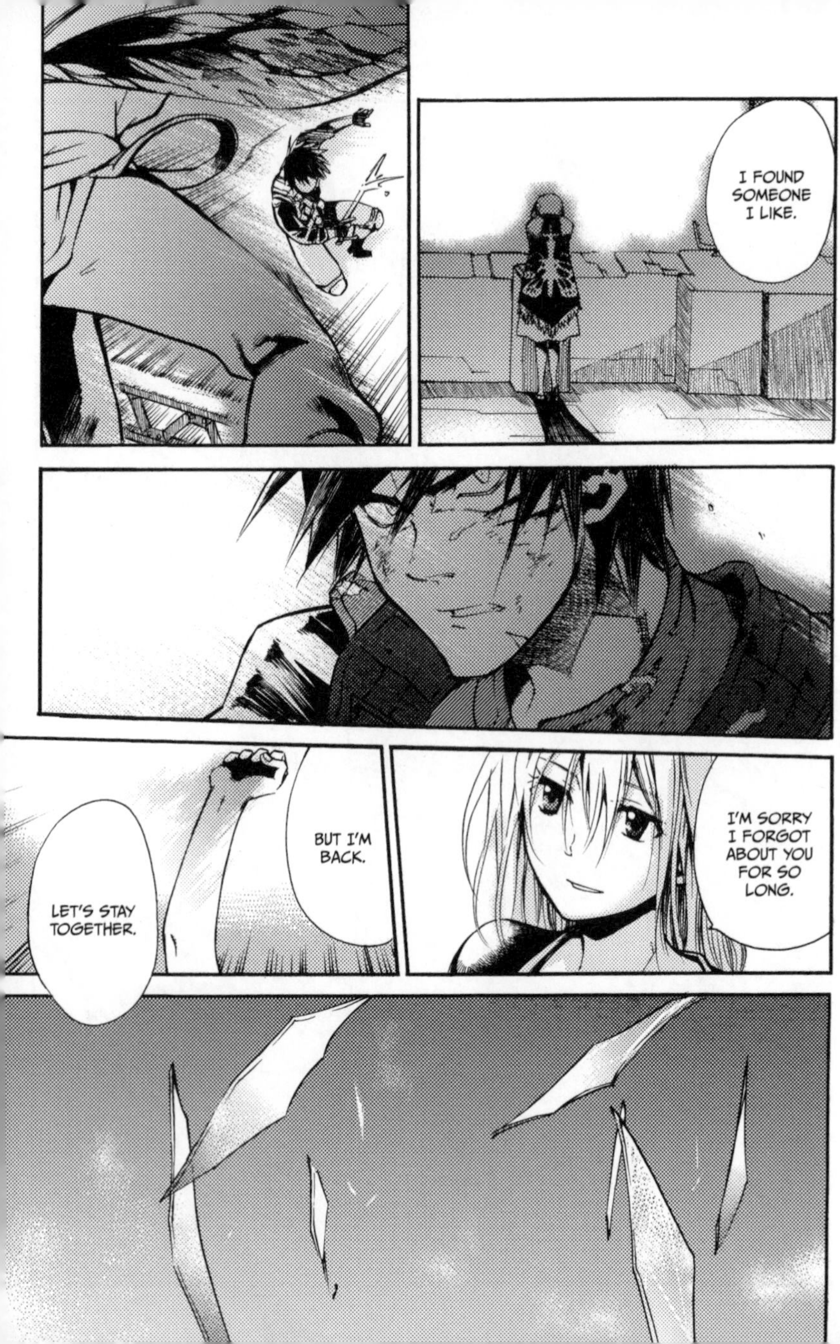
I FOUND SOMEONE I LIKE.
I'M SORRY I FORGOT ABOUT YOU FOR SO LONG.
BUT I'M BACK.
LET'S STAY TOGETHER.

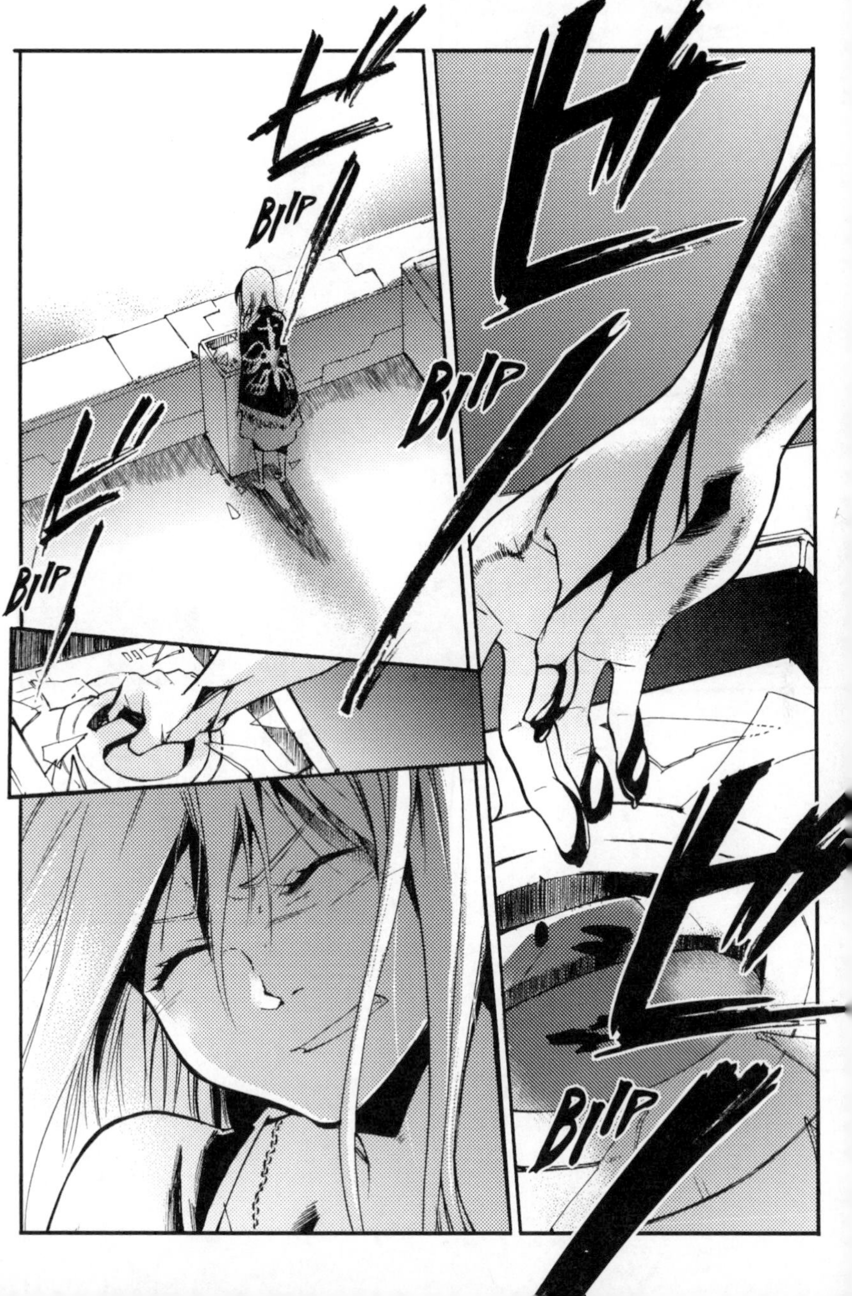
BIIP
BIIP
BIIP
BIIP

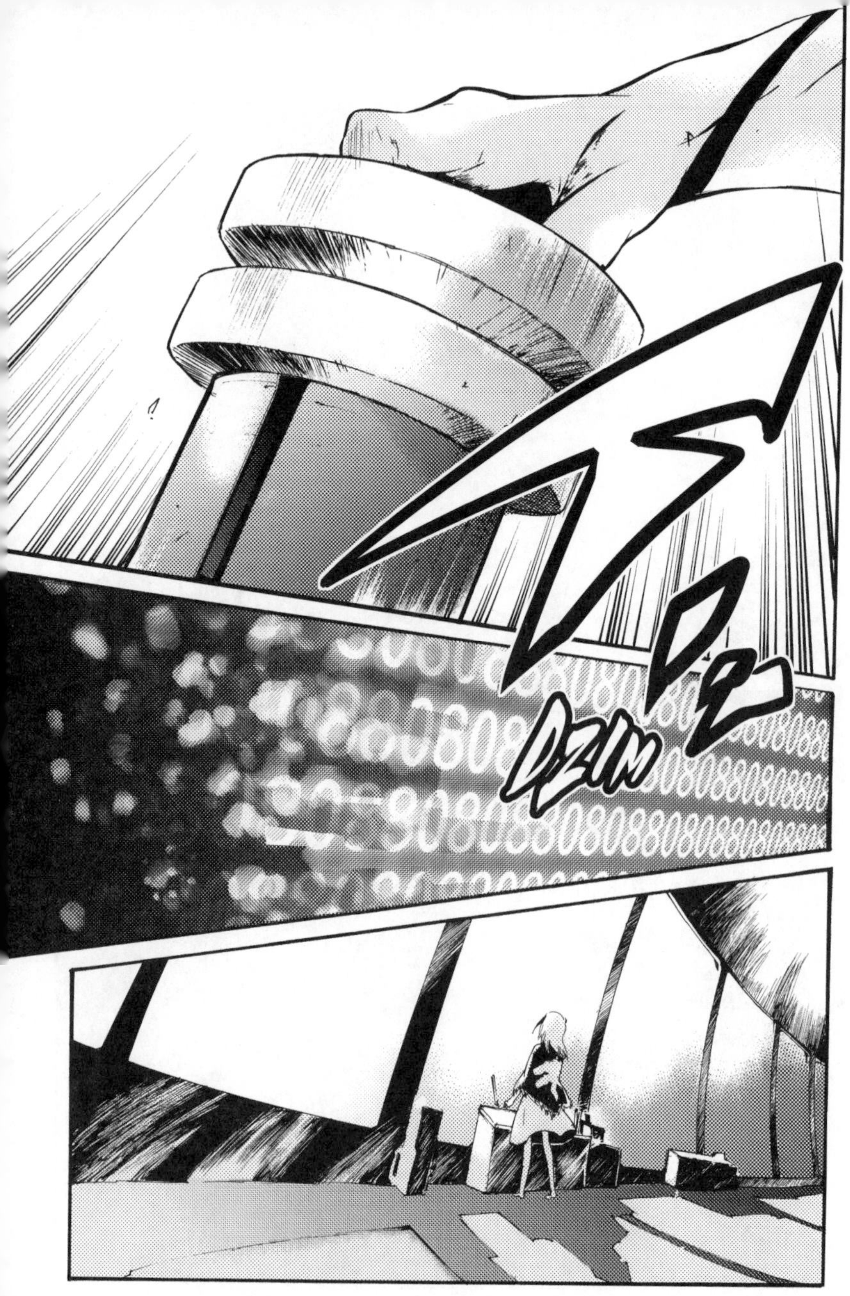
DZIM

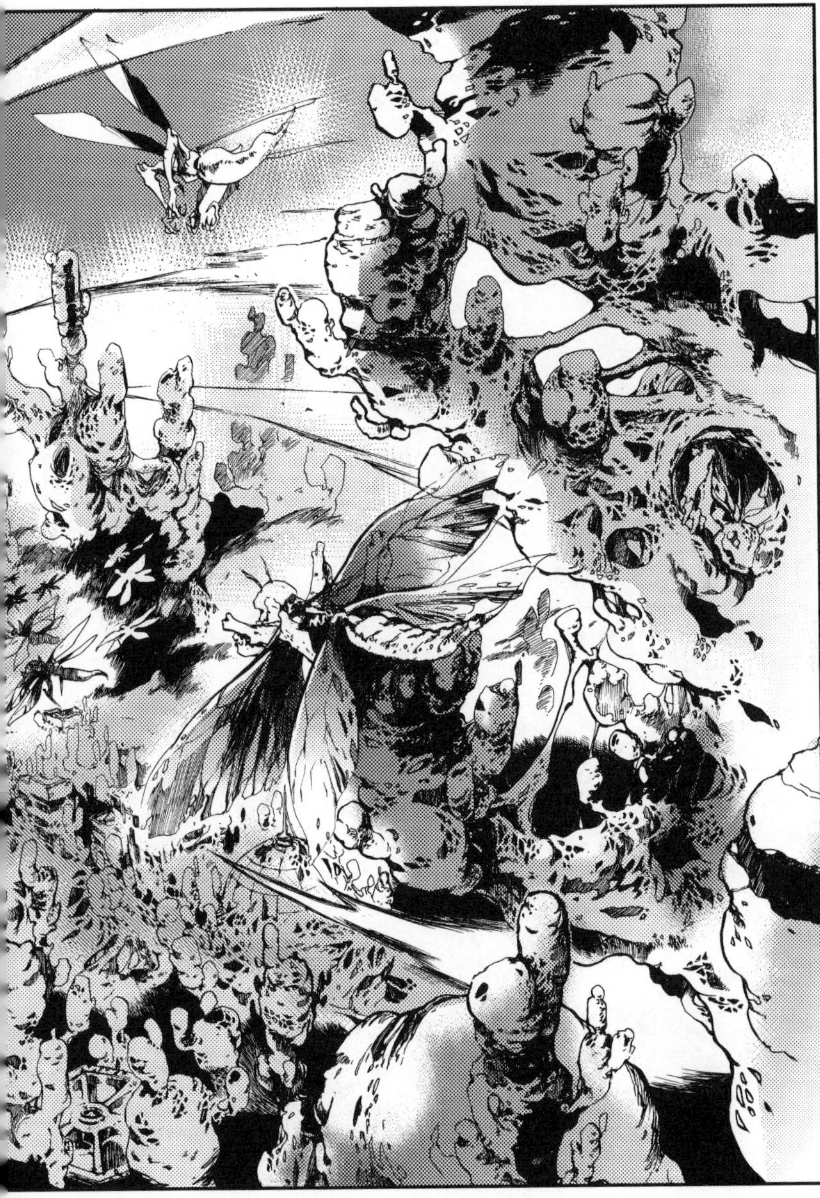

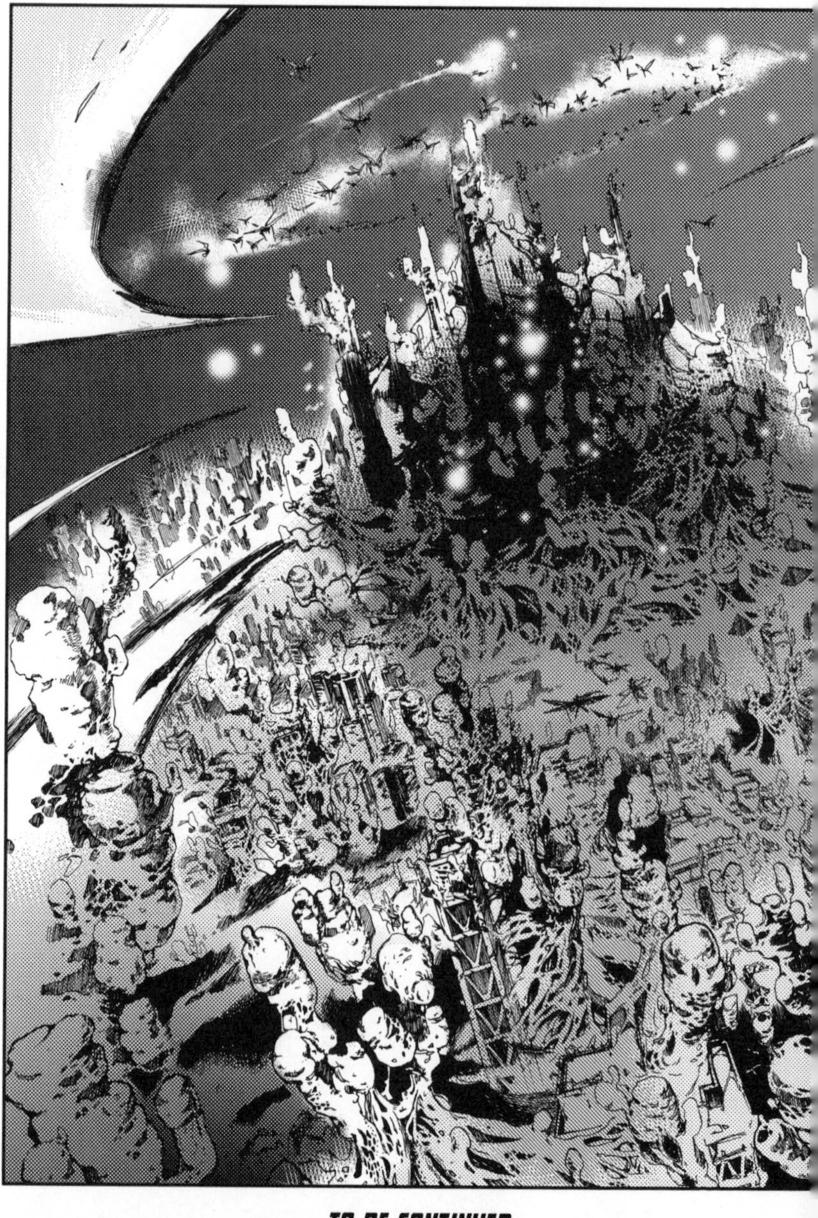

TO BE CONTINUED

ZIZS A.D.

30 YEARS HAVE PASSED SINCE THE BIRTH OF CAGASTER,
A MYSTERIOUS DISEASE THAT TURNS HUMANS INTO BUGS

THIS IS THE STORY OF A MINOR INCIDENT NOT FOUND IN ANY
RECORD THAT OCCURRED IN A SMALL TOWN IN THE EAST

CAGASTER
·QUICK GUIDE TO CHARACTERS·

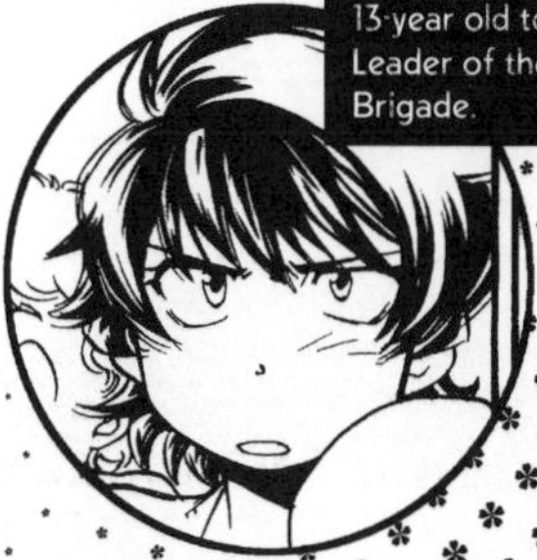

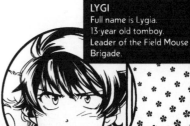

LYGI
Full name is Lygia.
13-year old tomboy.
Leader of the Field Mouse Brigade.

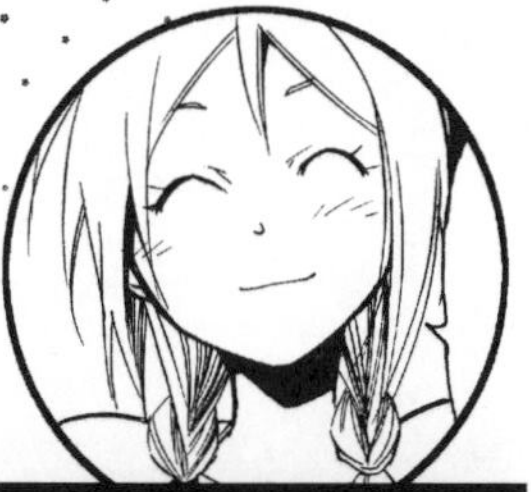

ILIE
Lives at Mario's establishment.
Friend of Lygi.
Seems to be keeping a diary full of embarrassing details she can't show to others.

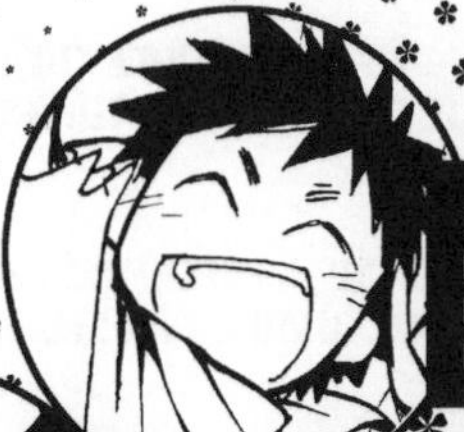

IASON
Member of the Field Mouse Brigade
Head of attacks

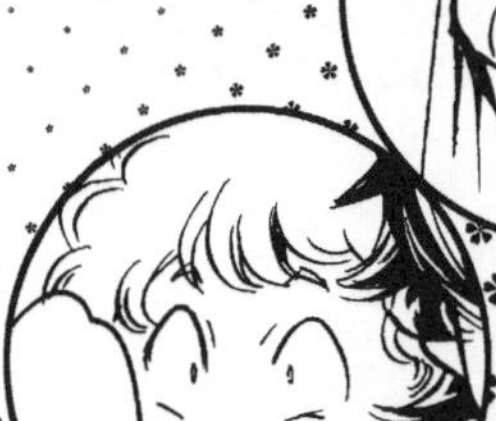

NIM
Member of the Field Mouse Brigade
Head of spying

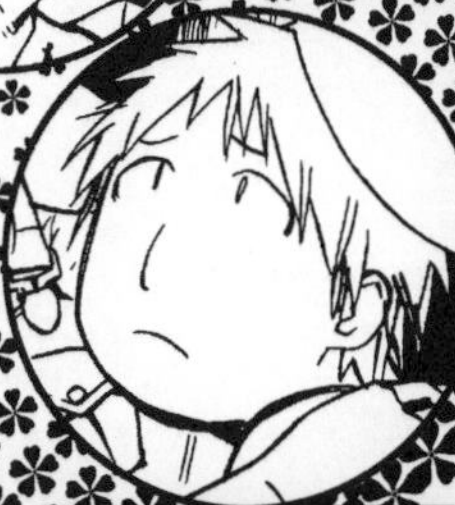

ROMUS
Member of the Field Mouse Brigade
Very quiet, but there is a sense of depth to him.

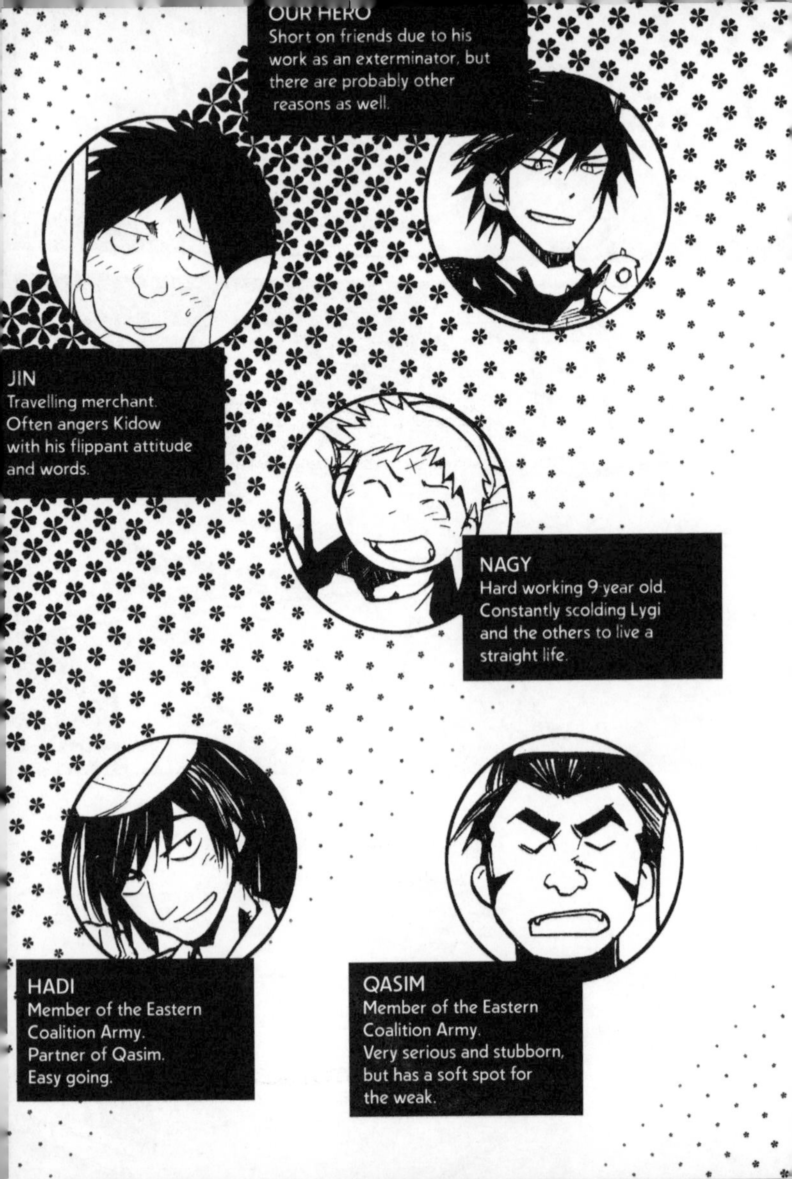
OUR HERO
Short on friends due to his work as an exterminator, but there are probably other reasons as well.
JIN
Travelling merchant. Often angers Kidow with his flippant attitude and words.
NAGY
Hard working 9-year old. Constantly scolding Lygi and the others to live a straight life.
QASIM
Member of the Eastern Coalition Army. Very serious and stubborn, but has a soft spot for the weak.
HADI
Member of the Eastern Coalition Army. Partner of Qasim. Easy going.

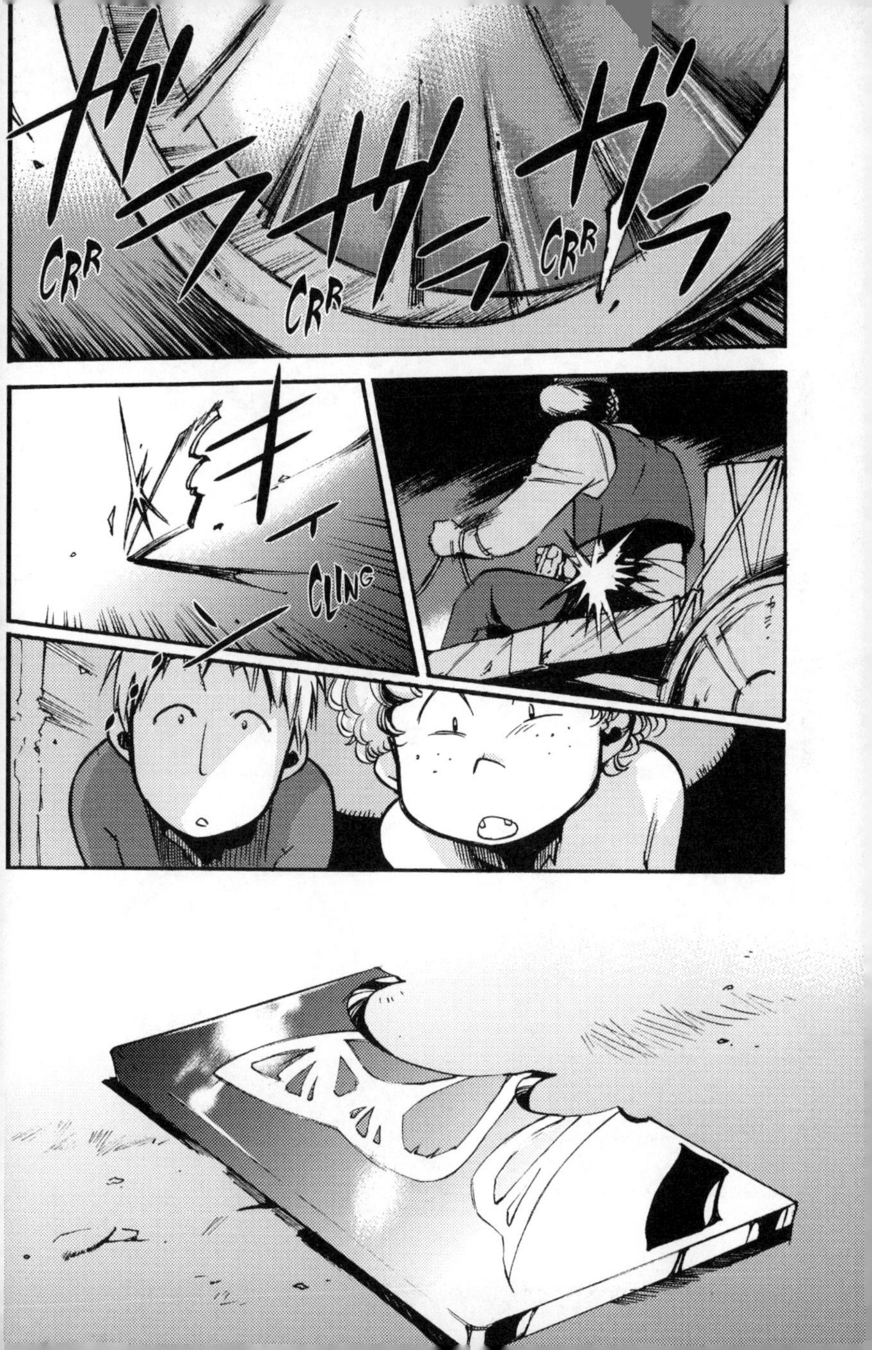
CRR
CRR
CRR
CLING

ADVENTURES OF PRINCESS BUTTERFLY

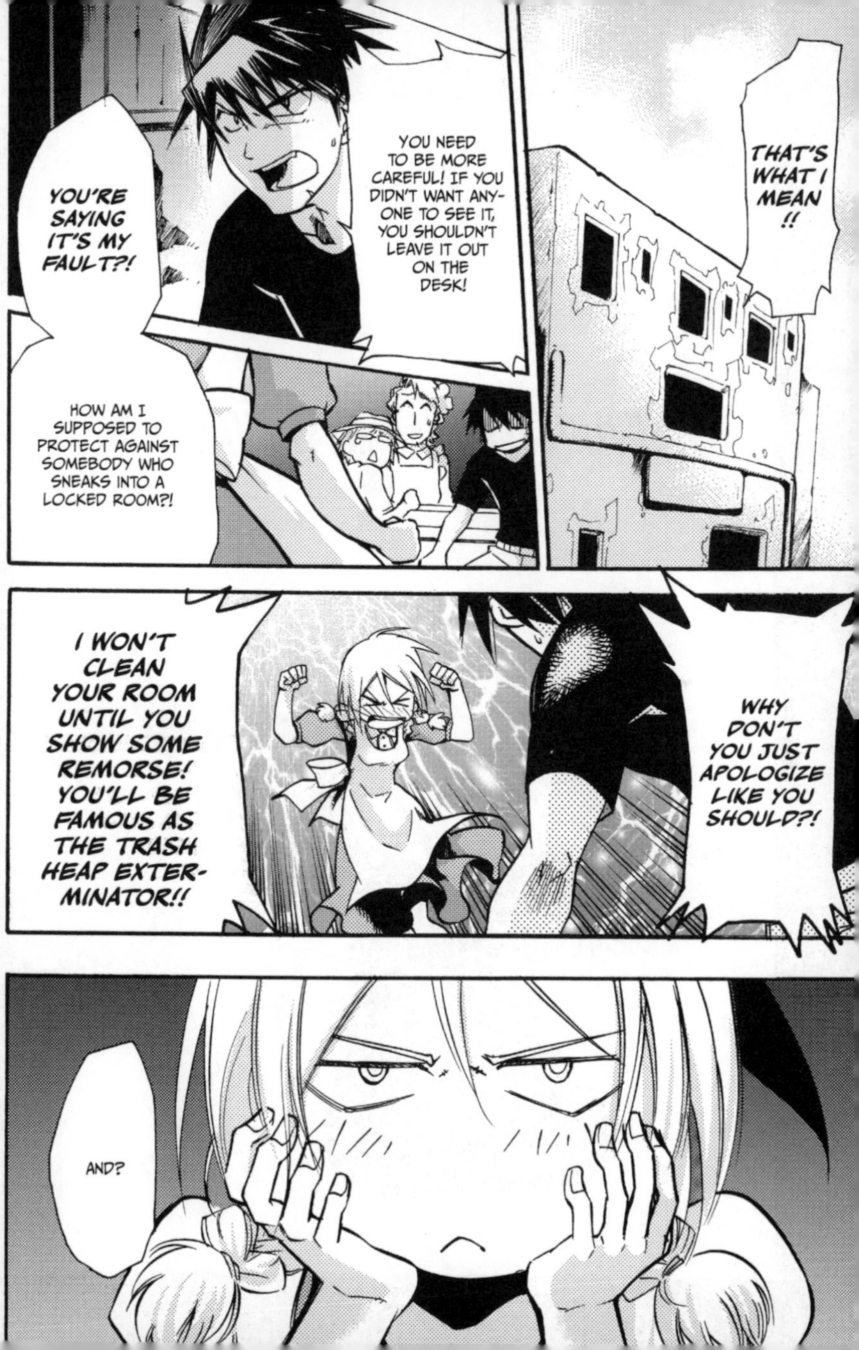
THAT'S WHAT I MEAN!!
YOU NEED TO BE MORE CAREFUL! IF YOU DIDN'T WANT ANYONE TO SEE IT, YOU SHOULDN'T LEAVE IT OUT ON THE DESK!
YOU'RE SAYING IT'S MY FAULT?!
HOW AM I SUPPOSED TO PROTECT AGAINST SOMEBODY WHO SNEAKS INTO A LOCKED ROOM?!
WHY DON'T YOU JUST APOLOGIZE LIKE YOU SHOULD?!
I WON'T CLEAN YOUR ROOM UNTIL YOU SHOW SOME REMORSE! YOU'LL BE FAMOUS AS THE TRASH HEAP EXTERMINATOR!!
AND?

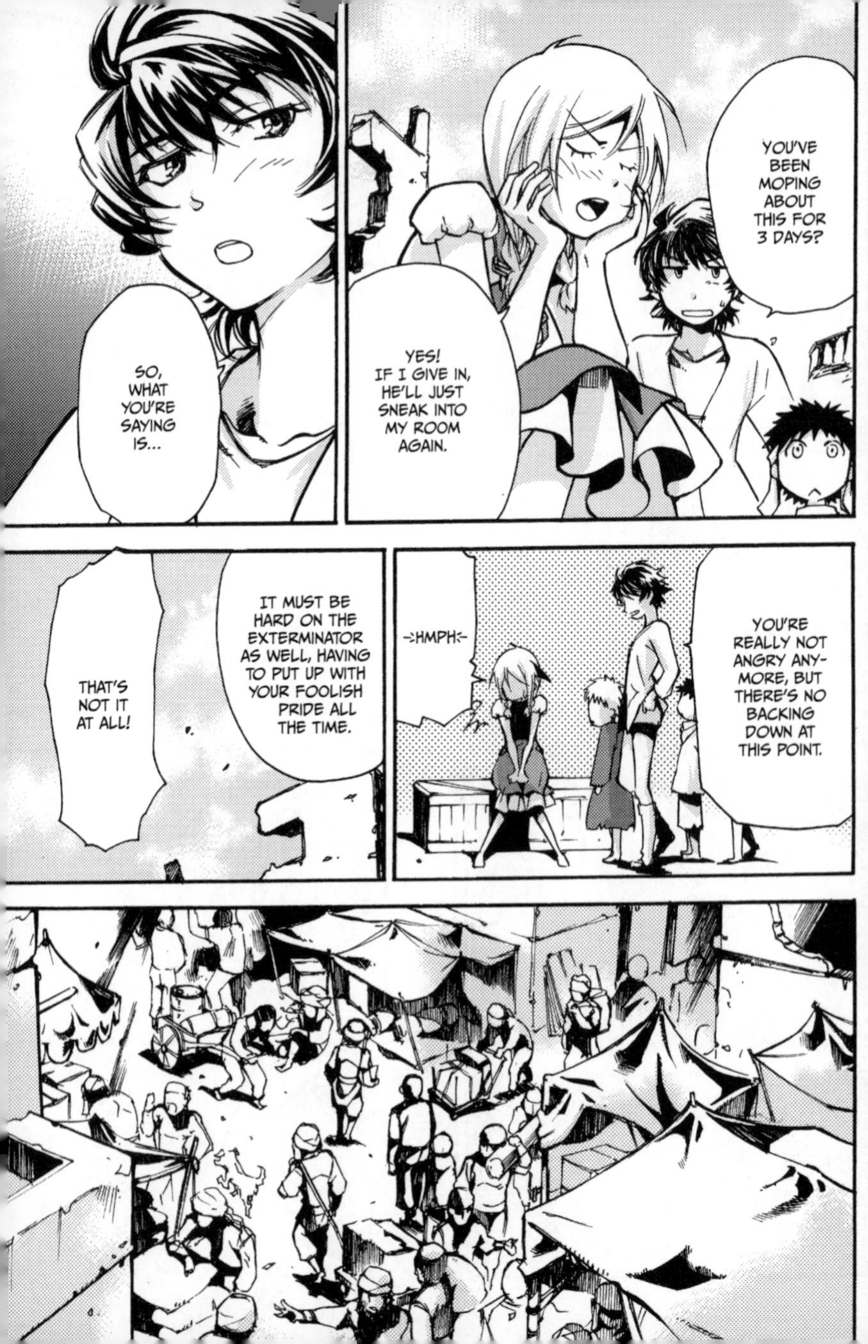
YOU'VE BEEN MOPING ABOUT THIS FOR 3 DAYS?
YES! IF I GIVE IN, HE'LL JUST SNEAK INTO MY ROOM AGAIN.
SO, WHAT YOU'RE SAYING IS...
YOU'RE REALLY NOT ANGRY ANY-MORE, BUT THERE'S NO BACKING DOWN AT THIS POINT.
HMPH
IT MUST BE HARD ON THE EXTERMINATOR AS WELL, HAVING TO PUT UP WITH YOUR FOOLISH PRIDE ALL THE TIME.
THAT'S NOT IT AT ALL!

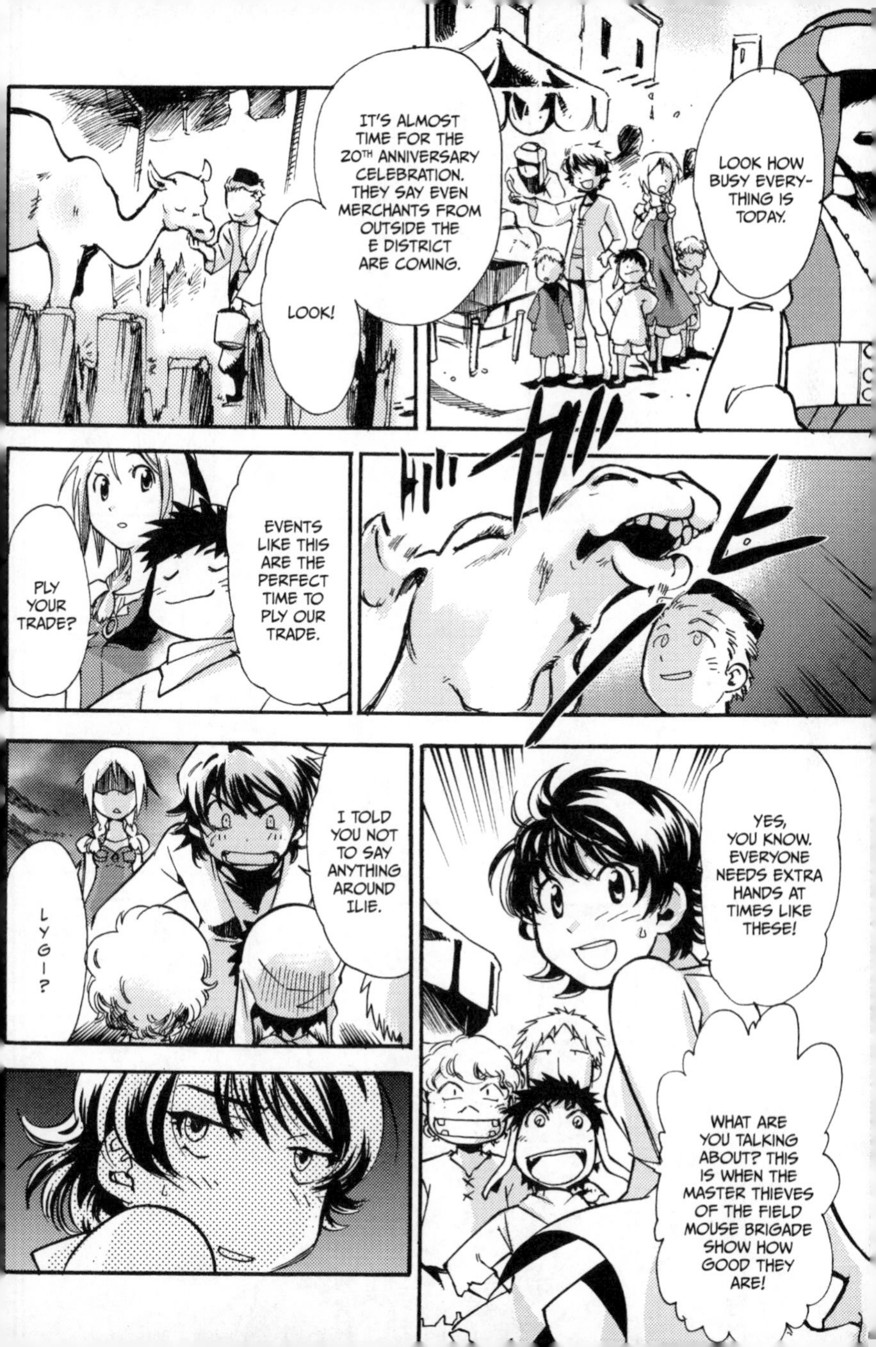
LOOK HOW BUSY EVERYTHING IS TODAY.
IT'S ALMOST TIME FOR THE 20TH ANNIVERSARY CELEBRATION. THEY SAY EVEN MERCHANTS FROM OUTSIDE THE E DISTRICT ARE COMING.
LOOK!
EVENTS LIKE THIS ARE THE PERFECT TIME TO PLY OUR TRADE.
PLY YOUR TRADE?
YES, YOU KNOW. EVERYONE NEEDS EXTRA HANDS AT TIMES LIKE THESE!
WHAT ARE YOU TALKING ABOUT? THIS IS WHEN THE MASTER THIEVES OF THE FIELD MOUSE BRIGADE SHOW HOW GOOD THEY ARE!
I TOLD YOU NOT TO SAY ANYTHING AROUND ILIE.
LYGI?

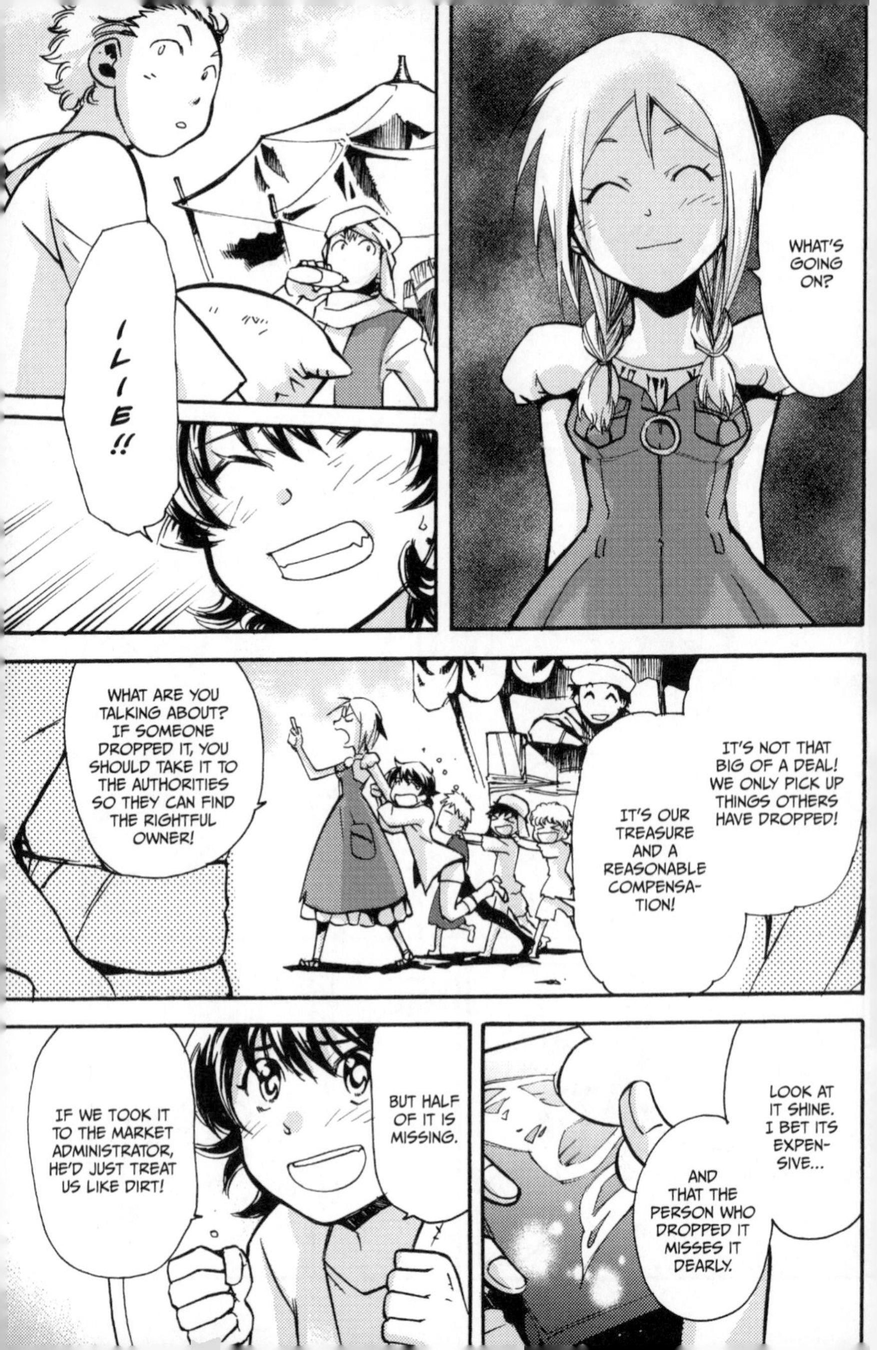
WHAT'S GOING ON?
ILLIE!!
IT'S NOT THAT BIG OF A DEAL! WE ONLY PICK UP THINGS OTHERS HAVE DROPPED!
IT'S OUR TREASURE AND A REASONABLE COMPENSATION!
WHAT ARE YOU TALKING ABOUT? IF SOMEONE DROPPED IT, YOU SHOULD TAKE IT TO THE AUTHORITIES SO THEY CAN FIND THE RIGHTFUL OWNER!
LOOK AT IT SHINE. I BET ITS EXPENSIVE...
AND THAT THE PERSON WHO DROPPED IT MISSES IT DEARLY.
BUT HALF OF IT IS MISSING.
IF WE TOOK IT TO THE MARKET ADMINISTRATOR, HE'D JUST TREAT US LIKE DIRT!

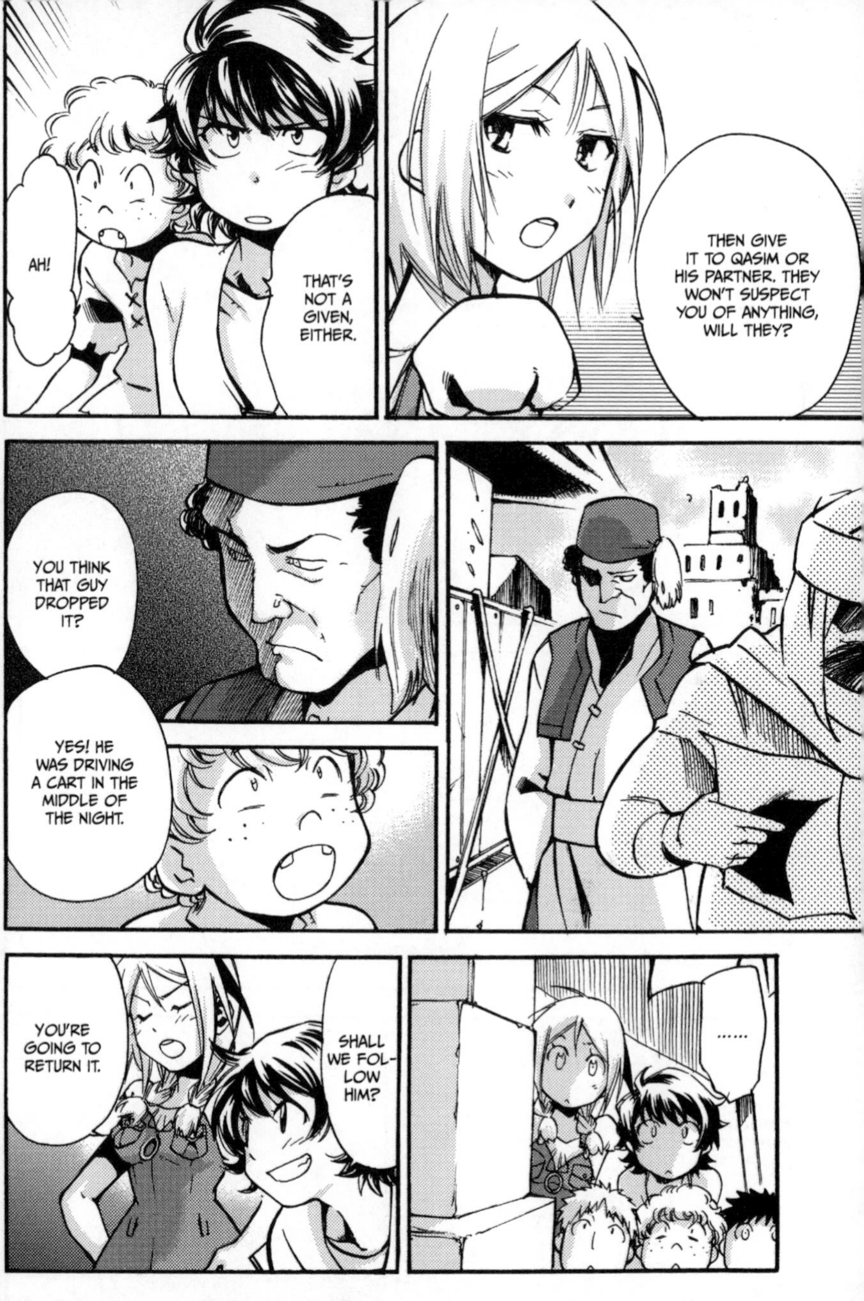
THEN GIVE IT TO QASIM OR HIS PARTNER. THEY WON'T SUSPECT YOU OF ANYTHING, WILL THEY?
THAT'S NOT A GIVEN, EITHER.
AH!
YOU THINK THAT GUY DROPPED IT?
YES! HE WAS DRIVING A CART IN THE MIDDLE OF THE NIGHT.
......
SHALL WE FOL-LOW HIM?
YOU'RE GOING TO RETURN IT.

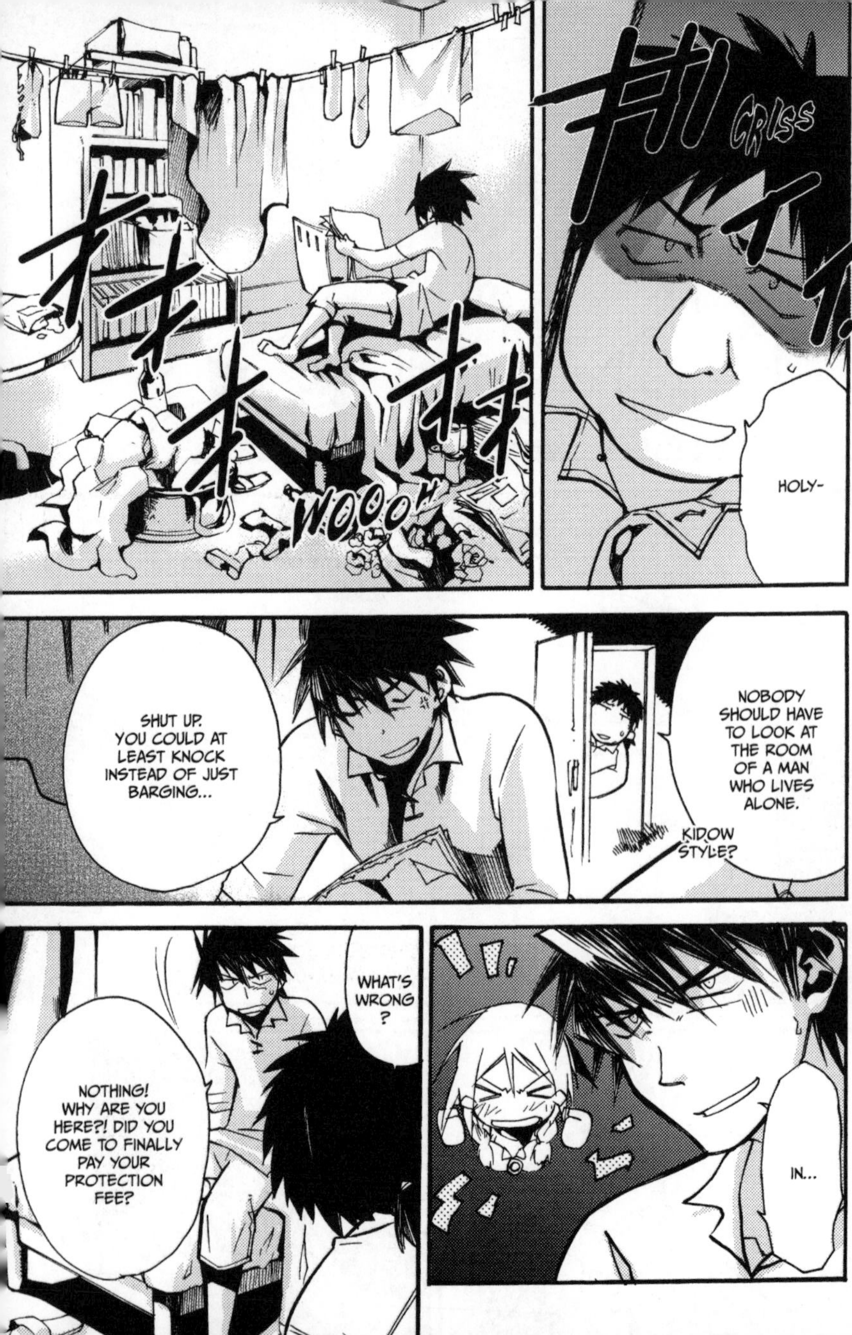
CRISS
HOLY-
WOOOH
NOBODY SHOULD HAVE TO LOOK AT THE ROOM OF A MAN WHO LIVES ALONE.
KIDOW STYLE?
SHUT UP. YOU COULD AT LEAST KNOCK INSTEAD OF JUST BARGING...
IN...
WHAT'S WRONG?
NOTHING! WHY ARE YOU HERE?! DID YOU COME TO FINALLY PAY YOUR PROTECTION FEE?

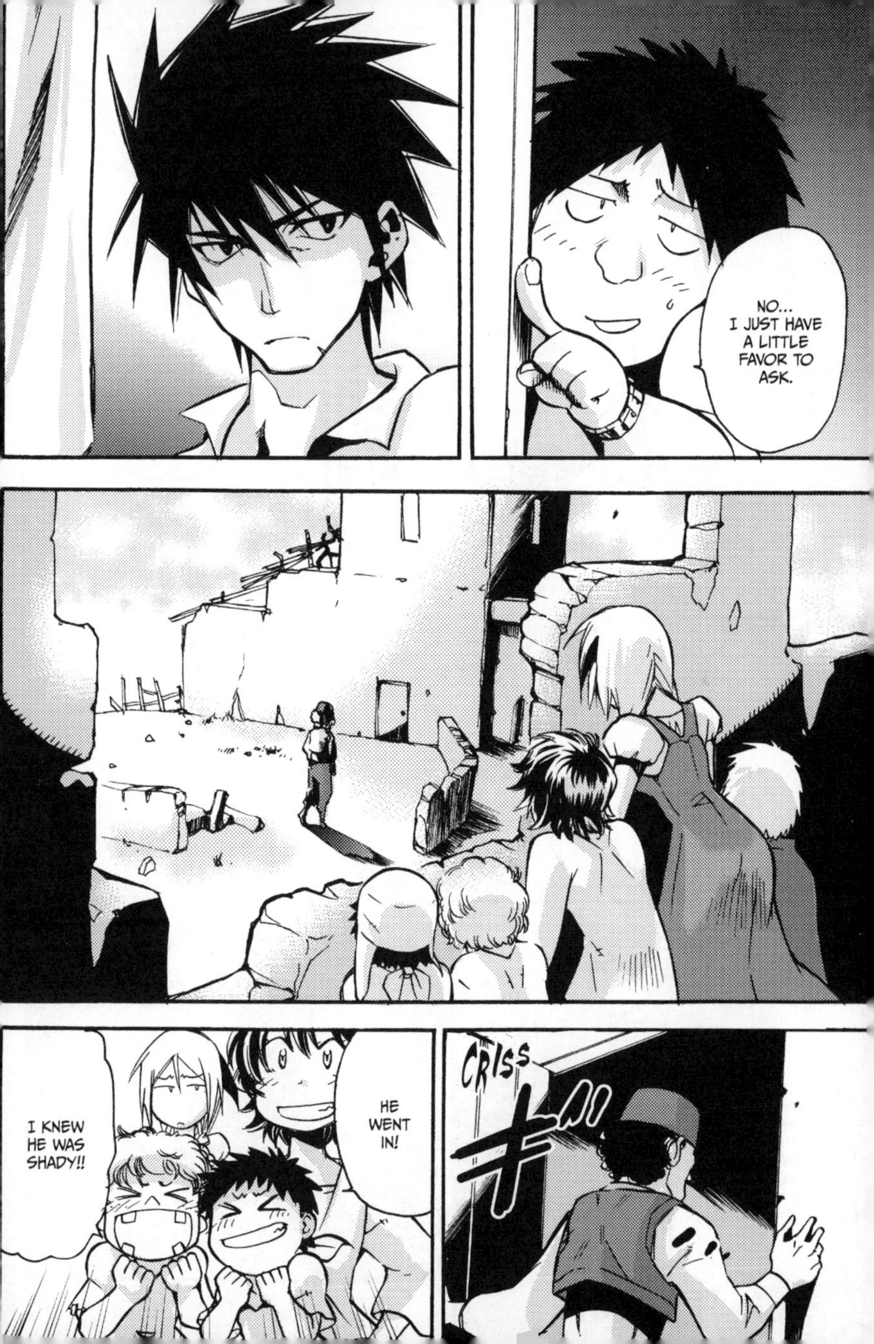
NO... I JUST HAVE A LITTLE FAVOR TO ASK.
CRISS
HE WENT IN!
I KNEW HE WAS SHADY!!

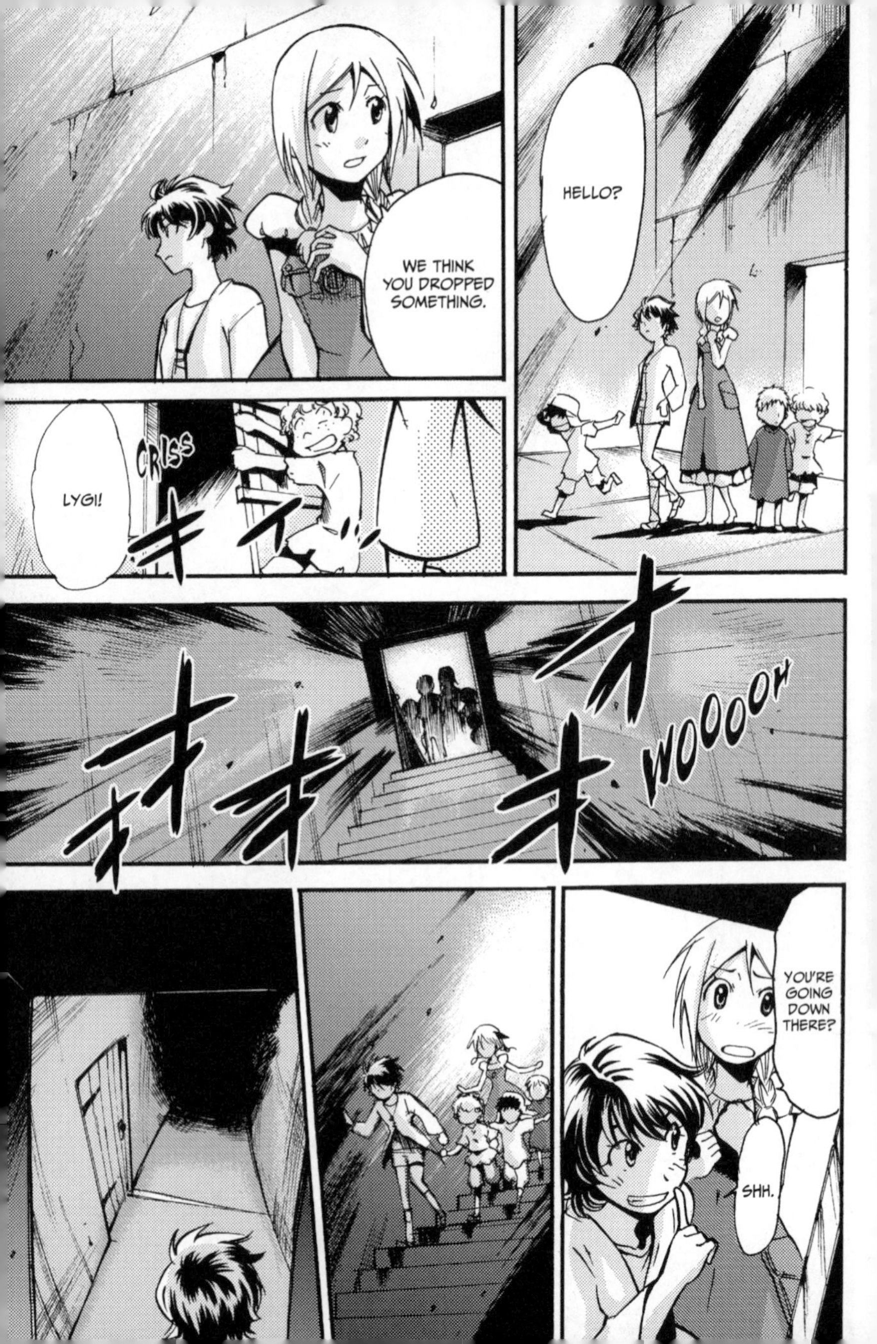
HELLO?
WE THINK YOU DROPPED SOMETHING.
LYGI!
CRISS
WOOOOH
YOU'RE GOING DOWN THERE?
SHH.

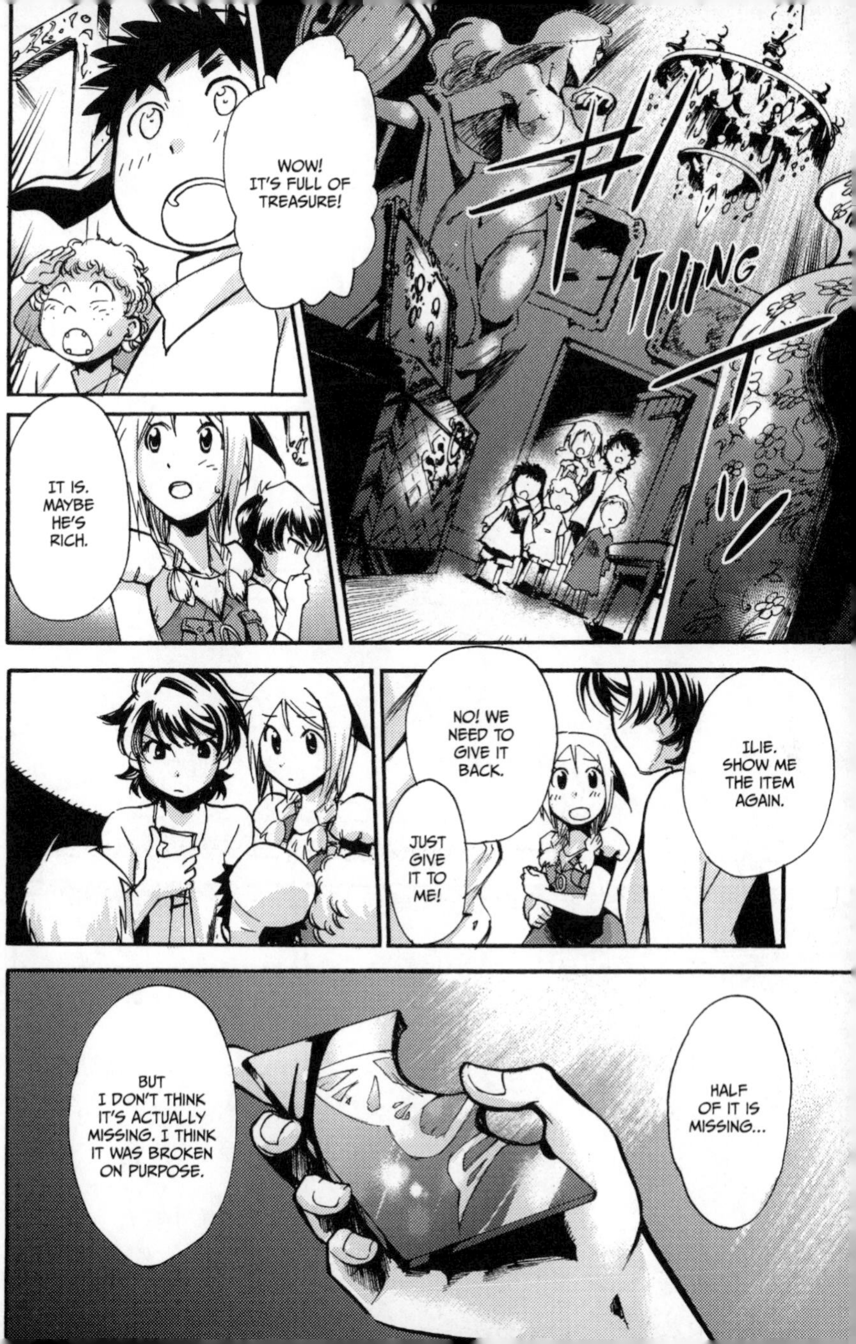
TIIING
WOW! IT'S FULL OF TREASURE!
IT IS. MAYBE HE'S RICH.
ILIE. SHOW ME THE ITEM AGAIN.
NO! WE NEED TO GIVE IT BACK.
JUST GIVE IT TO ME!
HALF OF IT IS MISSING...
BUT I DON'T THINK IT'S ACTUALLY MISSING. I THINK IT WAS BROKEN ON PURPOSE.

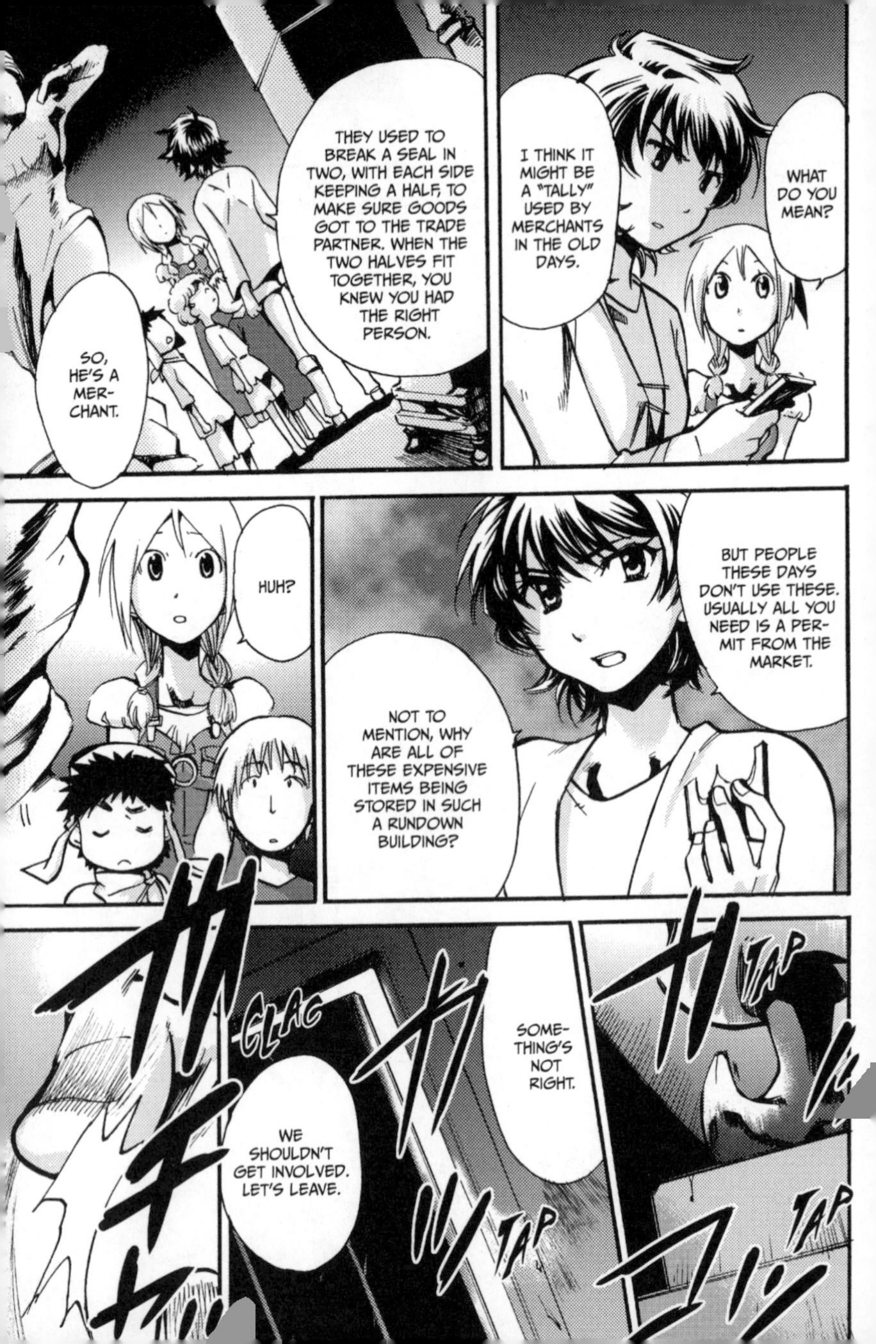
WHAT DO YOU MEAN?
I THINK IT MIGHT BE A "TALLY" USED BY MERCHANTS IN THE OLD DAYS.
THEY USED TO BREAK A SEAL IN TWO, WITH EACH SIDE KEEPING A HALF, TO MAKE SURE GOODS GOT TO THE TRADE PARTNER. WHEN THE TWO HALVES FIT TOGETHER, YOU KNEW YOU HAD THE RIGHT PERSON.
SO, HE'S A MER-CHANT.
BUT PEOPLE THESE DAYS DON'T USE THESE. USUALLY ALL YOU NEED IS A PER-MIT FROM THE MARKET.
NOT TO MENTION, WHY ARE ALL OF THESE EXPENSIVE ITEMS BEING STORED IN SUCH A RUNDOWN BUILDING?
HUH?
TAP
TAP
TAP
SOME-THING'S NOT RIGHT.
CLAC
WE SHOULDN'T GET INVOLVED. LET'S LEAVE.

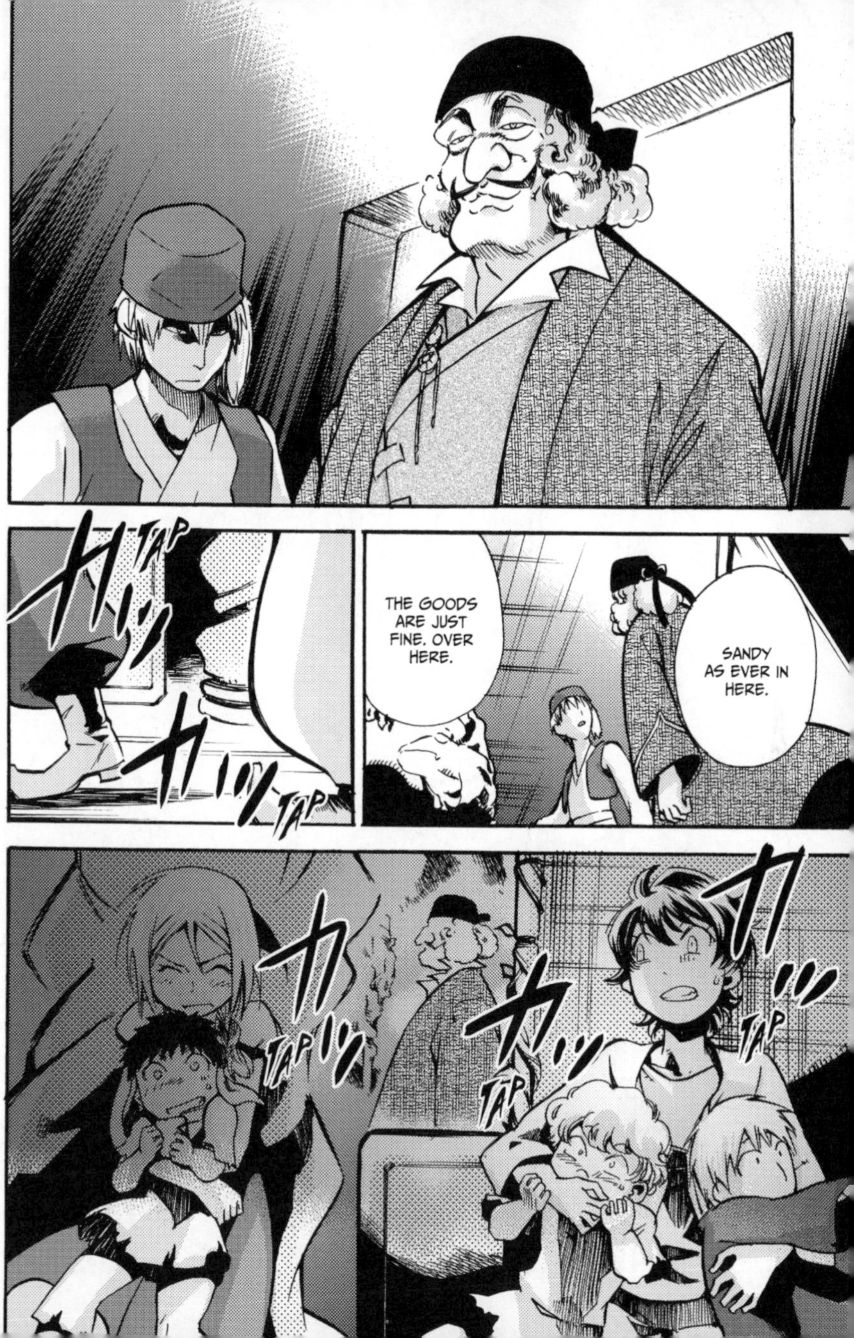
SANDY AS EVER IN HERE.
THE GOODS ARE JUST FINE. OVER HERE.
TAP
TAP
TAP
TAP
TAP

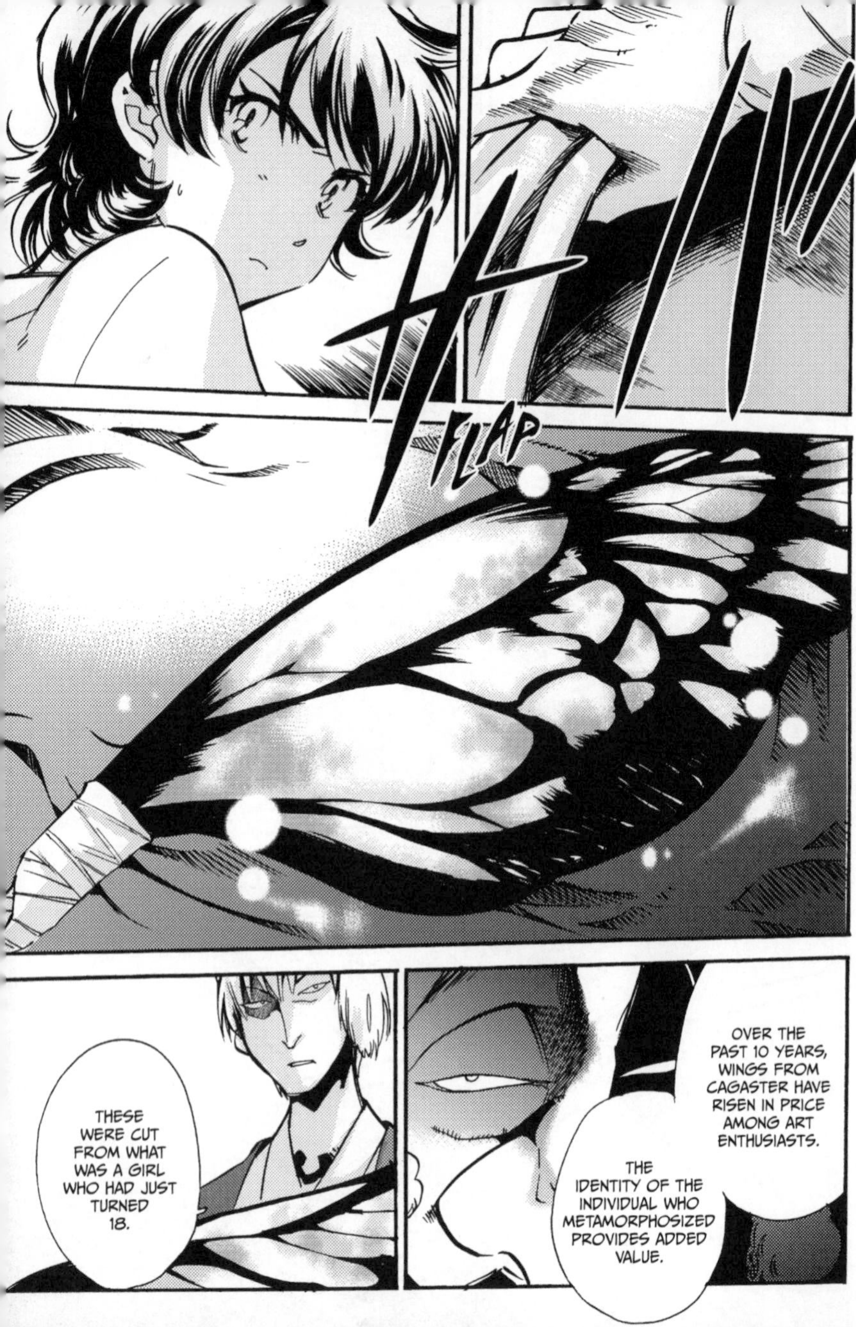
FLAP
OVER THE PAST 10 YEARS, WINGS FROM CAGASTER HAVE RISEN IN PRICE AMONG ART ENTHUSIASTS.
THE IDENTITY OF THE INDIVIDUAL WHO METAMORPHOSIZED PROVIDES ADDED VALUE.
THESE WERE CUT FROM WHAT WAS A GIRL WHO HAD JUST TURNED 18.

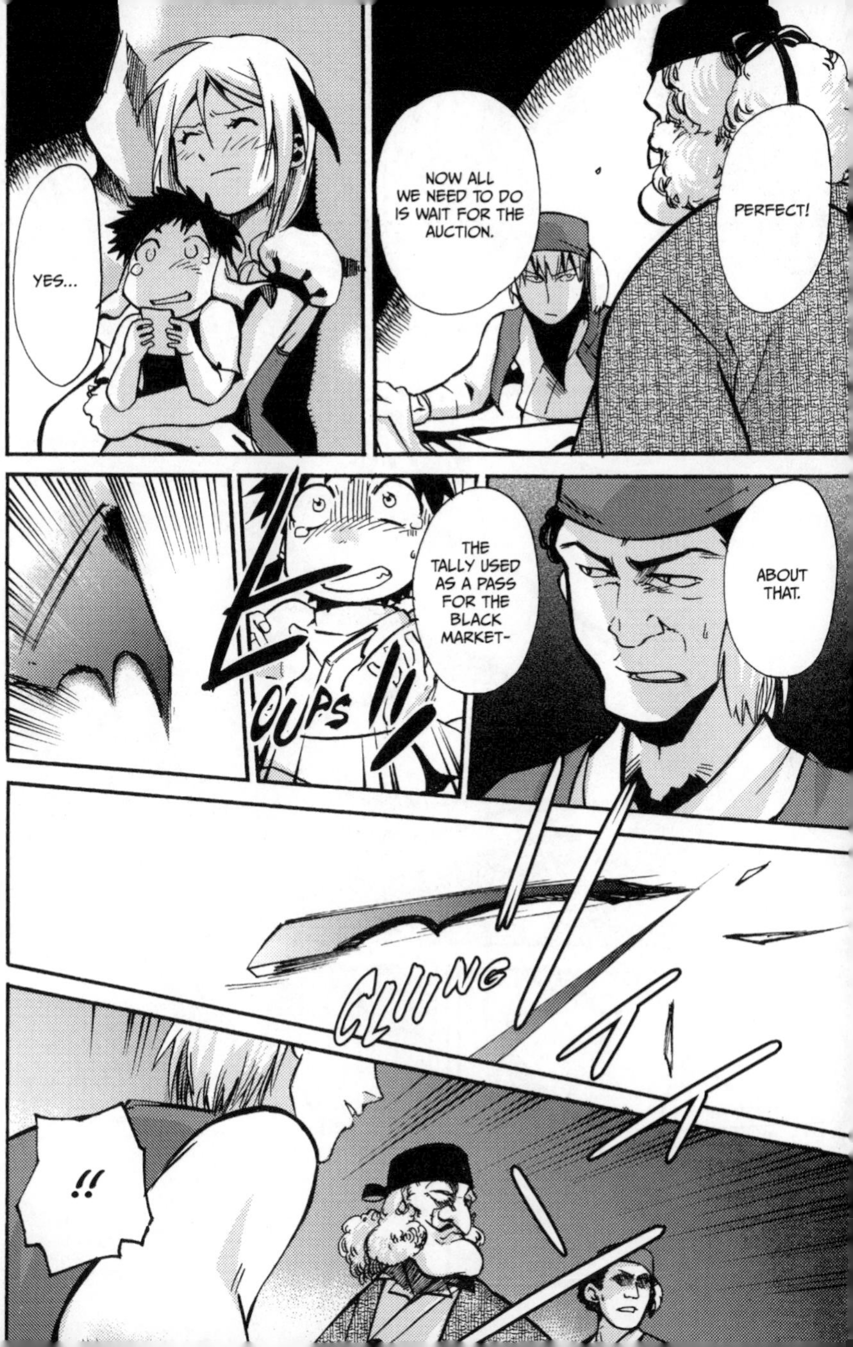
PERFECT!
NOW ALL WE NEED TO DO IS WAIT FOR THE AUCTION.
YES...
ABOUT THAT.
THE TALLY USED AS A PASS FOR THE BLACK MARKET-
OOPS
CLIIING
!!

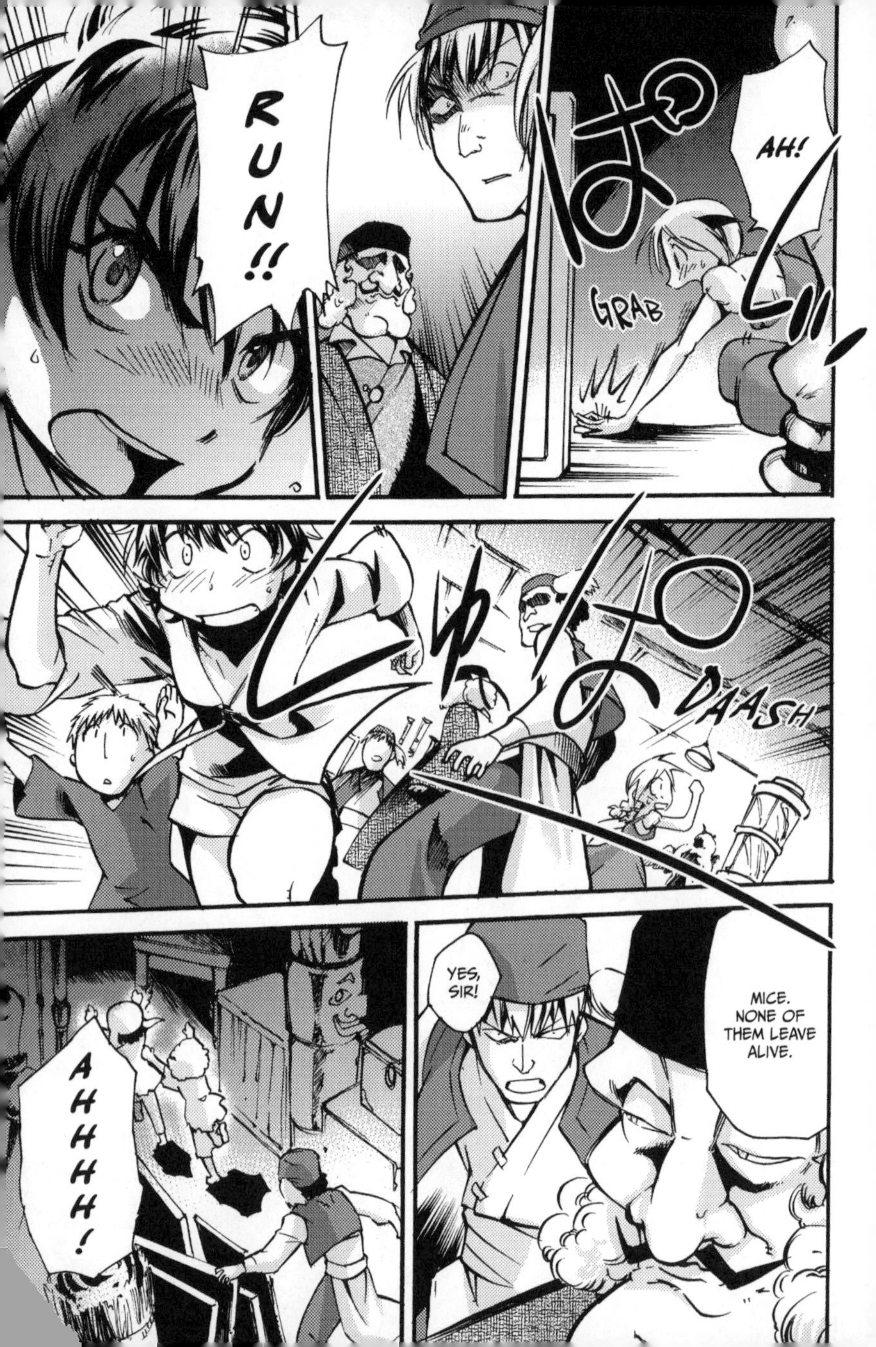
AH!
GRAB
RUN!!
DAASH
MICE. NONE OF THEM LEAVE ALIVE.
YES, SIR!
AHHHHH!

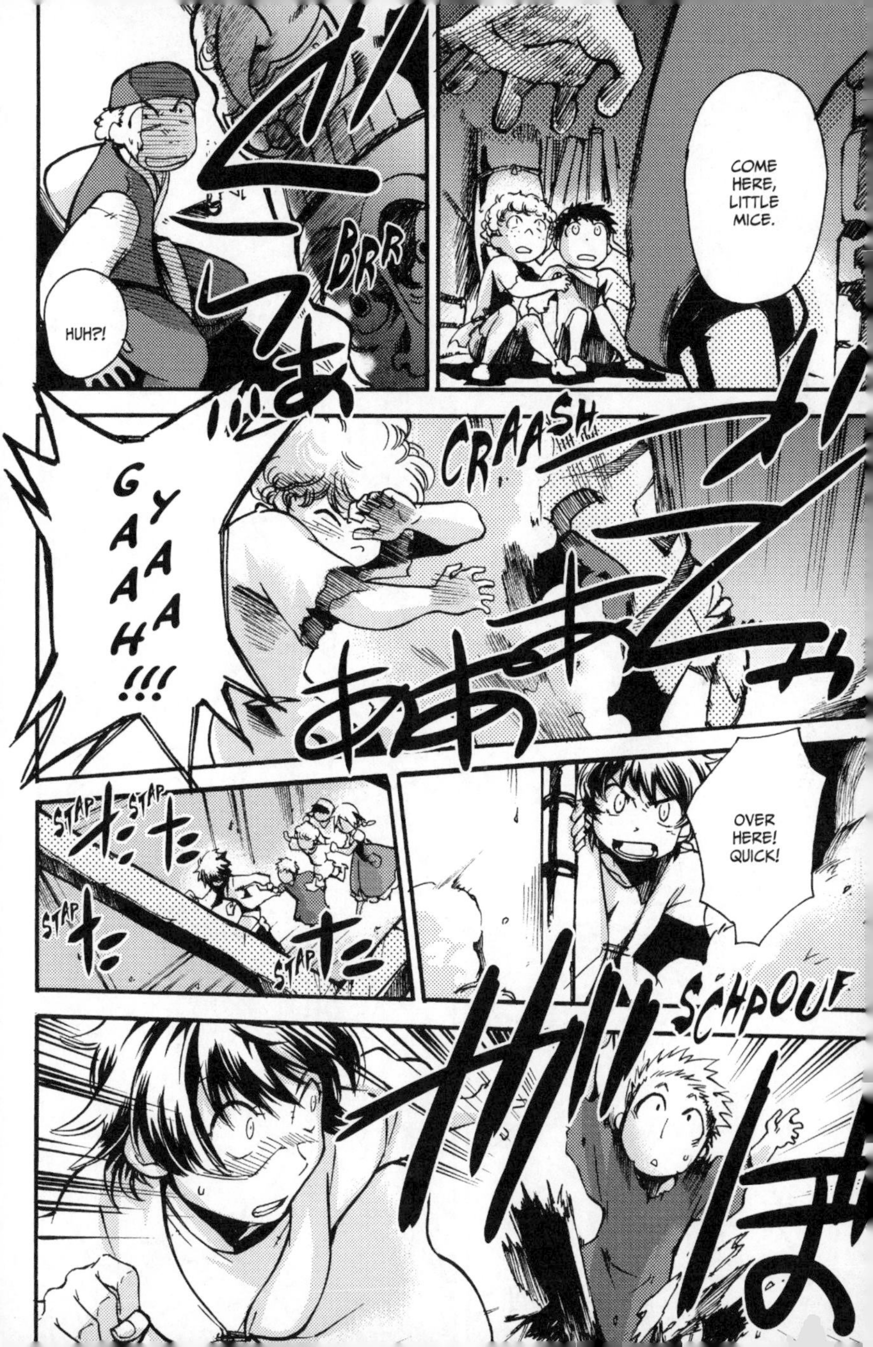
COME HERE, LITTLE MICE.
BRR
HUH?!
CRAASH
GYAAAAAH!!!
OVER HERE! QUICK!
STAP
STAP
STAP
STAP
SCHPOUF

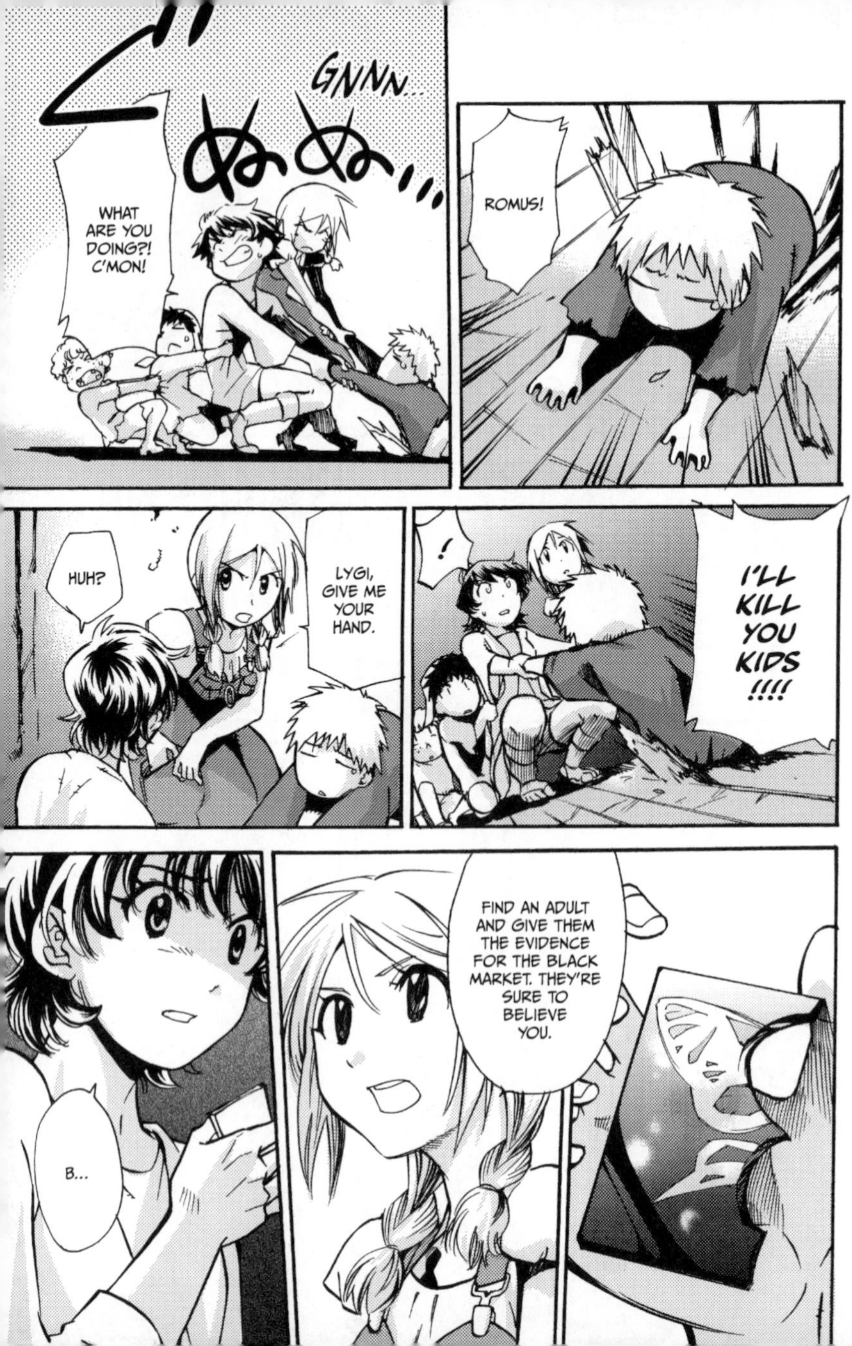
ROMUS!
GNNN...
ぬぬ
WHAT ARE YOU DOING?! C'MON!
I'LL KILL YOU KIDS!!!!
!
LYGI, GIVE ME YOUR HAND.
HUH?
FIND AN ADULT AND GIVE THEM THE EVIDENCE FOR THE BLACK MARKET. THEY'RE SURE TO BELIEVE YOU.
B...

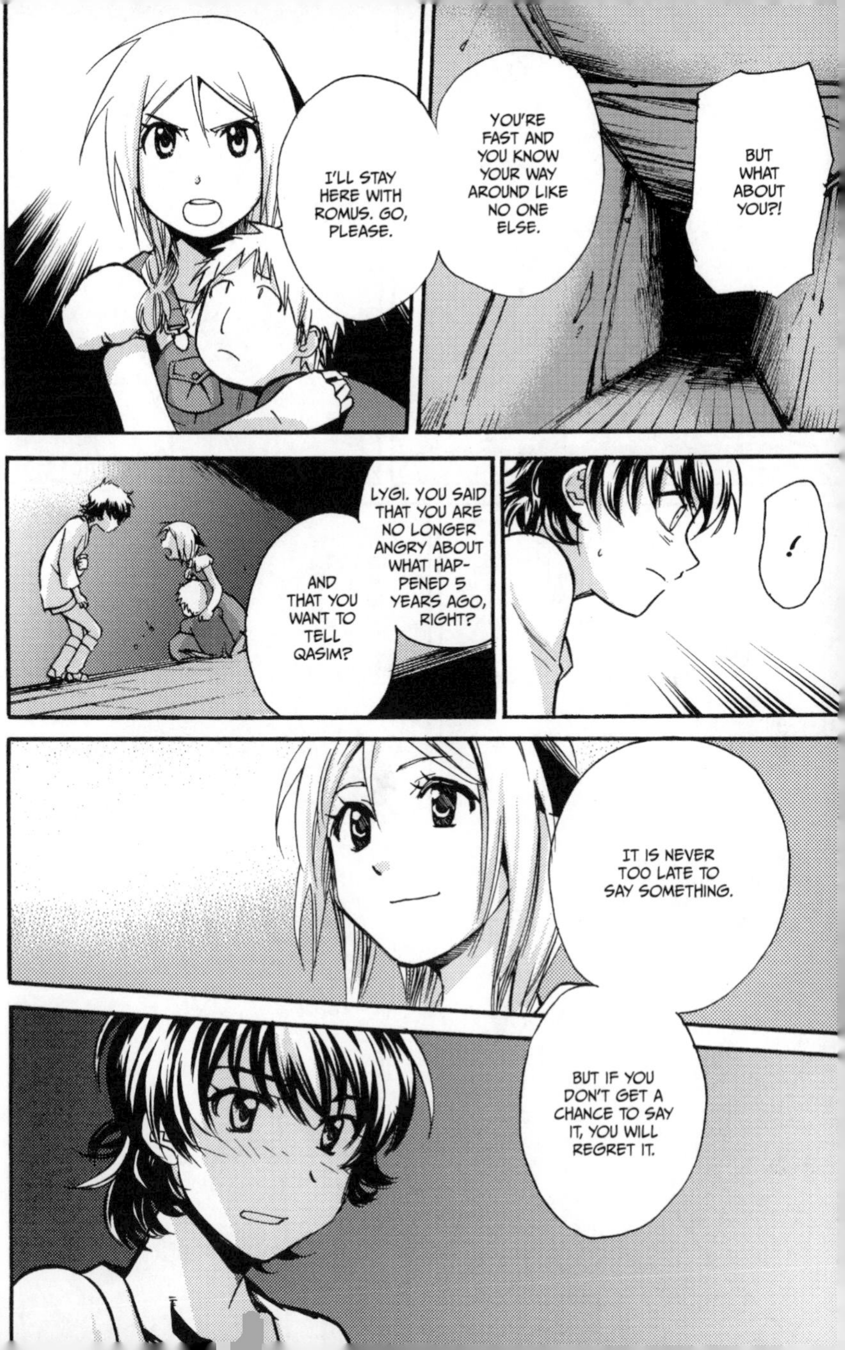
BUT WHAT ABOUT YOU?!
YOU'RE FAST AND YOU KNOW YOUR WAY AROUND LIKE NO ONE ELSE.
I'LL STAY HERE WITH ROMUS. GO, PLEASE.
!
LYGI. YOU SAID THAT YOU ARE NO LONGER ANGRY ABOUT WHAT HAP-PENED 5 YEARS AGO, RIGHT?
AND THAT YOU WANT TO TELL QASIM?
IT IS NEVER TOO LATE TO SAY SOMETHING.
BUT IF YOU DON'T GET A CHANCE TO SAY IT, YOU WILL REGRET IT.

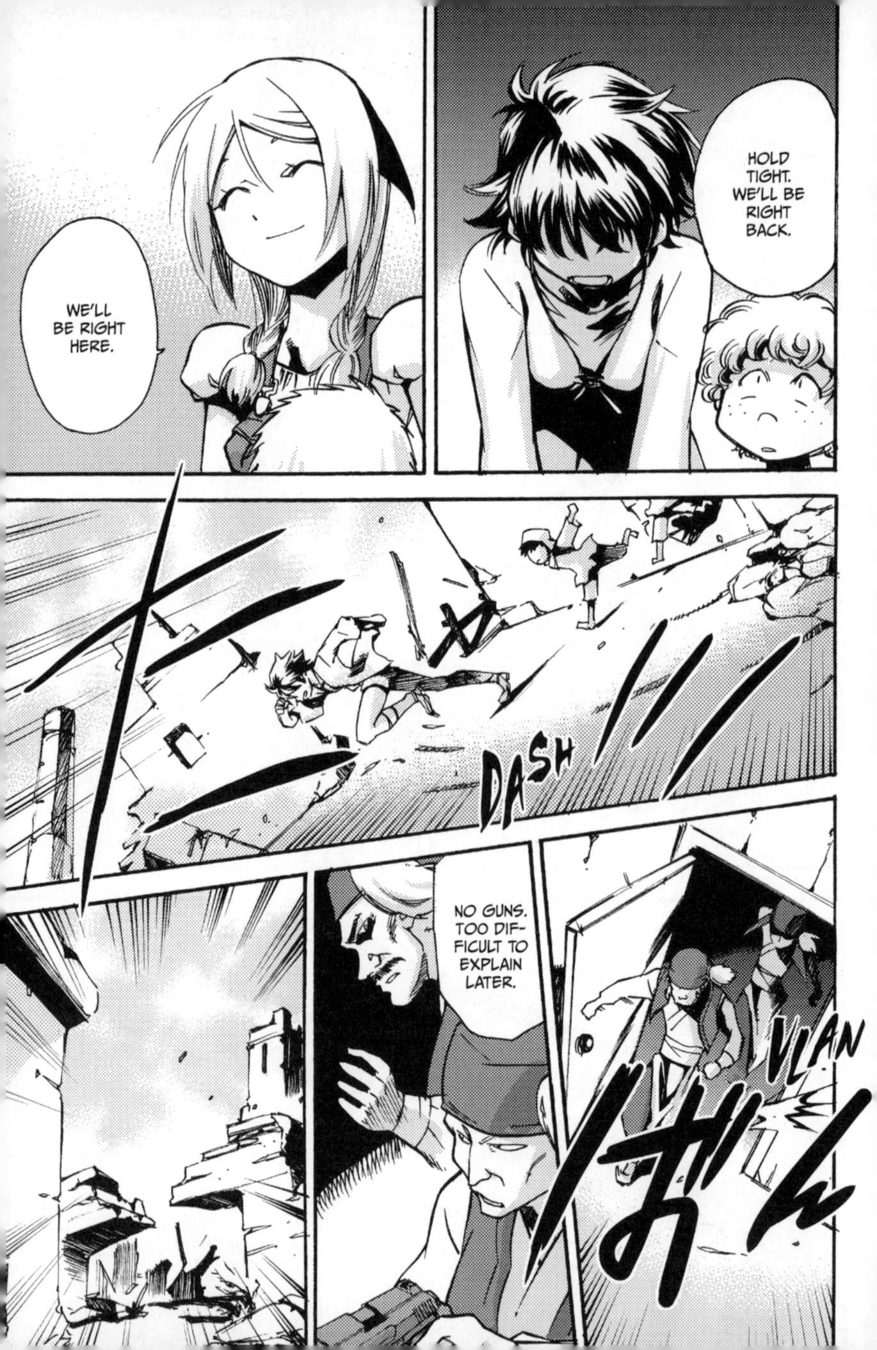
HOLD TIGHT. WE'LL BE RIGHT BACK.
WE'LL BE RIGHT HERE.
DASH
VLAN
NO GUNS. TOO DIF-FICULT TO EXPLAIN LATER.

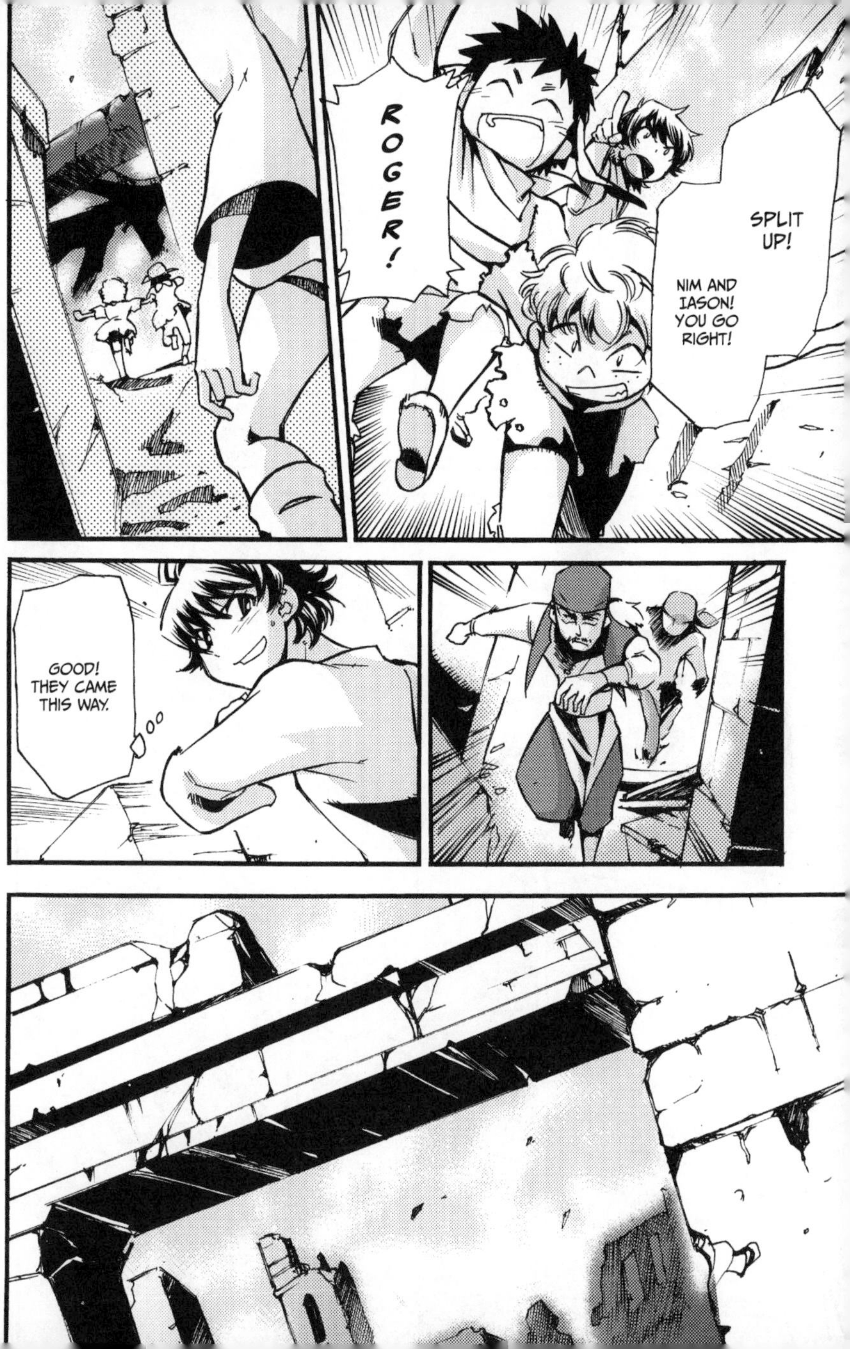
SPLIT UP!
NIM AND IASON! YOU GO RIGHT!
ROGER!
GOOD! THEY CAME THIS WAY.

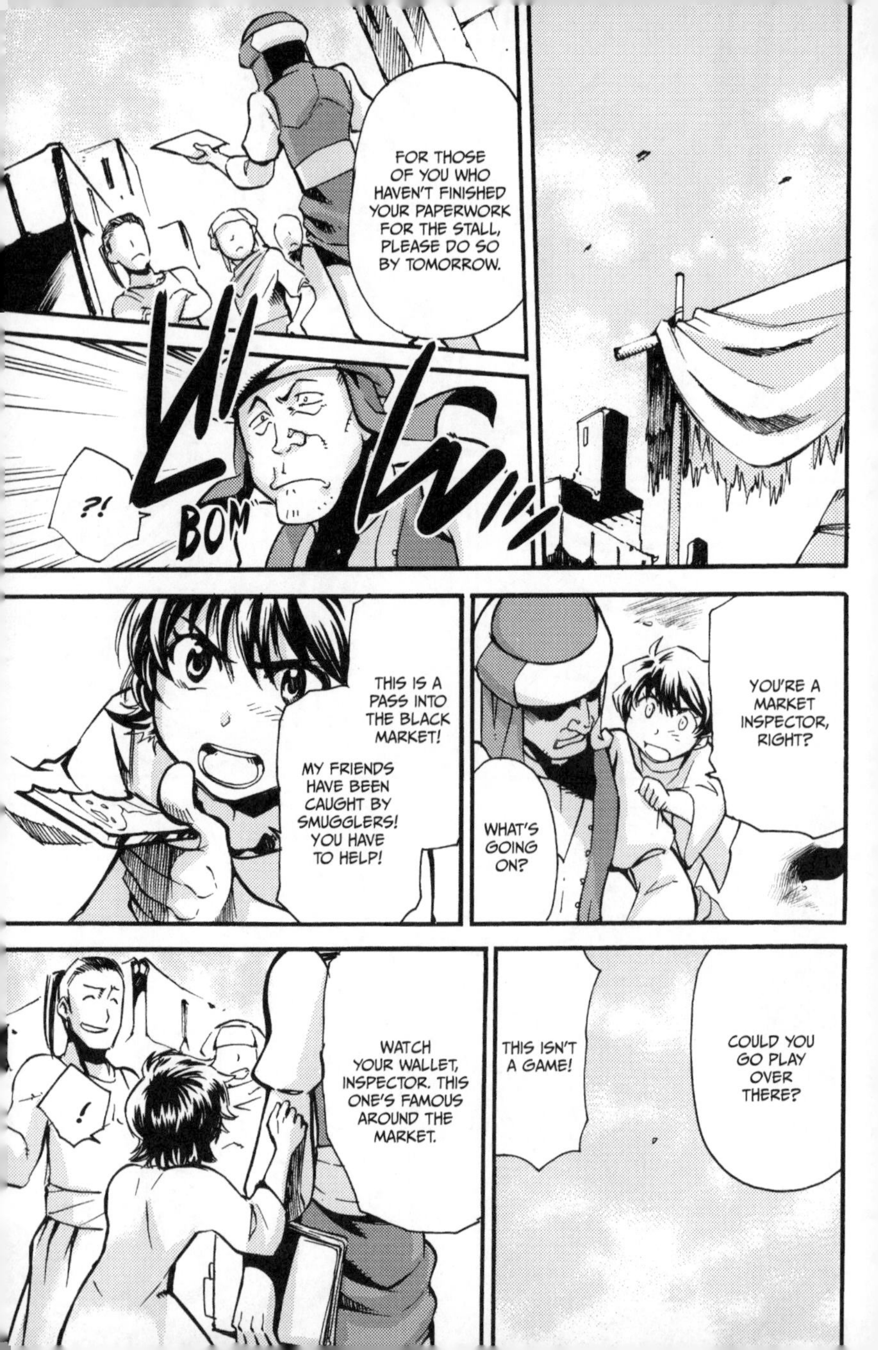
FOR THOSE OF YOU WHO HAVEN'T FINISHED YOUR PAPERWORK FOR THE STALL, PLEASE DO SO BY TOMORROW.
?!
BOM
YOU'RE A MARKET INSPECTOR, RIGHT?
WHAT'S GOING ON?
THIS IS A PASS INTO THE BLACK MARKET!
MY FRIENDS HAVE BEEN CAUGHT BY SMUGGLERS! YOU HAVE TO HELP!
COULD YOU GO PLAY OVER THERE?
THIS ISN'T A GAME!
WATCH YOUR WALLET, INSPECTOR. THIS ONE'S FAMOUS AROUND THE MARKET.
!

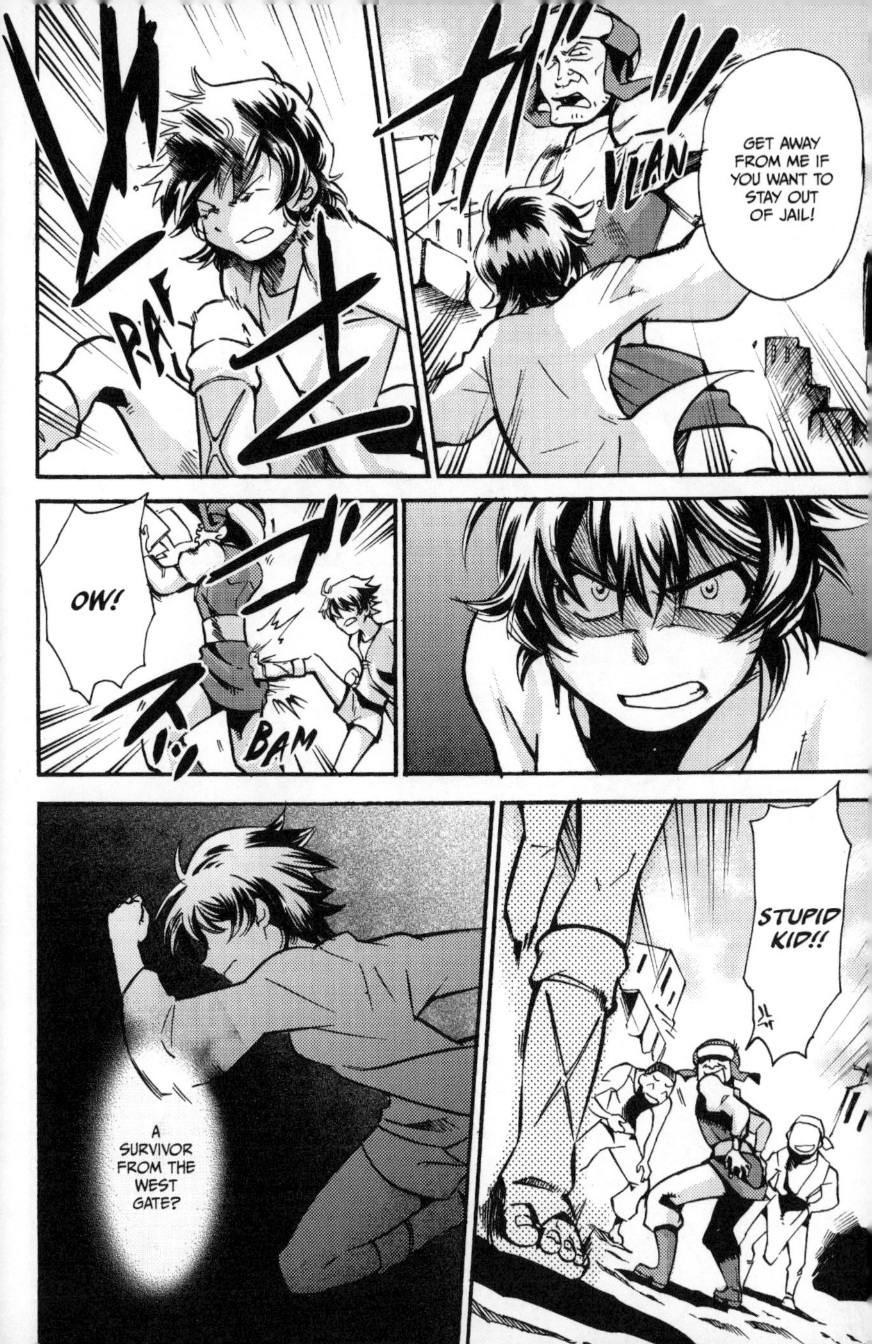
VLAN
GET AWAY FROM ME IF YOU WANT TO STAY OUT OF JAIL!
PAF
OW!
BAM
STUPID KID!!
A SURVIVOR FROM THE WEST GATE?

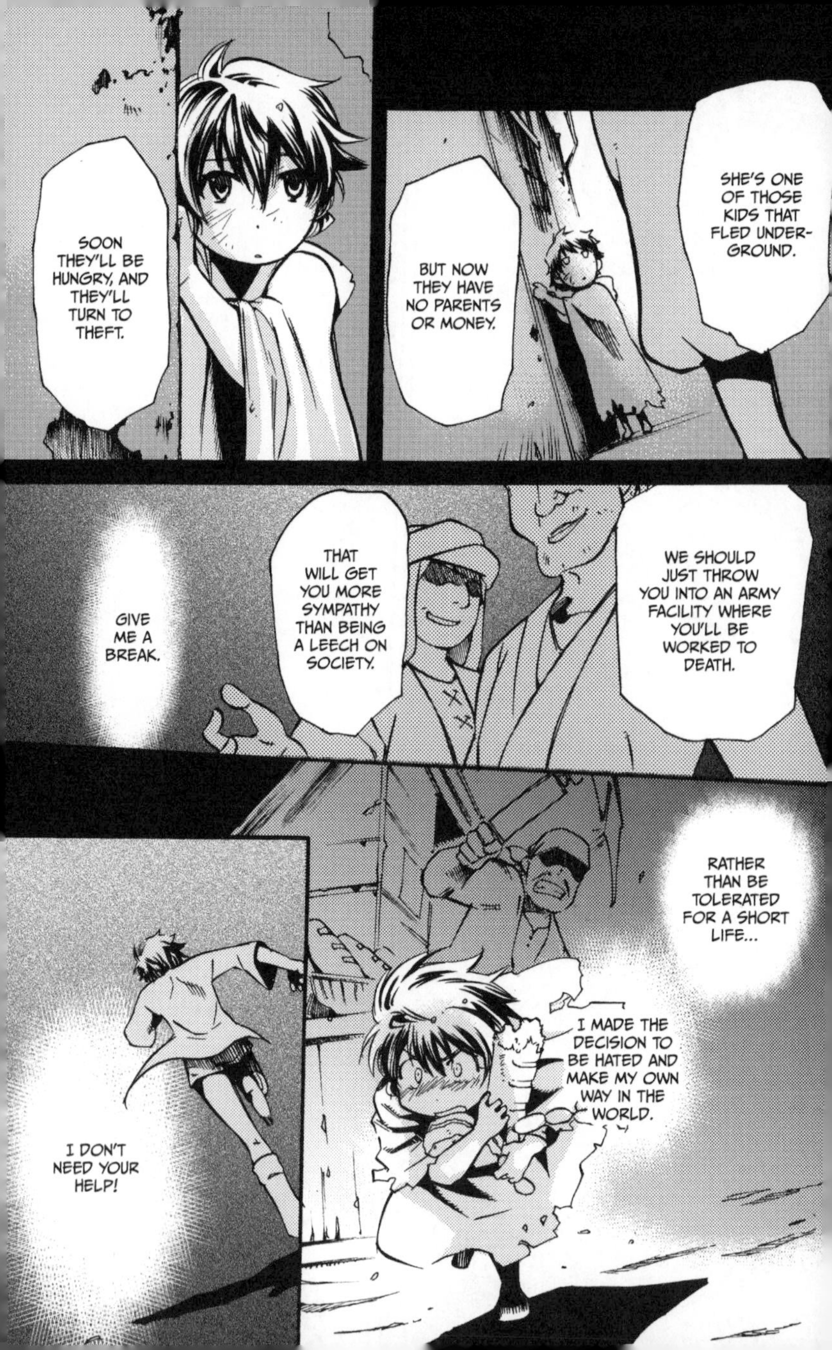
SHE'S ONE OF THOSE KIDS THAT FLED UNDER-GROUND.
BUT NOW THEY HAVE NO PARENTS OR MONEY.
SOON THEY'LL BE HUNGRY, AND THEY'LL TURN TO THEFT.
WE SHOULD JUST THROW YOU INTO AN ARMY FACILITY WHERE YOU'LL BE WORKED TO DEATH.
THAT WILL GET YOU MORE SYMPATHY THAN BEING A LEECH ON SOCIETY.
GIVE ME A BREAK.
RATHER THAN BE TOLERATED FOR A SHORT LIFE...
I MADE THE DECISION TO BE HATED AND MAKE MY OWN WAY IN THE WORLD.
I DON'T NEED YOUR HELP!

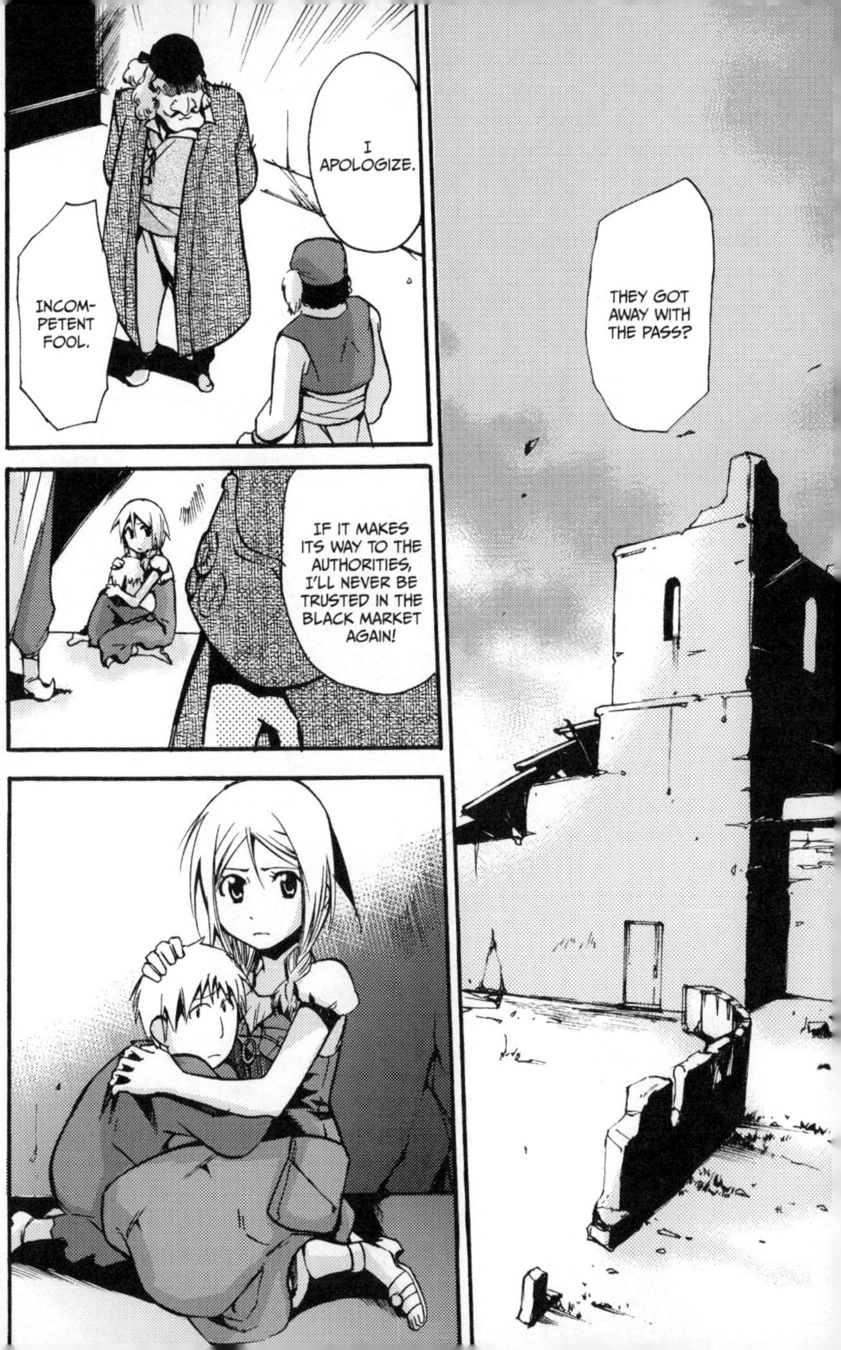
THEY GOT AWAY WITH THE PASS?
I APOLOGIZE.
INCOM-PETENT FOOL.
IF IT MAKES ITS WAY TO THE AUTHORITIES, I'LL NEVER BE TRUSTED IN THE BLACK MARKET AGAIN!

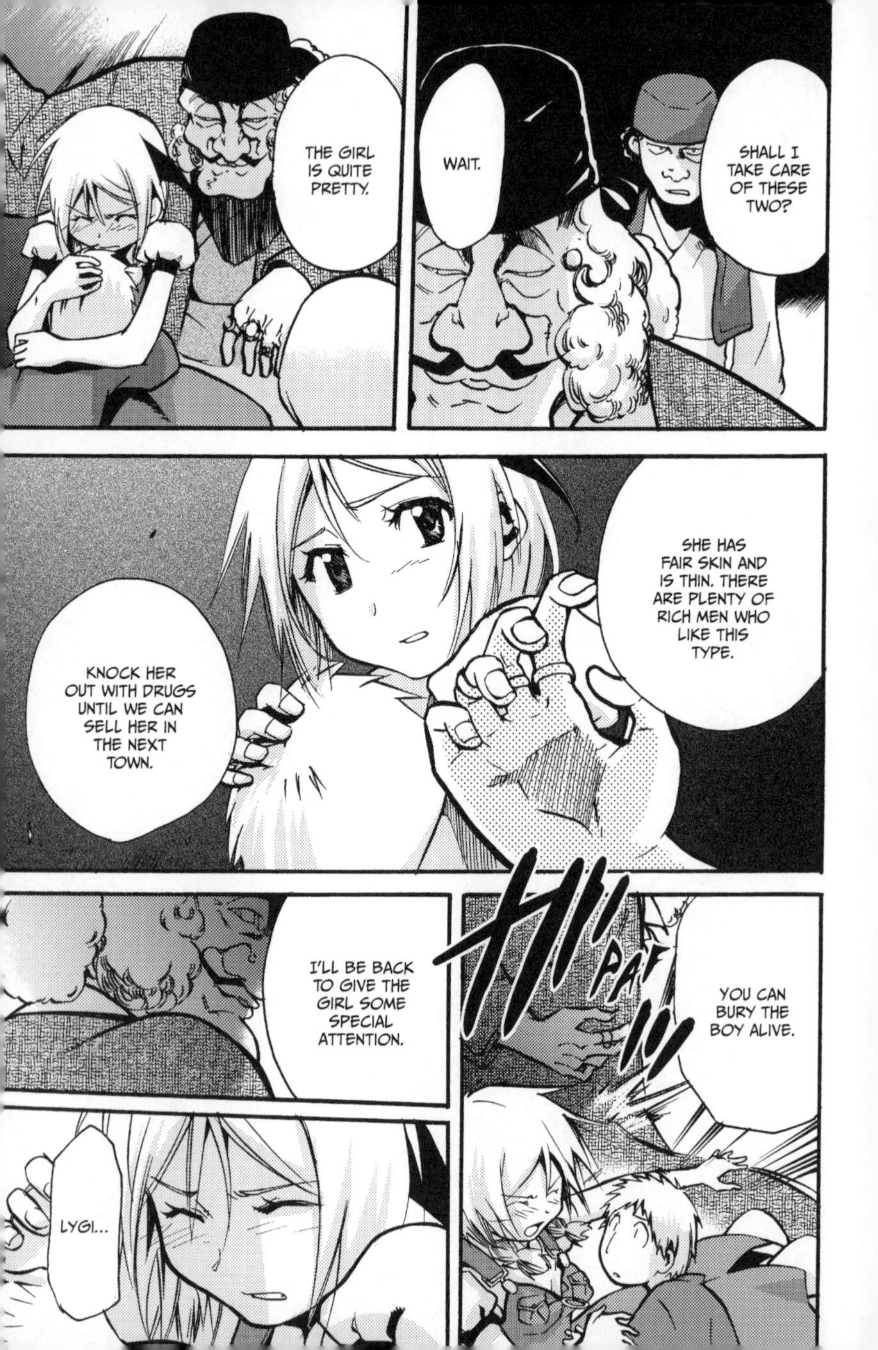
SHALL I TAKE CARE OF THESE TWO?
WAIT.
THE GIRL IS QUITE PRETTY.
SHE HAS FAIR SKIN AND IS THIN. THERE ARE PLENTY OF RICH MEN WHO LIKE THIS TYPE.
KNOCK HER OUT WITH DRUGS UNTIL WE CAN SELL HER IN THE NEXT TOWN.
YOU CAN BURY THE BOY ALIVE.
PAF
I'LL BE BACK TO GIVE THE GIRL SOME SPECIAL ATTENTION.
LYGI...

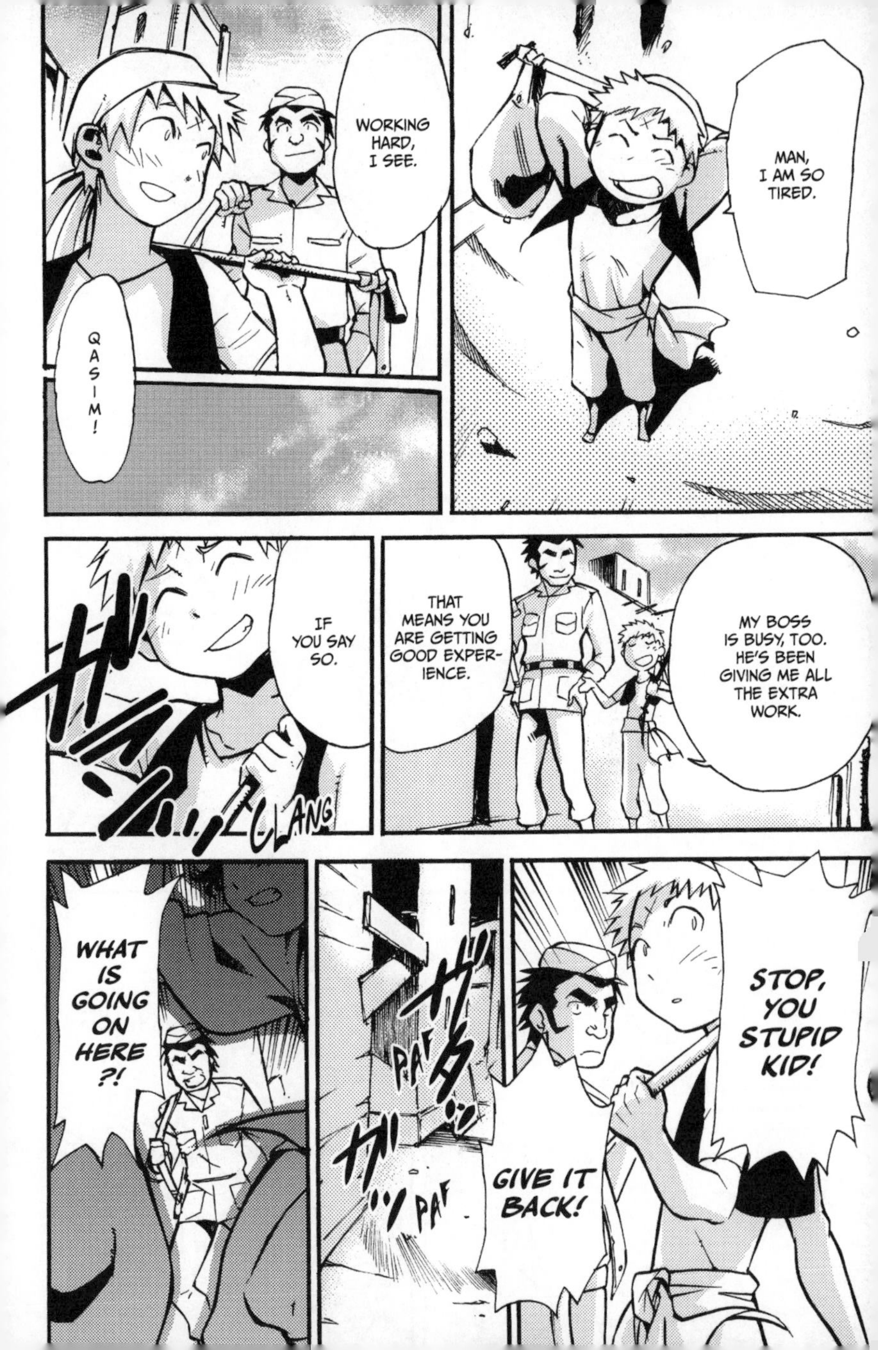
MAN, I AM SO TIRED.
WORKING HARD, I SEE.
QASIM!
MY BOSS IS BUSY, TOO. HE'S BEEN GIVING ME ALL THE EXTRA WORK.
THAT MEANS YOU ARE GETTING GOOD EXPERIENCE.
IF YOU SAY SO.
CLANG
STOP, YOU STUPID KID!
PAF
GIVE IT BACK!
PAF
WHAT IS GOING ON HERE?!

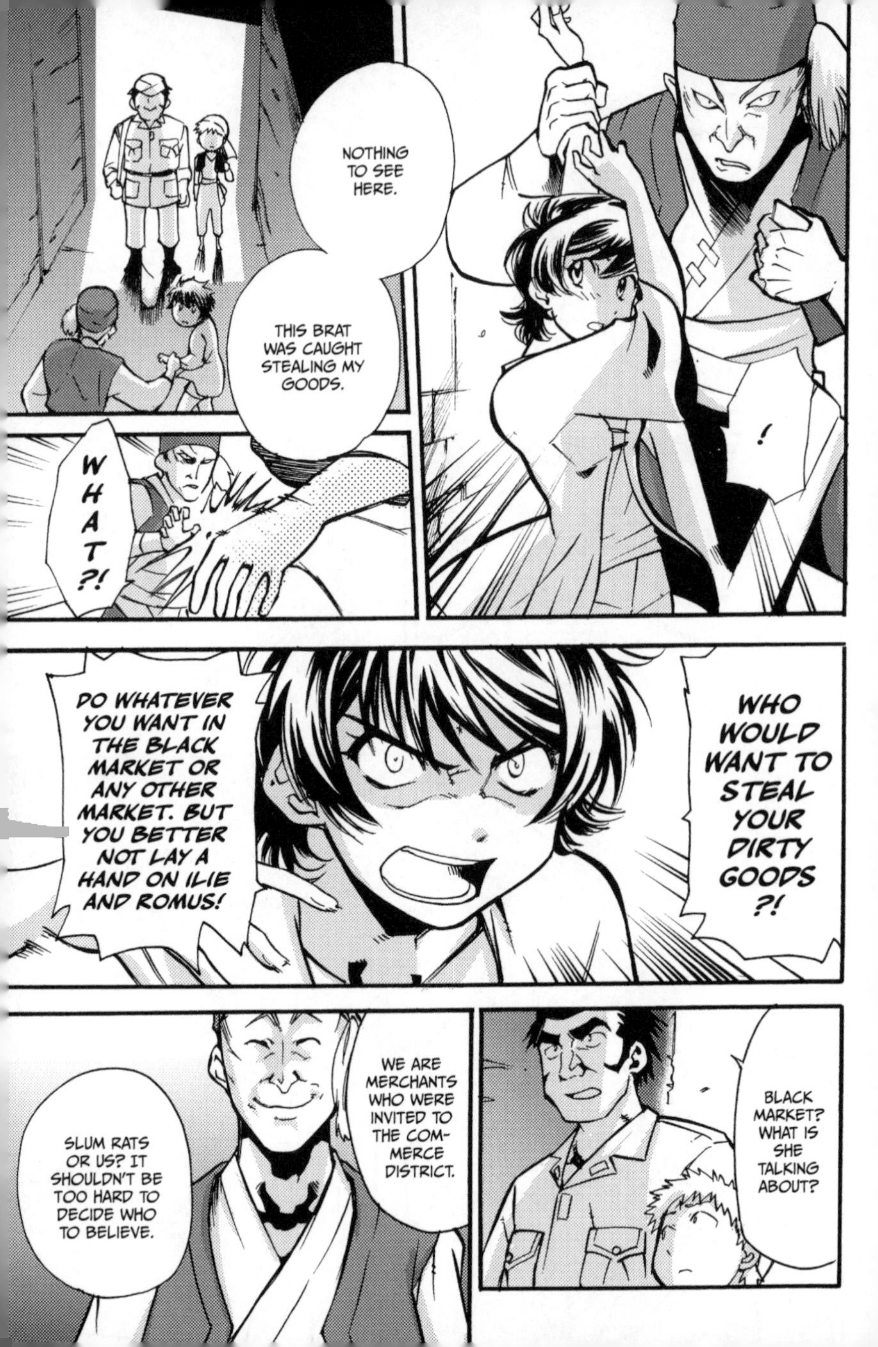
!
NOTHING TO SEE HERE.
THIS BRAT WAS CAUGHT STEALING MY GOODS.
WHAT?!
WHO WOULD WANT TO STEAL YOUR DIRTY GOODS?!
DO WHATEVER YOU WANT IN THE BLACK MARKET OR ANY OTHER MARKET. BUT YOU BETTER NOT LAY A HAND ON ILIE AND ROMUS!
BLACK MARKET? WHAT IS SHE TALKING ABOUT?
WE ARE MERCHANTS WHO WERE INVITED TO THE COM-MERCE DISTRICT.
SLUM RATS OR US? IT SHOULDN'T BE TOO HARD TO DECIDE WHO TO BELIEVE.

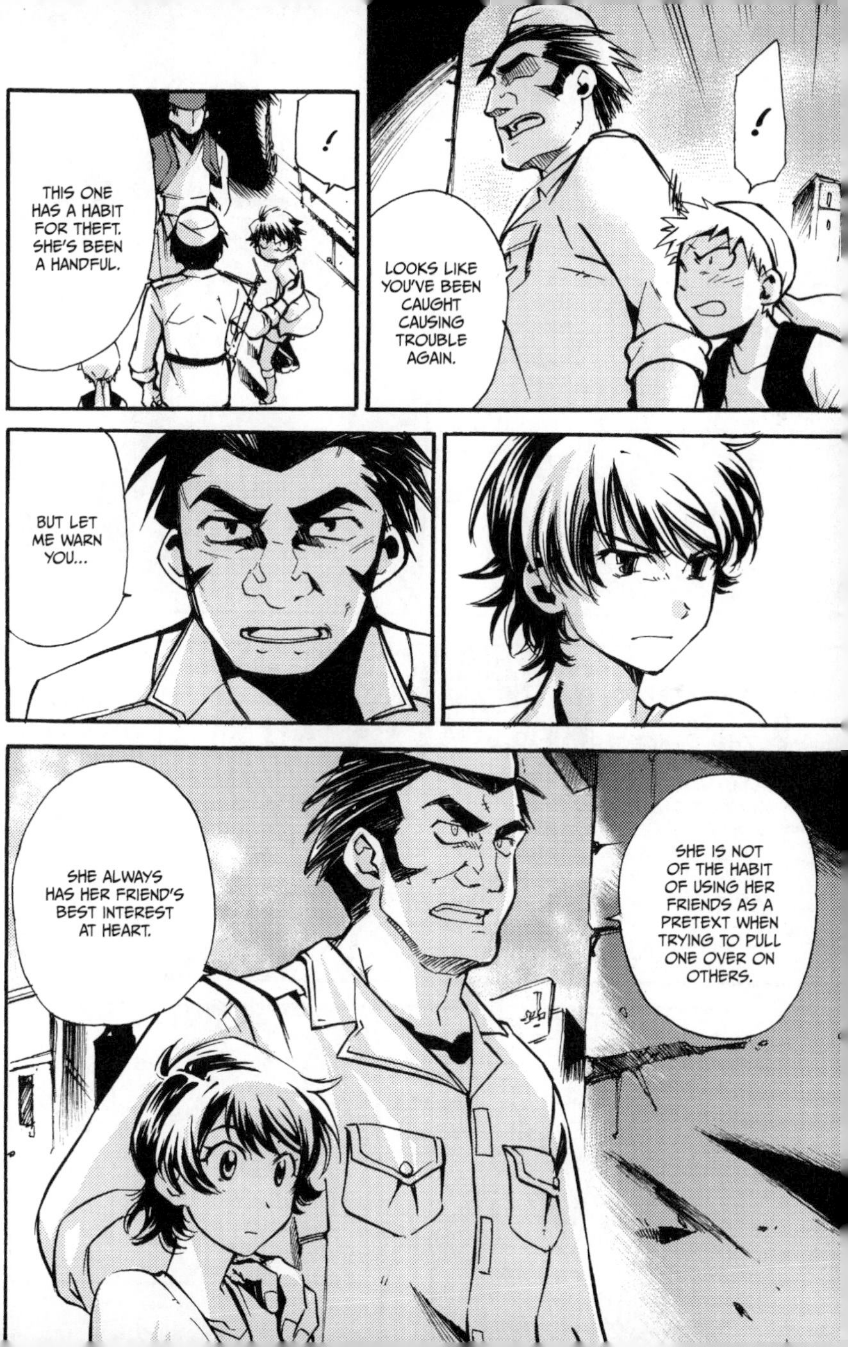
!
LOOKS LIKE YOU'VE BEEN CAUGHT CAUSING TROUBLE AGAIN.
!
THIS ONE HAS A HABIT FOR THEFT. SHE'S BEEN A HANDFUL.
BUT LET ME WARN YOU...
SHE IS NOT OF THE HABIT OF USING HER FRIENDS AS A PRETEXT WHEN TRYING TO PULL ONE OVER ON OTHERS.
SHE ALWAYS HAS HER FRIEND'S BEST INTEREST AT HEART.

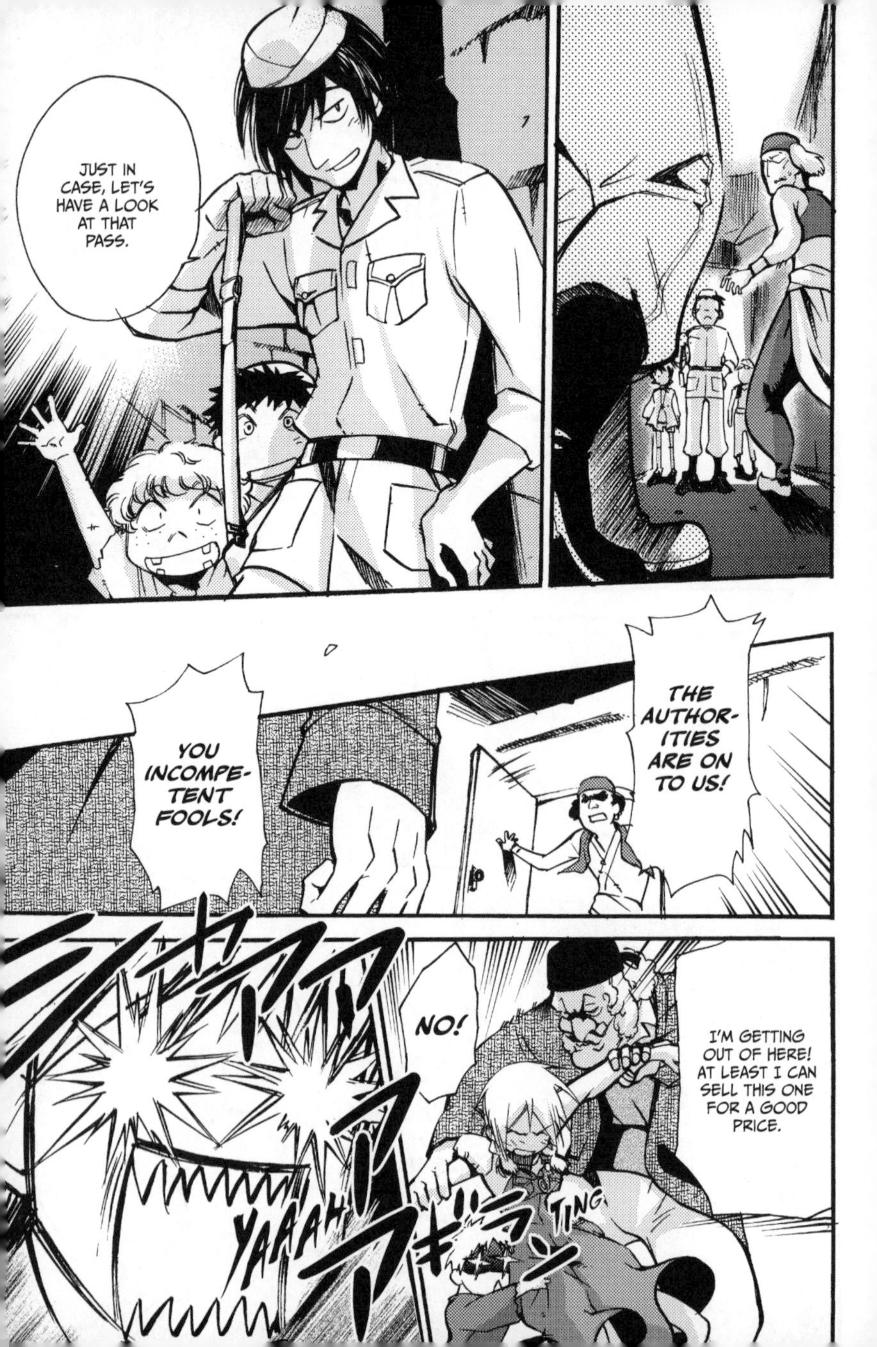
JUST IN CASE, LET'S HAVE A LOOK AT THAT PASS.
THE AUTHOR-ITIES ARE ON TO US!
YOU INCOMPE-TENT FOOLS!
I'M GETTING OUT OF HERE! AT LEAST I CAN SELL THIS ONE FOR A GOOD PRICE.
NO!
YAAAH!
TING

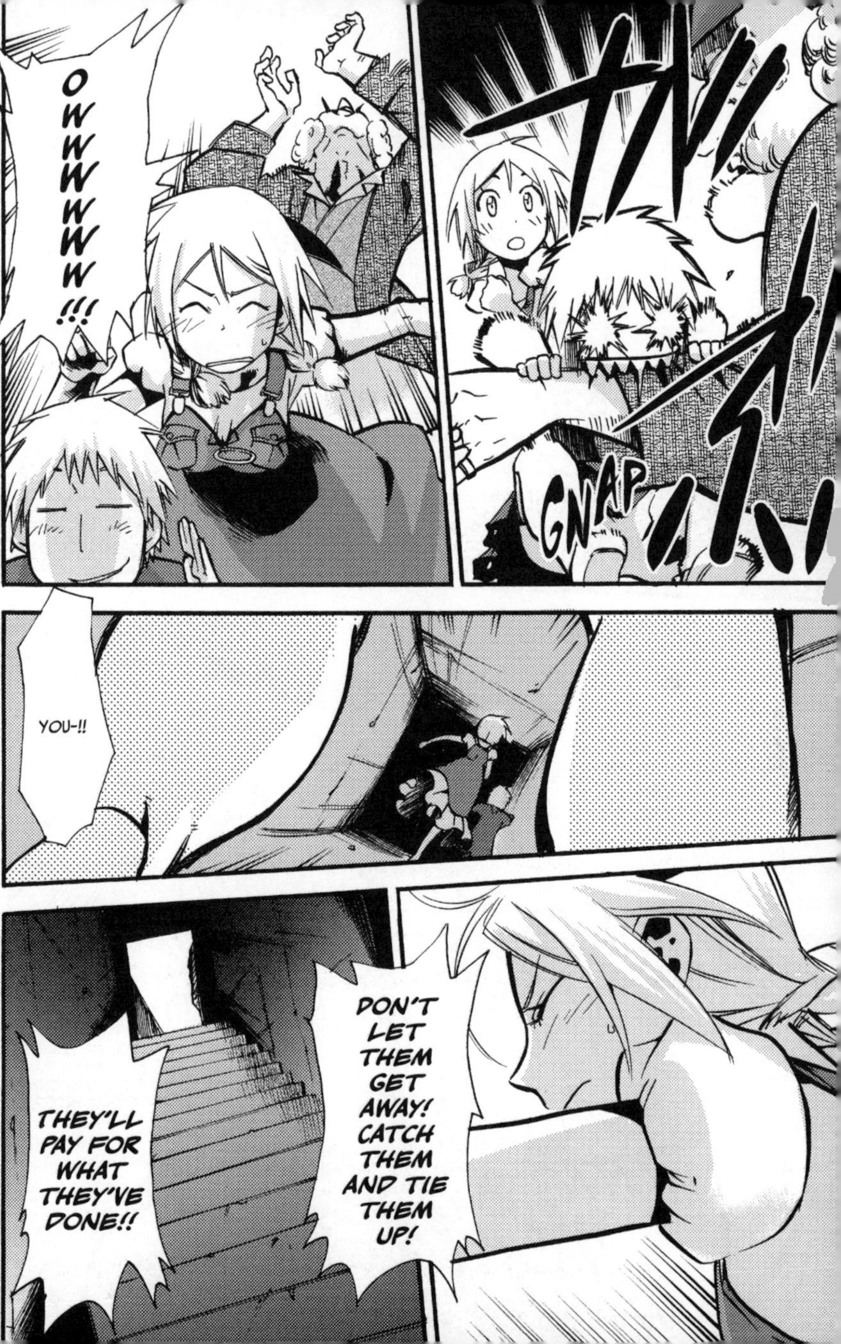
GNAP
OWWWWWW!!!
YOU-!!
DON'T LET THEM GET AWAY! CATCH THEM AND TIE THEM UP!
THEY'LL PAY FOR WHAT THEY'VE DONE!!

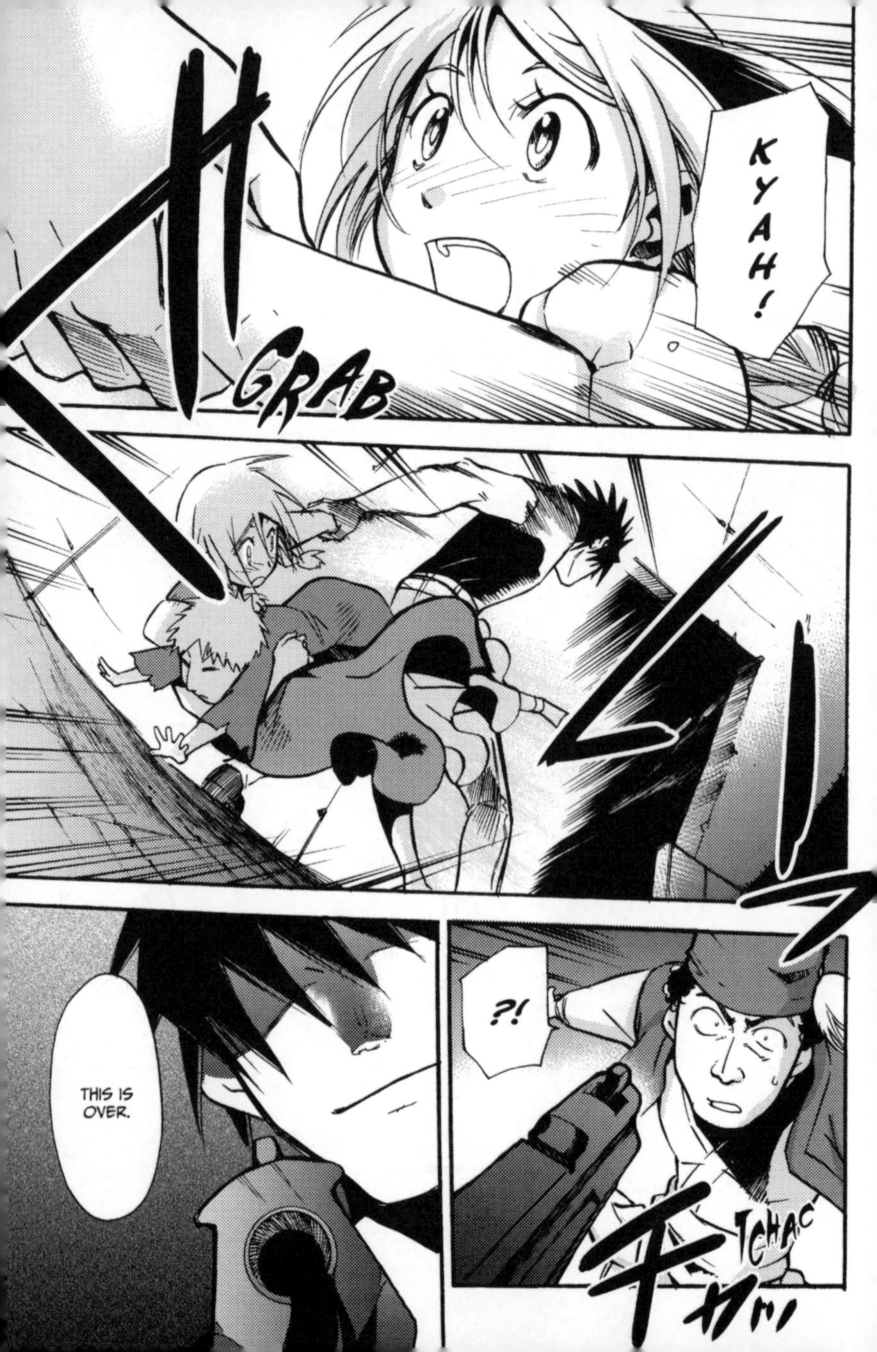
KYAH!
GRAB
?!
TCHAC
THIS IS OVER.

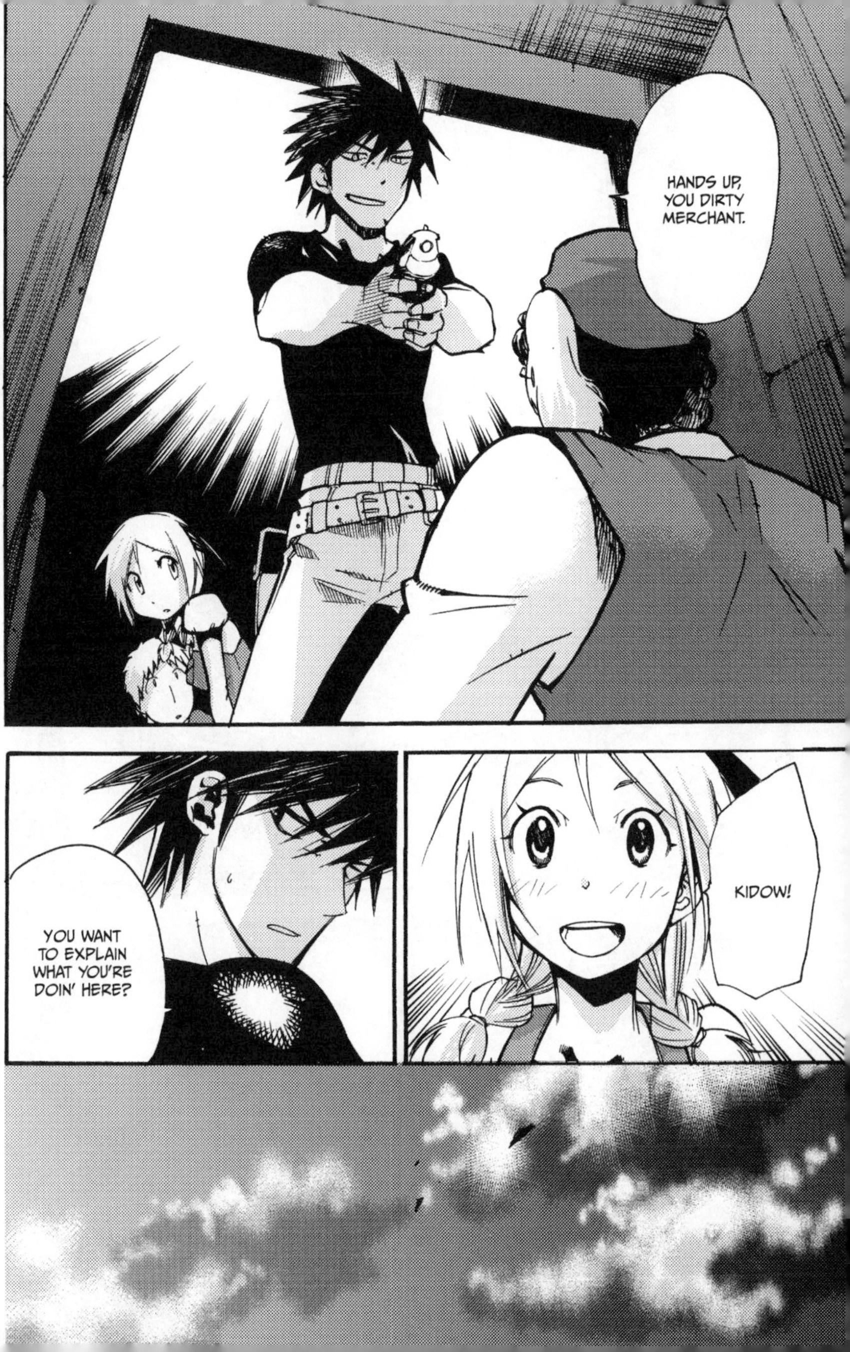
HANDS UP, YOU DIRTY MERCHANT.
KIDOW!
YOU WANT TO EXPLAIN WHAT YOU'RE DOIN' HERE?

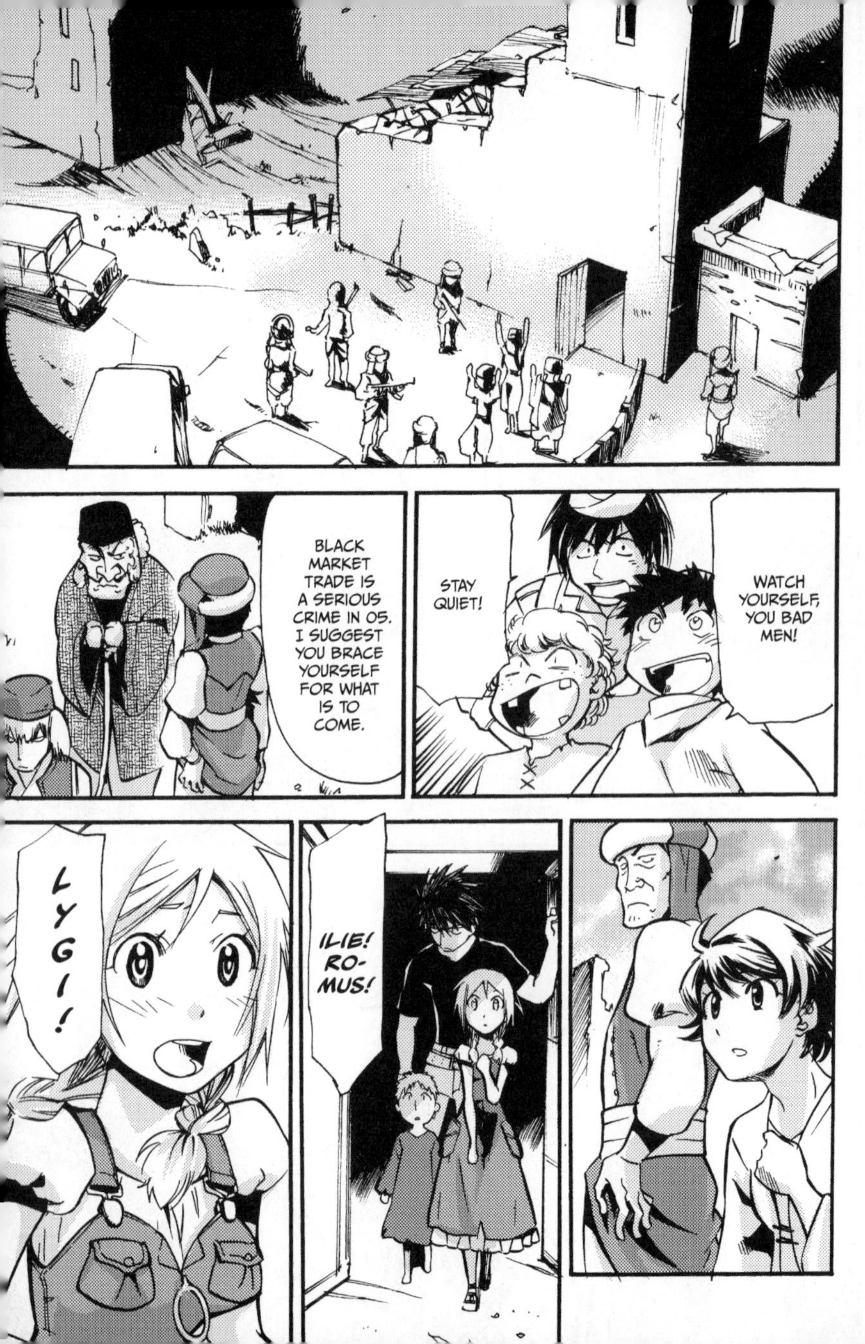
WATCH YOURSELF, YOU BAD MEN!
STAY QUIET!
BLACK MARKET TRADE IS A SERIOUS CRIME IN 05. I SUGGEST YOU BRACE YOURSELF FOR WHAT IS TO COME.
ILIE! RO-MUS!
LYGI!

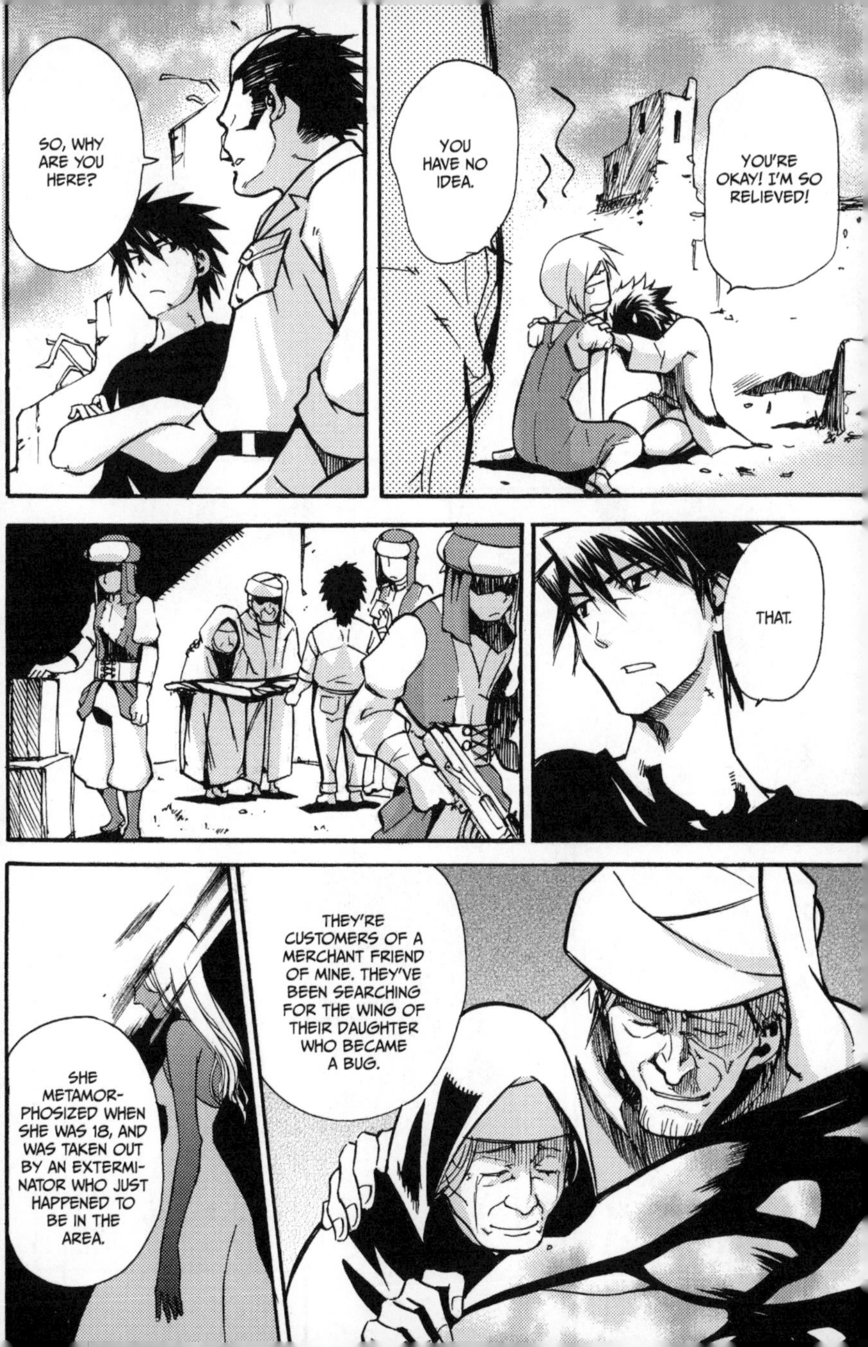
YOU'RE OKAY! I'M SO RELIEVED!
YOU HAVE NO IDEA.
SO, WHY ARE YOU HERE?
THAT.
THEY'RE CUSTOMERS OF A MERCHANT FRIEND OF MINE. THEY'VE BEEN SEARCHING FOR THE WING OF THEIR DAUGHTER WHO BECAME A BUG.
SHE METAMOR-PHOSIZED WHEN SHE WAS 18, AND WAS TAKEN OUT BY AN EXTERMI-NATOR WHO JUST HAPPENED TO BE IN THE AREA.

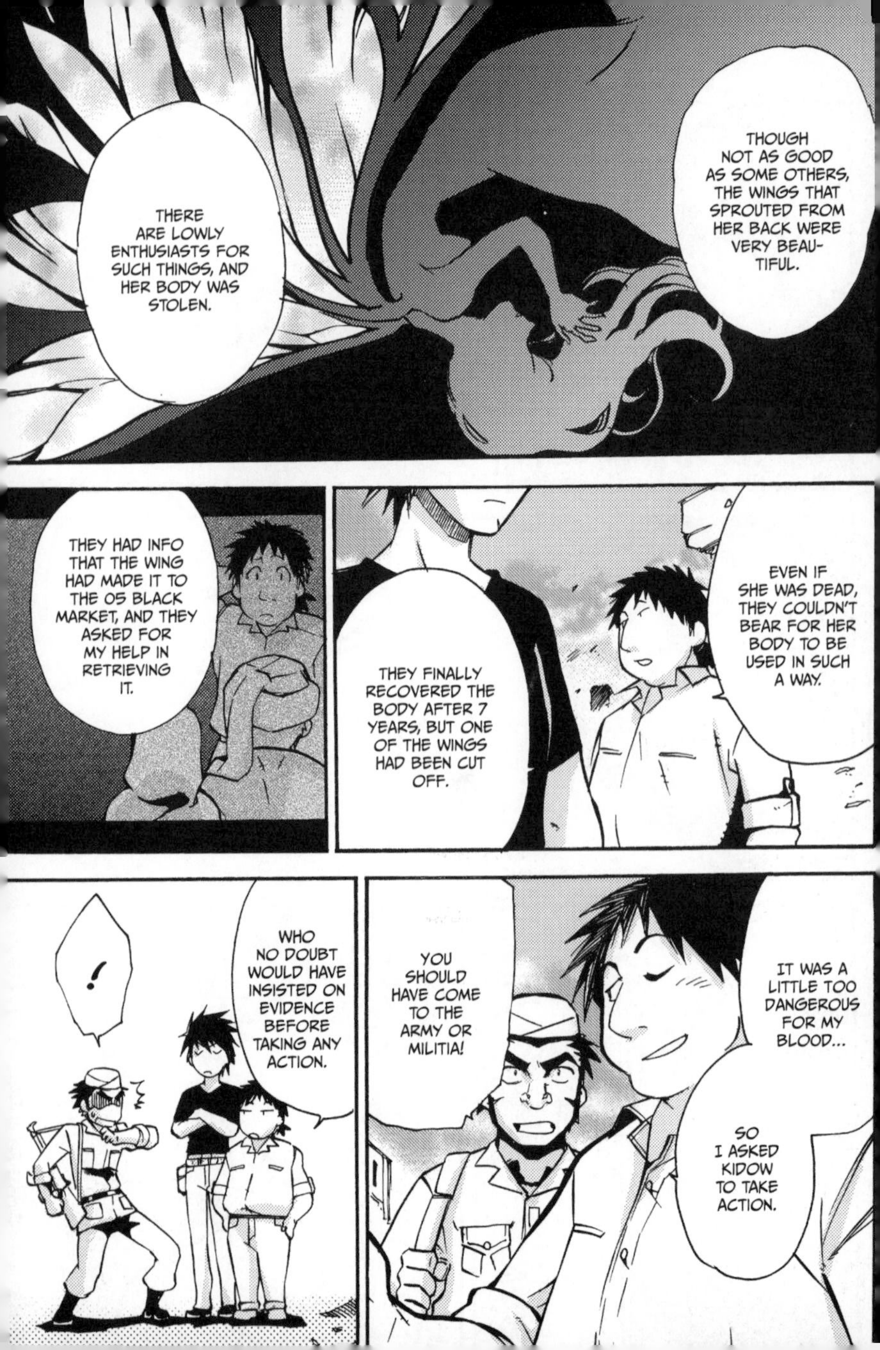
THOUGH NOT AS GOOD AS SOME OTHERS, THE WINGS THAT SPROUTED FROM HER BACK WERE VERY BEAU- TIFUL.
THERE ARE LOWLY ENTHUSIASTS FOR SUCH THINGS, AND HER BODY WAS STOLEN.
EVEN IF SHE WAS DEAD, THEY COULDN'T BEAR FOR HER BODY TO BE USED IN SUCH A WAY.
THEY FINALLY RECOVERED THE BODY AFTER 7 YEARS, BUT ONE OF THE WINGS HAD BEEN CUT OFF.
THEY HAD INFO THAT THE WING HAD MADE IT TO THE 05 BLACK MARKET, AND THEY ASKED FOR MY HELP IN RETRIEVING IT.
IT WAS A LITTLE TOO DANGEROUS FOR MY BLOOD...
SO I ASKED KIDOW TO TAKE ACTION.
YOU SHOULD HAVE COME TO THE ARMY OR MILITIA!
WHO NO DOUBT WOULD HAVE INSISTED ON EVIDENCE BEFORE TAKING ANY ACTION.
!

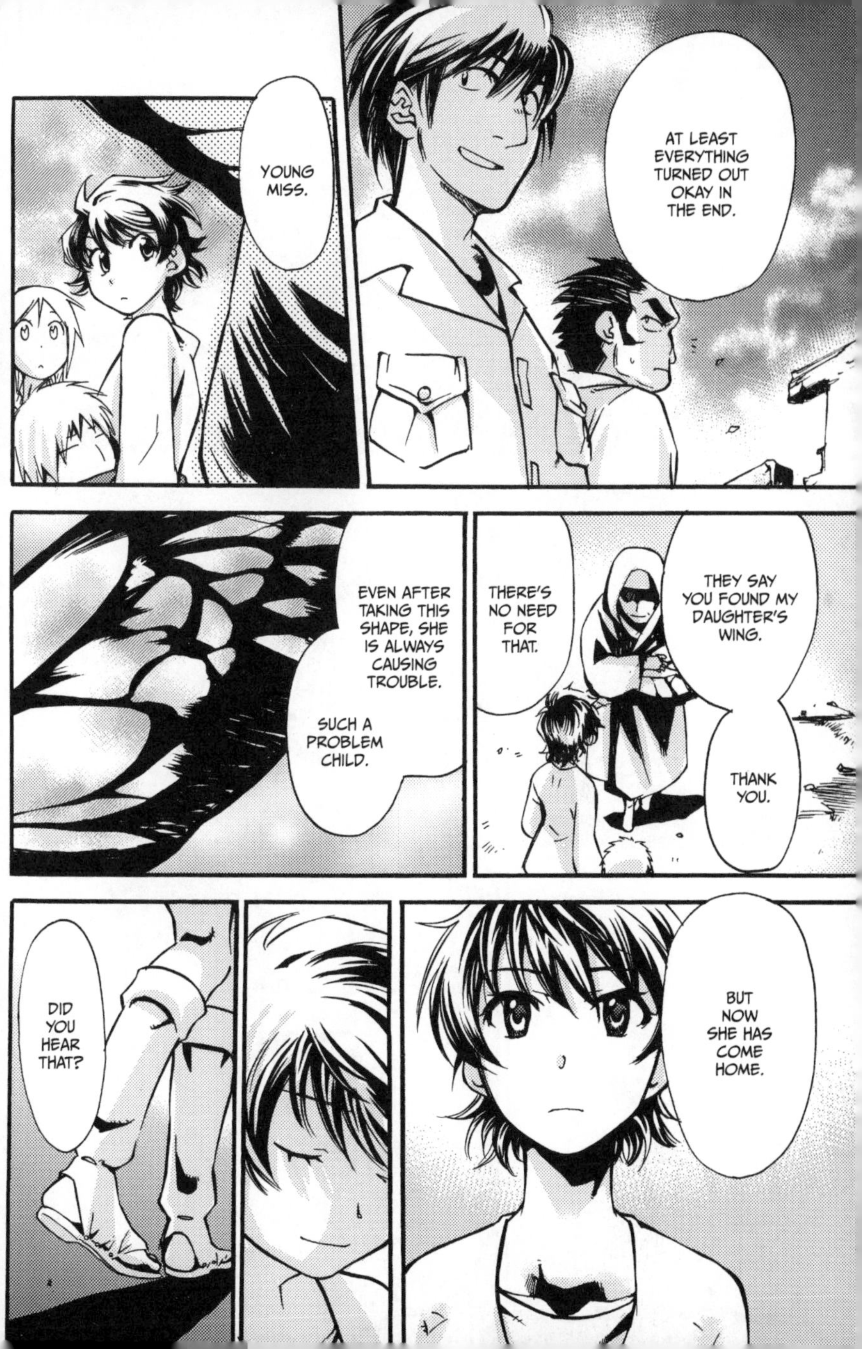
AT LEAST EVERYTHING TURNED OUT OKAY IN THE END.
YOUNG MISS.
THEY SAY YOU FOUND MY DAUGHTER'S WING.
THANK YOU.
THERE'S NO NEED FOR THAT.
EVEN AFTER TAKING THIS SHAPE, SHE IS ALWAYS CAUSING TROUBLE.
SUCH A PROBLEM CHILD.
BUT NOW SHE HAS COME HOME.
DID YOU HEAR THAT?

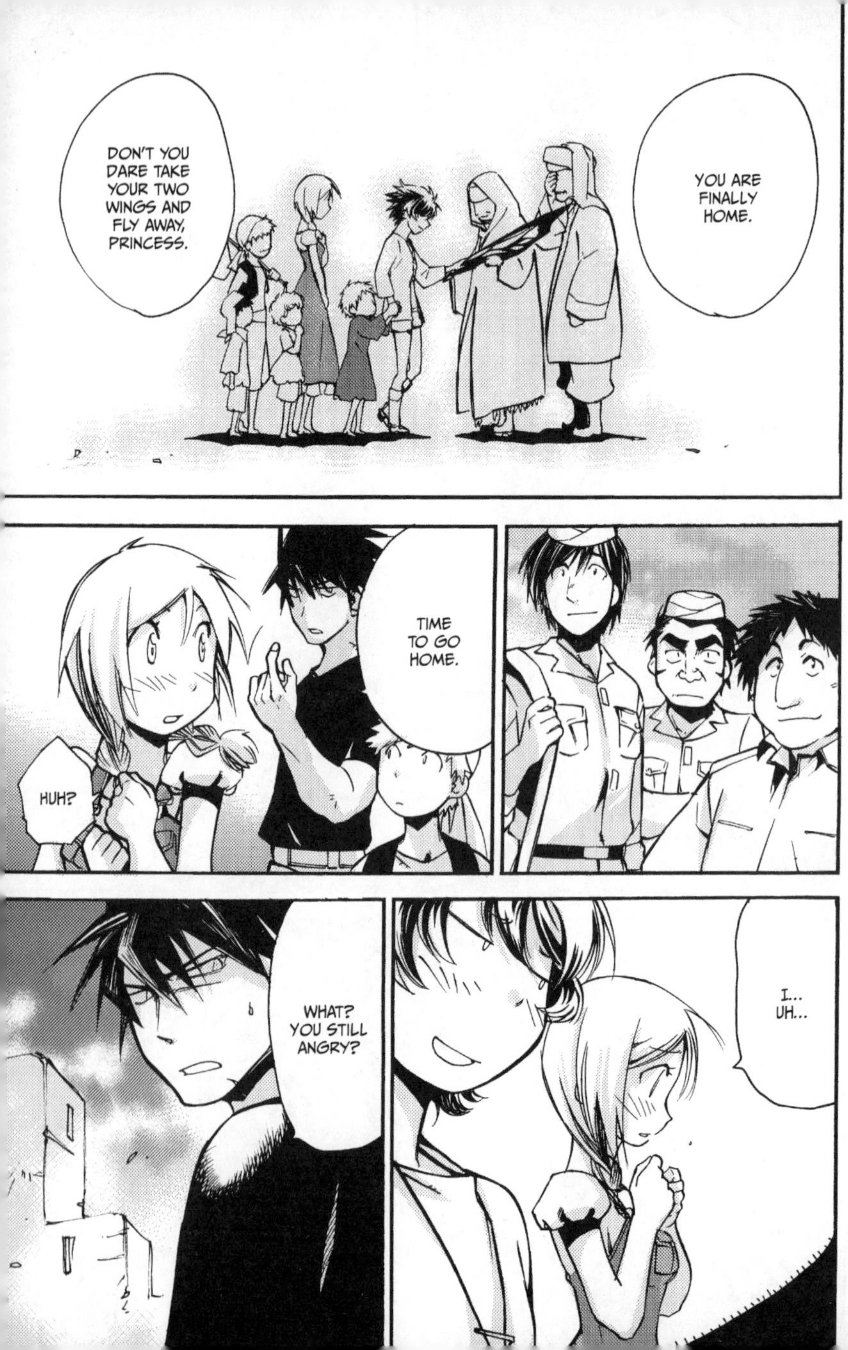
YOU ARE FINALLY HOME.
DON'T YOU DARE TAKE YOUR TWO WINGS AND FLY AWAY, PRINCESS.
TIME TO GO HOME.
HUH?
I... UH...
WHAT? YOU STILL ANGRY?

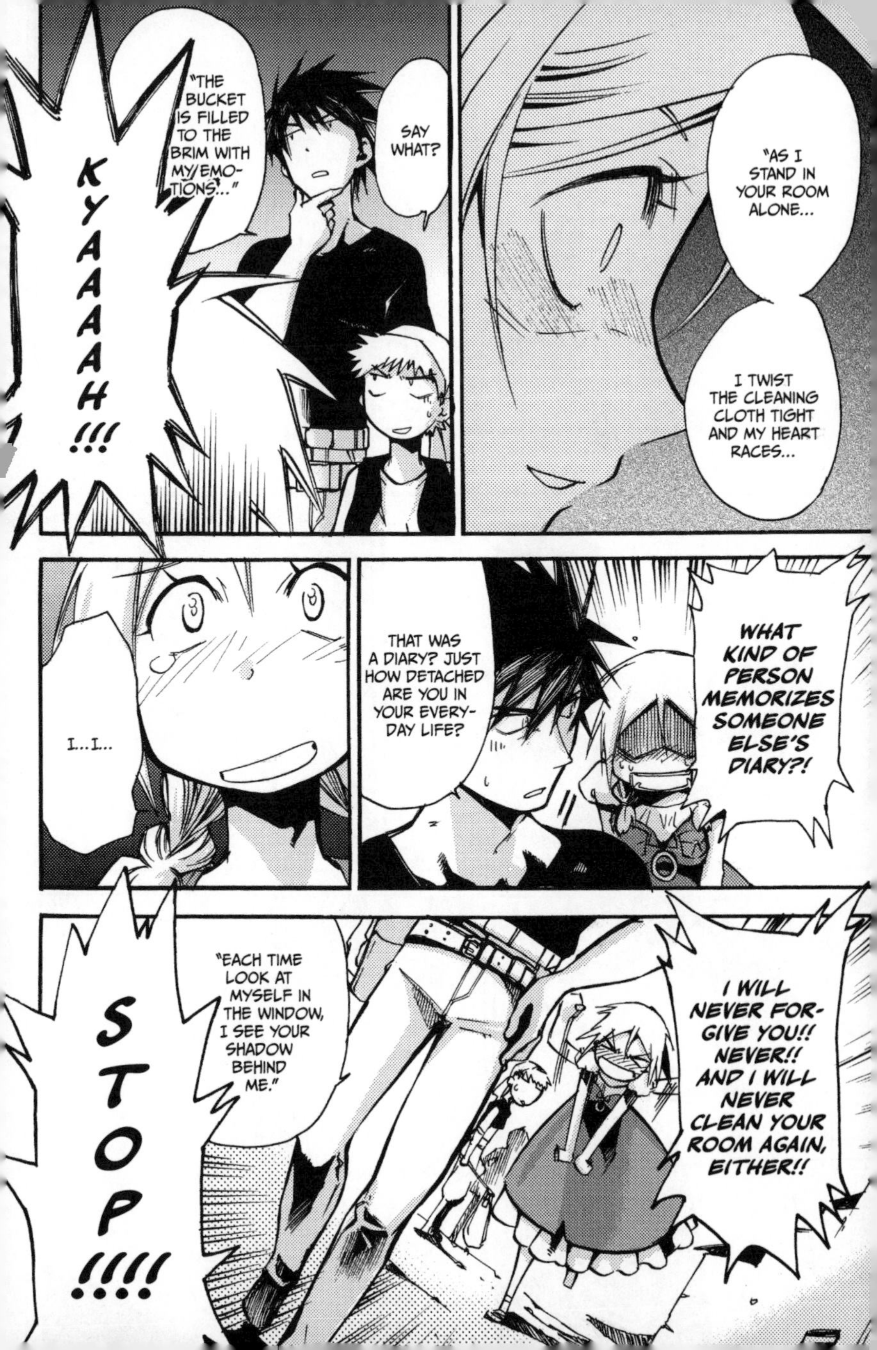
"AS I STAND IN YOUR ROOM ALONE...
I TWIST THE CLEANING CLOTH TIGHT AND MY HEART RACES...
SAY WHAT?
"THE BUCKET IS FILLED TO THE BRIM WITH MY/EMOTIONS..."
KYAAAAAH!!!
WHAT KIND OF PERSON MEMORIZES SOMEONE ELSE'S DIARY?!
THAT WAS A DIARY? JUST HOW DETACHED ARE YOU IN YOUR EVERYDAY LIFE?
I...I...
I WILL NEVER FORGIVE YOU!! NEVER!! AND I WILL NEVER CLEAN YOUR ROOM AGAIN, EITHER!!
"EACH TIME LOOK AT MYSELF IN THE WINDOW, I SEE YOUR SHADOW BEHIND ME."
STOP!!!!

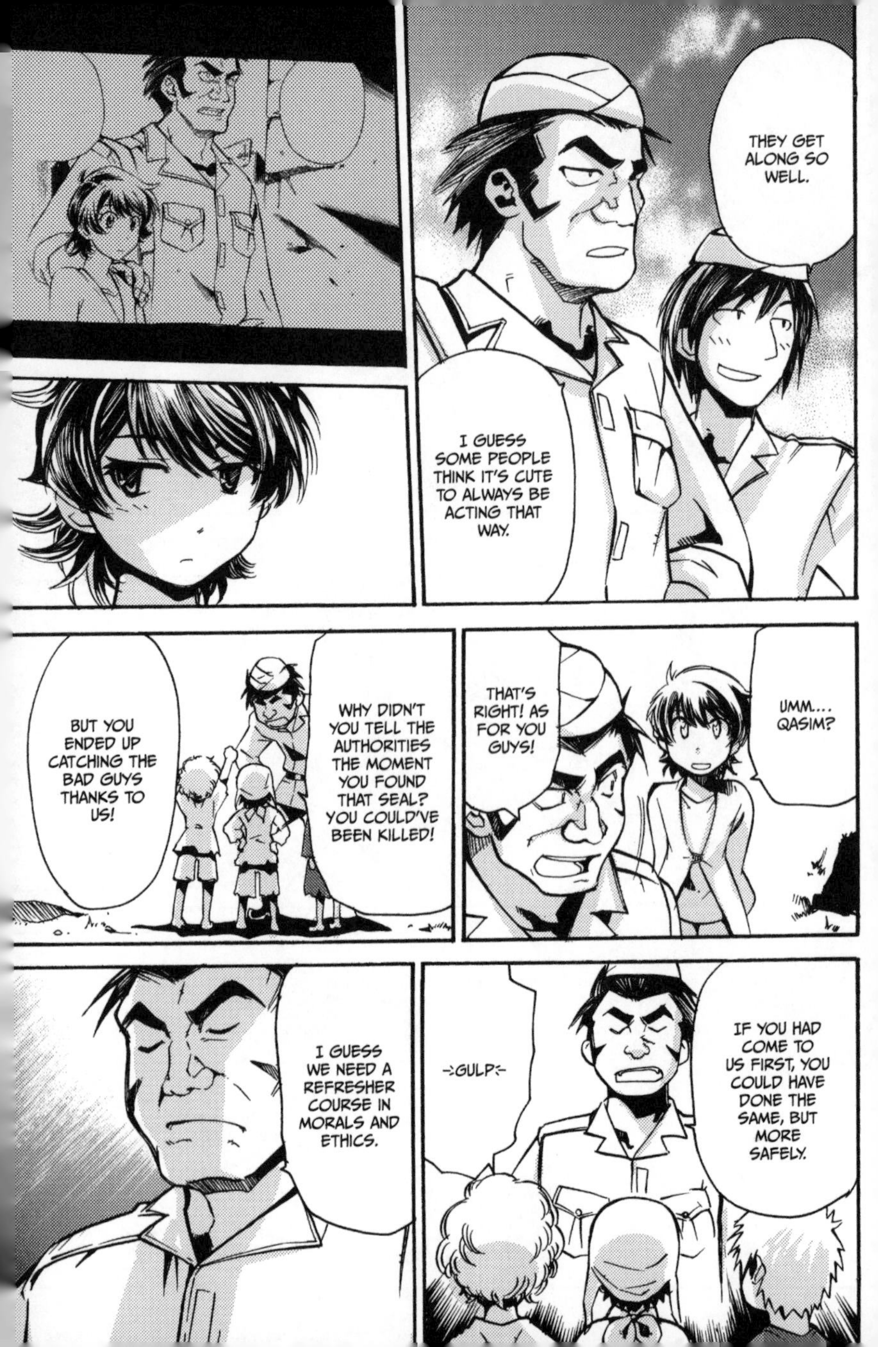
THEY GET ALONG SO WELL.
I GUESS SOME PEOPLE THINK IT'S CUTE TO ALWAYS BE ACTING THAT WAY.
UMM.... QASIM?
THAT'S RIGHT! AS FOR YOU GUYS!
WHY DIDN'T YOU TELL THE AUTHORITIES THE MOMENT YOU FOUND THAT SEAL? YOU COULD'VE BEEN KILLED!
BUT YOU ENDED UP CATCHING THE BAD GUYS THANKS TO US!
IF YOU HAD COME TO US FIRST, YOU COULD HAVE DONE THE SAME, BUT MORE SAFELY.
GULP
I GUESS WE NEED A REFRESHER COURSE IN MORALS AND ETHICS.

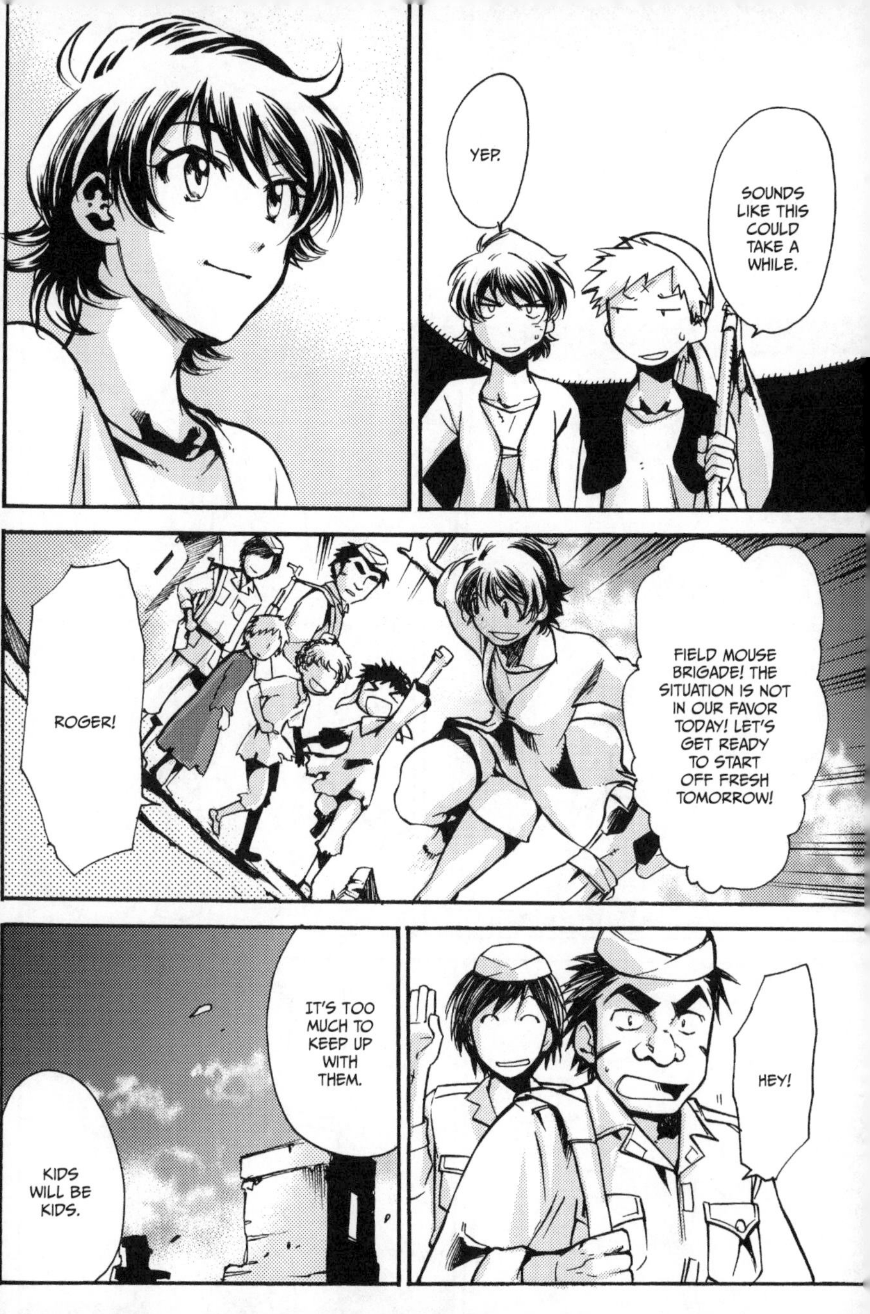
SOUNDS LIKE THIS COULD TAKE A WHILE.
YEP.
FIELD MOUSE BRIGADE! THE SITUATION IS NOT IN OUR FAVOR TODAY! LET'S GET READY TO START OFF FRESH TOMORROW!
ROGER!
HEY!
IT'S TOO MUCH TO KEEP UP WITH THEM.
KIDS WILL BE KIDS.

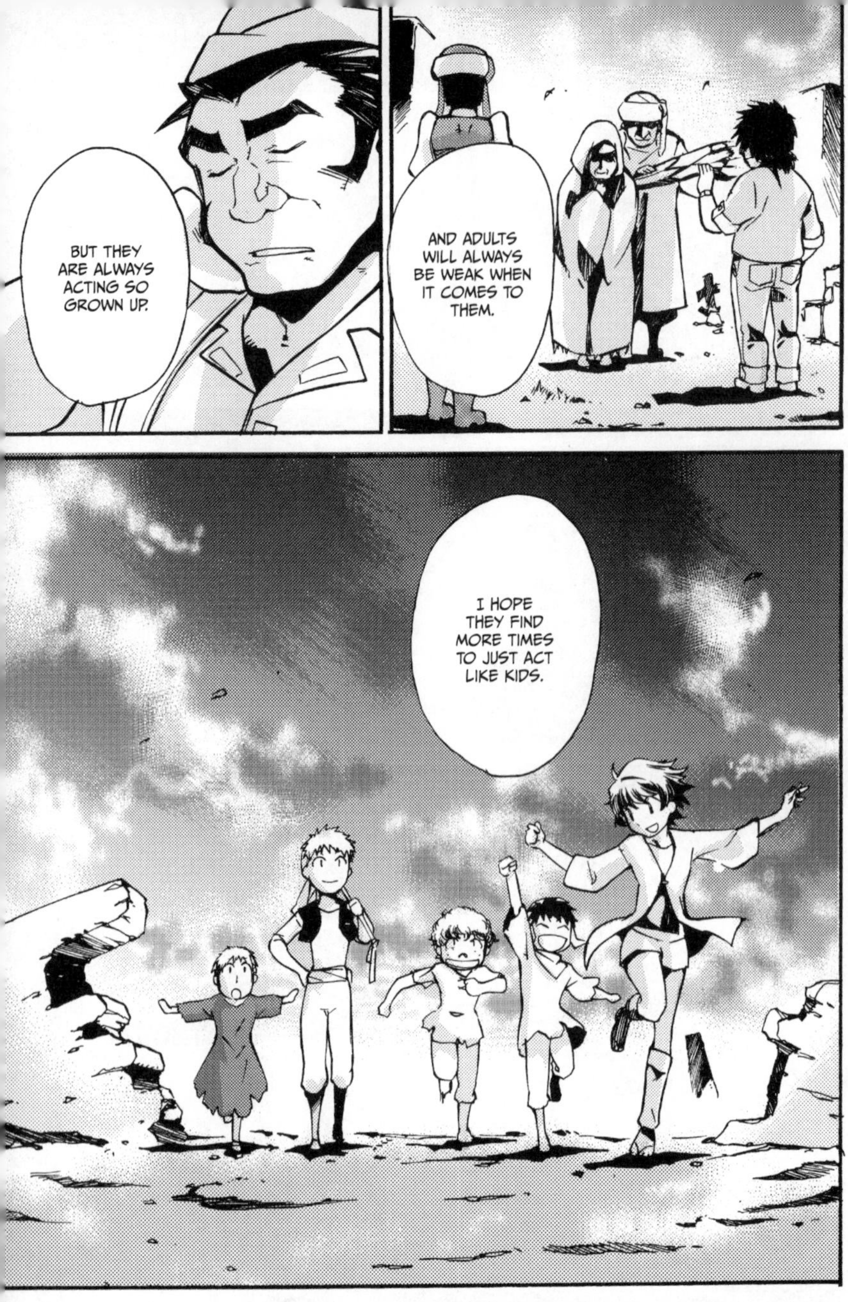
AND ADULTS WILL ALWAYS BE WEAK WHEN IT COMES TO THEM.
BUT THEY ARE ALWAYS ACTING SO GROWN UP.
I HOPE THEY FIND MORE TIMES TO JUST ACT LIKE KIDS.

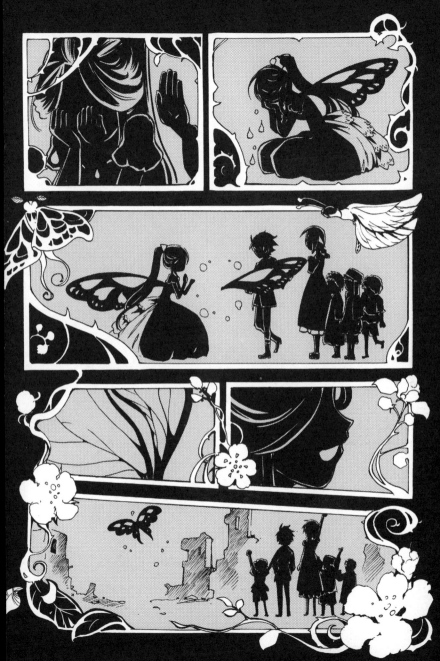

ADVENTURES OF PRINCESS BUTTERFLY
THE END

THIS IS A NEVER PUBLISHED SIDE STORY THAT HAPPENS BETWEEN CHAPTER 8 AND CHAPTER 9 OF THE CAGASTER MANGA.

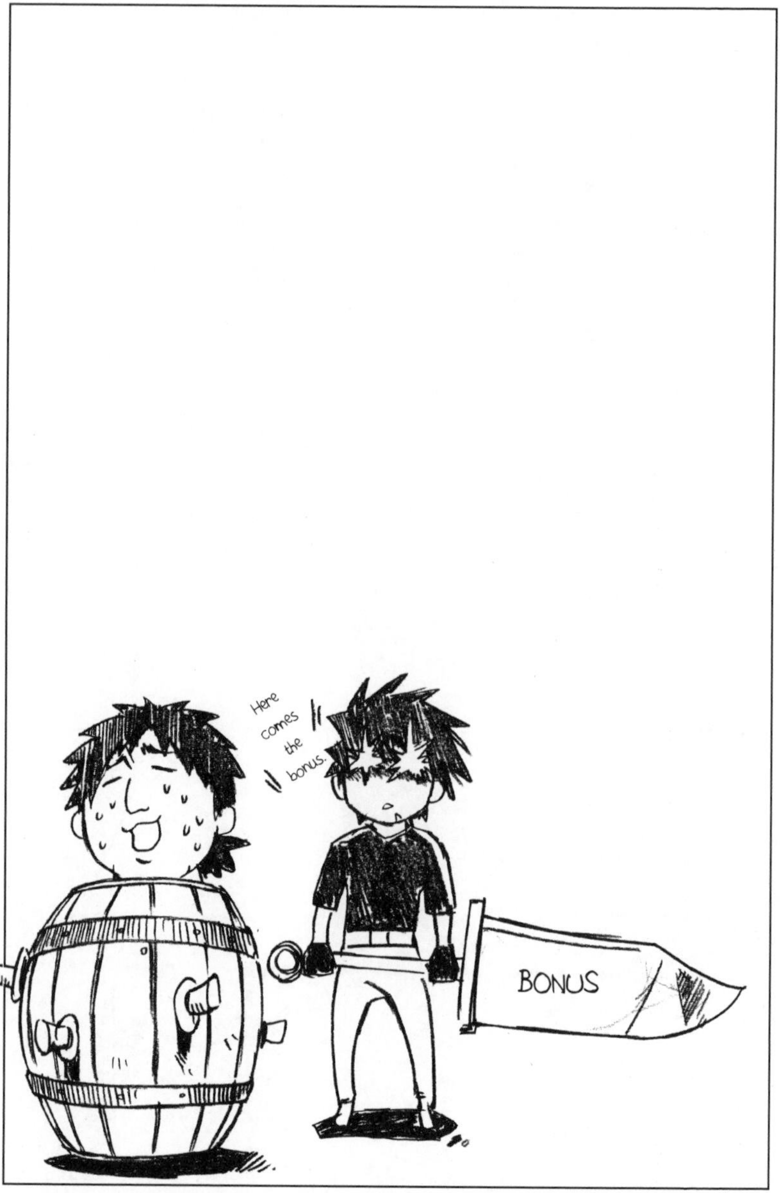
Here comes the bonus.
BONUS

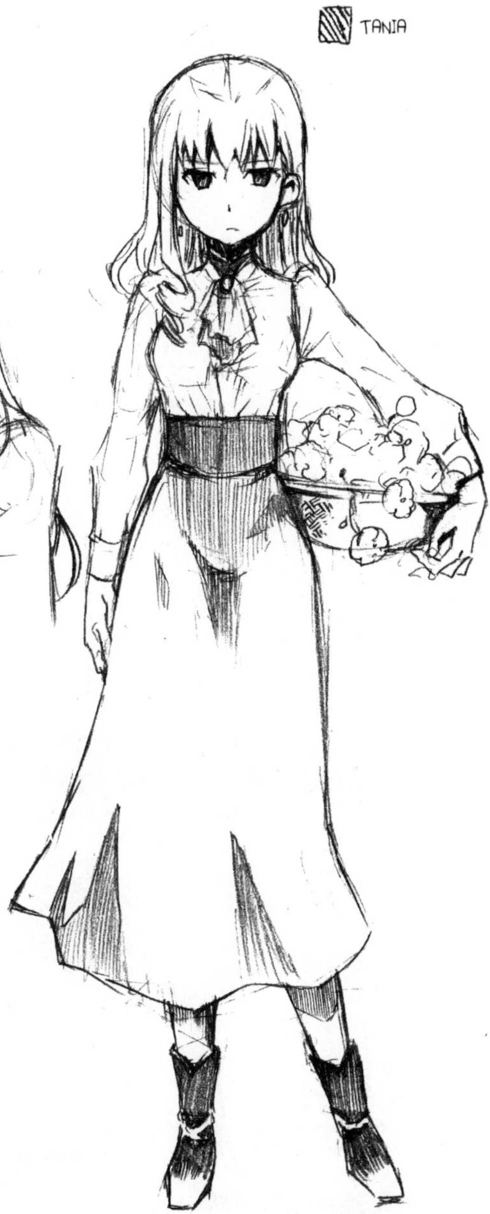
TANIA

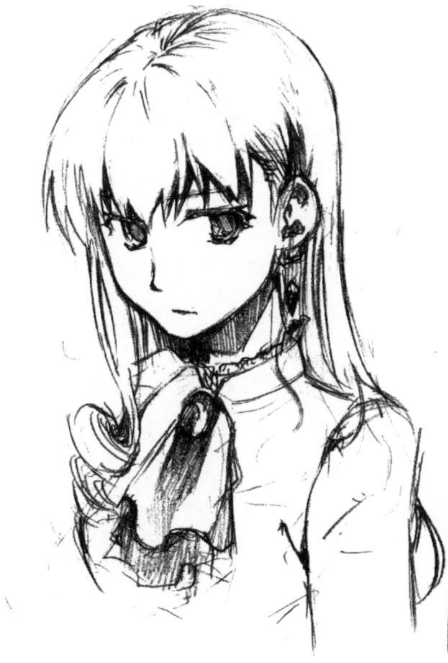

ILIE'S MOTHER.

Was 16 when she first appeared in
the flashback sequence.
Born from the womb of an insect,
and later sacrificed for the sake of research.

Her relationship with Acht is a
little difficult to understand, I think.
Acht was born solely from an ovum
taken from Tania, but he is not a clone.
Genetically, they are "brother and sister".

That would make Acht Ilie's uncle,
though they are very close in age.

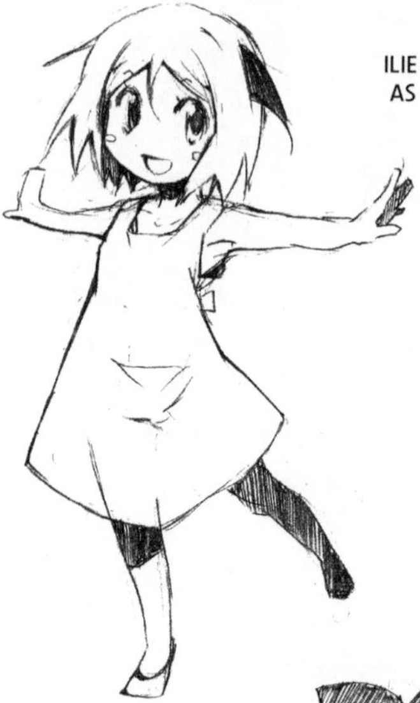

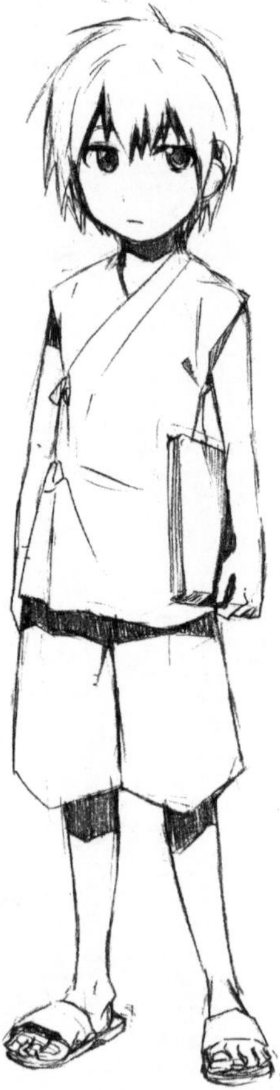

ILIE AND ACHT
AS CHILDREN

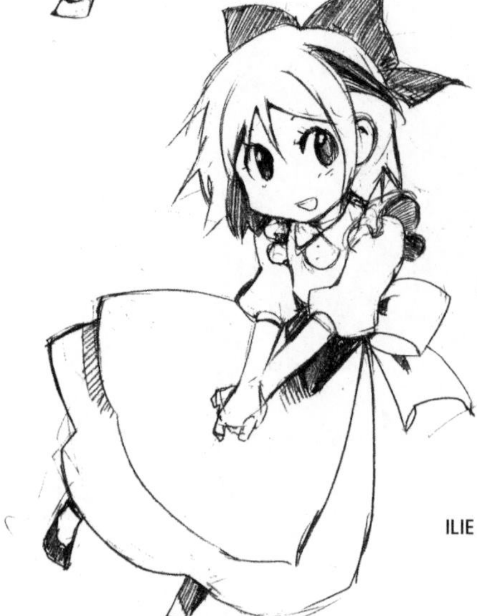

ILIE AS A CHILD IN A-47

GLIPHIS

Franz's assistant, and later the man who raises Ilie.

He dies at the very beginning of Vol. 1, but he is the center of the story during the flashback sequence.

While it seemed his life in the village was full of anguish, when you see the fine young girl Ilie has grown into, you can imagine how well he raised her.

I have a soft spot for characters like this who live normal lives but find themselves facing extraordinary circumstances.

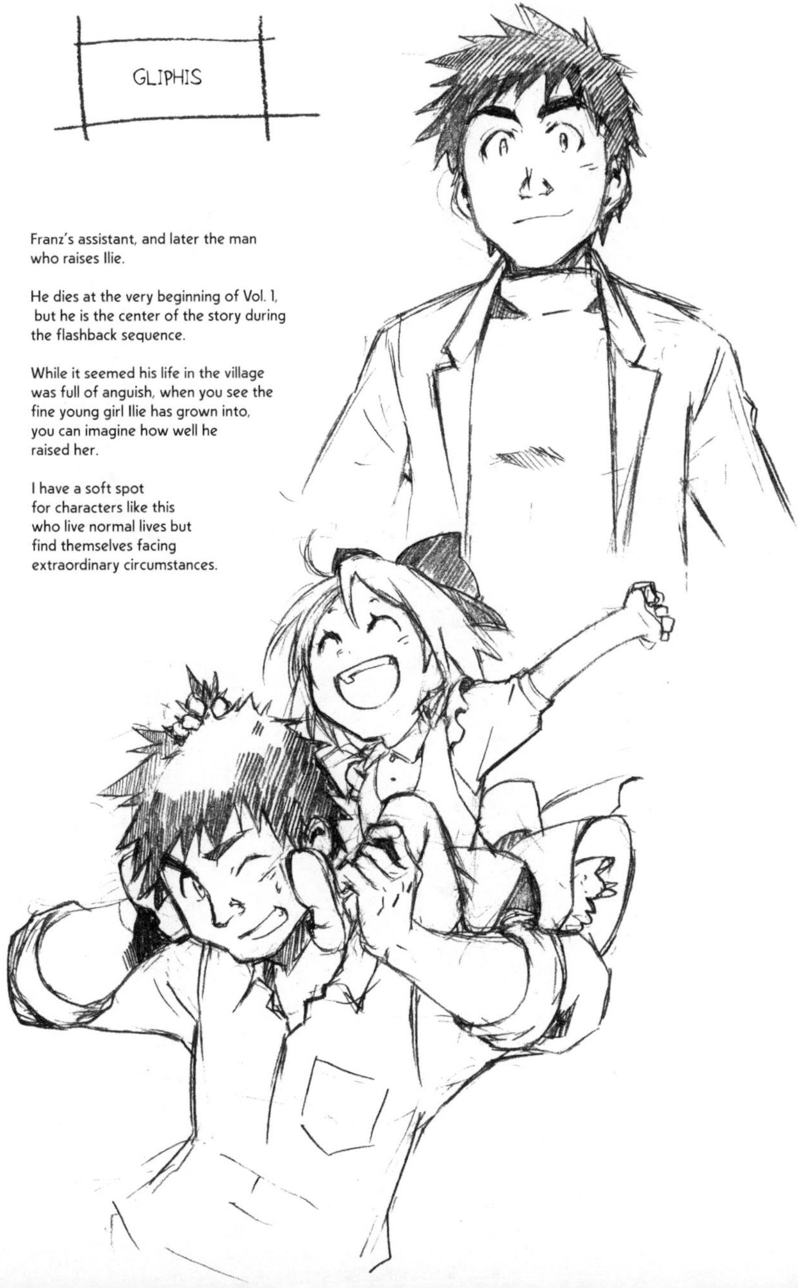

The son of Emeth Chilio and leading researcher of cagaster. Ilie's actual father.

His bangs are almost the same as Ilie's. He has dirty blond hair and greyish-purple eyes.

I designed Ilie to look like her father, and she inherited the color of her eyes from him.

FRANZ

LOOK, ACHT! I'M PRACTICING HOW TO FLY!

WOO HOO!

Having lost Tania and Gliphis, Franz may have been the only adult Acht could look to.

Acht is very quiet, so this must have made for one odd couple.

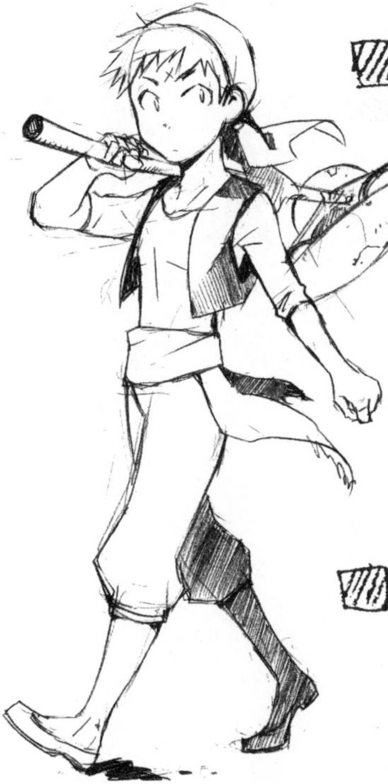

NAGY

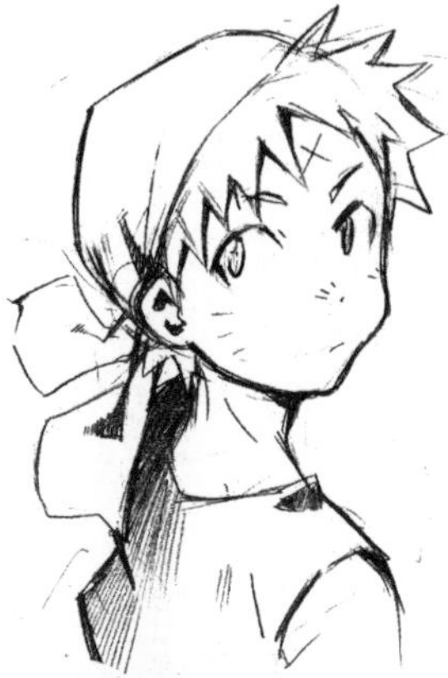

LYGI

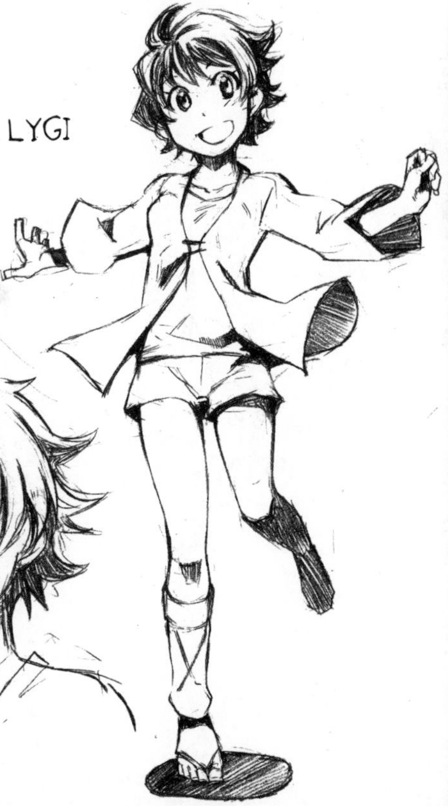

Nagy and Lygi, his friend who is much like an older sister. One is a mature 9-year old, and the other is still a difficult young teen.

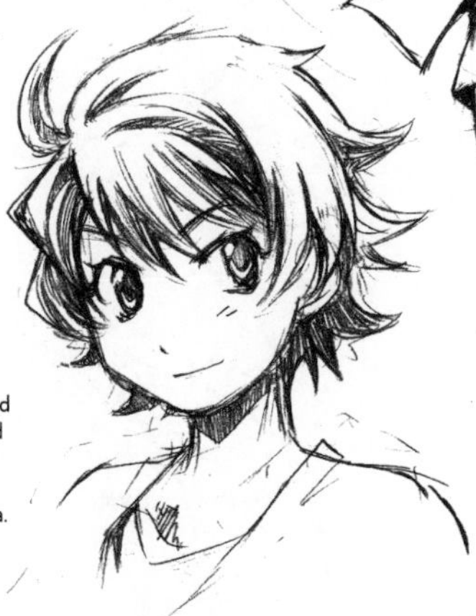

Lygi was originally two characters, a brother and sister, but I consolidated them into one.

Her actual name is Lygia.

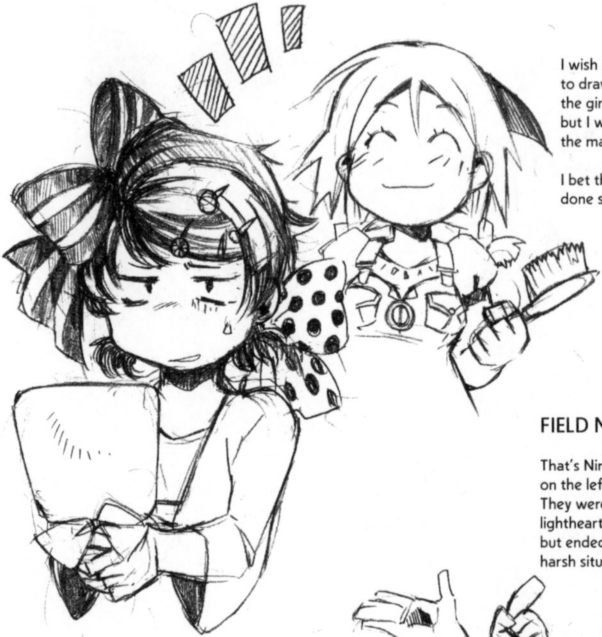

I wish I had the chance to draw more scenes of the girls playing together, but I was too busy with the main story.

I bet they would have done something like this.

FIELD MOUSE BRIGADE

That's Nim on the right, Iason on the left and Romus in the center. They were supposed to provide lightheartedness to the story, but ended up facing so many harsh situations.

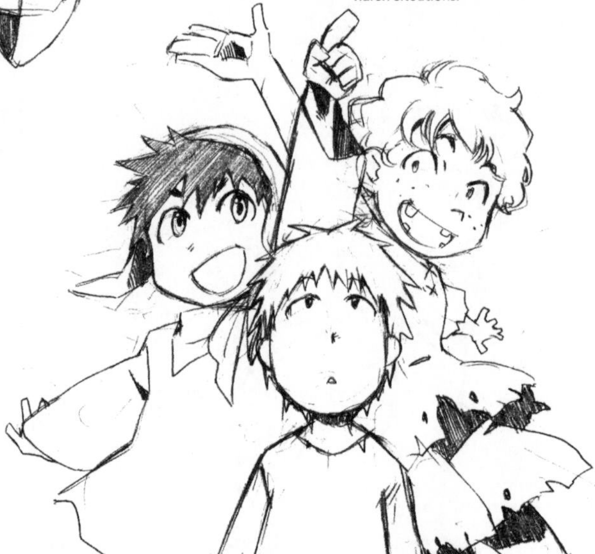

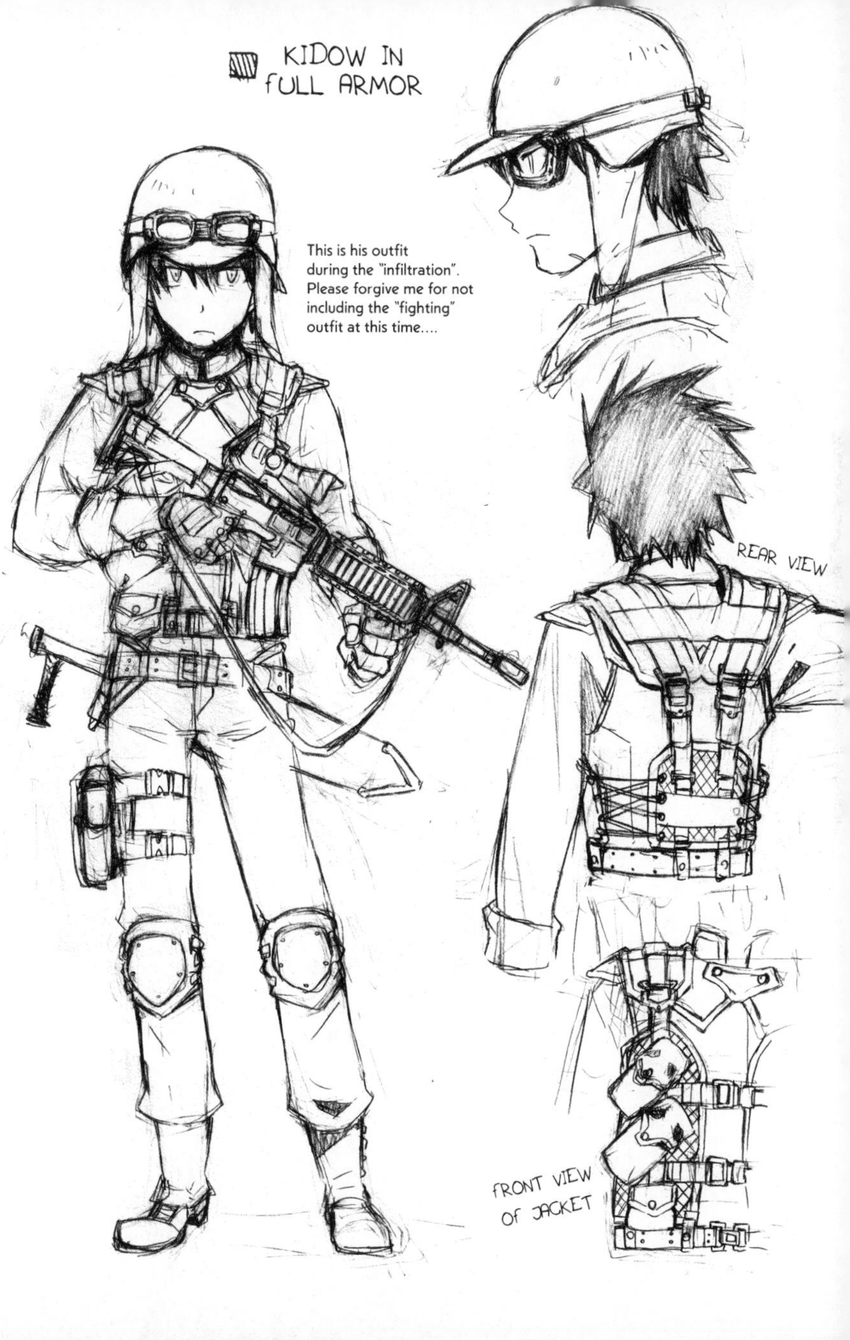
KIDOW IN
FULL ARMOR
This is his outfit during the "infiltration". Please forgive me for not including the "fighting" outfit at this time....
REAR VIEW
FRONT VIEW
OF JACKET

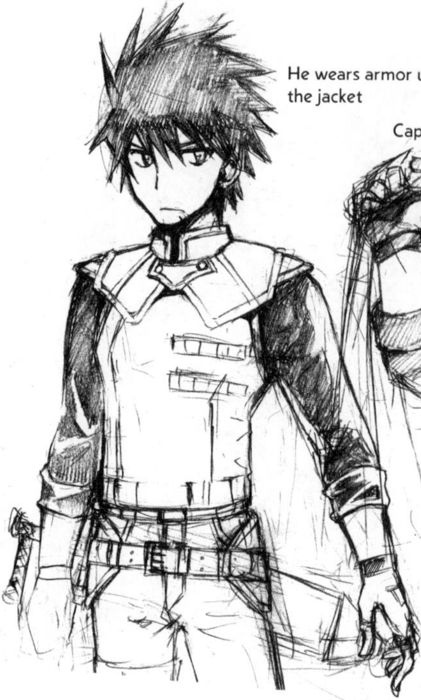

He wears armor underneath the jacket

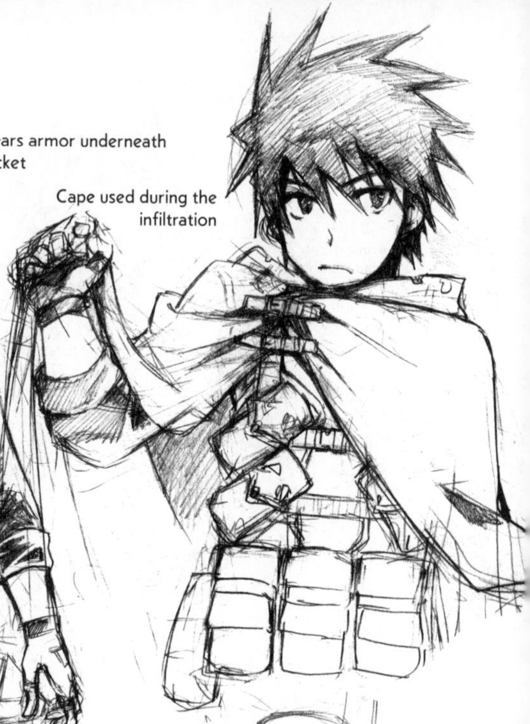

Cape used during the infiltration

The Acht costume used when infiltrating the cage. Though at first glance there are no major differences, the stitching up the back gives it away.

Not the best quality, especially if you were to ask pro cosplayers

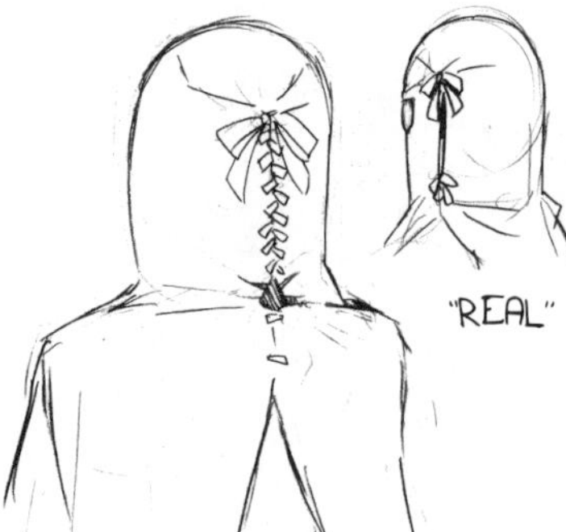
"REAL"
"FAKE"

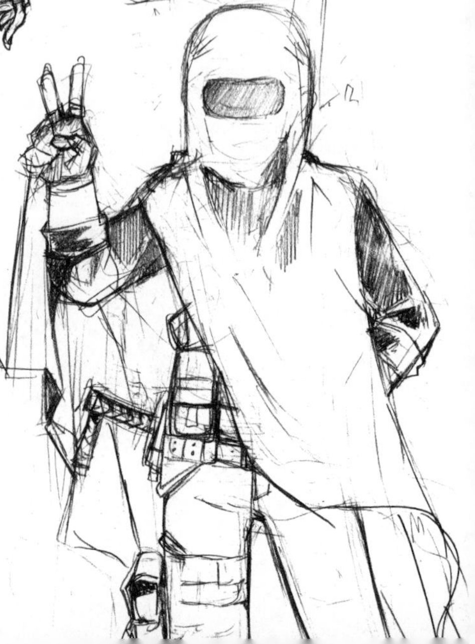

MILITARY TRIO

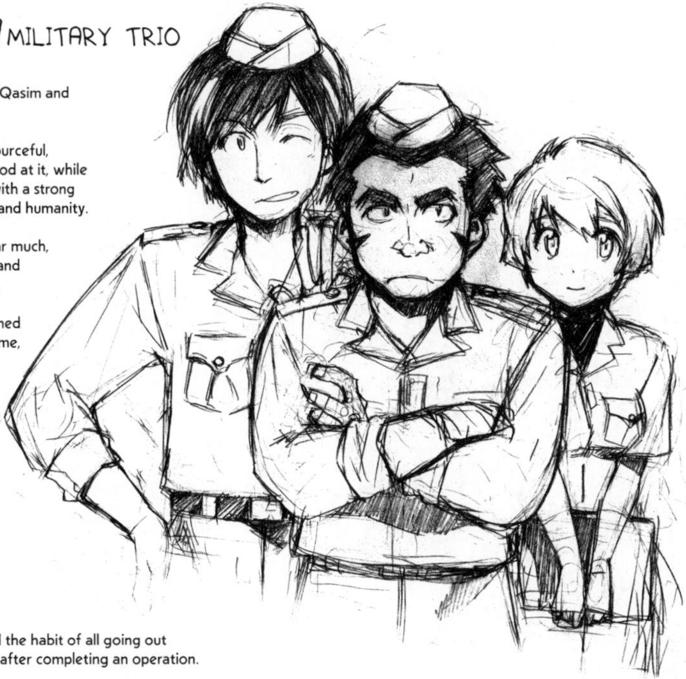

From the left: Hadi, Qasim and Aisha

Hadi likes to be resourceful, but is not always good at it, while Qasim is a fighter with a strong sense of obligation and humanity.

Aisha doesn't appear much, but she is a serious and dependable person.

They were all stationed in 05 at the same time, right around the incident at the West Gate.

I am sure they had the habit of all going out drinking together after completing an operation.

Aisha would down drinks to take out her frustration at daily sexual harassment, while Qasim would rather openly moan about failures.

And, of course, Hadi would be stuck looking after them. I'm sure these sessions weren't the stress relief he was looking for.

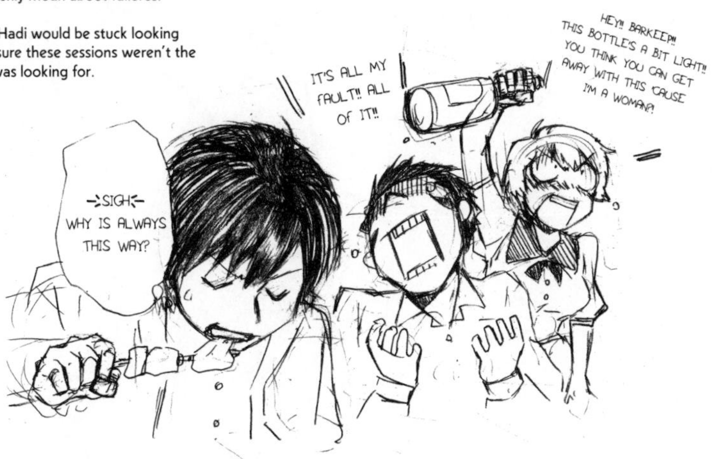
HEY!! BARKEEP!! THIS BOTTLE'S A BIT LIGHT!! YOU THINK YOU CAN GET AWAY WITH THIS 'CAUSE I'M A WOMAN?!
IT'S ALL MY FAULT!! ALL OF IT!!
SIGH
WHY IS ALWAYS THIS WAY?

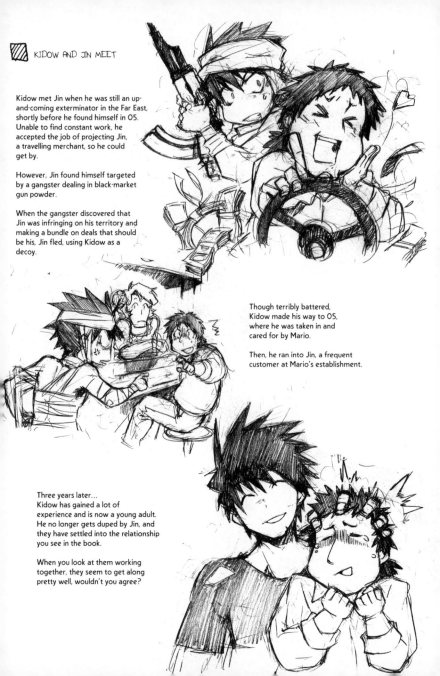

KIDOW AND JIN MEET

Kidow met Jin when he was still an up-and-coming exterminator in the Far East, shortly before he found himself in 05. Unable to find constant work, he accepted the job of projecting Jin, a travelling merchant, so he could get by.

However, Jin found himself targeted by a gangster dealing in black-market gun powder.

When the gangster discovered that Jin was infringing on his territory and making a bundle on deals that should be his, Jin fled, using Kidow as a decoy.

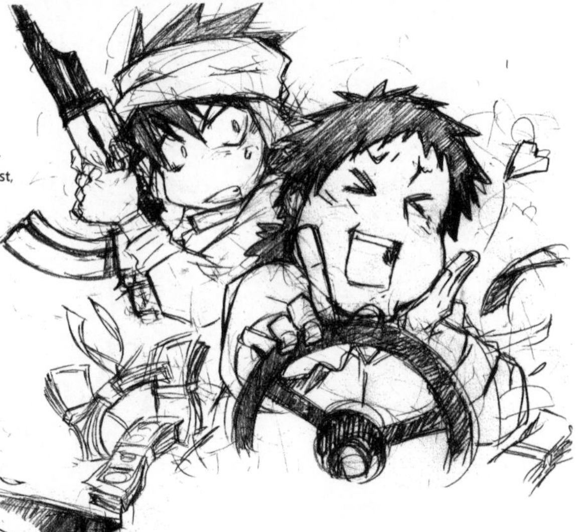

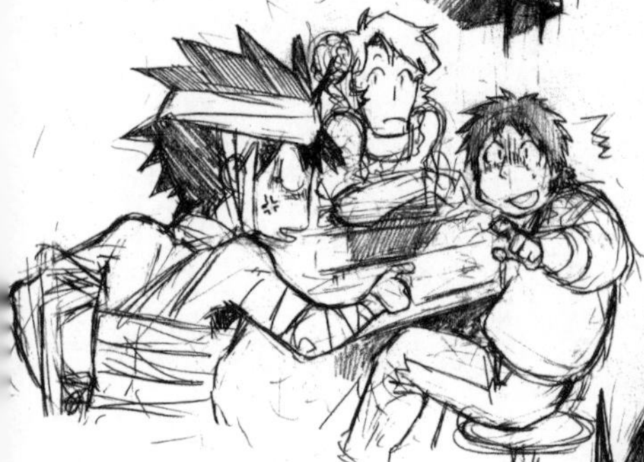

Though terribly battered, Kidow made his way to 05, where he was taken in and cared for by Mario.

Then, he ran into Jin, a frequent customer at Mario's establishment.

Three years later...
Kidow has gained a lot of experience and is now a young adult. He no longer gets duped by Jin, and they have settled into the relationship you see in the book.

When you look at them working together, they seem to get along pretty well, wouldn't you agree?

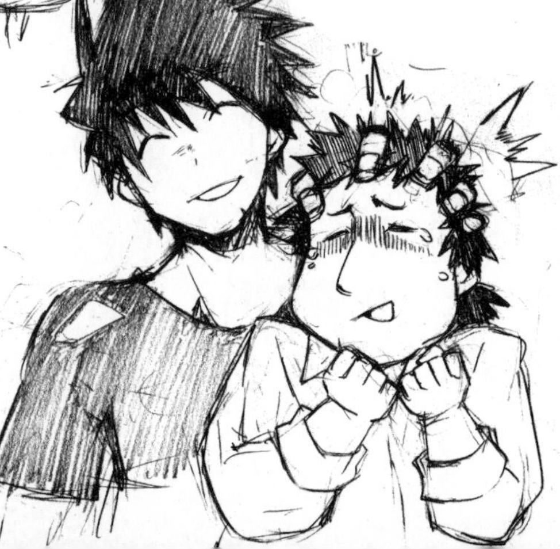

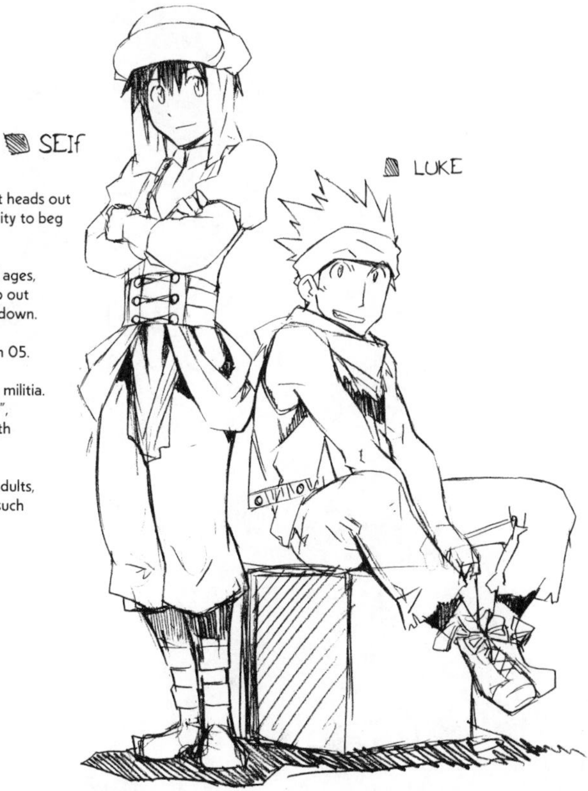
SEIf
LUKE

These two form the team that heads out to the commerce federation city to beg for help in Vol. 4.

They actually have names and ages, but I decided to keep that info out since it just bogged the story down.

Both are 16, born and raised in 05.

Seif is in his first year with the militia. Luke, a "pretend exterminator", would like to travel around with caravans.

They are treated basically as adults, but they are very new to the such a position in society.

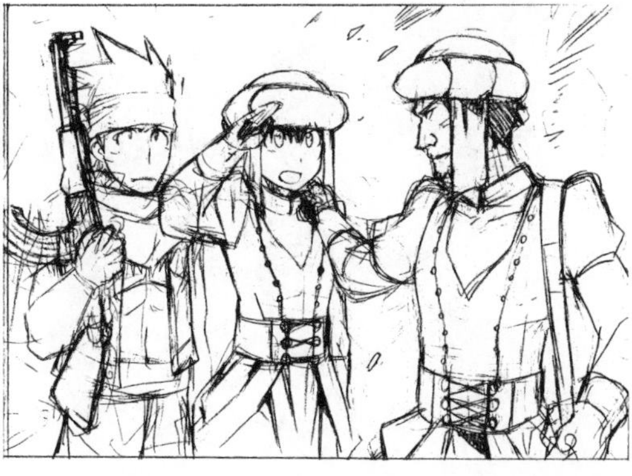

One scene that didn't make it into the book is "sending younger members for help".

The 05 militia is about to give up all hope, and decides that it needs to rely on its younger members if it is to survive. Seif, one of the newest members, is chosen as the messenger.

That way, even if everyone else died, at least someone would survive.

It seems as though the militia fighters were ready for what looked to be the end...

But the two young men sent off to find help were determined to succeed in their mission.

It would have been a good scene to include, but like I said earlier, it would have bogged down the story too much, so my short introduction here will have to suffice.

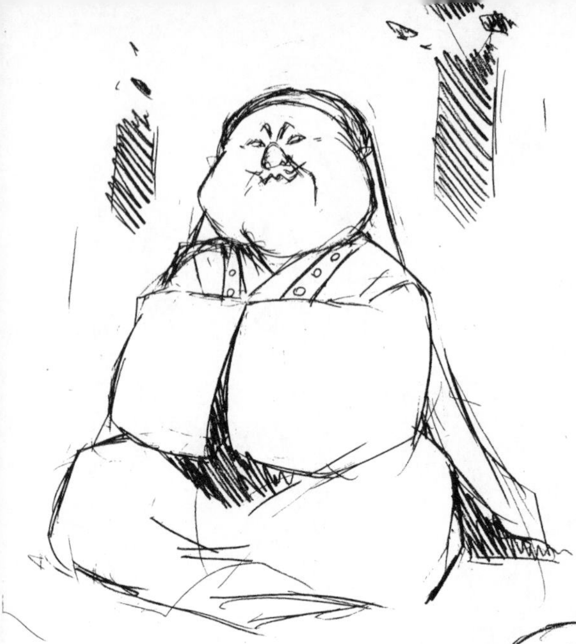

HEAD MERCHANT

The leader of E-05.
Sounds powerful, but the position changes hands every few years.
One member of the council of elders is chosen for the position, and is given the responsibility of overseeing safety and the flow of commerce in the city.

Still in his 50s, he's the young member of the council of elders, and has a hot-blooded temper.

Though he normally sticks to his shrewd and miserly ways that keep him among the rich, he has no patience for those who do not adhere to principles.

I guess that makes him kind of like a mob boss.

HARB ADHAM

The highest-ranked leader in the E District.
He rose to that position after being the No. 2 man in the Far East, and he has many connections in the financial world.

Though his ideas are fierce and extreme, he is also cool and patient enough to watch his plan take shape in secret over many years.

He was the guardian of Franz and Tania when they were young, and used them as tools for his own ends...

But it might be too much to say that he had no feelings for them at all.

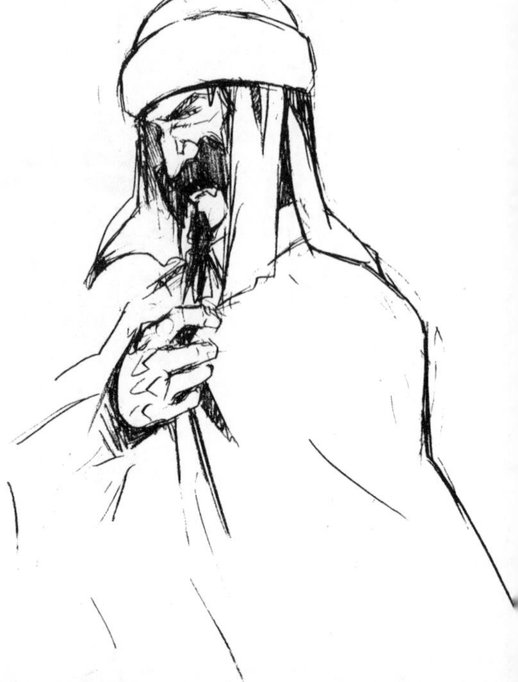

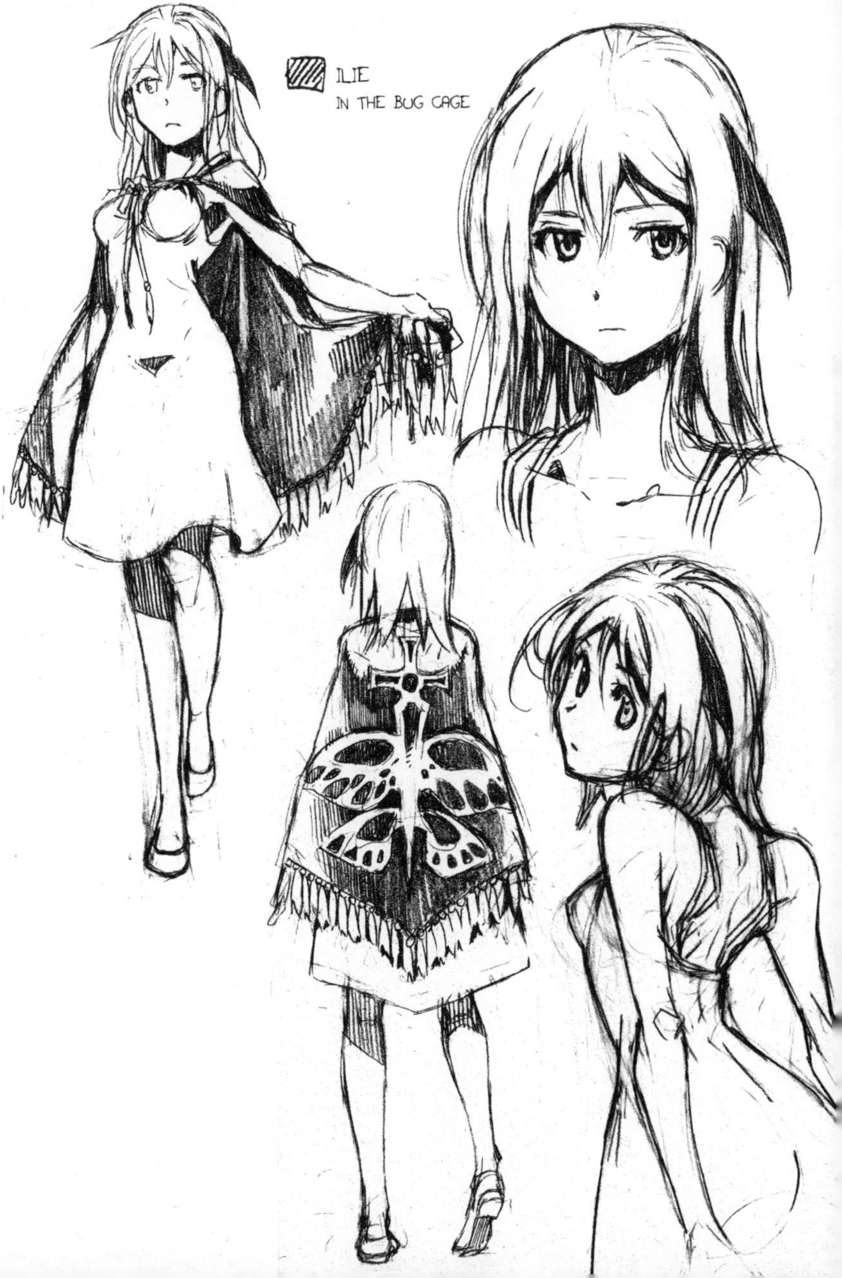
ILIE
IN THE BUG CAGE

INNOCENT ILIE AND SERIOUS ILIE

Once she starts remembering her childhood, Ilie changes so much she is almost a different person.

When her hair is braided, she is "country village Ilie", and when it is down, she is "princess Ilie".

Country village Ilie is pure and innocent, and her positive demeanor is expressed in the straightforward way, but princess Ilie is more distant, and even uses sarcasm.

This is not a separate personality, so her basic characteristics are not different, but her attitude has changed so much, it is a wonder that Kidow was not thrown off.

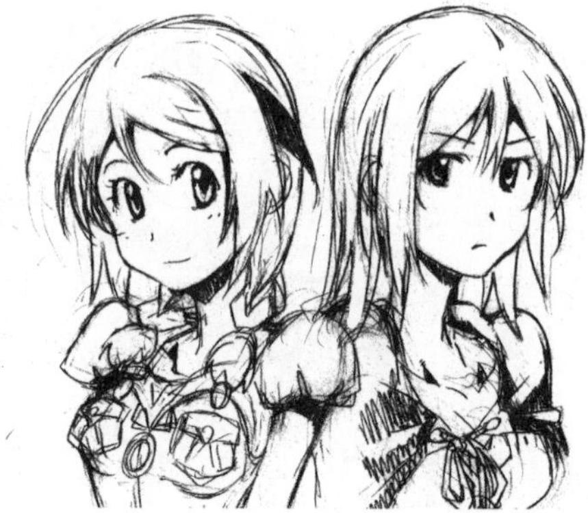

THE TRIANGLE

Kidow's current attitude is such that if Ilie had seen it when her crush was so strong, I bet she would have backed away quickly.

He did mention that princess Ilie is more his "type", but I have to wonder. Considering that Kara was his first love, he seems to have thing for those who are out of reach.

Even though he isn't exactly two-timing, two flavors are better than one. Still, it looks dangerous. Better watch his back.

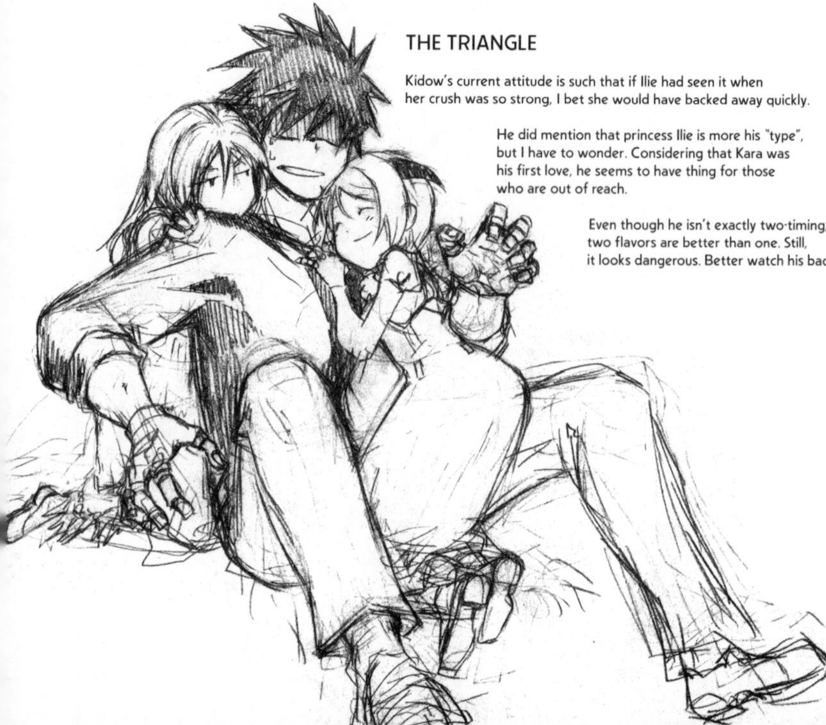

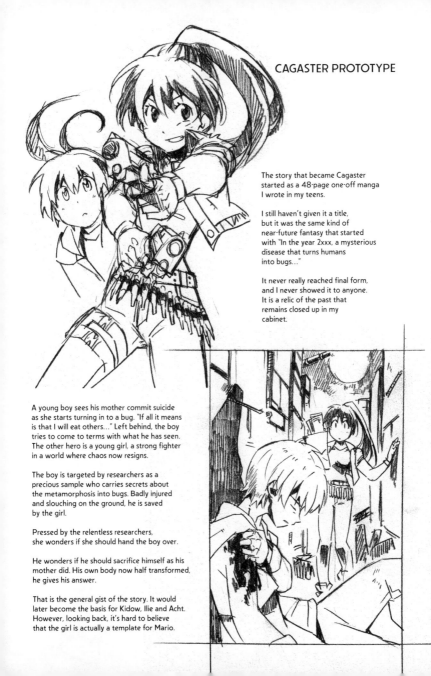

CAGASTER PROTOTYPE

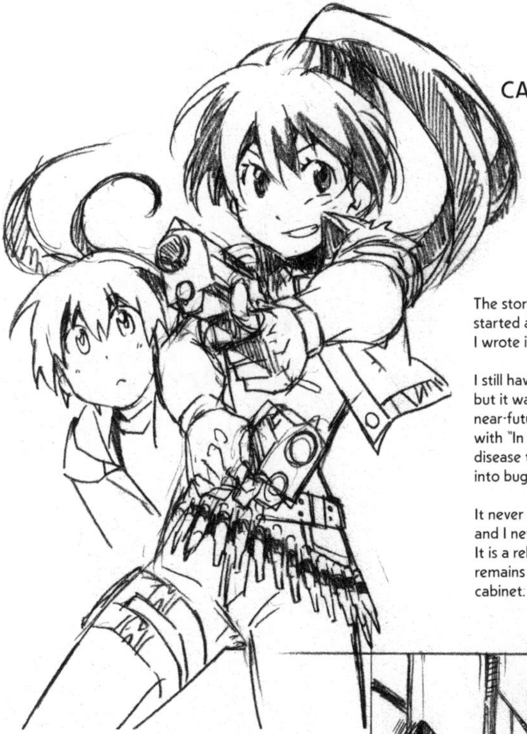

The story that became Cagaster started as a 48-page one-off manga I wrote in my teens.

I still haven't given it a title, but it was the same kind of near-future fantasy that started with "In the year 2xxx, a mysterious disease that turns humans into bugs..."

It never really reached final form, and I never showed it to anyone. It is a relic of the past that remains closed up in my cabinet.

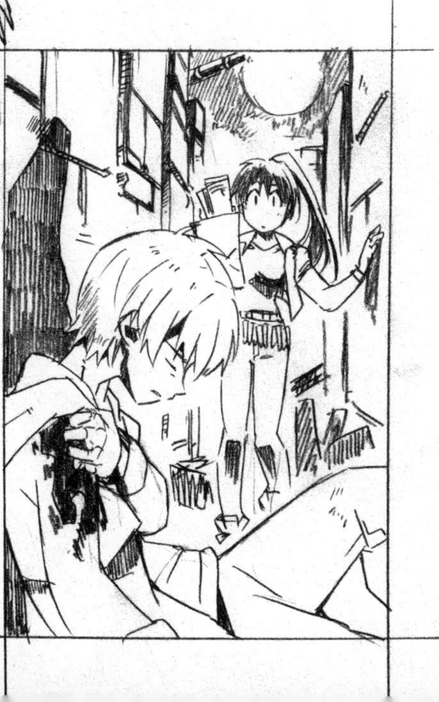

A young boy sees his mother commit suicide as she starts turning in to a bug. "If all it means is that I will eat others..." Left behind, the boy tries to come to terms with what he has seen. The other hero is a young girl, a strong fighter in a world where chaos now resigns.

The boy is targeted by researchers as a precious sample who carries secrets about the metamorphosis into bugs. Badly injured and slouching on the ground, he is saved by the girl.

Pressed by the relentless researchers, she wonders if she should hand the boy over.

He wonders if he should sacrifice himself as his mother did. His own body now half transformed, he gives his answer.

That is the general gist of the story. It would later become the basis for Kidow, Ilie and Acht. However, looking back, it's hard to believe that the girl is actually a template for Mario.

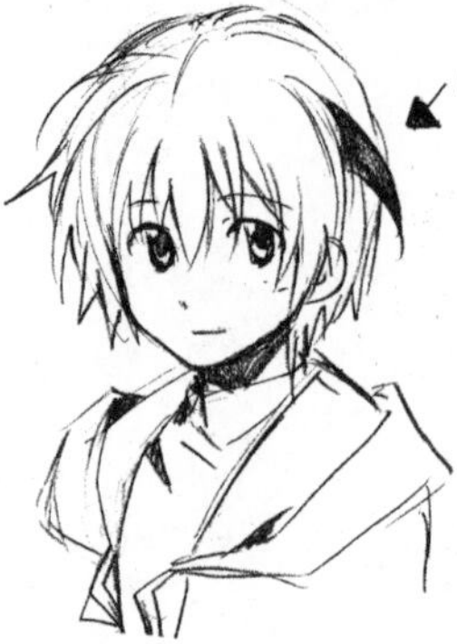
MYSTERY SUBSTANCE

The boy had the same mysterious lock of hair that Ilie does.

It doesn't have any deep meaning. The hero of a fantasy novel I like had "a single lock of red among silver blond hair", and that provided the inspiration. You can trace the look of Acht and Ilie straight to him. He was 14-years old.

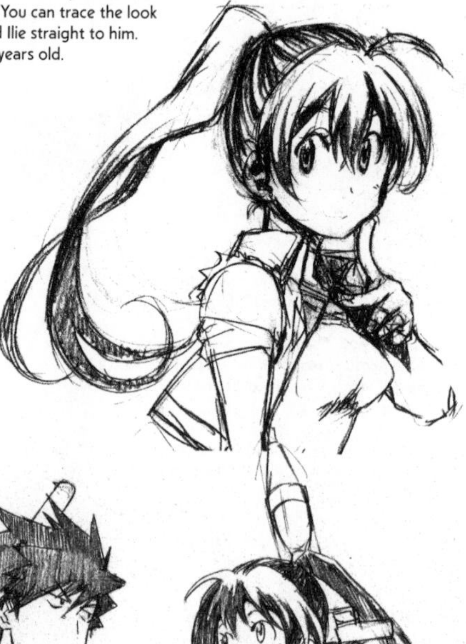

The girl had a black pony tail, and if I had to choose, I would say her personality was close to that of Kara. She was 17, just like Kidow.

She was cheery and straightforward, which makes me wonder how she shifted into that cynical young man. There is no female character like her that fights on the front lines in Cagaster, so her character is a somewhat refreshing.

In the end, the genders were switched for Cagaster. I do think that things have gotten better as I went along compared to how the characters were initially designed.

There wasn't even a love interest in the beginning.

I guess my purpose in life is to write at least one story where "a captured princess is saved".

No, I like that theme, so I don't think I'll stop at just one.

It will help if I don't have to draw so many tanks and guns next time.

Or large bugs...

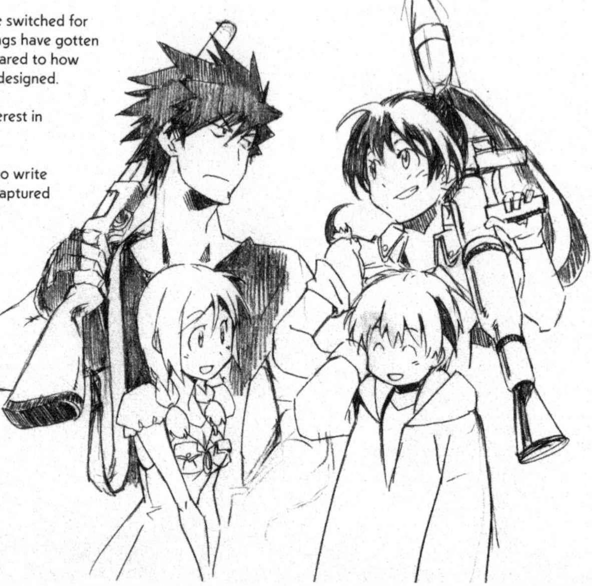

KAFKA'S "METAMORPHOSIS" AND MASTERPIECE THEATER

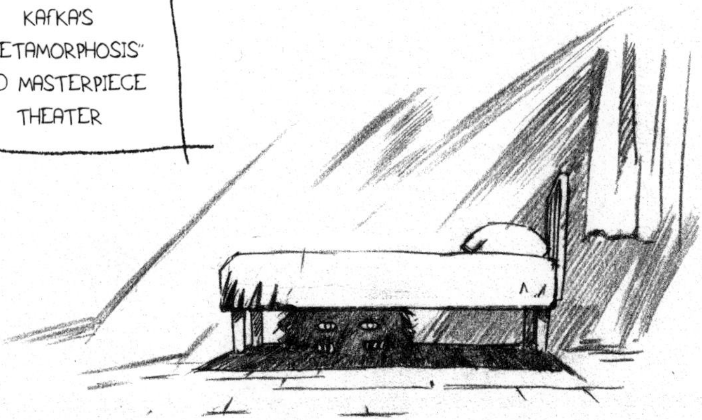

Cagaster, in which people turn into large bugs, is partly inspired by Franz Kafka's "Metamorphosis".

One morning, Gregor Samsa, who loves his family and younger sister, notices that he has metamorphosized into a large bug. His family is horrified, but he still worries about his sister.

Though it starts in a very sensational manner, everyday life in the book unfolds in a very matter-of-fact way.

"Why do they become bugs?"
This is not the focus of the story. Instead, as an homage to "Metamorphosis" (at least in how the story is set up), Cagaster puts more emphasis on "how do people react to a reality where people inexplicably change into bugs".

When you think of "Masterpiece Theater", it brings to mind the enduring heroines. The first couple of volumes could be shown to children without any problems.

Then things change, and there isn't a trace left of "Metamorphosis" or "Masterpiece Theater"...

It's out of the blue to bring it up now, but I really wish "Masterpiece Theater" would come back.

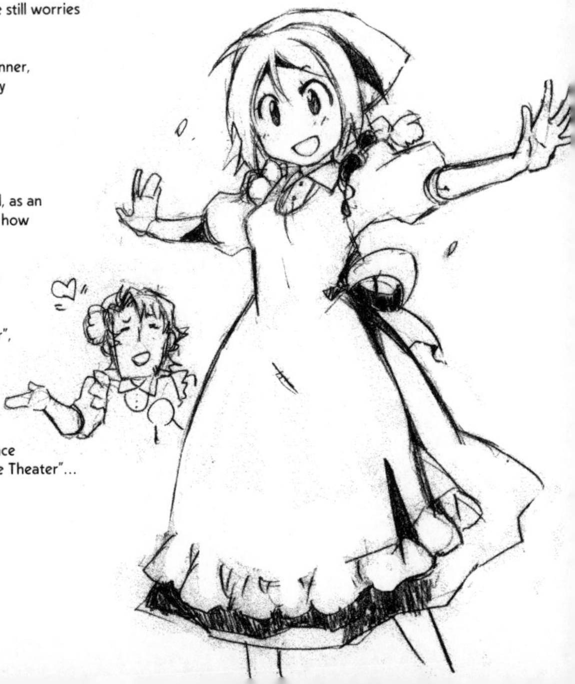

POSTSCRIPT

There is just one volume left. I had actually meant to finish the online version as I worked on the books, but now I want to go back and make some revisions to the online version. I hope that is done by the time this volume reaches you.

Kidow certainly has changed since Volume 1, hasn't he? I guess the same could be said for Ilie.

The story takes place over just 3 months, but it took me 7 years to write it. That is a long time to involved with the characters.

The next volume will bring the story to an end.

Thanks for sticking with me!
And be sure to pick up the last volume!

Hashimoto Chicken

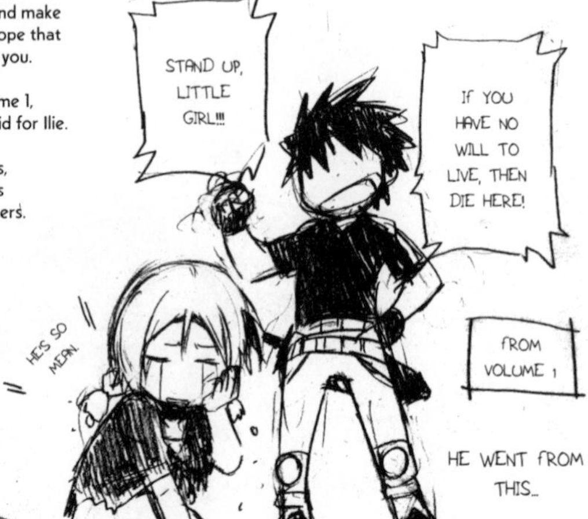

IF YOU HAVE NO WILL TO LIVE, THEN DIE HERE!
STAND UP, LITTLE GIRL!!!
FROM VOLUME 1
HE WENT FROM THIS...
HE'S SO MEAN.

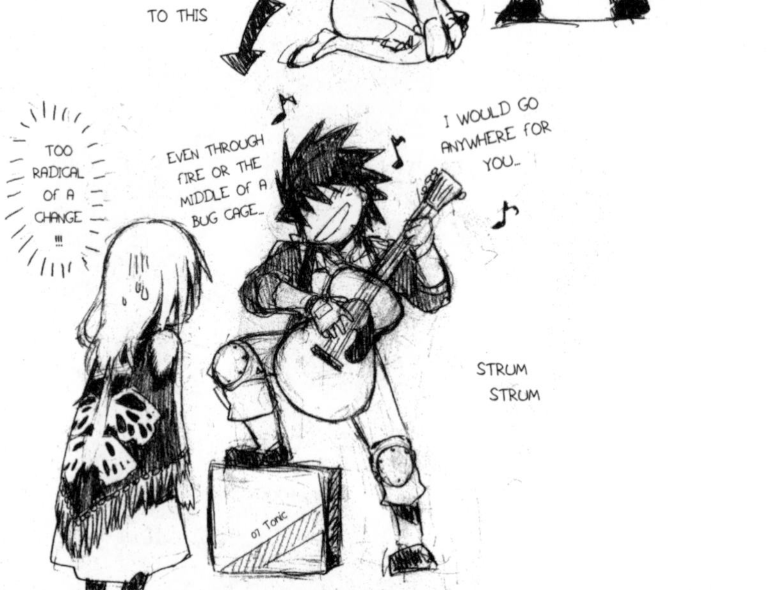

TO THIS
I WOULD GO ANYWHERE FOR YOU...
EVEN THROUGH FIRE OR THE MIDDLE OF A BUG CAGE...
TOO RADICAL OF A CHANGE!!!
STRUM STRUM
07 Tonic

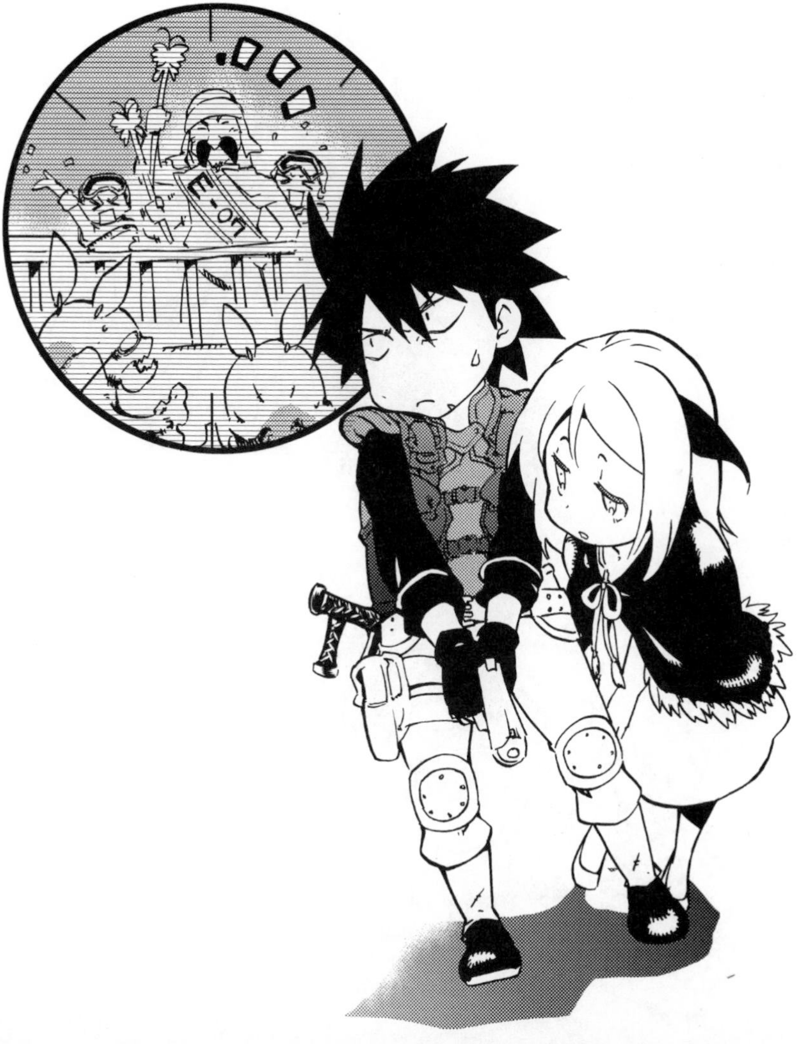

CAGASTER
by Kachou Hashimoto

Translation: Matthew Johnson
Lettering: Studio Makma
Editor: Rich Young
Designer: Rodolfo Muraguchi

CAGASTER, VOLUME 5. First printing. Published by Ablaze Publishing, 11222 SE Main St. #22906 Portland, OR 97269.

For advertising and licensing email: info@ablazepublishing.com

---

Publisher's Cataloging-in-Publication Data
Names: Hashimoto, Kachou, author.
Title: Cagaster , Volume 5 / Kachou Hashimoto.
Series: Cagaster
Description: Portland, OR: Ablaze Publishing, 2021.
Identifiers: ISBN 978-1-950912-11-7
LCSH Mutation (Biology)—Fiction. | Cannibalism—Fiction. | Insects—Fiction. | Dystopias. | Fantasy fiction. | Science fiction. | Adventure and adventurers—Fiction. | Graphic novels. | BISAC COMICS & GRAPHIC NOVELS / Manga / Dystopian | COMICS & GRAPHIC NOVELS / Manga / Fantasy COMICS & GRAPHIC NOVELS / Manga / Science Fiction
Classification: LCC PN6790.J33 .H372 v. 5 2021 | DDC 741.5–dc23

/ablazepub @AblazePub @AblazePub
ablazepublishing.com

To find a comics shop in your area go to:
www.comicshoplocator.com

STOP!

THIS IS THE BACK OF THE BOOK:

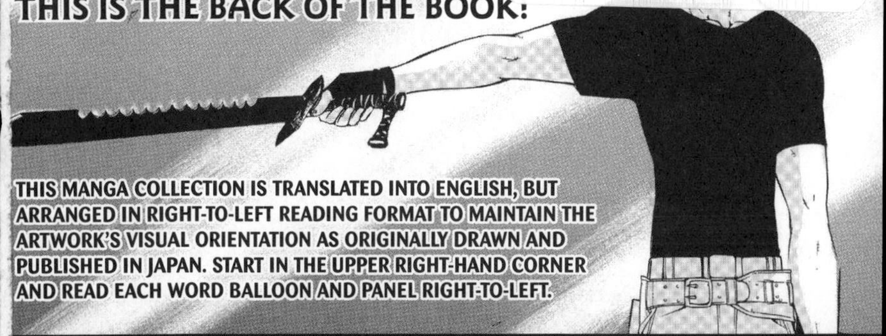

THIS MANGA COLLECTION IS TRANSLATED INTO ENGLISH, BUT ARRANGED IN RIGHT-TO-LEFT READING FORMAT TO MAINTAIN THE ARTWORK'S VISUAL ORIENTATION AS ORIGINALLY DRAWN AND PUBLISHED IN JAPAN. START IN THE UPPER RIGHT-HAND CORNER AND READ EACH WORD BALLOON AND PANEL RIGHT-TO-LEFT.

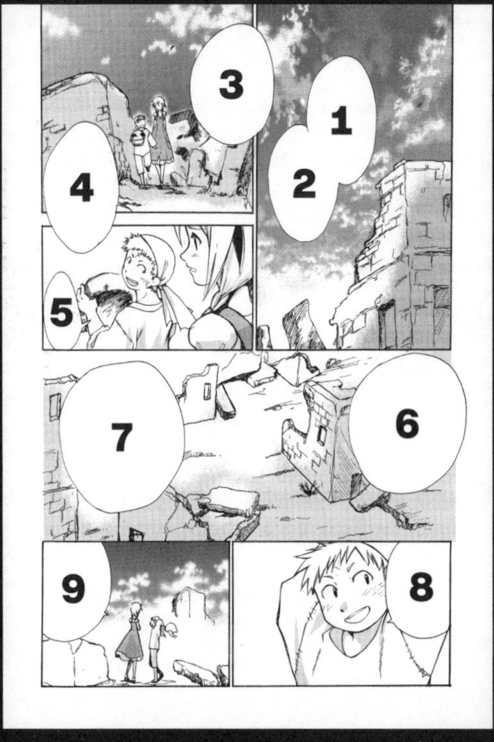
1
2
3
4
5
6
7
8
9